JUN 1 0 2020

W9-BLN-565

CAREFUL WHAT YOU CLICK FOR

ALSO BY MARY B. MORRISON

Head Games
I Do Love You Still
Careful What You Click For

The Crystal Series
Baby, You're the Best
Just Can't Let Go
The One I've Waited For

If I Can't Have You Series
If I Can't Have You
I'd Rather Be with You
If You Don't Know Me

Soulmates Dissipate Series
Soulmates Dissipate
Never Again Once More
He's Just a Friend
Somebody's Gotta Be on Top
Nothing Has Ever Felt Like This
When Somebody Loves You Back
Darius Jones

The Honey Diaries
Sweeter Than Honey
Who's Loving You
Unconditionally Single
Darius Jones

She Ain't the One (coauthored with Carl Weber)
Maneater (anthology with Noire)
The Eternal Engagement
Justice Just Us Just Me
Who's Making Love

MARY B. MORRISON, WRITING AS HONEYB
Sexcapades
Single Husbands
Married on Mondays
The Rich Girls Club

WRITING AS MARY HONEYB MORRISON
Pleasers: How to Sexually Satisfy Women
Never Let a Man Come First: A Woman's Guide to Understanding Male Behavior
Dicks Are Dumb: A Woman's Guide to Choosing the Right Man

CAREFUL WHAT YOU CLICK FOR

MARY B. MORRISON

KENSINGTON PUBLISHING CORP.

www.kensingtonbooks.com

To the extent that the image or images on the cover of this book depict a person or persons, such person or persons are merely models, and are not intended to portray any character or characters featured in the book.

DAFINA BOOKS are published by

Kensington Publishing Corp.
119 West 40th Street
New York, NY 10018

Copyright © 2020 by Mary B. Morrison

All rights reserved. No part of this book may be reproduced in any form or by any means without the prior written consent of the Publisher, excepting brief quotes used in reviews.

All Kensington titles, imprints, and distributed lines are available at special quantity discounts for bulk purchases for sales promotion, premiums, fund-raising, educational, or institutional use. Special book excerpts or customized printings can also be created to fit specific needs. For details, write or phone the office of the Kensington Special Sales Manager: Attn. Special Sales Department. Kensington Publishing Corp., 119 West 40th Street, New York, NY 10018. Phone: 1-800-221-2647.

Library of Congress Card Catalogue Number: 2019953573

Dafina and the Dafina logo Reg. U.S. Pat. & TM Off.

ISBN-13: 978-1-4967-1091-8
ISBN-10: 1-4967-1091-6
First Kensington Hardcover Edition: June 2020

ISBN-13: 978-1-4967-1094-9 (ebook)
ISBN-10: 1-4967-1094-0 (ebook)

10 9 8 7 6 5 4 3 2 1

Printed in the United States of America

R0457035385

To my literary guardian angel,
Walter Zacharius,
thanks for believing in me

Acknowledgments

Everything must change.

Pray with and for me as I will do the same for each of you. I have the best family, friends, fans, and publisher. Never could've made it this far without your love and support.

There are constants in my life. God. Faith. And my willingness to do the things I am most passionate about. I'm now doing film, television, nonfiction, public speaking, and operating my 501(c)(3) nonprofit, Healing Her Hurt, Incorporated, based in Atlanta, Georgia. If you shop on Smile.Amazon.com, please select our organization. Amazon will donate a portion of your purchase to HHH and there is no charge to you.

For the past twenty years, I've been with the number one literary company, Kensington Publishing Corporation. Steve and Adam Zacharius, Barbara Bennet, Selena James, and the entire staff, I'm eternally grateful for all you've done to elevate my career. This is (perhaps) my last fiction work, but it's also the beginning of a new chapter for us.

My son, Jesse Byrd Jr., joins me on the filmmaking trail and he's received awards for the Mom's Choice, 2018 Picture Book of the Year in London, Paris Book Festival Top 3, and other accolades. God gave me the right child. Jesse is a brilliant and compassionate human being with a love for penning and publishing children's books. Visit Jesse online at www.JesseBCreative.com.

Hamdy and Magda Abbass, thanks for giving life to two phenomenal women. I am blessed to have Emaan Byrd (my daughter-in-law) and Heidi Abbass (my daughter-in-law's sister). We have our unique bond.

When I think of home, Wayne Morrison, Andrea Morrison, Derrick Morrison, Regina Morrison, Margie Rickerson, Debra Noel, the late Elizabeth Morrison, and our unborn sibling, I think of our upbringing. We've each come this far by God's grace. I love each of you!

Pets are family members, too. "Mom, I want a Yorkie," my son said, and I protested to the end. Jesse was college bound and for the first time in nearly twenty years I didn't want anyone or anything to care for except myself. Turns out, KingMaxB was more loyal than any man I've dated (lol). If you have a pet, you feel me. As with rearing my child, I'm fortunate to have co-parents who love KingMaxB unconditionally.

Julie Brown, Princess Cole, Julien Edward Brown Perry, Shari Williams Brown, Eve Lynne Robinson, your co-parenting is priceless. Although KingMaxB lost his eyesight at the age of twelve, dude is still humping his stuffed animal girlfriend on the regular.

I add cars to my friendship train every year. At each junction, old friends ride along, new friends board. Others transition into another space. Energy can neither be created nor destroyed; therefore, wherever you are, I am with you and vice versa.

Kendall Minter, Kenneth P. Norwick, and Alan S. Clarke (my attorneys), Esi Sogah (my new editor), Karen R. Thomas and La-Toya C. Smith (my former editors), Christal Jordan and Tiffany Irene (my publicists), and John Williams of Worldstar, I don't want to imagine where I'd be if it weren't for you guys.

My gurl squad runs deep: Lieutenant Colonel Cassandra Guy, Judge Vanessa Gilmore, Felicia Polk, Koren McKenzie-John, Esq., Carmen Polk, Dr. Angela Davis, Dr. Rose Rowden, Lauren Davis, Rachelle "Slice of Pie" Davis, Vyllorya A. Evans (my mentor), Jo-Vanté Morrison, Derrianna and Derrianne Morrison, Anissa Rickerson, Michaela Burnett, Vanessa Ibanitoru, Brenda Jackson, Marissa Monteilh, Lilly Ortiz, Tina Celisa Robinson, Chantel Vallés, Marion Whitaker, Colonel LaNita "Nikki" Taylor, Yevonna "Missy E. the Partydoll" Johnson, Jessica Holter, L. Nyrobi Moss, Joelle Gracia, Charlene "Queen" Johnson, Sherri New, and Kimbercy Marie Harris-Jones. If I'm going to make this book longer than my list of gurlz, I have to stop here. Each of you have had a positive impact on my life.

Richard C. Montgomery, I love you, man.

Many of you have a story to tell. Some don't know where to start. Others have a difficult time committing to the process. Penning a book isn't for everyone, so I encourage you to do anything you're passionate about.

Roneagle4Life! McDonogh 35 Senior High Class of 1982 (in New Orleans, Louisiana), we are and forever will be #1.

What's life without social media? You can find me on Facebook, Twitter, Instagram, and Snapchat at @celebhoneyb.

Wishing each of my readers peace and prosperity in abundance. Visit me online at www.MaryMorrison.com. Sign up for my newsletter and follow me @celebhoneyb.

1.5 MILLION MISSING BLACK MEN
(in the United States)

—The New York Times

Online dating will be the best or worst decision you'll ever make.

CHAPTER 1

Kingston

He can't remember his face, yet he'd never forget his name.
The cap of his Arturo Fuente Opus X fell to the floor as he snapped the guillotine. Slowly he dipped the shoulder of his cigar into a shot glass filled with pure honey, placed the sweetest end between the enormous lips classmates used to ridicule him for having. Lighting the foot, Kingston suctioned a long drag of the savory tobacco smoke into his mouth.

Kingston stood. Clinched the tip of the seven-inch stick between his teeth, suctioned in the bold taste, then placed the cigar in a groove on the tray. His eyes were fixated on the guest who was seated on the maroon velvet sofa. Kingston walked to the living room's window, then closed the beige blackout drapes. Retreating to the bedroom, he removed his red designer fitted pants, black T-shirt, and green boxer briefs, then carefully lay each item on the plush king-sized bed. Optioning to keep on his red knee-high compression socks, he returned to the living room, reclaimed his seat in the black-and-white paisley-print barrel chair. Exhaling white clouds of smoke from his mouth and nostrils at the same time, he spread his legs.

Gazing across the room, he held in his darkest secret. It wasn't his fault.

"Get off the couch. Take off your clothes. Get on your knees.

And suck my dick," Kingston said in an apathetic tone, making more of a request than a demand.

A five-star hotel in Buckhead was Kingston's temporary haven. A place where he could be his authentic self. He placed his stick between his pointing and middle fingers.

Six feet, nine inches didn't make him a man. Becoming a multi-millionaire at the age of twenty-two hadn't altered his character. Being thirty and one of the blackest men in America, he feared three things: being killed by a white police officer, wrongful incarceration, and . . .

Suctioning the smoky smoothness, Kingston wondered how they'd made it to arrangement number thirteen. On the square table within his reach were his room key, phone, a brightly lit lamp, a torch device, and the ashtray where he placed the stogie.

He retrieved his cell, scanned the app BottomsUp, swiped left twice, right once.

Staring across the room into a beautiful set of large brown eyes, Kingston firmly said, "Sweetheart, I'm not going to ask you twice. Your only other option is to get out."

They'd met on the app BottomsUp. For Kingston, it was supposed to be a one and done. That was why he had to find a replacement today.

What does the kid that had performed fellatio on Kingston look like today? Slim? Fat? Tall? Short? Beard? Mustache?

Third grade. Janitor's closet. Between brooms and a yellow bucket on wheels filled with dirty water and a mop, his pecker is being sucked for the first time.

"You know I'm not going anywhere, silly. Stop trying to act all bad and stuff. I know you want me. The feeling is mutual." Theodore Ramsey rose in slow motion, approached Kingston, removed his shirt, twirled it in the air. He pranced to the sofa, neatly lay his pink polo across the back. Unfastening his belt, he pushed his pants to his knees, shuffled his feet back over to Kingston, then stepped out of his jeans. Theodore seductively swayed his dick left and right. "We need some music, baby," he said, reaching toward the table with the lamp.

Grabbing his cell, Kingston firmly reminded Theodore, "What'd I tell you about that 'baby' bullshit. Stop calling me that. And don't you ever make the mistake of touching my phone."

"I was *reaching*," Theodore said, emphasizing the word, then continued, "for the cigar. Come out of hiding and you won't have to worry about anyone finding out that you're—"

The janitor's closet is where his innocence was compromised. Inhaling the scent of wet mops, bleach, and pine, he watches the little boy lock the door. The light is on. Kingston's back is pressed against a cold metal stand with shelves overflowing with rolls of paper towels and toilet tissue.

"Say it and regret it!" Kingston sprung from his seat. "I'll put your ass out of my suite for good."

Theodore stepped two feet back. Shook his head.

Kingston sat center on the armless paisley chair, admiring his guest. Theodore was six-two with glistening skin that looked like he was dunked into a barrel of glazed caramel. His beard, mustache, and pubic hairs were shaved to a smooth shadow. Theodore's uncircumcised penis pointed toward Kingston's full lips.

Theodore knelt in front of him.

A call registered on Kingston's cell. It was his wife. Her timing was inconvenient. He tapped the red circle to decline hearing her voice. Placing his phone on the wooden table, Kingston gazed down at Theodore. "Sorry, man. You don't get it. I'm not that way."

Staring up, he said, "Your wife is the one who's not getting it or your dick. You're lying about your marital status to others. The only reason you told me was because you know I don't care anything about a pussy."

Lying was easier. How often did women search for validation? Most men and some women didn't care about a wedding ring.

Afraid of being a disgrace to his family, friends, and fans, Kingston found it was easier to live his life based on what others expected of him. There were things he admired about Theodore Ramsey. Primarily, his open sexuality, candor, courage, intelligence, sense of humor at times, and his not having a dark side.

Theodore leaned over; then he gently kissed Kingston's inner thighs.

"I still want you to come by my clothing store. I have a wardrobe for you that I know you're going to like, Mr. Royale. And I'll have my partner design you a branded signature look."

"Cool." Picking up his cigar and torch, Kingston held the fire at the edge, then sucked the tip several times, reigniting the fading flame.

It feels good. The wetness of the little boy's mouth on his pecker when they are alone in the janitor's closet.

Monet Royale wasn't going anywhere. He'd hit her back later. Kingston had an urgent hard-on to tend to.

His shaft grew wider. Longer. He reached toward his crotch, untucked his balls from underneath his butt. Too many encounters were beginning to lead to Kingston developing emotions for Theodore. Blowing smoke in Theodore's face, Kingston insisted, "Let's get this over with."

Theodore rested his butt on his heels, placed his hand on his hip, questioned Kingston as though Kingston had put a ring on his finger: "That was her, huh?"

Kingston had the best privacy screen for situations like this. No need to deny the truth. Nodding, he realized there was no competition between Theodore and his wife. Just differences. Kingston wished he could merge the best of both of them into one person.

He knows it is wrong. But he can't leave the janitor's closet for two reasons. He's never felt anything that has made his entire body tingle. And he is afraid of the rumors if someone sees them coming out together.

"If you want to get this over with, you can at least silence your damn phone." Theodore lamented, then politely added, "Please."

The most salacious male specimen Kingston desired—mind, body, and energy—slowly glided his tongue from Kingston's knee to his balls, causing his erection to stand at full attention.

Wow, Kingston thought, letting the second call from his wife go to voice mail. Staring at the sugary temptation before him, Kingston anxiously welcomed being Theodore's dessert.

Kingston leaned forward, slapped Theodore's ass. "Get the lemon cream pie out of the freezer."

"Cream and pie and it's frozen. You should've been said that, ba . . ." Theodore let the other half of the word resound in his head, then he saluted Kingston. He strutted barefoot on the chocolate hardwood floor. "You know I'm a headmaster, and tasty toppings bring out the beast in me." Theodore growled, "Grrr!" then snapped his teeth twice.

"Great. Then you won't make a mess," Kingston said, following up with a smile. He was ready to blast off a full load.

Nothing comes out of his pecker in that janitor's closet. Nothing.

"When have I ever made a mess, hon . . . I mean, Kingston?" Correcting himself, Theodore twirled, then tap-danced back to Kingston, balancing the pie in his palm.

Kingston smiled, but his enormous lips did not part. His eyes did not depart from Theodore's.

They were both perfectionists with problems. The military had trained Theodore to give and receive commands. Team sports made Kingston a standout and team leader of triple-doubles. Theodore was fighting a dishonorable discharge. Kingston was battling being honest about his identity.

Another call from Monet surfaced. Not prepared to give up his new lifestyle, Kingston had left her behind in Maryland, two months ago. Unwilling to admit that he loved the way Theodore loved on him, Kingston gazed into the windows of Theodore's soul.

Holding the pie, Theodore knelt between Kingston's legs. "What the fuck. I can't get no peace, so you ain't gonna get no peace with her. If we're keeping it real, you done with pussy. Leave her ass in Columbus. She'll be okay," he said, smashing the pie on Kingston's dick.

Kingston calmly corrected him. "It's Columbia. And . . . don't say a word." Then he picked up the phone and answered, "Baby, let me call you ri—"

Monet interrupted, "All I want you to tell me is you've found a house for us. We miss you, Daddy."

Leaning into Kingston's lap, Theodore opened his mouth, stuck out his tongue, wrapped his hand around Kingston's lemony creamy shaft, and began stroking up and down in slow motion.

"I knew I shouldn't have let you go alone. I'm coming to Atlanta, to help you find something," Monet insisted.

Selecting and decorating a home each time they'd moved, his

wife should've gotten her real estate license, instead of getting pregnant for him twelve years ago. Between stripper poles and human trafficking, there was no way Kingston was raising his daughters in the ATL.

Theodore buried his face in the filling, then alternated suctioning Kingston's nuts into his mouth one at a time.

Rising from his knees, the boy races out of the janitor's closet. Afraid to peep outside, Kingston closes the door. Crying, trembling, and sniffling, Kingston pulls up his pants, fastens his buckle, turns the lock, and starts counting to fifty. His grandmother taught him if you count to fifty before reacting, you'll make a better decision.

Watching Theodore's head go up and down, Kingston mouthed, "Stop it."

The last thing he wanted was to give Monet a reason to pop up on him. Theodore's head bobbed faster.

"Hold tight, baby. I'm close. Real close." To cumming. "Listen, baby. Lilly is helping me narrow it down to two mansions. One in Smyrna and the other in Conyers. Then you can choose one or the other. I'll FaceTime you tomorrow after church from both locations."

Monet's breathing became noticeably heavy with long pauses. Her voice softened. "I can retreat from the kitchen and FaceTime you now. I can use a naughty-girl tune-up."

A text message popped up from Victoria: **We're ushering the early service tomorrow.**

Inhaling deeply, Kingston quietly exhaled. "Not now. I'm at the gym. That's why I missed your other calls," he lied.

Kingston replied to Victoria's text: **Cool, gray or blue uniforms**.

Monet's voice escalated. "I know how the women in Atlanta are! I'm not losing my husband to a 'do anything for a piece of change' ho shaking her ass for a sponsor."

Gray, Victoria replied.

Theodore stood, started jerking his arms and swinging his hips at the same time. He twirled, then twerked, making his ass cheeks greet each other. His face was covered with melted cream.

Silently Kingston laughed, motioning for Theodore to get back on his knees. "You right. I'd never fuck them hos, baby." Kingston muted the call.

"Aw, shit!" Kingston yelled as Theodore's lips slid along his shaft. He felt Theodore's tongue slide, stop. Glide. Stop. Each time a chunk of pie was devoured. "You definitely know what the hell you're doing, man. Where'd you learn that search-and-find"—Kingston yelped his next word—"technique?"

"Do you hear me, Kingston? I'm coming to Atlanta without your permission," Monet retorted.

Theodore shook his head and wiggled his tongue.

Kingston was about to cum. Inhaling deeply, he held his breath. Exhaled. Thanks to the volume in Monet's tone, he didn't care that Theodore could overhear the conversation.

He told Theodore, "Don't say a word."

"You the one up in here screaming like a bitch. Not me," Theodore replied.

When he gets to fifty, Kingston slowly opens the janitor's closet door.

Is fifty the perfect age to come out? "Give me a minute. I'ma end this call in a sec and return the favor," Kingston said, unmuting the call.

Kingston rubbed the crown of Theodore's head, then told Monet, "Baby, ooh-whee. You need to bring it down an octave."

What would his wife, parents, and church members think if Kingston confessed that he enjoyed the company of men?

Kingston wasn't gay. No man had penetrated him, and no man ever would. Monet didn't enjoy performing fellatio. Theodore was his first male experience in Atlanta. But not his only.

Theodore started sucking, pumping, and licking vigorously.

Kingston took a deep breath. "Ba-by. The, is, break, I, ma, call—"

"Kingston!" Monet yelled. "I'm getting three tickets today. I'm bringing the girls. We'll be there tomorrow! I bet you heard that."

Ending the connection, Kingston shouted, "Shit! Shit! Damn, man! You are a fucking headmaster."

Kingston hadn't cum that hard with his wife. The edginess of having Monet on the phone and Theodore on the mic turned Kingston on.

Theodore stood. Swallowed. "You'd best tell your babies' mother to stay in Columbus, Co-lum-bia, wherever the hell she's at, or she's going to have to deal with me. I am not letting you go."

He had that right. There was nothing to let go of. Kingston was *not* dating a man.

Langston Derby. That is the boy in the janitor's closet. Where is he now? And how does he look?

CHAPTER 2

Victoria

"**S**hit." *Jesus, please take away the hot flashes or the insomnia. Praying for both might be too much.* Victoria flapped the white down-feather comforter to create a breeze. Her internal inferno was on the rise.

Glancing at her longtime seventy-one-year-old lover, William Copeland, who was lying beside her snoring, she retrieved her cell from the headboard, then lay on her back and bent her knees.

Every dick Victoria touched was an investment.

Heavenly? Cedric? Both? Neither? Victoria scanned their profiles on the app TuitionCougars; they were equally handsome juniors in college. Heavenly's major was communications. He was requesting $10,000 (for entertainment, a vacation, clothing, and car repairs) plus another $50,000 for next year's tuition and a new car. Cedric's field was engineering. His shortfall without a breakdown was cumulative of $80,000.

Goddamn, Victoria thought. *Why are the young educated men in Atlanta trying to get over on older women, too? Just because she was a sponsor didn't mean she was desperate.*

Considering there wasn't exclusivity, a ten-grand spread out over a year was reasonable. Eighty thousand was enough for a down payment on a house. Picturing Willy's gray pubic hairs, she in-boxed both of the guys: **Dinner or lunch at Capital Grille in Buck-head?**

Victoria kicked the sheet. She wasn't ungrateful for her gift, but out of all the spells she'd cast and broken, why-oh-why couldn't she prepare one potion for herself? The Lord had bestowed "private summers" upon seasoned women for what good reason? Victoria appreciated making it to sixty, but she certainly wasn't happy having had a decade of hot flashes *and* difficulty falling asleep most nights.

Expectedly, she went from a peaceful moment to what felt like a wildfire spreading inside of her. Sweat oozed from every pore. The prickling sensation along her scalp threatened to soak her freshly flat-ironed short hair, reverting it to her natural curls.

Victoria silently prayed, *Lord, hear my prayer. Make it stop. Now.* Her cell slipped from her saturated palms, hit her breast, bounced onto the carpet. Making a split decision, Victoria yanked off her head scarf, then slid from underneath the moist covers before her 140 pounds became 139. If she continued to lie down, the mattress would be drenched in minutes.

"Help me, Jesus," she said softly.

Why, Lord? Why? What's the purpose? she questioned, knowing He knew her thoughts. *Why don't men have a period? Menopause? Hot flashes. Babies? Anything. Something that would decrease or at least interrupt their sex drive other than erectile dysfunction, old age, or prostate cancer?*

Tiptoeing through the dimly lit room, Victoria tried not to disturb her companion, who'd temporarily stopped breathing. Abruptly he snorted, coughed three times, then resumed his snore. Willy denied having sleep apnea; he refused to do a breathing study or use an oxygen machine.

Victoria entered the bathroom, quietly closed the door before switching on the ceiling track lights. Covering her hair with a plastic cap lined with satin, Victoria quickly stepped into the shower and turned on the cool water. Adjusting four of the ten heads, she welcomed the mist spraying from her breasts to her knees.

With a sigh of relief, she softly said, "Thank You, Jesus."

It was too early to be perky. Too late to go back to sleep. "Please let it end, Lord. Forever, this time. This is the only thing I ask of

You every day. I know You hear me. But just in case, it's Your favorite child, Victoria Fox, Lord.

"It's me, it's me, it's me, O Lord, standin' in the need of prayer." The hymn transitioned to a hum.

Preparing for her cryotherapy, the liquid-nitrogen regulator was set to 192 degrees below zero. Victoria put on her special socks, boots, and gloves, then stood inside for 120 seconds exactly. Any device, workout equipment, serum, mask, or cream that prevented Victoria from wrinkling, sagging, or aging was somewhere in her four-thousand-square-foot mansion.

Stepping out of the freezing chamber, she said, "Thank You, Lord Jesus."

Growing up, Victoria was too poor to be rich. Too rich to be poor. Thankful that she never married, had two pregnancies—no births—Victoria was responsible for one person all her life. That was the way it would always be until her Lord and Savior called her to glory.

"You okay in there?" Brother Copeland called out from the bedroom.

Why, Lord? Why? What's the purpose of men, when most of them don't know how to make love and women are sexually self-sufficient? she questioned.

"Brushing my teeth," she replied, then traded her electric toothbrush for her Luxe Replenish 7-Function black stimulator.

Letting the silver vibrating tip rest on her clit, sixty seconds later, Victoria released a satisfying climax, as she'd done to start each day.

Victoria had resolved to being an opportunist at the age of sixteen. "Shit," she hissed. Now that he was up, her getting back to the TuitionCougars app to see if Cedric and/or Heavenly had replied wasn't happening soon.

Victoria had hoped the Lord would've given her just one more hour of relaxation. That way, Brother Copeland would've rolled out of her bed, gotten dressed, and walked out of their—more like *her*—house, which he'd bought, all cash, after his first wife died.

Victoria didn't have *much* to do with Brother Willy's wife passing unexpectedly.

Standing in the doorway, she replied, "I have to get ready for church, Willy Copeland. I'm ushering the *early* service this morning." That was the truth. It was seven o'clock and church started in two hours.

"Yeah, but we don't have a sunrise service, honey pumpkin. Come back to bed so Mz. Purrty can cuddle with Big Willy," he said. "Him beez lonely." A pouty mouth followed.

No need to deny her lifelong sponsor. Every woman needed at least one. Victoria had satisfied Brother Copeland through two of his marriages for a total of thirty-four adulterous years—plus a decade of fornication.

In the beginning, it was just the two of them, she'd thought. She was sixteen. He was twenty-seven. The Lord knew her heart. Willy didn't. If Willy had gotten her pregnant again or procreated with any woman, Willy would've lived the rest of his days itching and scratching his balls.

Victoria had voodoo potions of the best and worst kind, but she preferred the ones that agitated her enemies.

"Let's get this out of the way or you're going to have to wait until next weekend to cum," Victoria said, peeling the wrapper off of her favorite toy for Big Willy.

He was the only man she ever cared for. But Victoria's mother had told her: "If a man lies, he'll steal. If he steals, he'll kill. And once a cheater, always a cheater. It's not *if,* Victoria. It's *when* he'll do it again. Better to be the one he's cheating with than the one he's cheating on. And always get your money up front, baby."

Back when she was in her twenties, thirties, and forties, sex with Willy did not require forethought. He stayed ready.

"Work your magic, darling. You are the only woman that knows how to send Big Willy to the moon," he said. "I done took my medication. Half of your work is done, sugarplum." His belly jiggled when he laughed.

Willy was her seventy-one-year-old steady Saturday-evening, Sunday-morning companion. She had one younger man in her rotation. Rodney Hudson, a thirty-four-years-young—big dick for real—aspiring entrepreneur that would be in her bed beating her pussy up before sunset. Rodney gave her what Brother Willy Copeland no longer had to offer. There was no voodoo potion to make bad dick better and no concoction for hot flashes, but Victoria was relieved that putting a little coconut oil inside of her vagina helped alleviate the dryness.

"Close your eyes, Willy. I'm about to take you on a ride out of this orbit, honey!" Victoria exclaimed.

"Ooh-whee," he cheered, grabbing his manhood. "You heard that, Big Willy? Get ready."

Victoria refused to tolerate off-beat strokes from Willy every time his enhancement kicked in. He'd never learned to properly sex her, but his pockets were always deep and her long fingers were glued to the bottom of both of them.

"Lay still," Victoria demanded. "Turn onto your side, and—"

"I know. I know. Don't touch Mz. Purrty or she'll dry up. Get me off. I hafta go home and gets ready for church."

After his last wife passed, Victoria immediately gained legal entitlement to Willy's 401(k), military benefits, health insurance coverage, real estate portfolio, luxury cars, stocks, and bonds by catering to what Willy valued the most. His penis. What good would it do to bury Willy along with his benefits and leave his riches to a state that reinvested in the oppression of black people?

Victoria hated for any man to tell her what to do. "I've been handling Big Willy for forty-four years."

"You know what time it is, woman?" The side of Willy's belly flattened to the mattress as he rolled over. "I need extra time these days to get myself together. Shit. Shower. Shave. Sleep. Just wait until you turn my age. Come on, Victoria. I can't let this good Viagra go to waste."

If she was going to get excited, it was going to be for a virile man like Rodney. Or prayerfully for Cedric. Or Heavenly. Victoria was anxious to get back to the app.

"You sure you're ready for Mz. Purrty?" Victoria asked.

Opening the plastic shell, she removed an egg-shaped masturbation sleeve, tore the package of lubrication, squirted it inside, arched her back, then tilted her vagina toward Willy's erection. Firmly holding his shaft, she stretched, then eased the silicone over the head of his dick. Every man she used it on loved it, including her younger guys. The difference was they knew what it was. Willy did not.

"Aw, yeah," Willy moaned. "How do you stay so tight and wet, woman? Guess it's all those products you charge to my Black card."

Grazing her hairless labia against his pubic hairs, Victoria tightened her grip. She thrust back and forth; stroked Willy up and down, using the egg.

"You ready to make Mz. Purrty wet, Big Willy?" Victoria stroked harder. Moved a bit faster.

"Pow. Pow. Pow. That's all Big Willy got for you today?" he said, keeping his hands above his head. "After all these years, your vagina is the best I've had. If I didn't know any better, I'd swear you were trying to send me to glory on the express train, woman." Willy chuckled.

Stuffing the soiled masturbation sleeve back into its container, Victoria retrieved a black plastic bag from underneath the mattress, dropped the egg inside. "Lord Jesus, You know I'm tired. Big Willy, you wear me out every time," she lied, then told the truth. "I love you, Willy Copeland."

"Love you more. Always have. Forever will," he replied. "Nothing I won't do for ya."

Willy was generous with her in every way. Why not keep her old man happy?

Carefully getting out of bed, Victoria held Willy's seeds. He'd already begun snoring. Staring at Willy, she kissed his cheek. "No, I love you more. I just can't let you know it, big daddy."

If Willy overslept for church, it wouldn't be his first time.

CHAPTER 3
Chancelor

"Fake it until you make it," Pastor Baloney preached. "It's called practice. If you want to be a great basketball player like Brother Kingston Royale was, start working out daily. Athletes are strong. A lawyer like Sister Jordan Jackson—by the way, thanks for helping the church out with that legal matter—start by being a great debater and a better listener. Whatever you want, you can have if . . . you have faith in God and never give up. Degrees are nice, but mastering a skill set is better. Like it or not, some Instagram models are making millions. I don't know about the other religious institutions in Atlanta, but here at Hope for All Church, we want every member to become wealthy and healthy. God does not want you to be poor. Men and women who believe they are better than you, based on the color of their skin, will never inherit the earth. Why? Because they don't respect human life or God. We are going to move quietly. Register today for our upcoming HFAC Millionaires' Club. Keep this between us. I want my members to eat first. Be generous with your tithes as the ushers receive your benevolent offering. For you can never outgive who?"

The audience shouted in unison, "God!"

"Amen," Pastor Baloney said, then sat to the left of the podium.

Passing the collection basket to the deacon seated on the first pew, Chancelor licked his lips, then placed one arm behind his back. Standing six feet tall, dressed in gray slacks and vest, a white short-sleeved shirt, he spread his brown leather shoes apart, ran his hand over the short spiked locs (with blue tips) bunched on the top of his head. The sides and back were shaven and brushed into black zigzag pattern.

Victoria was on the opposite end facing him. That woman never had any of her natural strands—curly or straight—out of place. Today her hair was flat and smooth with a part on the right side. She was tall with legs that seemed to never end. Bragged about being a size four. Always wore dresses and heels. Her mocha skin was flawless and tight like a teenager's. Victoria didn't look as though she was close to sixty-one. She could easily pass for forty-five. She'd turned him down several times. Chancelor knew Brother Copeland couldn't be the only man hitting that pussy.

Chancelor shifted his eyes twenty-five rows to his left. There sat the church whore, Tracy Benjamin. He hated her ass.

Atlanta was that city where no one was on the real, but everyone wanted *r-e-s-p-e-c-t* and a microwave drive-thru relationship. He tried to fall in love with Tracy, but no. All she wanted was his money. Her ass needed to be first in line to register for the pastor's HFAC Millionaires' Club.

A chip in Tracy's ass was what she needed so Chancelor could scan how many dicks she'd encountered—forget in her lifetime—how about the last thirty days. Chancelor was done with treating whores like ladies. Where he'd grown up, those two things didn't go together, but he couldn't convince Tracy of that.

"Here, Brother Chancelor," the man on the sixth row said with bass in his voice as he nudged the wicker against Chancelor's abdomen.

"Oh, thanks, man," Chancelor said, sidestepping to row seven.

The member sitting on the end placed her donation envelope atop the others, took the basket, then passed it to her neighbor.

Scanning the congregation, his eyes shifted seventeen rows to his left. He'd discovered $3,000 too late that Tracy was a professional gold-digger. Chancelor stared at Tracy through his peripheral. She smiled while chatting with the man next to her.

Bitch! Chancelor's body count of six at Hope for All Church was higher than Jordan's and probably much lower than Victoria the-undercover-consummate-Christian whore's, who claimed she refused to lay where she prayed (for the exception of Willy). He'd bet they were all award-winning one-night-stand champions. He saw Victoria give Brother Copeland a friendly wink earlier. The only person in their usher/friendship quartet that hadn't reportedly scored at church was Kingston. Fair enough. He was the newest addition to their group. And the humblest celebrity/member Chancelor had met.

Standing beside the nineteenth row, Chancelor thought, *Sister Peaches need to be ashamed of herself for dropping $5 for the Lord. The Göt2b glue for her front lace from Atlanta Beauty Depot cost more than that.* Then he moved along to row twenty. Peaches always raved about her exclusively patronizing the black-owned wig shop in Smyrna and tried to recruit every wig and extension-wearing member. Maybe she could become a kickback millionaire.

Joining a mega church was not what Chancelor wanted when he relocated to Atlanta. Nor did he want a small congregation where regulars shared each other's DNA.

The wicker basket made it to the opposite end of the pew to his fellow usher-friend Victoria. They made eye contact before side-stepping to the next row. Kingston and Jordan were on the other aisles over. Kingston and Victoria were back-to-back.

Chancelor's anger toward Tracy intensified. His full lips tightened. Eyes narrowed with disdain for the woman that called herself a "child of God." He was in part to blame. When he saw she, too, had a profile on the app ChristianFornicators, he couldn't resist asking her for a date. The only thing Tracy had put out was her hand.

Slightly shifting his eyes to the left, he felt the soft laughter from Tracy to the man next to her was intended to agitate him. If Tracy fainted right now, Chancelor couldn't confirm he'd check to find out if she had a pulse. His cocoa-colored lips kissing distance from hers would never happen again. The moment had come for him to move to the last row, and his heartbeat had quickened with hatred.

Tracy was the fifty-seventh female Chancelor pursued after moving to Atlanta from Beverly Hills, Michigan. It was time for him to do like she'd done and move on.

"Hi, Brother Chancelor Leonard," Tracy said seductively with that fake-friendly smile that once lured him in.

He nodded, wanting to knock out her teeth with her red-bottom stilettos he'd bought. Chancelor hadn't given up on finding a good churchwoman to marry. But each time he expressed interest in a lady at their church, Tracy found a way to ruin it. Why did women let ex-girlfriends get in their heads? Hell, why was Tracy still on his mind? She didn't deserve him.

Forming a double-file, two-person line in the center aisle at the rear of the church, Chancelor followed Victoria, and Kingston was next to him, and behind Jordan. Marching to the altar, they stood while the pastor blessed the congregation's offering.

When the choir began singing, Chancelor noticed Tracy's hour-glass waist and big booty standing in the center aisle, facing the exit. Maybe he should give Tracy a second chance . . . he'd have to be the stupidest dude in Georgia.

She is fine, though. Maybe I misunderstood her or wasn't compassionate enough when she shared her childhood trauma of sexual abuse . . .

Interrupting his mental monologue, Brother Melvin stood behind Tracy, blocking Chancelor's view. He was so close to Tracy's ass, one more step and his dick would touch her butt.

Where the fuck did he surface from?

Chancelor wished he had a bowling ball; he'd strike with just enough force to tap Brother Melvin so he'd knock Tracy in the gutter, where she belonged.

"Ahem. Ahem." Victoria cleared her throat, then whispered, "Stop worrying about Tracy, she's part of the penis-welcoming committee."

Chancelor didn't acknowledge Victoria's warped sense of humor.

Under the volume of the choir's singing, Chancelor replied, "Why hasn't she recruited Kingston?"

Kingston mumbled, "Stop it, both of you. I'm steps ahead of her kind."

"Give her a minute." The music ended as Victoria added, "Tracy will welcome your penis, Kingston."

In the deepest voice, Pastor Baloney said, "Let. Us. Pray."

Following the blessing of the contributions, all of the ushers headed to the back.

"I need a drink," Chancelor told Victoria, Jordan, and Kingston. "This conversation is going to be continued at Bar Purgatory."

"Our usual stop it is," Kingston said. "Meet y'all there in an hour."

"Why're you always an hour late, man?" Chancelor questioned.

Kingston replied, "My pattern ain't changed, bruh. This is your crisis, not mine. I need to switch out of these slacks, vest, tie, and this white shirt, man. You should do the same sometimes. The bar isn't going anywhere."

Jordan chimed in, "Kingston has to call his wife. Or as he claims, babies' mother, Monet."

Nodding at Jordan, Kingston squinted, then asked, "What's wrong with that? I raised her up to keep the media out of my face. I'm not legally married. Okay?"

Victoria said, "Then Kingston, in the name of God, you need to honor and marry the mother of your illegitimate children."

Holding up his palms, Kingston took a step back. "I don't have to explain myself. I'm single."

"The man acknowledged his status. He's single. Damn, what's wrong with women?" Chancelor lamented.

"Everything and nothing." Kingston gently patted Chancelor on the back. "Depends on who you ask. See y'all in a few."

CHAPTER 4

Kingston

Sitting in the black-and-white paisley chair in his hotel suite, Kingston searched BottomsUp to find a nearby guy seeking to have a quickie. A text registered from Theodore: **Why are you still on here?**

Definitely not to stalk him, Kingston thought, not responding.

Damn! Kingston drooled over the guy, who showed his body from the upper lip arch down to the defined dip of his abs, which led to the barely exposed pubic hairs. Was he an athlete, too? Didn't matter. They were both on the app. Kingston messaged: **Want some adventure right now?** along with a picture of his dick.

232323 replied, **If the pic is real, I'm wide open**, then pin-dropped his location.

Kingston made a quick wardrobe switch. Out of the usher uniform into all black: button-down shirt, a pair of denims, tennis shoes, and a zip-up hoodie despite the ninety-degree temperature outside. He then grabbed a box containing designer shoes. In less than fifteen minutes, he was headed to his interim destination.

One of the fifty private parking spaces located in the rear of the adult-entertainment establishment on Cheshire Bridge Road was all he needed. Flipping the hood of his jacket over his head, Kingston eased on a pair of dark sunglasses to shield his identity, then secured his cell phone in the armrest compartment of his black-on-black Mercedes SUV with tinted windows.

Hurrying inside, he stuffed his hands into his pockets. His chin touched his neck as he eagerly strolled past the cashier; he was anticipating what was to come. He wasn't there to finger the vagina of the silicone human-sized sexbot displayed at the entrance or purchase a glass-blown dildo enclosed in the case. He was there for the real thing. Kingston bypassed the exotic-toys section, then trotted downstairs to the dimly lit basement. Lifting his eyewear to his brows, he scanned the room, identifying what appeared to be a few women and lots of men, but he was solely interested in the latter.

Kingston quickly trolled the entire area one time, spotted a male image slumped in the corner. Watching the guy massage his thighs up and down sparked a rise in Kingston. The dude's dick pointed north without assistance.

Lowering his shades to his nose, Kingston sat on the bench beside the stranger, then whispered, "Triple twenty-three?"

"Yup" was all he said.

Kingston realized he was going to be in and done in less time than it took him to change his church clothes. "I'm pitching. If you're catching."

"You must be new at this. I told you. I'm wide open," he answered.

Enough procrastination. "Let's go to a private playroom." There was no need to discuss his health status; both of them knew what they were there for. Occupying one of the bedrooms wasn't necessary.

Real men didn't require missionary, foreplay, or afterglow. As he entered the standing-room-only space, the click of the lock reminded Kingston of being in the janitor's closet.

Erasing the childhood memory, Kingston snipped a tiny split in the edge of the condom packet with his canine teeth. The guy pulled down his sweatpants, leaned against the wall, spread his feet. Kingston unfastened his belt, let his jeans rest below his knees. Unrolling the latex over his shaft, he stepped out of his pants, then hung them on a hook. Squatting, he tilted his pelvis. Slowly he swiped his head between 232323's tight butt cheeks, then penetrated him.

Images of Theodore eating cream pie off of his dick while Monet was on the phone heightened Kingston's sex drive from stiff to rockhard. The more he replayed his last session with Theodore, the greater he struggled to dismiss his feelings for Theodore.

Was Theodore letting a man do to him what Kingston was doing to 232323?

Rapidly pounding again and again, the hood of his jacket slid down to the nape of his neck. His sunglasses slid to the tip of his nose. Kingston's secret shielded his truth. Kingston continued thrusting, praying this would be the last time he sexed a random.

Why did I enter the janitor's closet? What did I think would happen that day? Certainly not what Langston Derby had done.

Ten minutes later, Kingston released himself. He carefully removed the condom. Trashed it in the can filled with liquid that destroyed DNA on contact. Quickly he cleansed his genitals with a moist towelette. Putting on his pants, he placed his hood over his head. Pushed his frames to the bridge of his nose.

Cumming inside of that man felt more gratifying than ejaculating raw inside of his wife, but only during the act. Now that the orgasm was over, Kingston felt empty.

I'm not gay, he told himself, questioning his sexuality. Certain his wife had called him at least three times by now, he headed toward the exit. Kingston had to develop a plan to keep Monet in Columbia until he'd gotten out of his system the urge to sex men. Another month or two should suffice. But how was he going to end his situation with Theodore?

Triple twenty-three wasn't as good as Theodore, but Kingston's mission was accomplished. Rushing to his car, Kingston headed to Bar Purgatory to meet up with his church friends. His dick felt sticky against his boxer briefs.

Transit time was best for him to call Monet. Having a destination gave him a valid reason to get off the phone shortly.

"What took you so long to call me back?" his wife complained.

"Baby, church. Today was my Sunday to usher the late service." Decreasing his speed to a complete stop, Kingston looked to his left.

The driver stared. Breaking eye contact, Kingston looked straight ahead. Adjusted his tacky shaft from his inner thigh toward his abdomen.

"Hey, Daddy," Israel shouted.

Nairobi echoed her older sister.

Saved by his girls. "Hey, my beautiful little angels. I'm sending you special-edition backpacks. One is pink and the other is purple. Don't fight over them. The one with the cell phone in it is for Nairobi," Kingston said, knowing if Monet disapproved she'd be the bad parent.

Israel countered, "What's in mine?"

"Guess," he said. Kingston kept the conversation going, hoping to run out of time to talk with his wife.

"Clothes?" Israel said.

"What kind of clothes?" Kingston hadn't purchased anything—backpacks, cell, clothes—for the girls. Not yet.

Israel stated, "Tennis shoes with lots of rhinestones?"

"You are a mind reader," he said.

Monet was quiet. The girls screeched with excitement.

"I know Mommy isn't happy with my being away from home," Kingston stated, then explained, "I have to stay busy in order to keep focus on our goals of finding a place here."

Kingston parked in the lot at the bar. Texted Lilly, **I need you to pick up four, make that five gifts. I'll drop off $10,000 and the list to you later.**

Np, Lilly messaged back.

"Daddy, I don't want to move," Nairobi protested.

"I don't want to make new friends," Israel said with attitude. "People in Atlanta are plastic."

"And fake," Nairobi added.

A call registered from Theodore. Kingston loved his wife, but his children made his decision to take his time easier. Ignoring the flirtatious female in the car next to his, he drove off.

"That's Lilly calling about the house. Let me call you back, baby. Love you guys," he said, thankful to end the conversation.

"Hey, man. What's up?" Kingston answered.

"It's your wife," Monet retorted.

Damn. He hit the red circle this time to end the call. Kingston looked at his cell, then dialed Theodore back and said, "Hey, man. What's up?" with the same enthusiasm.

"How about I bring over dinner and dessert tonight," Theodore suggested. "But I ain't giving you this delicious dick. We're chilling and watching a movie."

Sensing there was a smile on Theodore's face, Kingston's lips curved upward. "I'd like that. I need a friend in Atlanta, bruh."

"And you think I don't know that," Theodore replied. "See you at seven . . . man."

CHAPTER 5

Monet

Monet released the cell from her grip, letting it fall into a fruit basket in the middle of the island. "Stop jumping right now!" Her eyes shifted from one to the other as she yelled at her daughters.

If anyone deserved to be happy, it was Monet. The thought of hurling her smartphone across the kitchen at one of the many family photos hanging on the wall throughout their home was on the tip of her brain. Every room in their house was built with her husband, kids, or her mother in mind.

Four happy feet skipped lightly around the dining table. "I said stop it. Right this minute!" Monet slapped the bar-height island as she stared at her girls.

Wide light brown eyes beamed at Monet. Israel's full lips, were like her dad's, and high cheeks, mirrored Monet's. Her onyx skin shined from an excessive application of shea butter. She didn't blink when she asked, "What's wrong, Mother?" Resembling a skinny replica of her father, Israel stood five feet, five inches, at eleven years old.

Monet's anger wasn't her children's fault. Kingston cutting her off to talk to his boy pissed her off. Not returning her call. Not telling her "I love you" first thing in the morning, before bedtime, or saying it prior to ending their conversation had become more frequent. No more phone sex. Or FaceTime. His coldhearted tone was new and hurtful.

Monet's mother quietly sat at the island on one of the six barstools. She'd changed, too. Helping less with the girls. Siding more with Kingston.

Deep breaths filled Monet's lungs. Slowly she exhaled out of her nostrils. She picked a ripe mango from the bowl, then squeezed it hard. Juice splattered onto her mother's arm and onto the perfectly squared crystal-blue island's tiles.

Her seven-year-old, Nairobi, slowly approached her. "If Daddy doesn't send you anything, you can have my backpack." Nairobi was four feet, nine inches. She was a foot shorter than Monet, and she resembled her. Light complexion, almond-shaped eyes, and moderately plump lips. Nairobi wrapped her short arms around Monet's curvaceous hips and smiled. "But I'm going to need my phone. Please, Mommy."

Monet uncurled her fingers, letting the mango fall onto the island, then dampened a paper towel. Slowly she wiped the crystals.

Israel handed her grandmother a paper towel. Three feet of separation across the island, Monet wanted her mother to say something. Anything. But Trinity remained silent as she wiped the juice off of her arm.

This time her children deserved to see the outburst Monet often hid, like the lonely nights she wept on his pillow. Bracing her forearms on the tiles, tears streamed down her cheeks.

"Don't cry, Mommy." Nairobi dried Monet's face using the cotton of her mother's orange maxidress.

Monet firmly spoke. "Brunch is over, girls. Put your plates in the sink. Go to your room and pack an overnight bag. We are going to Atlanta to visit your father."

She retrieved her phone, then texted her travel agent: **I need 3 round-trip airline tickets from BWI to ATL leaving after 6pm today returning tomorrow evening for me and the girls and a hotel suite where you booked my husband. Drivers on both ends.**

Monet's impromptu decision was based on her gut instinct that something was wrong. That, and she was fed up with Kingston's procrastination of finding their family a new home. And she needed to meet their Realtor, Lilly, eye-to-eye.

Nairobi skipped to the table, stood next to her sister. Israel's eyes filled with sadness. She shook her head.

They lived south of Baltimore, north of Washington, D.C., where her husband had played professionally. Columbia was ideal for family living, when she thought Kingston would finally become a full-time father. Six bedrooms. Eight bathrooms. Six thousand square feet of living without him was depressing.

Sunrays beamed in her direction through the vertical ceiling-to-floor patio blinds. Shimmering crystals danced along the tiles.

"What about my friends in Jack and Jill? And the Girl Scouts, Mother?" Israel enunciated every syllable. "My perfect attendance at school will be ruined for an overnighter." She nudged her sister.

"Mine too," Nairobi blurted.

Israel added, "Daddy is always gone."

"And he always comes back." Nairobi's eyes were wide.

True. They'd primarily grown up without their father around, but damn, it was only for one day. Basketball practice, games, constantly on the road. Monet looked forward to her husband being home when he could. That had changed after he'd recovered from his injury. For the first time—for four consecutive months—Monet was no longer parenting alone. Two months ago, Kingston reverted to the familiar. *But why?*

"One day from school won't keep you from getting into a new private school, where both of you will have a clean record." Undoubtedly, it would ruin the girls' perfect attendance in Columbia, but no educational institution in Atlanta would care.

Nairobi didn't move from the dining area. Israel poured homemade lemonade in four glasses, then handed one to her sister, mother, and grandmother.

"Thank you, baby," the grandmother said.

As she placed her glass on the counter, Monet's eyes drooped as she looked to her mother, Trinity Baptiste, and pleaded for help.

Her mother stood. "You girls go to your library and read a book. Do not choose one you've already read . . . and I want an oral report when I come upstairs."

"Yes, Grandma," Israel and Nairobi said simultaneously. Both of Monet's daughters hugged her, then their grandmother, before racing up the steps.

Waiting until the girls were out of sight, Monet waved her hand over the trash can. When the lid opened, she slammed the mango inside, washed her hands, then cleared the serving dishes from the table for six, which had two empty seats, sometimes three when her mother wasn't dining with them.

Her mom sat tall on the barstool, arched her back, then crossed her legs. "When did you become so selfish, Monet Baptiste-Royale? Have you ever stopped to think that maybe Kingston needs alone time? He didn't leave the game because he wanted to. He's dealing with a lot and you need to give him space."

Whoa. Wait. "Mother, time and distance? My husband being in Atlanta for two months straight without as much as a visit from his family is dangerous. He hasn't even come home for a few days." Her voice escalated as she slapped the tiles. "Anywhere but Atlanta. He wasn't gone that many consecutive days when he was in the league. You've seen the reality shows. Those famished whores will stop at nothing to get at a tall, dark, and handsome man. Especially a celebrity with money."

Monet had decorated their home with original paintings throughout. The finest imported furnishings. High-end fashion was the norm for her and the girls. Kingston was more fanatical about his clothes. Her husband wouldn't die in a pair of tennis shoes, unless he was on the court.

Her mother had no comparative basis for love or marriage. Monet missed her husband. He was her truest best friend.

"I'm telling you what I know. Keep acting up. Don't be surprised if your husband begins to pull away from you. Kingston has given you everything you've wanted—and two beautiful children. He could've walked away and not married you when you got pregnant in college. Give—"

Monet interrupted, "You told me to trap him before he graduated from high school. I could've gotten locked up for having sex with a—"

"He was seventeen going on eighteen, and every university was courting *him*, Monet. You were twenty-three, single, and looking like a teenager yourself. And his parents were Christians from a small Southern town. I told you that boy was going pro and that the odds were in your favor, and I was right, just like I'm right, right now. My son-in-law earned credit for loving us unconditionally. He could've said no to making an honest woman of you when you intentionally got pregnant with Nairobi right before he was drafted from college—"

Interrupting her mother again, Monet said, "You told me to have his second and get the ring that counts!"

"Show respect, Monet. Haven't I proven Mother knows best? That boy put that rock on your finger. He let you choose every house you've lived in. Bought me my own mansion. Let the man exhale, Monet, damn," Trinity said with disdain. "He's never lived alone. Let him get it out of his system."

As she wept in disbelief, Monet's tears fell onto the tiles. "I can't replace him. If I lose him, Mother, I'll die. My husband is my best friend."

"Stop being dramatic," her mother replied.

Having Kingston's babies was strategic, but Monet wouldn't have wanted to nurture any other man's seeds. Every cell in her body loved Kingston. He was the only man she'd ever had sex with.

"I'm not overreacting. I've never lived alone, either, Mother."

Trinity stood. Walked around the island. Swatting at a bug flying in the air, Trinity asked, "Are you being his best friend right now? Seriously." Trinity held Monet's hand. "No matter how good you are to him, a man gets tired of the same thing, baby."

"Same thing or same woman?" Monet questioned, pulling her hand away from her mother's.

"No matter how great the sex is, they get bored of having the same pussy the same way. Calling him twenty times a day. Why, Monet? The two of you have been together for twelve years." Circling back to her seat, Trinity picked a banana from the bowl. "He doesn't have a prenuptial. Half of all he owns is yours. Trust your husband to do whatever he's going to do, and whatever you do, do not show up in Atlanta without his permission or with my grandbabies."

Peeling the fruit from the bottom, she pulled away each leaf, then broke the banana in half before eating it.

Monet's phone rang. Quickly she retrieved her cell from the bowl, placed it next to her ear. Sniffling, she answered, "Hey, baby."

"I apologize for hanging up on you earlier, but that was my boy, Theodore, calling. I'm leaving the bar en route to the stadium. Theodore got us tickets to some event, and after that, he wants me to stop by his store so his partner can design me my own clothing line. That's good news. Don't cry," Kingston said.

"I'm not," Monet stated, quieting her sniffs.

"I'm going to find the perfect home for us, baby," her husband claimed.

Monet looked at her mother as Trinity consumed the last of the banana, then spoke to Kingston. "Theodore who?"

Kingston hesitated, then answered, "Ramsey. You don't know him. He goes to my church. He invited me to his store. His partner is going to design a clothing line for me."

"What's his partner's name? First and last." Monet's memory didn't require a pen and pad.

"I don't know," her husband answered.

"You don't know?" she stated.

Kingston firmly replied, "No."

"Well, I can't wait to meet our new friends. Take as much time as you want. We're good. Besides, I don't need to mess up the girls' perfect attendance and have them mad at me, too." Monet placed the call on speaker.

Trinity nodded, then whispered, "Good response."

Rolling her eyes at her mom, Monet insisted, "Say hi to your best friend. She's right here."

"Hey, baby," Trinity said.

Placing her cell on the island, Monet walked a few feet to the nearest full-length mirror. She turned her back to her mom and focused on her own image.

"Hey, Mama-T," Kingston replied with enthusiasm. "Thanks for helping Monet with the kids."

What man wouldn't want all of this? Monet fingered the edges of her golden-brown highlights; not a strand was out of place. A part centered atop her head. Her hair, smoothed to the sides and slicked to the back, was gathered into a long, loose-waved ponytail that was all hers.

Looking at her mother's reflection through the mirror, Monet noticed her mother staring at her.

"You know, once I find a house that my wife approves of, I have to buy you a home in the same neighborhood."

Trinity's smile curved high, making her cheeks lift. "Take your time and find really nice homes for your families. I'm heading up. The girls owe me an oral book report. I'll let you talk to your wife."

"Have a good day, Mama-T. You know I love you. Thanks for having my back. And tell my wife, she's my best friend."

"You do know I'm right here," Monet told Kingston as she watched her mom effortlessly climb the steps until she was no longer visible.

"Love you more!" Trinity shouted.

Retrieving her phone, then stepping out on the patio, Monet sat in a lounge chair beside the pool. She texted the travel agent— **Cancel all plans**—then removed the call from speaker. "Baby, can you at least give me a time frame? Or come home for a few days and tune up your pussy?"

Jokingly Kingston sang, "Your mama's gon' take our kids out of the house because I'ma beat my pussy up 'til you scream my name."

"That was a great freestyle, but what are we waiting for?" she stated, relocating to their bedroom on the first floor, then locking the door. Monet eased out of her purple thong, let her maxidress fall to the floor. She slid her fingers along her clit, then moaned, "Mmmm. You just made her wet. FaceTime me so I can show you."

"I'm driving, Monet. And I only have a few minutes to talk," her husband said firmly, declining her request to video. "I'm meeting back up with some church friends after the game, so this is the last time I can talk with you today."

"Friends, huh? Every week it's the same thing. You don't know those people, Kingston. A couple of months and you've joined a church, and whoever these so-called friends-slash-drinking buddies are, y'all do this every Sunday. Now it's twice on a Sunday. I don't trust them. Besides, I thought you were meeting up with Lilly the Realtor today, remember her? Kingston, are you cheating on me?" Disgusted and sexually frustrated, Monet put on her dress.

"The only lips of any kind that mine have touched are yours, baby." Kingston sounded sincere.

Monet stepped into a fresh pair of underwear. The heaviest sigh escaped her mouth.

"Don't do that. Lilly had to reschedule. I'm getting out of the car to meet up with Victoria, Jordan, and Chancelor," he confirmed. "And, yes, we do meet up every Sunday."

Monet flopped onto the edge of the firm mattress. "I thought you were headed to a stadium."

"Yes. After I leave the bar. Keep up," he said, then laughed.

Her husband was the one who needed to keep up with his lies. "Where are you? What's the name of the bar?" she questioned, waiting to add the location to her mental Rolodex. "One better. Drop me a pin with your location."

"Doesn't matter. It's always some new spot," he told her.

Changing her tone, Monet calmly mentioned, "It's cool, Kingston. Do you."

Her husband had gotten to a point where he couldn't recall his lies. Monet wasn't naïve.

"I'll have Lilly e-mail you the houses. I just need a little more—"

"Shut up! I'm beginning to believe there is no Lilly." Monet began crying. "I'm the one combing hair, washing clothes, dropping and picking up our girls from school, cleaning, homework, dental appointments, bedtime stories. I'm not going to be fine until we are living under the same roof. Going to sleep and waking up together. You hear me? *Together.* If you don't want me to come to Atlanta, you need to come home for at least a week so we can discuss face-to-face how we're going to move forward."

"Pretend I'm still under contract. That'll help," Kingston said, then added, *"Muah!"* right before he ended the call.

Monet dried her tears. Self-pity wasn't going to bring her husband home. Atlanta was not that far. If she took the first flight out in the morning, Trinity or her girlfriend Bianca could pick up the girls from school, and Monet could be back home in time for dinner.

CHAPTER 6

Jordan

"Trust and believe. We're never going to find true love in Atlanta." Jordan curled her neatly French-manicured nails into her palm, pounded her hand on the round dark wooden table, then shouted, "Ever!"

The liquid inside of Chancelor's snifter and Victoria's long-stem wineglass swayed.

"Damn, girl," Victoria replied. "You're out of order. This is not a courtroom."

"That's pent-up frustration," Chancelor commented. "Let me take the edge off that marinated pussy," he joked.

Ignoring Chancelor, Jordan hit the table again to emphasize her point. "Men in Atlanta want women to pay them for dick. Even the ones who can't fuck worth a damn."

Victoria laughed out loud. "We do have most of the money and all of the pussy. Meow," she said, sounding like a cat. "The problem is, too many men are acting like females. They want women to suck their nipple, get on top and ride it, get them hard, kiss and hold him after she's done all the work. That's worse than paying for dick."

"That's a lie," Levi yelled from behind the bar.

There were four eight-inch rounds in the bar section of the

restaurant, plus eight barstools at the counter. Levi was aware of everything happening at all times.

"Some of the trans are sexier than a lot of y'all born with the real thing," Levi stated. "They keep themselves up. Hair. Nails—"

"And what else they're keeping up, Levi? Huh?" Jordan's voice projected across the bar. Levi needed to stay out of the conversation with his fake-ass relationship with Queen. None of them had met her.

Flinging her lustrous, kinky curls away from her sweet toffee skin, Jordan's shoulder-length hair bounced back in place. Makeup beat to perfection, her facial features were pronounced. She knew that her left eye was smaller, right ear sat higher, and her narrow nose barely had a bridge. Nothing foundation, concealer, eye shadow, and lipstick couldn't alter beautifully.

She thanked her mother for her flat ass. At least men weren't objectifying her based on what was behind her. And though she was 150 pounds, only five feet, five inches, her hips were wide, her waist was small, and her skin was smoother than a baby's. What she lacked in the rear, she made up for with her double-F boobs. This time Jordan slapped the table.

"Whoa." Chancelor quickly gripped his snifter. "Don't spill the cognac."

Staring at him, Jordan replied, "How many times must I tell you? What you drink is brandy. Kingston is a cognac connoisseur."

Successful men wanted to cum and go leisurely—no accountability or responsibility to a woman—the same as broke guys, except the ones with nothing played head games in order to drain gullible women of their tangible and intangible assets.

Jordan directed her attention to her friends at the table. "I've been here fourteen years, dated six professional men, and all of them were on that MGTOW nonsense until it came time to fuck." She pronounced the Men Going Their Own Way acronym as "mag-tow."

"Mag what?" Chancelor had a habit of laughing and frowning at the same time. When he did, his forehead wrinkled and brows almost touched. "That law degree has you making up words now? Lower your standards or keep sleeping by yourself," he told Jordan.

A seasoned attorney, Jordan moved to the ATL to practice, find a good man, and partake in a robust lifestyle she never had in her hometown of Rome, Georgia, which had a population of less than forty thousand.

"Lower my standards. Like you did. And let men use me the way Tracy used you," Jordan said to Chancelor. "No thanks. You might want to try screwing fewer women at church." She waved to the mixologist. She held up her second bottle of the imported red wine she'd brought in from her collection for Levi to uncork.

Defending his rights to smash whomever he wanted, Chancelor responded, "Why do you think women go to church? To find a man like me. I'm helping them out."

Credit card theft, unauthorized bank and CashApp transfers, jewelry heisting, auto title pawning, failure to repay personal loans, marrying without prenuptials—the list of things women were forgiving and doing to get a man in Atlanta kept growing. If Chancelor continued chasing beautiful women who were hustlers, he was bound to get robbed. For real.

Jordan Jackson, of the Jackson, Johnson, and Jones law firm, represented countless intelligent ladies that were scam artists and those that were victims of con guys. She was admiring the original paintings hanging on the wall adjacent to the entry, and Corey Barksdale's colorful abstracts stood out among the rest in the bar area. She knew what type of man she didn't want and the must-have prequalifications she demanded before dating anyone exclusively.

Jordan articulated, "I need a wealthy, *highly* educated man with great character, and a sense of humor. The kind that prefers lobster and fish over beef and chicken. Cork over a twist-off cap. Flying to a destination for vacation over cruising with port pit stops. The beach over a cabin in the woods. A man that would stand up for justice and not ignore the struggle of his people."

The mural off of the downtown connector—Interstate I-75/85—of U.S. Representative John Lewis mirrored her type of guy, inside and out. She hadn't come close to finding that man.

"Here I am. Next round on me," Kingston said, entering the bar. He was wearing a black short-sleeved, button-up shirt, denims, and gray-black-and-white snakeskin hard-sole shoes. He sat in his usual seat, spread his thighs.

Victoria stared at Kingston's dick imprint. Kingston really was working with a salami. Not a wiener like Chancelor's.

"See something you like?" Chancelor mumbled across the table at Victoria.

"Women are always in trap mode trying to find a husband. Men don't look for love. Love looks for us," Kingston said, sliding his chair forward. Winking at Victoria, he added, "That's why I stay single."

Kingston is fine and fuckable, Jordan thought as she shook her head. *He is too attractive. And if he slings good dick . . . He's trouble with a capital "T."*

The blackest man she'd ever met had the whitest teeth. Tall. Athletic. Ripped abs. Tight, round ass. And he appeared to have a big dick! Kingston Royale was perfection personified.

A whiff of masculine cologne greeted Jordan every time he was near. But with his having two young kids by the same woman, crossing the line with Kingston, knowing the attachments he had, Jordan was not risking losing the friendship of a celebrity.

"Excuse me, Kingston. Can I get a picture with you?" a gorgeously voluptuous woman asked.

"Not now, baby. Maybe later," Kingston replied, then said to the group, "Monet dropped our first baby on me when I was a senior in high school. She knew what she was doing. I knew, too. But I didn't want to be a ghost to my kids, like some of my teammates' dads were with them. My folks are Bible-toting parents. That's why finding a church family was at the top of my list. Monet's dad wasn't around. When she got pregnant with our second child, I felt obligated to do right by her," Kingston commented.

"What? How do you define 'obligation'?" Jordan questioned. "What's the right thing when you still haven't married her? How do you consider that—"

Kingston interrupted as he slapped his chest, saying, "I take care of mine. Isn't that what you black women want? A provider. Not a ring. Or a husband."

And there you have it, Jordan thought. *Another entitled black man.*

Bulging biceps, super-succulent lips (that she knew would feel amazing on her clit), and he was intellectual . . . and wealthy. "Hmm." Without ever seeing Kingston naked, she could almost feel the tip of what she visualized as his ginormous head poking the opening of her vagina. But his cocky personality aligned with the professionals she'd dated. They all wanted two things: pampering and pussy. That was easy. It was the heartbreaks Jordan hated.

Chancelor spoke then. "Men look for love, too, but we don't get it. And when we do, we end up with a fucking user, like Tracy!"

Levi yelled from behind the bar, "Bring it down, bro!"

"That's a lie. I've loved Brother Copeland for forty-four years," Victoria commented. Sweat beaded on her face, arms, shoulders, and neck at the same time.

"Damn, I'm glad I'm not a woman," Kingston said. Reaching across the table, he handed Victoria the white square paper napkin that was in front of her.

Levi placed two clean goblets on the table, then opened Jordan's bottle of wine. He eye-measured six ounces for both. Sat one in front of Jordan. The other by Victoria. "You need to get your sweat glands fixed. There's a surgical procedure for that. I'll be right back with more napkins."

Holding the stem of her glass, Jordan stared at Victoria. Swirling the wine, she contemplated telling Miss Know-every-damn-thing-in-the-name-of-Jesus-but-fornicated-and-committed-adultery-on-the-regular. "Wait. Levi, bring a glass of ice, please," Jordan said.

"I'll have my usual cognac," Kingston mentioned.

Levi smiled at Kingston. "Anything for you, boss. I bet you still got it. You should join my Pro-Am team." Before Kingston replied, Levi asked Chancelor, "Ready for another, my brother?"

With his eyes fixed on Victoria, Chancelor nodded.

"Whew. I'm okay, y'all. Just another private summer," Victoria explained. "I've been trying not to do hormone replacement therapy, but I may need to. Ten years of this, with no foreseeable ending. I can't."

Levi returned with the glass of ice. Placed it near Jordan. Set the napkins in front of Victoria. Looking at Chancelor, then Kingston, Levi said, "I got y'all cocktails coming up. Anyone need anything else?"

Everyone shook their heads.

"Perfect." Levi walked away.

"Give me your arm," Jordan told Victoria.

She placed the inside of Victoria's wrist against the condensation on the cold glass.

"Oh, my gosh. That feels great." Victoria sighed in relief. She frowned at Jordan, Kingston, then Chancelor. "It stopped. Oh, my Lord. Thank You, Jesus."

"Give credit where it's due," Jordan said.

Victoria countered, "I did."

Should've kept letting her sweat it out. "I'm a lawyer. I research things," Jordan confidently mentioned to the group, then told Victoria, "Start adding a pinch of matcha green tea powder to sixteen ounces of room-temperature or hot water. Use a bamboo whisk to mix it up or shake it up in a bottle. Drink it first thing every morning. Your hot flashes should decrease. Maybe stop altogether. And although you don't need to, you might lose weight."

Chancelor laughed. "You sound like a commercial advertisement."

Men. What did they know about menopause? Studies had shown matcha green tea powder could help prevent cancer, protect the heart, liver, and kidneys, was a great antioxidant, and could improve brain function. Jordan wasn't waiting for premenopause to invade her body. At forty, she'd already started a daily routine. Plus, Jordan realized her grandmother and great-grandmother were her most valued resources for natural health remedies.

Victoria took the glass from Jordan. Set it in front of her, then said, "Why didn't you tell me this sooner? You know I've been dealing with hot flashes since I've known you."

Jordan smiled. "I was waiting for God to take care of it for you. We all know that you tell Him what you want."

Kingston laughed.

Chancelor nodded. "Right. Right."

Jordan scanned the faces of everyone at the table. She focused on Victoria. "You need to ask God for some young dick. Nothing ages a woman faster than an old impotent man."

Victoria countered, "How do you know Willy is impotent?"

CHAPTER 7

Chancelor

"Nothing angers a man more than a serpent with her hands in his pockets twenty-four/seven," Chancelor lamented. Appearing relaxed, Victoria quietly sipped her vino.

No one outside of his mother gave him anything. Kelly Leonard was his rock. His mom put him in private school. Had his college scholarship fully funded. She taught him how to treat women respectfully.

Tracy Benjamin wasn't the first Atlantan to get over on him, but she'd be the last.

Kingston laughed out loud. "I should introduce you to Monet Baptiste. First I had two hands on my millions. Now I have six. I'm glad I have one baby mother and I'm happy I got fixed. Get used to taking care of females, bruh. That shit ain't gon' change long as you want pussy."

Chancelor wet his lips with brandy, held the snifter in front of his chest, propped his elbow on the table. There was no solace in Kingston's words. Tracy had taken Chancelor for four figures in the first week of their one-month relationship. Chancelor was CEO of his marketing-and-advertising firm. The two weren't the same. Had to teach his clients that. Paying a woman's bills and giving her money wasn't a problem. It was the tricks he hated.

"Excuse me. I'm leaving. Is now a good time, Mr. Royale?" the gorgeously voluptuous woman asked.

Kingston hesitated. Glancing around the bar, he said, "Just lean in and get it. If I stand up, others are going to want a pic, too."

"Thanks," the woman said. She snapped a selfie, then exited through the door.

Shaking his head, Chancelor confessed to his friends for the first time, "Y'all don't understand. I wanted to marry Tracy."

"After one week?" Kingston laughed.

"Month. It was a month. A woman that fine gotta be put on lock-down quick." Chancelor was serious. "I did everything I could to help her ass. When her mother was killed in a car accident—"

The rim of Jordan's goblet missed her bottom lip. Quickly she pulled the glass away, avoiding staining her uniform.

"Watch yourself," Chancelor told Jordan, then continued, "I CashApped her fifteen hundred dollars to go to the funeral in Texas. Another thousand for her to buy a nice tombstone. Then I sent five hundred dollars to pay for a bleeding heart. And—"

"And . . . stop. I can't," Jordan said, holding her stomach while crying tears with laughter.

Victoria squealed, uncontrollably gasping in between as though she was hyperventilating.

"What the fuck is so funny? That's the problem with you fe-males. Y'all disrespectful to a man when he's opening up his heart. Then you want to know why we don't open up." Chancelor's next swallow of liquor was a gulp.

Jordan held her waist as she raised her hand. "It's funny because Tracy's mother—"

Victoria squeaked, then added, "Dies every month."

"That's how she pays her mortgage, car note, and credit cards," Jordan said.

What the fuck? Chancelor thought. "So Brother Melvin is on first?" he asked.

Victoria and Jordan nodded in unison.

"Don't be angry. Consider it restitution." Jordan chuckled.

Isn't shit humorous! Chancelor didn't want to become the man that used women, but he understood why some guys turned opportunist. "I'm forty-two and I'm not getting any younger. I want a wife and kids. Kingston, you're a *d-o*-double-*g*. How do you recommend I handle these bitches?"

Kingston stretched his neck sideways. "Fuck 'em where you find 'em. Leave 'em where you fuck 'em. That's the ballers' mantra. Your problem is, you're trying too hard. Hos ain't loyal. That's why I—"

Levi interrupted. "Everybody good?"

Everybody at the table ignored Levi, stared at Kingston.

That was definitely the wrong answer. "I can't get no wife that way, man." Chancelor believed in treating women the way he'd expect men to treat his mother. He was never part of a team, nor was he ever a standout athlete. He didn't even have employees. Contractors only. In order for him to screw over a chick, he'd first have to disrespect his mom.

"If you're looking for marriage you have to set one lady aside. One that you really like," Jordan explained. "Make her your friend. Your best friend."

Victoria added, "That you can be totally vulnerable, open, and honest with. Don't fuck her right away. Just be her friend."

"And don't mislead her. If you wouldn't do something to Victoria or myself, don't do it to her," Jordan said.

Chancelor laughed, rubbed his brows, then looked to Kingston, hoping he had something solid to share. The ladies were trippin'.

Kingston advised Chancelor, "Most importantly, fuck whomever you want, but never let the reserve bitch know you're getting your nuts drained elsewhere."

"That's just it. I'm not a dog like you. Levi needs to pass his golden bone to you." Chancelor held his snifter high in the direction of Levi. "Bring that bone over here and hand it to our man Kingston!"

"I have an idea," Jordan interjected. "Have any of you been on a dating site?"

Kingston choked on his cognac, cleared his throat, then responded, "Ballers have groupies. We don't need apps to get laid. I could've fucked that chick who asked for a photo with me."

What kind of inconsiderate answer is that? "No" would've sufficed, Chancelor thought. *Who raised him?*

"Whatever, Kingston. Let's all agree to do online dating. I have a friend who met his wife on a dating site," Jordan commented.

Jordan could try it, but she'd never have luck, let alone find love online. She was too picky. Chancelor reflected on her long list of requirements.

"Casting a net online is one step away from mail-order dick!" Victoria exclaimed. "That's how trifling-ass Levi met, then moved in on Queen. The woman we have yet to meet. He's got her on house arrest while these women in the bar emptying their purses, thinking he's a filmmaker who's going to make them famous. He gets more pussy than he serves cocktails."

Kingston cleared his throat again, but didn't add to Victoria's comment.

"All mixologists are whores," Jordan said. "Let's just try online dating and see how it works out for us. This might be what we all need. Let's start by revealing our body count. Mine is twelve. Half of that was while I was in law school."

Liar, Chancelor thought. *Women never tell their real number.* He was not revealing his body count to those three. Nor did he want to see their profile on ChristianFornicators. The fact that he'd been on a dating site for years was his little secret.

Setting a fresh drink in front of Kingston and Chancelor, Levi said, "Jordan, you're sitting in my bar talking about me. I keep my Queen first. Post that on your social." He dug in his pocket, set the golden bone in front of Kingston.

Kingston picked it up, shook his head, then handed the bone back to Levi. "I'm good."

Jordan defended herself. "How about you post a picture of Queen on your page and tag us in it. I imagine Queen is happy being first in your lineup of whores—"

"Don't go there, Jordan," Levi insisted. "I know everybody's personals." Giving Kingston a quick glance, Levi emphasized, "*Everybody's.* Jordan, your bar body count is closer to—"

"I'll draft the rules for how we're going to move forward," Jordan said, rolling her eyes from Levi to the group.

Kingston told Levi, "Next round on me."

"It's already taken care of," Levi said, walking away as he stuffed the bone in his pocket.

"God knows my heart. I'ma pray about this online dating," Victoria told the group. "I don't like putting myself out there."

Jordan eagerly replied, "C'mon. I don't want to do this by myself. I'll do the research, compile a list of sites, create a compatibility spreadsheet for each of you, draft the rules, and I'll run background checks on our dates before we go out with them."

Kingston stated, "I'm good with everything, and I don't need background checks. I can handle mine in person."

Damn, she is doing everything except an AncestryDNA test. Chancelor decided to go along with Jordan to find himself another dating app. He needed a new fuck pool.

"Count me in," Chancelor said. "I'm ready for something different."

Victoria replied, "In the name of Jesus, leave me out. I already have to answer to God for my sins with William Copeland. But you've got my blessings, Jordan. Let the church say, 'Amen.' "

CHAPTER 8

Monet

"Thanks, Mother, for helping me. I really need this girls' day out." Monet's silky, wavy high ponytail flowed down her back, stopping above her perfect Brazilian butt lift, which was included in her push gift of a mommy makeover. "Excuse me, Mom, it's Bianca calling."

"Hey, Bianca. I'm on my way," Monet confirmed, then quickly ended their call.

Monet stood in the living room on a—blend of light and dark blue, purple, and pink hues—pure silk Persian area rug. All white Italian leather sofas and several high-back chairs were centered between two seventy-inch television screens that hung on opposite walls.

The real sports bar—pool table, two-player arcade basketball game, movie theater, wall projector, stripper stage, pole, full kitchen—was secured downstairs in Kingston's man cave, where the girls were forbidden to go and which he'd seldom used.

Why in the hell did women have a damn "she shack"? Monet called her hideaway "Monet's Diva's Den," but like Kingston with his hideaway, *she* seldom used it. Perhaps it was time to host another overnight lingerie pleasure party and let her daughters stay at their grandma's house.

"You look beautiful," her mother complimented. "But—"

"It's only a spa day, Mother." Monet relocated to the living room's full-length mirror; "boss lady," "rich bitch," and "baller's wife" best defined Monet's attire.

A $1,200 designer sleeveless red fitted jumpsuit, $1,800 nude platform six-inch heels, a $20,000 wristwatch, $20,000 diamond hoop earrings, $150,000 wedding set, and a limited-edition designer bag valued at over $14,000 decorated her from head to toe. The nonnegotiable bonus was her tubal ligation after birthing Nairobi.

"You need pampering. It'll relieve your stress," Trinity stated, sitting in one of the tall chairs. She crossed her legs, leaned back. "Be sure to text me when you arrive at brunch, at the spa, and when you're on your way home. And turn on your location for me."

Trinity hadn't worked a day after Monet gave birth to Israel. Having her mother help raise the girls was a blessing, but the older Israel and Nairobi became, the less Trinity did with and for them. Trinity claimed she dated, definitely never married, but she'd never brought a man around Monet or the kids. Monet never met anyone on her father's side of the family, including her dad. All she knew was his name. John Bernard Baptiste.

Israel and Nairobi raced down the stairs and hugged their mother at the same time.

Stepping back, Israel said, "Mommy, let me take a picture for my 'gram," holding up her phone.

Nairobi's face drooped. "When is Daddy sending my cell phone? I need it," she whined. "I'm the only one in my class without social."

Monet hadn't verified that, but Nairobi was probably being truthful. Was it better to give in or continue to try to protect her daughter from online predators? Nairobi probably had a page, just not a cell.

Trinity answered, "You can have one in—"

"Three more years!" Nairobi cried. "That's a lifetime. Why am I the only one at my school without a cell *and* social media page?"

Monet's ponytail swayed, side to side. Israel snapped a head-to-toe picture of their mother, then handed Nairobi the cell. "Here, let me teach you how to post it with a caption."

Nairobi's frown turned upward. Her eyes beamed bright. "Mommy, I want to look just like you when I grow up. And I want a rich husband like Daddy. And I want you to treat my two daughters just like Grandma takes care of us."

Monet stroked the top of Nairobi's head, thinking how innocent her children were. Being the wife of a celebrity athlete was a step away from single parenting. Having an expensive home, multiple cars, designer clothes, and expensive jewelry had been a trade-off for her husband's time and affection. Especially now when he was investing his energy elsewhere.

"Go get dressed, girls. The driver will be here in a half hour. We're going to the Smithsonian to meet Ruth Carter," Trinity said.

Nairobi's pink painted nails covered her innocent face as she gasped. "She's my idol. I want to design costumes like her. I'm going to bring my sketchbook. I hope she'll sign it, Grandma."

Israel's smile couldn't possibly grow wider. "I love her, too! I have lots of questions for her. Thanks, Grandma!"

Racing up the stairs, the girls screeched.

Standing, Trinity reiterated, "You look beautiful, baby. Refrain from calling Kingston. And if he calls you, don't answer. This is your day. Be in the moment with your girlfriends." Her mother held her tight. "I love you so much."

Girlfriend, Monet said in her head. She didn't know the others. They were Bianca's friends. Embracing her mother, Monet said, "I love you more."

Exiting the house, she sat behind the wheel of her Porsche SUV. Monet drove toward B-W Parkway. She commanded Siri, "Call Daddy."

"Hey, baby, I just unlocked my phone to call you. How's everybody?" Kingston asked.

"Great. Mama's at home with the girls. They're getting ready to meet Ruth Carter and I'm heading to brunch with Bianca and a few of her girlfriends."

Bianca knew her better than Kingston.

"That's what's up. Pick up the tab for everything . . . on me," he said cheerfully, then hesitated before adding, "Let me call you—"

Monet interrupted, "Wait. The kids want to send you something they made. What hotel are you at?" Monet asked nonchalantly.

"I switched to an Airbnb. Got tired of living in one room. Hold the gift for me. I'll be home soon," Kingston insisted.

"How soon?" Monet questioned, then asked, "Are you looking at houses for us today?"

"Of course. I'm meeting Lilly at her office at one o'clock. I'll FaceTime you from the properties," Kingston stated. "Oh, that's right. You're hanging with your girls. Don't let me make you late. I'll keep you posted. Let me call you—"

"I'm sure Lilly Ortiz is doing her job." His lies weren't worth acknowledging.

No reservation or hesitation. Kingston answered, "Cool," as though he was relieved, but his response didn't apply to her last statement.

"Okay, baby. I love you." Before Monet could say "Bye," Kingston ended their conversation.

Monet altered her destination, daily parked at BWI, and texted her travel agent, **Book me on the next direct flight to Hartsfield.** Her next message went to her personal assistant: **Get me ALL contact information for Kingston's Realtor, Lilly Ortiz, in Atlanta.** The last was for Bianca: **Change of plan. Will explain later. Don't contact my mom.**

By the time Monet arrived at check-in, her reservation was confirmed. Monet breezed through TSA PreCheck, boarded her first-class nonstop flight to Atlanta. Awaiting takeoff, she logged into their Airbnb account. There was no reservation for Kingston.

Signing into their travel account, he'd checked out of the Waldorf Astoria days ago. No new reservation was listed for the Four Seasons, W, Ritz-Carlton, or Whitley for Kingston Royale.

Monet's ten o'clock flight was scheduled to land at noon. A message from her assistant with the office address for Lilly Ortiz registered, along with Lilly's home location and two cell numbers.

Monet's arrival should put Kingston and her at Lilly's business suite at the same time.

CHAPTER 9

Kingston

A text registered from Lilly: **Monet showed up at my office unan-nounced. What do you want me to do?**

Lying on his back, Kingston stared at his phone. He'd picked it up to check the time, and now his wife had the potential to ruin the moment. **Hold tight. That can't be right,** he replied.

An attached photo was returned of Monet in a red jumpsuit wearing diamond hoop earrings he hadn't seen. If he had to iden-tify his wife or kids by the last thing they were wearing, Kingston didn't see them often enough to know what was in their wardrobe collection or how they dressed daily.

It wasn't his fault that his appetite for men had increased. "Hold tight, man. I have to handle something," he said to his naked lover, who was lying beside him.

If he could erase the day he'd stepped into the janitor's closet, perhaps he would've never been on BottomsUp. Maybe if his par-ents weren't devoted Christians, or the hometown pastor hadn't made him believe gay people were going to hell, then telling his truth would've been easier.

Why would it be that Monet was in Atlanta? He'd spoken with his wife a couple of hours ago. Kingston texted Lilly, **Show her the door!!**

If she walks out of mine, she's going to knock on yours, Lilly answered.

What the hell? Out of all the years he'd been married, Monet never popped up on him.

Kingston messaged Bianca, **I can't reach Monet. I called her four times. Is she with you?** He copied, then pasted the same inquiry to Trinity, adding, **Did you tell Monet where I'm staying?** Lilly and Trinity were the only two with the address to his Airbnb.

Lilly replied, **She knows. Or at least that's what she said.**

Why the fuck did you tell her where I'm at! Kingston texted Lilly.

I didn't! Lilly replied.

Then the only other person he trusted had betrayed him. If Trinity had given Monet his location, then she might have told her daughter the real reason he was in Atlanta. Setting him up for divorce would free Monet and Trinity. He didn't care as much about that. But Monet leaving him with half of everything wasn't happening. Adultery was a reason for an automatic divorce in Georgia, but it generally worked in favor of the husband. She'd probably gain more than half if Trinity told the lawyer he was gay.

What was Monet trying to prove? Kingston got out of bed, told Levi, "I have unexpected company in town. Thanks for not outing me on Sunday at the bar."

"No problem. Holding secrets is part of my job. That, and we're living in the same glass house, my brother. Being in a relationship keeps the females interested. But don't get me wrong. I'll hit Queen's pussy every now and again to see"—he paused, held his dick—"if my man here is still interested."

That was wrong of Levi when he knew he didn't want a real commitment of any kind.

"Who told you about me?" Kingston asked.

"Confidential. But if you're looking for a conservative app to explore prospects, check out VirginsSeekingVirgins. It's for professionals like ourselves. No one posts pictures of themselves. If you like a guy, you make an arrangement to meet up. And stop taking your ass over there on Cheshire Bridge Road. Nothing good comes out over there. Literally."

It was convenient. Quick. Like a drive-thru. Long as he didn't linger, Kingston believed he'd be okay with the quickies.

Kingston bit his bottom lip. Stared at Levi's long, flaccid penis. "Why do you stay with Queen?"

"She does any- and everything for me." Levi put on his socks first. "What man doesn't want a live-in maid?"

"And if she found out you go both ways? Then what?" Kingston had no intentions of coming out to Monet. And he didn't want to be that dude who got caught naked in bed with a man doing things God intended for husband and wife.

Trinity's message registered: **Monet is okay. You concentrate on getting it out of your system so you can find us a new place to live. You good?**

"You don't get it," Levi said. "If she left me, for any reason, her replacement is already in the lineup. Lots of females in the ATL don't care about bisexuality. They eat more pussy than me."

That isn't hard to do, Kingston thought, then laughed. "You're the one who don't understand. If Monet walks, she'll cash out with twenty-five million dollars."

Levi stumbled as he put on his slacks. Hopping on one foot, he nearly fell to the floor. Regaining his balance, he sat on the edge of the bed, slipped on his shoes, then buttoned up his shirt. "Never tell anybody else that shit. And never fuck a man or woman who has nothing to lose. This town ain't for everybody, but they all moving here. See you at the bar Sunday. I'll let myself out."

Kingston, what's up? I'm not babysitting a grown-ass woman!

Ignoring Lilly's text, Kingston sat on the side of the bed and stared down at his limp dick, wondering why God gave man built-in temptation. He logged into his phone. Downloaded the app for VirginsSeekingVirgins, wondering if Theodore had a profile.

Will the little boy inside of me ever come out of the closet? Kingston wondered if Langston Derby was gay, bi, or straight.

I just put your bitch out of my office.

Kingston replied that was good, then messaged Trinity: **I need a new Airbnb. Now.**

CHAPTER 10

Victoria

Fresh out of a steamy shower, Victoria prepared to make herself squirt.

After spreading a disposable water-resistant pad atop her comforter, she lit a lavender-scented soy candle, which was on the dresser, then dimmed the lights.

Placing her pink Luxe Replenish 7-Function and Precious Metal Slim-10 on the bed, Victoria reclined flat on her back. She closed her eyes, inhaled deeply, then slowly exhaled, repeating her breathing pattern three times.

Victoria powered both stimulators to her preferred vibration; then she returned her breath to normal. Gapping her thighs as her legs remained flushed against the bed, she inserted the metal Slim-10 into her vagina just beyond her G-spot, then left it there. She didn't squeeze her muscles to hold it in; no, she simply relaxed.

Teasing her clit with the Replenish 7, Victoria closed her eyes and enjoyed the dual action that pleased her. Moving the Replenish to the upper right inner labia, she felt a cool waterlike sensation flow throughout her vulva. The upper right inside of her labia majora was her most sensitive spot.

As the excitement heightened inside of her, Victoria took a deep breath, exhaled, and relaxed. The urge to push grew more pressing, but she wasn't ready to squirt. Not yet. She lifted the Replenish vibrator away from her vulva area, waited a few seconds, took a few deep breaths, then resumed pleasuring her clitoris.

The Slim-10 buzzed nonstop inside of her vagina. When the device slid out a little, Victoria pushed it back in. Repositioning the Replenish toy to her favorite spot, she began stroking up and down along her inner labia. This time the vibration brought her closer to squirting, giving her a stronger urge to push, as though she were mimicking giving birth.

Relaxing, she lifted the Replenish again. Reconnecting to the spot that gave her that coolest sensation, Victoria heaved, pushing lightly from her belly. She relaxed, then heaved again. This time she felt the fluid leak from her urethra indicating it was time. She inhaled. Bent her knees. On the exhale of the third heave, Victoria pushed as hard as she could.

The Slim-10 ejected from her vagina. Ejaculate fluid shot in the air and came showering down all over her body and the water-resistant pad. The sensation was a gratifying release that was different from the screaming orgasmic climax that she only achieved with younger men or by herself. The days of Willy making her cum were long gone, but thanks to the Lord, her God, she didn't need a man to make herself squirt and cum at the same time.

Victoria tossed the pad in the trash, showered, stroked her hair into a wavy pattern with a wide-tooth comb. Slipping into a floral summer sundress and comfortable heels, she headed to Pappadeaux's for lunch.

Soon as she sat at the bar, she heard, "Give her whatever she wants, Jerome, on me." The gentleman sat next to Victoria and spoke to the mixologist. "I'm picking up to-go today, man."

"Feeding the staff again?" Jerome asked, then said, "Hey, Victoria. Long time, no see. How's the real estate business?"

"I appreciate my people," the guy replied.

"You a good dude, Noel," Jerome complimented.

Hmm. Looking straight ahead toward the opposite side of the bar, Victoria scanned Noel's body out of her peripheral. "Business is great, Jerome," she answered.

Young. Handsome. Light complexion. Slim with a flat stomach. And his cologne was manly. Inviting. Not cheap. Noel's pheromones were strong enough to engage more than her intellect.

Though Noel sat on the edge of his seat, his feet barely touched the floor. Victoria didn't care about his height. In bed the length of a man's frame wasn't what mattered most.

Incoming call was announced on her Bluetooth. Victoria pushed the button to accept the call.

"Make sure you put in your order," Noel said.

Victoria nodded at him, pointed toward the Bluetooth in her ear. "Hey, I was getting ready to text you. I'll meet you at 15555, then we can drive over to 29411. Based on the neighborhood, both properties are good short-term investments if the acquisition price is right. Hold on for a sec."

Jerome set her usual cocktail, a frozen Swamp Thang, in front of Victoria, then smiled at her.

Placing her phone on mute, Victoria said, "Thanks, Jerome. I'd like to have the fondue pot, and the alligator bites with an order of fries."

"Hey, Jerome," Noel said, "put everything she's having on my tab."

"I got that the first time. Your to-go should be up in a minute," Jerome said, then asked Victoria, "Bread pudding to go. Ice cream for here?"

Unmuting her phone, Victoria nodded, then confirmed with her client. "I'll meet you at 15555 at one o'clock. I've got to catch this call. Bye."

There was no incoming call. Lying was her polite way of ending a business call. That, and her tactic always made her appear busy. Indulging her unsolicited sponsor, Victoria said, "Thanks for your generosity."

Quickly she confirmed her date with Henry inside the app Tuition-Cougars: **See you at 4:00 p.m.** Then she sent him her address. She'd bantered back and forth with the twenty-three-year-old for two days. It was time to see how much he was worth to her.

"Are you available tonight?" Noel asked.

His confidence intrigued her. "Depends on why you're asking."

Noel followed up with, "You like jazz and live music?"

His spirit was good. Jerome was familiar with the young man. Noel had a staff, which meant he owned a business. "Yes," she replied.

"Pick you up at nine-thirty," Noel said.

Jerome placed Victoria's fondue pot and alligator bites on the bar; then he placed three large to-go bags in front of Noel.

"Jerome, my man. I'ma need you to get those fries for my lady friend like right now. Make sure they're hot," Noel insisted.

Victoria sipped her icy drink. She smiled at Noel; then she slid her hand up his inner thigh. *Oh, shit!* she thought. His flaccid dick met her hand halfway.

Noel smiled.

Victoria did, too, on the inside. Short-and-long might not be bad. Maybe she was going about finding a younger man the wrong way. "Why don't I give you my number and you text me the location. I'll meet you there."

"That works. See you tonight," Noel said. Locking in Victoria's number, he signed his tab, then handed Jerome a $20 bill. "Keep what you think you're worth and give me back the rest."

Jerome kept the money, tapped the bar. "See you tomorrow, man. Thanks."

Impressed by Noel, Victoria sampled her food, got the leftovers and her dessert to take with her.

Touring both properties, she wrote an offer for both. Heading home, she showered, slipped into a red teddy, and waited for Henry.

Five minutes early, he buzzed from her gate.

"Park in the circular driveway," she said.

Greeting him at the door—oh, how she did enjoy hugging his hard body. "Come in and take off all your clothes."

Henry nervously laughed. "Wow. You don't waste time."

"Time is money, Henry," Victoria said, escorting him to a guest bedroom. "The sooner you learn that, the richer you'll become."

Easing atop the comforter, Victoria unsnapped the garment, spread her legs, and moaned, "Touch me."

Henry stood at the foot of her bed, stared at her pussy. Victoria locked eyes with him.

"What?" she questioned.

Her profile included a decade shaved off of her age, because she knew she didn't look a day over forty-five. MamaKnowsBest was her username. Hobby: World Traveler. The site appealed to her because there were handsome young men under forty seeking assistance to either pay their tuition or pay off student loans. At this pace, Henry wasn't getting a dime.

"Where?" he asked.

"Sweetheart, if you're going to get your bills paid you're going to have to use your imagination."

"Okay. I don't see any gray pubic hairs. I like them. I'll start with your feet," he said.

Was the young man serious? He didn't, and wouldn't, see any graying on Victoria ever. She'd had permanent hair removal done at Beauty by Bowers years ago. It wasn't that temporary laser treatment where hairs grow back after eight weeks. It was gone for good. But she gave the young man credit for appreciating an older woman's assets.

Pressing his thumbs into the arch, he massaged her foot in small, circular motions. "How's that?"

Thank You, Jesus. He should've rotated his fist in her arch, but what he was doing felt orgasmic. She had a good four hours before putting Henry out of her house and meeting up with Noel. Relaxing on her back, Victoria sighed as she pulled the lingerie over her head. A man who took his time was refreshing, but this guy was kind to a tortoise. Victoria didn't get a background check from Jordan, but she'd learned over the phone that Henry was a four-year army veteran and a freshman in college. The longest he'd gone without seeing a woman was three consecutive months.

Thanks to Jordan, Victoria had a new pleasure. "Go to the kitchen and get a cup of ice." She stroked her pussy, thinking she might have to incorporate a few toys with Henry.

"I've never done anything like this before," he said, returning holding a glass of cubes.

"Where are you really from?" she asked.

Placing the glass on the nightstand, he scooped an ice cube into each palm. "Small-town Mississippi boy, ma'am." His shaking hands slid from her ankles to her knees. He rubbed the ice up and down.

If Henry only dialogued and caressed her with those big, strong hands, Victoria would make good on her promise to pay him $500. Was it Henry's innocence that excited her to the point of climaxing without penetration? She reached toward the nightstand, picked a cube, then circled it atop her nipple. His eyes widened as he watched her go from soft to hard.

Taking a deep breath, she admired the young man. Victoria moaned. He did, too.

"I take it I'm doing a good job?" Henry asked.

"Better than that," she acknowledged.

Nestling his hands in the arch of her thighs, he gently grazed her outer labia. "You mind if I use a cube here?"

"Not at all," she replied.

"I'm enjoying you." He helped himself to a melting cube, placed it in his mouth, then pressed his lips to hers. She redirected him to her vagina.

She wasn't sure if it was the excitement of the coachable young man, or the matcha green tea powder she'd started taking every morning, which had stopped her flashes, or the fact that she hadn't been touched that delicately in years . . . *But thank You, Jesus,* she thought . . . then screamed, "Thank You, Jesus!" as she climaxed so intensely, her juices flooded his mouth.

He yelled, "Shit!" wiping his face.

"Great job, Henry. You just drew nectar from a woman's well," she told him. "That makes you a pussy pleaser."

Henry started grinning. "I'm a what?"

"You heard me, Henry. Stay hungry," Victoria said.

CHAPTER 11

Jordan

Dickless by default, Jordan hadn't felt sparks in any part of her vulva or a man's penis in 469 days. With or without her friends' support of online dating, it was time for her drought to end.

At forty, she was percolating at her sexual prime, but the men in Atlanta—irrespective of their single status—most were not willing to make a commitment to a relationship, and definitely not to marriage. If she wanted to put her pussy back in action, she was the one who needed a major attitude adjustment.

"Yes, Mr. Ealy. Your hearing is set two weeks from today. We need to Skype next week. I'll have Tia contact you to arrange a time." Jordan powered off her laptop, stored it in her tote.

"I can't go to jail for killing my father. He deserved it. He came to my house inebriated and belligerent, demanding money. What had he ever done for me? I'll tell you," he cried, then answered his own question. "Beat my and my mother's ass every time he showed up at my mother's house drunk, looking for what? Money from my mother!" Mr. Ealy shouted. "I'm grown now, and I don't owe him a motherfucking thing! If this was Florida, I would've been standing my ground!"

Mr. Ealy was emotional and he was right. But Georgia wasn't Florida. His father was trespassing, but his dad was unarmed. Jordan had to prove Mr. Ealy's father was a threat. Calmly Jordan advised him, "We just learned who the solicitor on your case is. I'm going to speak with her in the morning."

"I don't want a plea deal or probation. I want my case thrown out," he cried.

The strongest men became infantile when they realized they could be sentenced to years in the state penitentiary. The upside for her client was he owned a billion-dollar corporation that invested millions into Georgia's economy. His downside, he was a seventy-year-old black man who'd killed a ninety-year-old black man. Since it was a black-on-black crime, the color wouldn't matter as much to a jury. It was his father's age that would be the biggest challenge. Her client's trump card was his case was in Fulton County, where Jordan's firm had key connections.

Jordan glanced at her wristwatch. If she was going to be on time for her date, she had to get Mr. Ealy off the phone. "We're entering a plea of not guilty. Your corporation feeds a lot of homeless people in Georgia. The court of public opinion supports you, but we cannot make it seem as though we're trying to influence the judge or the solicitor. The solicitor is numbers-driven and she's seeking to keep her reputation of lowest cases lost."

"Zero?" he asked.

"No. But don't worry. We got you. Go play golf. Take it out on your balls." Jordan laughed.

Mr. Ealy did, too. "That's why you're worth every cent. I'm heading to the country club. Talk with you in the morning."

Ending the call feeling good, Jordan secured her office; then she told her assistant, Tia, "I'm leaving early today. With the exception of the Wilson Ealy case, take messages. I'll return all other calls tomorrow."

"Will do, Ms. Jackson. Have a good rest of your day," Tia said politely.

Exhausted from giving her love and trust to a prestigious guy that would say whatever he thought was clever to maintain her interest, Jordan's last "situationship" with Donovan Bradley left her in emotional turmoil for nine months (long enough to have given birth to a child).

Suggesting that the group online date was more because she did not want to be the only one talking about her encounters. Jordan's first date on CelibateNoMore was requested ten minutes after creating her profile. Twenty minutes into her membership, her inbox was flooded with opportunities. She'd narrowed it down to three entrepreneurs. It was easier for her to conduct background checks on established men than those who were trying to chase a dream. After she learned their net worth, Terrence Russell outranked the other two.

No intentions of deviating from her standing hair appointment with Dwayne Xavier, Jordan gave herself an extra hour to deal with traffic from downtown to his salon inside Perimeter Mall.

Parking near Dillard's, she entered the store, bypassed the shoe department, exited into the mall, then walked, instead of taking the elevator, to the second floor.

"Hey, my gorgeous Nubian Queen of Lady in Red! How are you doing, darling?" Dwayne asked in his normal jovial voice. "Over-the-top" was an understatement for Dwayne's upbeat personality and his designer taste in fashion.

"Perfect. But I don't need to ask, I can see you are fabulous as always," she told him, then strolled to the shampoo room in the rear.

"I need you to blow this hair all the way out. Make these curls super-triple-X silky straight to every strand." Jordan snapped her fingers in Dwayne's face.

Terrence had a lot of ones: kid, ex-wife, home, S-Corp, car, yacht, and a misdemeanor. A black man under forty without an arrest record was an anomaly. Prejudgment free, Jordan opted to get to know the new guy face-to-face at Bar Purgatory. If things didn't work out, she could stay and talk with Levi. Jordan planned on looking into Terrence's eyes and observing his body language to determine if he was truthful or a liar, like Donovan.

Placing his hand on his hip, Dwayne swayed his pointing finger at Jordan. "Bitch, don't tell me the well is about to get wet." He snapped the black plastic in front of Jordan as though he were a matador. "Let me see his picture." He flapped the cape once more before covering her body from the neck to her knees.

Glancing at her watch, Jordan told Dwayne, "I don't want to be late. Blow and flat iron it."

"Excuse me, Ms. Attorney. A real man will wait, and you need to make an *entrance*. When I'm done, go downstairs to the MAC store and let 'em beat your face. You have to slay, bitch." Dwayne spun. Stopped. "Loose curls pent up, with a few dangling. Okay?"

"That's old-fashioned," Jordan countered.

"Men love it!" he said. "I'm not trying to have you looking like a reality-television star. Men know when they see a real woman. And you, Ms. Jackson, ain't no joke."

"Okay, all right," Jordan conceded, leaning her head back. Closing her eyes, she melted at the sensation of Dwayne's fingertips massaging her scalp. If only Terrence could make her feel as good tonight.

Jordan entered Bar Purgatory. Glanced around.

"Oh, shit. Levi, you're overpouring my drink," a customer at the bar said, scooting her stool back.

"Sorry, babe." He noticed nothing had spilled on her clothing, but she was a great tipper and a regular. "Your tab is on me. I got you," Levi said, wiping the counter as he stared at Jordan.

"The lady is in all red and bouncing curls, too. Hurt him. Hell, hurt me, Ms. Jackson. Let me knock the dust off that pussy." He laughed. "Seriously, you look incredible," Levi said, wiping off the countertop with a dry cloth. "Your gentleman friend Terrence awaits. He's at your reserved table, number twelve."

No need to inquire how Levi knew Terrence's name. Not many people slipped through the door of his place of employment and remained unknown.

"Thanks," Jordan answered.

Having been a waitress during the summer between high school and college at Hampton University, Jordan was familiar with the layout and table numbering of the restaurant side of the bar. Heading toward the table in the corner with a view of the entire room, she noticed her date stood immediately, then pulled out her chair.

Crossing one stiletto over the other, Jordan stepped slowly in her fitted dress as she swayed her hips.

"Wow! Your photos do not do you justice. You are breathtaking," Terrence acknowledged, standing approximately two-inches below six feet.

Scanning him face-to-feet-to-face, Jordan replied, "Thanks." With her five-inch heels on, she was kissing height with the cleanest-shaved gentleman, who was dressed in a navy suit with lime green pinstripes and a tie that matched her attire.

This time her approach would be different. Jordan would start off letting Terrence Russell salivate over her. If his enthusiasm for her should fade after date one, two, or three . . . that was fine. Jordan wasn't emotionally investing in another man. At least not first.

"You were definitely worth the wait." Terrence eased the chair under her before sitting to her left. "What do you prefer? A bottle of champagne or wine. Order whatever you'd like," he said, handing her the cocktail list.

His paying the bill was understood, as Jordan never touched her purse or went on a date where she suspected the man wouldn't pick up the tab. Removing her cell from her tote, she placed it in front of her.

Approaching them, Levi stood with his hands behind his back, then asked in a deep voice, "A bottle from your private locker, Ms. Jackson?"

"Hmm," Terrence commented.

Shaking her head, Jordan replied, "I'll let my date decide," wanting to poke Levi in the stomach for his being silly. Bar Purgatory didn't have private cellars. Capital Grille did.

Terrence ordered a bottle of champagne and the seafood trio.

"Are you married? Cohabiting? Attached? Engaged? Or in any form of situationship with a male or female?" Jordan asked her date.

Terrence smiled. She raised her brows.

"I can't blame you for being direct. I like that," he confessed. "I'm very single. Have been celibate for over six months. I meditate and pray daily. I'm more spiritual than religious. I believe in God. And I'm hoping to meet a woman that is ready to be romanced without nuisance. We're the same age, let's explore if we want the same things. I want your mind and your heart's undivided attention. Are you intimately or physically involved?"

"I am—"

An incoming text interrupted Jordan's response. Levi returned with the champagne. A waiter placed the dish of calamari, crab cakes, and seared scallops in the center of the table, along with two setups and small plates.

Jordan read, **Baby, I need you!**, then angled her cell where Levi could see the message. She placed it on the white tablecloth. She scanned the room. Perhaps her ex was dining at the restaurant also and being an inconsiderate, jealous asshole.

"Pardon that." Jordan silenced her phone, then explained. "I have to make myself available for a top client my company is representing. That's the only call I must take. Back to your question. I am—"

Her screen lit up. Same person, who didn't seem to be in the restaurant, texted the same message. Levi shook his head, placed the champagne in the ice bucket before walking away. Staring at her screen, Jordan pressed the lock button. Reaching for her flute, her ex's face appeared with an incoming call this time. Jordan ignored his FaceTime attempt to contact her.

Exhaling, Terrence commented, "You're what?"

"Single and interested in getting to know you better. Cheers," she said, holding up her glass, then asked what she already knew. "Where do you live?"

Again. Her ex Donovan Bradley's face appeared. Again, attempting to FaceTime her.

"Why don't you take a moment to respond, to minimize our interruptions," Terrence suggested.

She hadn't heard from Donovan in over fifteen months. What could be so pressing that he relentlessly reached out? Answering the call, she placed it on speaker as she had nothing to hide from the man she wanted to know . . . and potentially have sex with. Tonight.

"What do you want, Donovan?" Jordan asked with annoyance, then mentioned, "I'm on a date."

"Baby, I need you," Donovan said, sounding desperate.

"Call me tomorrow. I said I'm on a—"

Donovan cried, "Turn on the news, baby. Our son, DJ, was just shot and killed by a police officer. Jordan. Please," he pleaded, "fuck that date. Your man needs you now, baby."

Why in the hell had she placed the call on speaker? Now other diners redirected their attention toward her. Donovan knew she wasn't the mother of his child, nor was he her man. She told Donovan, "Give me a minute. I'll call you back."

Shaking her head, Jordan said, "Listen, Terrence. I apologize. Donovan is my ex."

"And the kid? He's an ex, too?" Terrence asked.

She Googled "Donovan Bradley Jr." and the headline read: PO-LICE OFFICER ALLEGEDLY SHOT AND KILLED TEENAGER FOR REFUSING TO GET OUT OF A SUSPECTED STOLEN VEHICLE.

Jordan cried. "I used to call him my son when I dated his father. But he's not my biological."

Being an attorney was tough. Jordan was desensitized toward almost every professional and personal situation, including Wilson Ealy's. Business. Every legal situation was business. But not DJ. She loved him so much, it hurt both of them when Donovan Sr. insisted she stopped communicating with *his* son.

DJ was smart, thoughtful, loving, and kind.

Tears streamed down her once-perfect makeup, splattering onto the lap of her red dress.

Levi approached the table. Placed his hand on her back. "I just saw on the flat screen. Get up. Dinner is on the house, Terrence. I'm taking Jordan home, man."

"What about the bar?" Jordan asked as she stood.

"Fuck the bar. I can serve drinks anywhere. Our friendship is worth more than this job to me," Levi said. "Let's go."

CHAPTER 12

Chancelor

"I have one question for you, Tracy. Why? Why? Why?" Chancelor sat in his car and yelled at the call box at her home. Before Chancelor could mentally move forward, he demanded closure.

He got out of his car, left the engine running, took ten steps to the black-and-gold-painted wrought-iron gate. Grabbing the bars, he shook it hard, then yelled, "Why?! Tracy!"

"Why what, Chancelor? I can hear you from my living room." Her voice resonated from the box that was behind him.

Hurrying back to respond, Chancelor commanded, "Let me in. We need to talk."

She'd broken his heart and it was her responsibility to mend it. He'd given her his all. Now she was approaching him like he was shit on the bottom of her shoes that he'd paid for. Prancing toward him, she posed inside of the fence. Tracy placed her hand on her hip. Her eyeballs scrolled right to left, along with her neck.

Retracing his footsteps, Chancelor grabbed the bars again. "Why you used me? Why you lied about your mother?" His voice escalated. Holding on to the fence, he leaned back. His face absorbed the early-morning sunshine as he yelled toward the clear blue sky. "Why are you a fucking whore?!"

Tracy shifted her weight to the opposite hip, propped her hand on the other side, and stared him up and down.

Damn, she fine. Why she gotta act like this? he thought.

He looked around, went to his car, got his cell. Tracy's nearest neighbor was at least one hundred yards away. Chancelor opened his social app. Started a live video. Pointed the camera at Tracy.

"Let's see how you act now. You, live ho!" he said, keeping the phone pointed at her.

Calmly Tracy replied, "Call me a 'ho,' loud as you want. That's what you think I am? I'm not going to stand here and call your mama or any other woman a 'whore.' I am a queen."

A gardener off in the background surrounded by purple crocuses, yellow daffodils, and white tulips appeared in the corner of the video. Dude stared up at Chancelor, then at Tracy. What he needed to do was put his fucking shirt on. Who toils soil half-ass naked before noon? It wasn't even hot yet.

Comments started scrolling on Chancelor's live:

Damn, he fine!

I need my lawn manicured.

How much for the gardener?

Chancelor shifted the camera to screen dude out.

"Tracy," Shirtless called out. "Are you okay?"

"'Tracy. Are you okay,'" Chancelor mimicked. "Who the fuck you looking at, man? You hittin' that community pussy, too?" Chancelor added "too," but, honestly, he'd never seen Tracy without her being fully dressed.

She waved at dude. "I got this bitch ova here. Keep working, handsome."

Handsome? Chancelor kept the lens focused on Tracy. "I don't think. I know for a fact that you're a ho. That's what you call a woman that fucks for money! Accept it! You are a fucking whore, Tracy Benjamin."

There! Now no man would want Tracy and she'd have to beg him to take her back. Moving closer to his cell, Tracy said, "You have never seen me naked. You're mad because I never fucked you. Guess you're going to have to find another adjective to describe me. Thanks for the three-thousand-dollar sponsorship. Good-bye, Chance—"

"Don't you walk away from me!" he shouted.

Comments, GIFs, and memes flooded his screen as Tracy slowly swayed her big booty in front of his camera:

Dam!!!!!!!!!!!!! Dat Ass Thou.

ICYU outta of control, nigga! She need a man like me!

TRACY . . . I GOT 5K ON THAT AZZ #HOLLAATME.

I don't have 5K, but my DIK is on swole.

Back dat azz all the way up to my salami!

Fuck dat bitch-ass nigga, u need a real man! Tracy #inboxme I'll CashApp just to see your fine ass on my phone.

Squash all the wannabes trying to steal my girl, Chancelor thought. "Come back here! I'll bulldoze this gate with my car if you don't. Let me in your house!" Chancelor yelled. "We need to work this out."

Fearing he'd ruined all chances of winning Tracy back, Chancelor's heart thumped in his chest. Just when he was about to end the live video, slowly Tracy turned and began walking toward him.

"You love me, baby?" she asked, all seductive.

Chancelor didn't want to fall in her trap. His eyes filled with tears that clung to his lids. He nodded so no one could hear his answer.

"Come close." Tracy placed her lips between the bars. "Kiss me."

Chancelor held his phone to the side for all of his haters to see his tongue in Tracy's mouth.

She stepped back. Looked into his camera. "You have no idea how many men have fucked me over." Tracy spoke confidently. "I've been raped. Molested. I've had my bank accounts, with an *s,* emptied by a man that I trusted. Y'all watching might not be that type of guy, but you have male friends that abuse women, so if you're your brothers' keeper, you're guilty by association. I don't feel sorry for you or any of the other men that sponsor me. And if my mother dies every other day, bitch . . . she's *my* mother."

Chancelor wanted to hate Tracy, but he couldn't. He'd never thought about her pain and suffering. He ended the live video, then asked, "Is your mother alive?"

Tracy turned, glanced over her shoulder. "I'm behind on my

mortgage. CashApp me four thousand dollars and I'll invite you over for dessert."

"I'll send it right now. I love you, Tracy." Chancelor watched her begin to walk away. She climbed one step at a time, then stood on her porch.

"I love you, too, Chancelor," Tracy said, then shut her front door.

CHAPTER 13

Kingston

Entering the code on the keypad, Kingston stepped aside to let Theodore in the house. Theodore suddenly looked up from the keypad before crossing the threshold.

"I need to handle some business. Keep busy until I'm done," Kingston stated.

Theodore said, "No problem. I see the yard from here. I'll be out back on the deck, sipping on a little something. When you're done, join me."

His purple fitted skinny pants had half-inch black cuffs at the ankles. The black button-up shirt had purple sleeves that were tapered above Theodore's biceps. A brown designer belt matched his shoes.

Kingston headed into the master bedroom, locked the door, sat on the side of the spa tub, then called Mama-T. Soon as she answered, he asked, "Is this a good time?"

"Why do you need a different Airbnb, Kingston?" Mama-T scolded as though he were her child. "You're taking this 'get it out of your system' thing too damn far, son-in-law."

What he'd done for too long was lived his life for everyone except himself. And he'd generously kept Mama-T in a lifestyle she acquired off of his success. This was the first time he'd requested a favor of her.

"Mama-T, I'm not making this up," Kingston explained. "Monet came shitless close to rolling up on me in an uncompromising position. All she needed was the address and code and I could've been caught with . . . I can't chance my wife discovering my current location. After all, she is your daughter. If you do this solid for me, I'll be indebted to you for the rest of our lives."

If Monet found out he was sexing men, she'd divorce him. "You do understand that I can't have my wife popping up on me. It's not about me. It's to protect her and the girls. My children will be ridiculed at school. Or worse. Ostracized everywhere they go. Your friends will talk about you behind your back. And me? I'd leave the country and never come back."

Mama-T was eerily quiet.

He owed Lilly a solid for showing Monet two properties that Kingston knew his wife wouldn't approve of. His backup plan was to ask Lilly to get him a place and pay her all cash. But if she learned his truth, that would risk his being exposed or perhaps blackmailed. The truth was, he wasn't ready to go home to Monet and his kids.

"You're becoming paranoid. Monet didn't pop up on you, Kingston. My daughter took a spa day, a much-needed one, may I add, with her girlfriends. Don't start making up lies about my child."

Mama-T was starting to piss him off, but he needed her to protect his image. Traditionally, Mama-T would side with him or remain neutral. Now she was indirectly calling him a liar.

Mama-T continued, "She left in the morning, texted me throughout the day, and she was back home by midnight."

The fact that Monet was in Atlanta was history. Sending Mama-T the picture Lilly sent him of Monet sitting in a chair with a white wall background wouldn't prove he was telling the truth. Kingston was tired of trying to make Mama-T believe him.

"Mama-T. Haven't I always taken care of you?" he asked.

"You have," she answered.

"And have I ever asked you for anything?" he asked.

"You never had to," Trinity said. "Who do you think raised those girls? And who do you feel deserves credit for bringing your wife out of depression every time she felt like a failed mother and wife?"

"De—"

Mama-T interrupted. "Listen to me, Kingston. You ballers think millions can buy everything. No amount of money can cure mental instability, postpartum, loneliness, or prevent suicide. Bianca and I were here for Monet through her hardest times. You don't even know your wife."

Tears fell. Monet had considered committing suicide. Why hadn't she told him? He knew what he had to do—go home and visit his wife—but he couldn't do it right away.

"Just to be safe. I can't use our account. You know Monet has access. I need you to book me a different Airbnb in Buckhead and don't tell Monet where I'm staying," he pleaded. "I'll make things better on the home front. Soon. I promise, Mama-T."

"I'll do it, but you need to bring your sabbatical to an end in thirty days," Mama-T said. "Your absence is taking a toll on your wife. I might not be able to talk her off the ledge if there's a next time."

"Thanks. I'll be home soon," Kingston lied, then said, "Bye."

Third grade. Langston Derby. In the janitor's closet. That is where his urges began.

Kingston fell to his knees, cried, and silently prayed. *Lord, please make my attraction to men go away. Please. Lord, I'm begging You. Please.* He repeated the word "please" at least a hundred times.

Theodore. Private meetups with strangers on the app Virgins-SeekingVirgins and BottomsUp. Basement encounters on Cheshire Bridge Road. The common denominator was men. Some of them were like him. Not gay. So, what made them have sex with him?

Logging into their Airbnb, Kingston found a house, copied the link, then logged out.

With all the fine females in Atlanta, being in the company of Victoria-the-Undercover-God-Worshiping-Freak and sexy-ass Jordan each Sunday, his dick only got excited when Levi came to their table.

He texted Mama-T the link to a three-bedroom spacious home with a gated entrance. As he packed his suitcases, a confirmation from Mama-T with the gate and house codes registered. Kingston loaded up his trunk, then went out back.

"Let's go, man," Kingston said.

Theodore abandoned his cocktail, followed Kingston outdoors, then sat in the passenger seat. "You okay?"

"Yeah. Decided to stay in the ATL a lil longer, but I had to check out of that location," Kingston said, driving without an immediate destination.

"You're doing the right thing," he said. "If you didn't have kids, I'd say never tell Monet shit. And live the rest of your life with me. Let's go to my shop."

Following Theodore's turn-by-turn directions, Kingston parked in the space reserved for the manager.

Theodore unlocked the back door. "After you," he said, relocking the door. "Yo! You here!"

"Who?" Kingston asked.

"Who else? My partner," Theodore said. "I was calling out to see if he was in the back so I could introduce you."

Disappearing into a room with a curtain, no door, Theodore called out, "There's a complimentary bottle of cognac behind the counter, ba . . . I mean Kingston!"

When Theodore reentered, Kingston was standing by the door. "Nice shop. Man, let's go."

Kingston didn't want to risk Theodore's partner walking in on them if they were to have sex. Knowing Theodore, Kingston knew Theodore was definitely going to suck his dick.

Locking up the shop, they got back in Kingston's car. Quietly he drove to the new Airbnb.

"Wanna talk about it?" Theodore asked.

Kingston remained silent, hoping God would give him a sign to take Theodore home, drop him off, and never communicate with him again.

Entering the code on the gate keypad, Kingston cruised up the driveway to his new temporary residence. Kingston retrieved his luggage from the trunk. He pressed 467109# to unlock the front door. Theodore walked in first, went upstairs.

Kingston called out to Theodore, "Come downstairs."

"Found this by the bed." Cabernet in one hand, wine opener in the other, Theodore suggested, "Let's christen the couch first."

Ignoring Theodore, Kingston walked outside. Inhaled the fresh air. The enclosed wraparound porch had a swing and rocking chairs overlooking the private backyard lawn and pool. He sat on the right side of the swing.

Holding two goblets by the stems, Theodore handed one to Kingston, then filled each with red wine. "We make our own rules," he said. "Salute. Follow your heart. You'll find your way."

They swayed and sipped until the sunshine traded places with the moonlight.

Kingston turned to Theodore and whispered, "I want to know what love feels like."

Theodore took Kingston's glass. He went inside, returned with a thick comforter. Spreading it on the porch, he held Kingston's hand. "Stand up."

Undressing Kingston, then himself, Theodore said, "Lie down. Relax. I got you."

CHAPTER 14

Monet

"**D**o you miss your daddy?" Monet asked Israel. If she were legally going to become a single mom, she had to understand which parent her girls would tell the judge they wanted to live with. They might choose their father if they thought he'd have all the money.

Sitting in their home salon, fingering a homemade curl serum into her daughter's hair, Monet reflected on her eight-hour visit to Atlanta. Never had she felt more abandoned by Kingston. Ending a call early when they were almost seven hundred miles apart mattered, but not as much as their being in the same area. He'd deliberately put her off on Lilly Ortiz. He didn't make it to either of the showings. And Monet hated both properties.

"Sometimes. But he's always gone. Most of my friends are daddy's girls. I'm a mommy's girl," Israel replied in a matter-of-fact tone.

Would that remain true if Monet weren't entitled to half of Kingston's assets and the girls had to downgrade their standard of living?

Earlier, Monet had prepared the girls scrambled eggs and cheese croissants, a fresh bowl of strawberries and blueberries, with a glass of almond milk, for breakfast.

Lilly was nice. It was obvious she'd protected Kingston. But why?

Women in Atlanta were known for sleeping with someone's man and acting as though they didn't know him that well when in the presence of the wife.

Tears clouded Monet's vision. She blinked repeatedly. Smoothing Israel's thick mane away from her face, she wrapped a cotton-candy-pink band twice around her daughter's hair to keep it in place. "Tell your sister to come in."

Monet removed the drape that covered Israel's solid pink shirt. A flat solid green ribbon extended from underneath her collar. Forest-green pants with pink stripes were loosely fitted down to her ankles. Pink rhinestones covered her designer tennis shoes.

She closed the lid on Israel's products, opened Nairobi's hair spritz. Her girls' textures were unique combinations of Kingston's kinky and her silky. Israel's was kinkier. Nairobi's silkier. Nairobi skipped in, wearing a green uniform dress with a flat pink ribbon underneath the collar. Her shoes were identical to her big sister's.

"Mommy, may I have a part down the middle with two big pretty braids, one on each side? And can you tie bows on the ends? I want the same color ribbon as Israel," she said, sitting in the chair.

Securing a cape over Nairobi's uniform, Monet asked, "Do you miss your daddy?"

"I miss Grandma. When is she coming over?" Nairobi asked. "We haven't seen her since she took us to see Ruth Carter. If I had a cell phone, I—"

"She's on vacation," Monet lied.

Trinity had distanced herself after Monet confessed to her mother that there was no girlfriends' day out at the spa and she'd gone to Atlanta. Trinity said she was outraged because she believed Kingston wasn't telling the truth, and Monet had disobeyed her. Although her mom was vehemently upset with her for lying, Monet had hoped that she'd understand.

"If I had a phone, I could call her," Nairobi explained, then glanced over her shoulder at her mom.

"Turn around, little girl." Monet took a deep breath. "I'll call her while you're at school to find out when she'll be back." She hated making up stories, but sometimes not being completely honest with her children was best.

Maybe Monet was overreacting. Perhaps her mom was right and Kingston did need time alone. But he could've respectfully shared his feelings with her over lunch or dinner while she was in Atlanta.

"Okay, go get your sister. It's time to go." Monet said.

Leaving the salon on the first floor, Monet stood in the doorway of the master bedroom. Black decorative pillows were neatly placed atop the gold satin comforter. As she gazed into the room, her spirit felt empty.

"Mommy!" Israel called out.

"Coming!" Monet replied.

Monet went to her en suite, stared at her reflection. Her natural hair hung behind her shoulders. No ponytail today. She painted her lips red. "I need an eyelash touchup." She texted Pamela Y. Smith, **I need a fill-in lady.**

Feeling melancholy, Monet was getting tired of being the only one fighting to spend time together. Her thin denim jumpsuit clung to every curve of her hourglass figure. Turning sideways, she admired her shapely ass.

"Let me find out Kingston is sexing another woman. All this fineness," she said, caressing her body, "will be for someone else."

"Mommy!" This time Israel was in her bedroom. "What are you doing? We're going to be late for school. Three tardies equal one absence. Come on."

Whenever she went into a depression, her mother made sure the girls got to school timely. Who could she depend on now? Bianca was her best girlfriend, but she was happily living the single life.

The second she'd given birth to Israel, Monet's entire life was spent catering to someone other than herself. A few days' getaways over the past eleven years, she could count on her fingers and toes.

Monet followed her daughter to the garage. Israel and Nairobi placed their backpacks in the trunk, then sat in the bucket seats on the row behind Monet.

"Buckle up, girls." Monet looked over her shoulder (as she'd always done) to make sure the girls' seat belts were secure.

Dropping them off at school, Monet hugged and kissed her babies the way she had since their first day of school. Her next stop was the grocery store, then back home to prep for dinner. Dicing squash, zucchini, mushrooms, to make a vegetarian lasagna, her phone rang. No need to check the caller ID. It was her husband's ringtone.

Flatly Monet answered, "Hi, Kingston."

"Baby, what's wrong?" he asked. "You sound down."

"I'm good. What's up?" she replied.

"I think Lilly is closer to finding us a house. One I know you'll like," he said. "I don't want you to be down about this. Everything is good."

"Kingston, you don't need me. You decide. That's why you're in Atlanta. Right? I have to take care of our children. By myself." Monet gently floated the noodles one at a time in the pot of boiling water.

"I don't like it when you talk this way," her husband admitted.

Her voice was monotone. "Is there anything else, Kingston? I have to finish preparing dinner, pick up the girls in a few hours, help them with homework, make sure they bathe, put them to bed, read them a story, get up early, cook them breakfast, prepare their lunch, comb their hair, drop them off at school, go to the store, figure out what's for dinner, get home, cook dinner. I have to do this five days a week with no help from my husband. And, thanks to you, without my mother."

"Baby, treat yourself on the weekends," he said.

What world was her husband living in?

"Oh, I guess Israel can drive the red Ferrari and take her sister to Brownie activities and then drive herself to her Girl Scouts meeting and pick up their friends for sleepovers on the weekends. Or I can go on an app, hire a babysitter I know nothing about, and let him or her cater to our girls while I entertain myself. What in the fuck is wrong with you?! Get your ass home and help me." Monet wanted to hurl a knife at their family photo. She might as well carve her husband's image out and flush it down the garbage disposal.

"Why isn't Trinity there?" Kingston asked in the same calm tone. "Mama-T always helps you out."

Lowering her voice, Monet told Kingston. "Find yourself a home. We're staying in Columbia."

"I promise. It won't take much—"

Ending the call, Monet opened the phone app, clicked on her favorites, pressed edits, and deleted her husband's number. Rethinking what she'd done, she reentered Kingston's information into her list of favorites, then pressed BLOCK THIS CALLER.

CHAPTER 15

Victoria

Victoria laid a black hand towel across her nightstand in her guest bedroom. Black satin sheets covered the king-sized mattress and pillows.

Filling the Crock-Pot with hot water, she set it next to her bed, plugged it in, then turned the knob to a medium temperature. Victoria added an ounce of coconut oil, then placed two face towels, one crystal vaginal egg, and a four-ounce glass bottle of honeydew sensual massage oil, mixed with lavender, inside the pot. She placed her second crystal egg in the bottom of a short glass, topped it with crushed ice, then placed the glass on the nightstand next to the Crock-Pot.

Victoria texted Kingston, Chancelor, and Jordan, **See everyone at church tomorrow. We're ushering the late service. Gray uniforms.**

She turned on her Bluetooth speaker, selected her favorite playlist of Isley Brothers, Trey Songz, and Kem. Before stepping into the shower, she covered her hair with a leopard plastic cap that had a silk lining. Warm, pulsating water splattered against her back. Victoria covered her body with an oil-based scrub, gently rubbed herself all over. Removing the handle from its holder, she switched the temperature to cool. Increasing the pressure, she lowered the showerhead to her pussy.

Inhaling. Exhaling. Again and again. Victoria enjoyed elevating her libido. Excitement rose from her vagina, to her abdomen, all the way to her throat. Wiggling the wand between her labia made her want to climax. "Okay, that's enough," she told herself aloud, on the verge of having an orgasm.

Self-pleasuring in the shower was a libido booster she'd discovered when her sex drive started decreasing. Using clit stimulators, dildos, vibrators, and vaginal crystal eggs kept her desire to have orgasms on edge without needing one of those G-spot injections that claimed to make a woman squirt every time she had sex. She worried that hormone replacements would not only increase her risk of getting cancer, but that it might eliminate her desire to have multiple orgasms with much younger men.

Exiting the shower, she texted a guy she'd met on Tuition-Cougars: **My gate code is 579. See you in 20 minutes. I'll leave the front door unlocked.**

If their relationship progressed, Victoria would be doing doubles every Saturday. Mornings with a handsome, hot, hard-body youngster and Saturday nights with Big Willy.

Moisturizing her freshly showered body with a mixture of shea butter, avocado, and black seed oils, she stared at her glowing reflection in the full-length mirror. Her once-ultraperky boobs were drooping, but just a little. Victoria placed a cotton swab under each breast. They vanished from sight. A decade ago they would've fallen to the floor. Hoisting her DD-cups, she wondered if she should get a lift. Turning sideways, she suctioned in her stomach. Maybe she should consider butt implants if she was going to keep fucking twentysomethings.

"Let's see," Victoria said softly, searching through lingerie with tags attached.

All-yellow stockings, garter, thong, and low-cut bra dangled in her hands. "Do millennials and the Z-generation even care about such?" She kept the thong, swapped the attire for a simple red baby doll negligee. The thong disappeared between her butt cheeks, making her ass appear bigger. "That's the look," she said, pleased with her decision.

Her ringtone for her garage gate commanded her attention. Victoria smiled, tapped # for her guest to enter. Standing in her doorway, she motioned for him to come inside.

"Wow. You are so beautiful for your age. I can't believe you're fifty," he said. "I brought us a bottle of Hennessy."

"How thoughtful. I'll fix us a drink while you go to the bedroom." She pointed toward the open door, then continued, "Get undressed and lay on top of the satin sheet. Facing up."

Getting some glasses for their imbibing, Victoria poured a hefty portion of liquor into his snifter; then she halfway filled her goblet with red wine. There was no such thing as too early to enjoy libations with a young handsome man. Nor should she delay her sexual gratification with small talk.

Returning to the bedroom, she set the drinks on the other nightstand. Removing a towel, she twisted until the last heated drop of excess water plopped in the Crock-Pot, then gently cleansed her lover's genital area.

"That's hot!" he exclaimed.

"So are you. Turn over so I can cleanse you," she said, then firmly rubbed his ass and his asshole.

"This is why I love older women. My dick and my ass feel amazing," he said.

Victoria retrieved a large condom from the nightstand's drawer, opened the packet, tossed the wrapper on the black-and-white towel, then commanded, "Turn onto your back." She quickly suctioned in the tip, then slipped the prophylactic inside her mouth.

Victoria inserted the warm crystal egg into her vagina to start her natural juices flowing. While the egg got her wet, she drizzled Kama Sutra oil over his chest and down to his feet, then began rubbing him all over.

"What's that that you put in your pussy?" he asked.

She mumbled, "This will feel better if you hold your question until we're done." Firmly stroking his shaft, she ejected the egg using her muscles, eased the condom over his corona with her mouth, rolled it down to the youngster's pubic hairs, using her lips, then straddled her lover. "Put this big, hard, beautiful dick inside this wet pussy," she commanded.

Holding his penis, he asked, "Where'd the raincoat come from? You real quick."

Victoria slid her hand under the pillow, located her Slim-10–speed gold metallic vibrator. Pushing the button, she circled the smooth tip around his nipple.

"Oh, shit!" He held her wrist. "What's that?"

"Let go of me and relax. You'll get used to it," she said, moving his hand.

Victoria increased the speed a level, reached behind her back, then slowly slid the Slim-10 along his perineum. She rocked back and forth, grinding on his stiffening erection. She felt his shaft expanding inside of her.

"Oh, my God, lady! I never did this," he exclaimed. "This feels amazing!"

The more she explored his sensitive spots with varying vibrations, the harder his dick became. Reaching underneath the pillow again, she pulled out a vibrating cock ring, then powered it on. Quickly sliding it over his head, she put his penis back inside of her.

"Lady! What else is under that damn *pillow!*" the twentysomething shouted.

Victoria pinched his nipples hard, then focused on him. Reaching behind her, she moved the pulsating device from his perineum to his rectum. Holding it at the opening, she switched from the constant vibration to a pulsation, then tightened her vaginal muscles.

"Lady, I'm about to *cummmm!*" He shouted the last word for about ten seconds.

"Thank You, Lord Jesus!" Victoria exhaled as she climaxed with him. "God is good."

Her lover stared at her with wide eyes. "I feel like I need to pay you. When can I see you again?"

Well, there was no rest for the weary. She had to get ready for dinner with Willy.

"You were fantastic, young man. I'll CashApp you five hundred dollars for your books. Everything you need to freshen up is in the guest bathroom to your left. Use the towels on the vanity. When you're done, toss them in the hamper. Oh, and take the rest of your Hennessy with you."

CHAPTER 16

Jordan

"Thanks for coming." Jordan handed the church collection basket to Terrence Russell, who was seated on the end. She glanced around Kingston, across the aisle on the last row. Chancelor's head was bowed and his attention was fixated on Tracy Benjamin.

"My pleasure, Ms. Jackson. I appreciate the invite," Terrence replied, placing a $100 bill on top, before passing the collection to the woman at his right.

"It's better to give than it is to receive," Pastor Baloney preached. "Give freely for you cannot outgive God. That includes everyone." Pastor stared in Tracy's direction. Or maybe he was singling out Peaches.

Hope for All Church had fallen into a shameful pit, syphoning its parishioners into a black hole. Most of the congregation knew the pastor had slept with the choir director. She—the same choir director—had committed adultery with the first lady. Jordan remained a loyal member because everyone was a sinner, and no ministry was without challenges. That, and she'd witnessed how the pastor had increased the profits of his people.

Tracy took the wicker basket from Melvin, then passed it to Chancelor without dropping anything inside. Chancelor bit his bottom lip, then mouthed "you see this whore" to Jordan. Every member watching Chancelor probably could make out what he'd said. Jordan placed her finger on her mouth.

Forming a double-file line, the four of them marched toward the altar, then faced the congregation. Jordan stared at Terrence. Soon as the doors of the church were closed and service had ended, she made her way to him.

"I really want to thank you for being here," she said, holding his hand as they exited to the sidewalk.

Terrence was dressed in a tan suit. The eighty-two degrees seemed too high for any type of jacket. Jordan wondered if his attire was ever casual. His clean-shaven face was well moisturized. She was attracted to his dark brown skin, full perfectly shaped brows, and she could tell he was muscular by the outline of his physique. Terrence stood face-to-face with Jordan. Held her other hand.

"After I left the bar, I heard on the radio that your friend's son was killed. When I got home, I saw Donovan Bradley and a picture of his deceased son on practically every news channel. I understood why he'd called you. I would've done the same, had I been in his position. I like you, Jordan." Terrence squeezed her hands. "A lot. And I'd appreciate an opportunity to spoil you."

Jordan welcomed the comfort of this man. His words seemed sincere, but she wasn't emotionally investing in him yet. Terrence was operating off a feeling that she was all too familiar with. *Love. A love void.* She knew more about him than he did about her. One more heartbreak could be devastating and could leave her jaded for the rest of her life.

"Who's this handsome specimen?" Victoria asked, standing next to Jordan.

"Terrence Russell. Jordan's friend," he politely said, extending his hand in Victoria's direction.

Responding in kind, Victoria smiled at Terrence, then told Jordan, "See you in a few."

"Okay, girl," Jordan answered. "But I might have to leave early." Her eyes shined brighter than the sun.

Watching Victoria head toward the parking lot, Jordan looked at Terrence. "He . . . Donovan wants me to represent him."

Sharing that information was a leap for Jordan, as she normally refrained from divulging professional details of any kind with a new acquaintance. It would be nice to have a man lie in bed next to her and listen to her after a long day in the courtroom.

Terrence said, "You sure that's a good—"

A man's voice erupted, "Get your hands off of her, man, before I whup your ass!"

Jordan's neck snapped in the direction of the commotion. "Oh, shit!" Running down the steps in her heels, Jordan got to Chancelor the same time as Victoria and Kingston.

"Let me go! You're hurting me! *Ow!* Somebody help me!" Tracy yelled, seemingly more for attention. Or to substantiate a lawsuit.

"Chancelor, let's go. Now!" Kingston grabbed Chancelor from behind by his biceps, hoisted Chancelor in the air. Did a one-eighty turn.

Facing Victoria and Jordan, Chancelor shouted, "She's a whore, y'all! That's what I'm trying to tell Melvin." Chancelor kicked his feet. "Put me down, dude."

Melvin raced around Kingston, punched Chancelor in the stomach several times. Chancelor kicked. Hit Melvin in the face. Melvin spat blood and a tooth into his hand.

"Oh, you gon' pay for this." Melvin opened his mouth, eased his finger inside the empty space. "This ain't over, nigga."

Thank God, Kingston released Chancelor, then stood between Melvin and Chancelor.

Kingston grabbed Chancelor by the back of his vest. "C'mon. You're riding with me. See you ladies in a few. Melvin, bruh, you struck first. You come for my boy, you come for me, too," Kingston said.

Turning to Terrence, who stood beside her, Jordan shook her head. "I'm so sorry, Terrence, but I have to go. Chancelor needs counsel and a group intervention. Thanks again for coming. Hope to see you next Sunday."

CHAPTER 17

Jordan

"Levi, open both bottles at the same time," Jordan insisted. She plopped down in her seat between Victoria and Chancelor; Kingston was on time and in uniform, like the rest of them, because he'd brought Chancelor directly from church to the bar.

"Y'all look a mess." Levi placed two goblets on the table, removed an opener from his vest pocket, peeled the foil tabs, then uncorked each bottle. "Be right back with a double brandy and double cognac, fellas."

Jordan immediately chastised and counseled Chancelor. "Don't ever put your hand, hands, dick, lips, or any parts of your entire being on Tracy ever again. Do not call or text Tracy ever again. Do not mention her name ever again. Pray she doesn't charge your ass with assault and sue you for pain and suffering. That dumb live you did outside her home went viral. Refrain from social media posts. She has lots of proof and witnesses and you gave it to her. For what? What are you trying to prove?"

Chancelor sat with his arms folded high across his chest.

"Yeah, bruh. Let it go," Kingston added. "We all play the fool sometimes. That chick has got you out of character. I ain't tryna fight a dude over a female that's not even your girl."

Chancelor's posture and lips were stiff, as though he disregarded every word.

"Not you, my brother. You're nobody's fool." Levi handed Kingston his drink first. Placed Chancelor's on the table in front of him, then left.

"Kingston, don't be so quick to protect Chancelor," Jordan said. "You might get sued by Melvin. He could claim you picked up Chancelor so Chancelor could kick him in the face. Melvin spat his tooth into a handful of blood. Did anyone besides me see that?"

"Good." Chancelor nodded upward. "I had the right to defend myself. Y'all saw him punch me first. One of our church members have to have that on video."

That was the damn problem with men. They thought they could justify their way out of any situation, even when they knew they were wrong. They always thought about the consequences of their actions *after the fact,* when shit got too complicated for them to deal with. Jordan had intentionally stood back so no one could hold her responsible. Victoria had kept a good distance as well.

"Thank the Lord, He showed you the real Tracy before you proposed," Victoria joked. "Where did you find her? In Bankhead? We need to clone Tracy's pus—"

"Shut up, everybody," Chancelor demanded, handing his cell to Jordan. "Since you're the background expert, fuck Tracy Benjamin. Set me up with my future wife."

That wasn't a bad idea. "Oh. Wait." Jordan stared at his screen. A dating app was open. She read aloud, "'ChristianFornicators'? Really, Chancelor?"

Victoria took Chancelor's phone from Jordan. Kingston snatched it from Victoria, then returned it to its owner.

Chancelor passed it back to Jordan. "I never said I wasn't on a dating site. That's where I met that ho."

Jordan's phone rang. She held it to her ear. No hi or hello. "I told you I'd consider representing you. Your calling every few hours isn't helping. If my firm takes your case, we'll need a fifty-thousand-dollar retainer."

"A what? I don't have that kind of money!" Donovan exclaimed.

Liar. More like he believed under the circumstances she should represent him for free. Perhaps she would've if he hadn't acted as though they were going to get married and have a baby, while he knew he didn't want to marry or impregnate her. Or if he hadn't used her for sex. Or toyed with her emotions. Or if he hadn't faded to black and stopped responding to her calls and texts after she'd given him an ultimatum.

"Bye, Donovan," Jordan said. Ending the conversation, she announced to the group, "I'm blocking him the way he did me. There."

"Damn," Kingston said. "You a boss. The man's son was killed, Jordan. By a white female cop. You have to take his case."

Changing the subject, Jordan said, "I've drafted the rules for our online dating. E-mailing them to each of you right now. Done."

"Chancelor, you need to find a different app." Jordan opened the document and read aloud, " 'Each person will create at least one profile. Establish and share your relationship goals with the group. Go out on at least one date a week. Text a photo of your date, along with their full name, cell number, turn on your location while you're on the date, and text your group partner when you get home.' I got Kingston. Victoria, you're with Chancelor."

Levi approached the table, refilled Jordan's and Victoria's glasses. Handed a snifter to Kingston and one to Chancelor. "Jordan, what you need is for a man to stuff you with good dick and a baby. Ain't no grown person doing all that."

A lot of people went wrong with dating apps because they didn't have goals or regulations. "Victoria, you start. What do you want to accomplish?"

Victoria sipped her wine, then answered, "The Lord knows my heart."

Jordan sighed. "Fine. I'm the only one taking this seriously."

"Too seriously," Kingston added. "Levi is right. We're adults."

"Okay, but can we at least pair up for some checks and balances?" Jordan inquired. Knowing she'd failed to get anyone's buy-in the first time, if no one agreed, she'd let it go.

Levi stood behind the bar. "Damn, girl. That's what's wrong with females. Y'all have too many damn rules. My Queen don't trip."

"Anymore?" Victoria added.

Jordan understood what it felt like to compromise herself behind closed doors. She was strong in public, but she'd had a few private weak and embarrassing moments trying to hold on to Donovan.

A man dressed in a brown suit, white shirt, and hard-sole shoes burst through the door. Scanned the bar. Rushed over to Jordan.

Kingston quickly stood in front of Jordan. "Hey, bruh. Back up. I'm not going to tell you twice."

"What, Donovan?" Jordan slowly placed the rim of her goblet to her lips, then tilted the glass up. Her eyes focused on Kingston's back as she remained seated.

"Oh, that's him. Sorry for your loss, man." Kingston returned to his seat.

Donovan opened a gym bag, removed a white envelope, slammed a stack of $100 bills on the table in front of Jordan. He said, "Here's ten thousand dollars. I promise to get you the rest as soon as possible. This should be enough to get you started. I demand justice for my son." Donovan shouted as though he was announcing it to everyone in the bar. "Anne Whitehall is a killer cop and she deserves to be behind bars! Not on administrative leave!"

Atlanta was an eclectic community. No one in the bar reacted to Donovan's outburst, including Levi and everyone at her table.

Donovan's owning a chain of boutique hotels made him rich, not famous. Picking up the money, Jordan handed it back to Donovan. "It's not just me who would be working your case. I have partners. If we are going to represent you, I need fifty thousand dollars. That's nonnegotiable. I'm sorry about your son, but this is business."

How quickly men forgot their asshole behavior when dating. Donovan started out making plans, showing up on time, offering to do things around her home. Then he downgraded to coming over after midnight. Departing two or three hours later. He went from texting her back right away to responding a day or sometimes two later. Two days had stretched out fifteen months. And now he had the audacity to make demands of her.

Why should she care about him? One thing Atlanta was not short on was lawyers.

"Damn, Jordan! Fine." Donovan shoved the money in his bag, then took a step back. "The hell with your acting as though we never dated."

"We didn't," Jordan said. "Now please leave. I'm trying to be polite."

The group at the table stared back and forth between Jordan and Donovan.

Levi approached the table. "Is there a problem, man? The lady said leave, and she asked you to leave now. I'm not asking. I'm telling you to get the fuck out. Or get knocked the fuck out."

Kingston stood, then nodded in agreement. "Now, bruh."

CHAPTER 18

Chancelor

"I'm originally from Austin, Arkansas. Where're you from?" Chancelor asked.

Getting to know a new female, Chancelor increased the volume on the Bluetooth, which was in his ear. He sat in his car with the rear passenger door open. His feet were on the grass.

Every day she proved him right. Parked a half mile away, he flew his drone over Tracy's house. Chancelor zoomed in on her driveway. Melvin had arrived with a large bouquet of yellow roses. Tracy opened the door, grabbed the bouquet by the stems, let Melvin in, then kissed him before closing the door.

"Yuck!" Chancelor said prior to her response.

"Yuck, what?" the female asked.

"Oh, nothing. Just saw something repulsive," he replied.

Why hadn't he thought to send Tracy flowers after he'd kicked snaggletoothed Melvin in the face. That kiss was supposed to be his. Chancelor had a few more days before Sunday service. Fingering his controller, he did a 360-degree lap around the house to every open window to see where Melvin had disappeared. There were laws that prohibited flying drones within the city limits, but the chances of his getting shot down by the government were slim.

"Born and raised in the ATL. I have one opening in my weekly schedule. You cool with Tuesday date nights?" she asked.

Exactly how many men were being inducted into Tracy's little sponsorship program? One day some dude was going to pay her back. Was the home security alarm he saw throughout her place real or a deterrent?

"Ho," he said to the chick on the phone.

"What's wrong with black men? Why I gotta be a 'ho'?" she questioned.

Having met Tracy at church, the dating app he was on started to feel like an extension of Hope for All Church. Based on the behavior of the pastor and first lady, he might have to start calling the tabernacle, "Whores for All."

Why in the hell was the chick on the phone upset? Chancelor emphasized, "Don't you mean ho-tation?"

"Monday and Thursday after I get off from working a nine-to-five, I have night classes. I'm getting my master's. Wednesday, Bible study. Friday and Saturday, I do in-home care. And Sunday, I'm at church most of the day," she lamented.

"Charge it to my heads," he said, thinking of Victoria.

Victoria was a one-man whore. Jordan was waiting to get back on the ho stroll, trying to drag everyone else on her sinner's mission. *Blame it on Tracy*, he thought, tempted to lower the drone to Tracy's bedroom window. "I apologize. You didn't deserve that. Since I've been in Atlanta, so many women are schemers. I've heard about how y'all rotate men on a schedule. I gave my last girlfriend three grand in the first three weeks because her mother died," he paused, then added, "But she didn't tell me her mom had died . . . again. And wait. Her mom is now among the living."

Laughter exploded in his ear. "If you're feeling less generous, my cell phone bill is due. All I need is sixty dollars." She continued laughing.

Wasn't shit funny. Chancelor had labored intensively to assist start-up companies with marketing and advertising. He worked long hours for his money. Terminating the call, he programmed his drone to return to home base. He dialed another female that had sent him her number.

"Hello?" she answered, sounding sweet.

"Hi, this is Chancelor from *CF*," he said.

"Well, hello, Chancelor. I like your pro—"

Interrupting, Chancelor said, "The only thing I'm paying for is food."

"Praise the Lord, you are a child of God. Of course, you won't be expecting any gratuities. When and where would you like to meet?" The smile in her tone was evident.

Unlocking his trunk, he put the drone and the remote inside. Closed it, then sat in the driver's seat. Chancelor wondered if Melvin's dick was inside of Tracy's pussy.

"You seem dickstracted. Have a nice evening, Chancelor," girl two said, ending the call.

The first chick might be the type of woman he needed. He called her. Soon as she answered, he said, "It's Tuesday. How's seven o'clock? Capital Grille, Buckhead. I'll order you an Uber round-trip. Or if you prefer not to give me your address, I can reimburse you when you arrive. And your name—"

Softly she said, "Shanita Williams."

Sha who? Sha what? Aw, hell no, Chancelor thought. What was he getting himself into? With a name like that, she was probably putting out pussy every Tuesday. However, he was tired of jacking off.

"On second thought," he said, "let's go to Harold's. You like fried chicken, right?"

CHAPTER 19

Kingston

Living in Atlanta felt better when Monet cared about him being gone. His wife had become the despondent one.

Each day Theodore gave Kingston a reason to file for a divorce. But what would his family, friends, and fans think of him if he told them he was bisexual? That was his new truth. Maybe. There was a sure way to find out.

Getting out of the Lyft, Kingston told the driver, "Pull up to the code box." He entered the digits. The gate to his house in Columbia, Maryland, opened. "Drop me off at the front door."

Kingston retrieved two backpacks—one pink, the other purple—off the seat, then shut the rear passenger door. He stared up at the home he'd bought, trying to figure out how any woman living in luxury could be depressed.

Standing on the top step, he realized almost three months had passed since he'd seen her face, hugged his girls, or kissed his mother-in-law on the cheek. Something inside of him felt strange. Perhaps he should return to the hotel, collect his baggage, head to the airport, hop back on his chartered jet, and return to Atlanta.

Kingston sat on the swing bench on his porch. Looking at his front lawn, he wondered if he'd ever be comfortable with himself. Being black was hard. Being a black man in America was harder. The odds of him being anything other than an athlete were against him. He didn't want to be an entrepreneur, a businessman working for a company, a coach, or a family man.

If he could do anything outside of basketball, Kingston didn't know what else he was great at. A good husband? Nah, he was an awesome provider. The perfect dad? He wasn't close to his girls. Honestly, he didn't know his children very well. He definitely wasn't the perfect son. He failed at that. He'd heard that men marry into their wife's lifestyle. For him, that wasn't true.

Kingston had traveled too far to avoid the inevitable. Pressing his thumb against the keypad, his fingerprint registered, and the light flashed green. Kingston heard the familiar click. Slowly he placed his palm on the oak wood, then nudged. He quietly closed the door behind him, glanced around the foyer, holding a backpack in each hand.

The one thing Kingston didn't have concern regarding was another man in his bed with Monet. He wished he could give her the same assurance.

Monet appeared from the kitchen area. "Put your hands up, motherfucker!" Monet shouted, pointing a .45 Glock at his head.

The backpacks dangled high in the air before falling to the floor. "Don't shoot! It's me!"

"Shit!" Securing the safety on the gun, Monet held her left hand over her heart, then said, "Damn, Kingston. You can't pop up on us like this. I didn't know who was coming in here unannounced."

The way she'd aimed at his face, he felt his wife might have wanted a justifiable reason to commit homicide. She had to have seen on the home monitor that it was him. "Baby! Girls! Daddy's home!" Kingston shouted, hiding the gifts behind the sofa in the living room, before sitting in a high-backed white leather chair to admire his wife.

Monet wore jean shorts that barely covered her cheeks, a fitted white tank top with no bra, her hair was in a high ponytail the way he liked it. She wore big hoop earrings and ruby-red lipstick.

It was six o'clock in the evening. Sniffing the aroma of good cooking, he smiled at his wife. He hadn't had a tasty home-cooked meal since he'd left her.

"Daddy! Daddy!" the girls shouted, running toward him.

Israel sat on his left thigh. Nairobi on his right. They hugged his neck and planted kisses on his cheeks.

Monet sarcastically said, "Oh, hey, Kingston. I see you have the girls' backpacks. Where's my gift?" Not awaiting a response, she went directly to the kitchen.

Israel stared her dad in the eyes. "Really?"

Kingston told his girls, "Go watch television. I'll be upstairs in a minute."

Soon as Nairobi opened her mouth, Kingston spoke with authority. "Now. Both of you."

Entering his kitchen, he asked his wife, "You're not happy to see me?"

"Of course I am, but I run this household," she said, then shouted, "Girls! Come down." Monet opened the refrigerator, asked him, "You hungry? Or thirsty?"

Kingston was confused. About his wife, not about his appetite for his wife. "Yes, I'm famished." For food, he knew, but wouldn't dare say.

Nairobi ran to her dad, wrapped her arms around his waist. "I miss you, Daddy. Before you made us go upstairs, I wanted to ask you where's my cell phone?"

"And our backpacks?" Israel questioned with a hint of an attitude.

Looking at Monet, slowly she moved her head side-to-side. Kingston dug deep into his pocket. Handed his girls five $100 bills each. "Daddy loves you."

Monet quietly stirred the pot while staring at him. Having his daughters present might be the only thing keeping his wife from cursing him out. Monet turned her back to him. Suddenly the room became cold.

Kingston picked up Nairobi. He lowered his cheek toward Israel. "Give Daddy a kiss."

"How long are you here for, Daddy?" Nairobi asked, hugging his neck.

Easing her to her feet, Kingston didn't answer. Monet didn't look over her shoulder at him.

"Girls, go read for twenty minutes," Monet said with her back to them.

Pretending to hold a cell to her ear, Nairobi tilted her head, then stared at her dad. "When is Grandma getting off of vacation?" Nairobi questioned her mother.

Israel added, "Yeah, she's been gone forever. We miss her," motioning as though she'd placed a backpack over her shoulders.

A couple of days past two weeks was how long he'd been living at the Airbnb with Theodore. Kingston knew that Monet was aware that Mama-T was not vacationing. Mama-T was at her home less than five minutes away.

Whatever had happened between his mother-in-law and his wife wasn't his fault. Kingston retrieved his cell from his pocket, then messaged Mama-T, **I'm in Columbia at the house, come by. My girls want to see you.**

Are you spending the night with her? I didn't fly with you to Columbus to stay in this fancy Baltimore hotel by myself. Don't make me come get my—, Theodore messaged.

Kingston approached Monet. "Do you want me here?" he asked in front of their girls. Putting his arms around her waist, he kissed the top of her head.

"Mommy, say yes," Nairobi excitedly said.

Monet looked at the girls. If they'd gone upstairs to do as she'd told them, they'd almost be finished. She knew how to get the girls out of sight. "Get your backpacks from behind the sofa and take them to your room."

Israel's and Nairobi's eyes widened. They raced to the living room.

"Thank you, Daddy!" Israel shouted.

"Oh, my gosh! I finally got a phone! Thanks, Dad!" Nairobi screamed.

"Up. Now," Monet said, then added, "Or I'm taking everything." The girls vanished immediately.

Shuffling to the left without giving him eye contact, Monet flatly replied, "It's your house, Kingston."

"I know that, but the way you're acting, it doesn't feel that way. You want me to leave?" he asked.

Monet remained silent.

"I hear ya. It's cool. Why don't I give you your space." Kingston moved closer to the living room.

He needed his wife to fight for him like Theodore had done. Kingston needed to be needed.

Monet picked up a butcher's knife, sliced an eggplant into strips, layered them inside of a clear plastic container, poured marinade on top, then placed it in the refrigerator.

Kingston pressed his lips together. Watched his wife stir the pot again. "Monet."

He'd feel better if she'd curse him. Slap his face. Cry. Something.

"I'll come back tomorrow," he told her.

Monet didn't acknowledge him.

CHAPTER 20

Monet

No mention of finding them a home. No conversation about when he'd planned to relocate them to Atlanta. And she was supposed to be happy to see him?

Monet turned off the burner, poured a glass of red wine, positioned the bottle within arm's reach. Sitting at the island, she inhaled Kingston's cologne. The loudest voice she heard was inside her head. What happened to the man she married?

She texted her mother, **Is Kingston at your house?**

Monet connected her Bluetooth, called her best girlfriend since high school.

"Hey," Bianca cheerfully answered. "I was just about to call you. I'm up here in Baltimore. Guess who I just saw in the hotel lobby?"

Irrespective of the fact that her husband was five years her junior, twenty-three was too young for her to get pregnant. The most fun part of dating Kingston was pre-motherhood, being courtside at his high-school games, cheering him on . . . until she delivered Israel. Speaking on camera as a family made Monet feel like a celebrity on her campus. When she had her baby and her man in front of reporters after a big win, spectators asked for her autograph, until Kingston's parents immediately squashed her three minutes of stardom.

Sadly Monet told Bianca, "Don't get pregnant unless you really want a child. Kids change your life. Forever."

Why did it have to take her pretending like she didn't love her husband to get a reaction from him? Monet wasn't crazy. Kingston showed up to make sure she wasn't planning on leaving him.

"But your girls are the best," Bianca stated. "Obviously, you're not going to guess who I saw."

Picking up the dish towel, Monet slammed it against the countertop repeatedly, then squeezed a ripe plum until it burst. Tears streamed down her cheeks. She trashed the towel and the fruit before leaving her phone on the blue crystals and retreating to her bedroom, where the girls couldn't witness her tantrum.

"Why is he treating me like he doesn't love me anymore?" Monet cried.

"Oh, Lord. Don't hang up. I'm still in Baltimore. I'm on my way," Bianca told her.

Bianca's home was in Laurel, Maryland. A short ten minutes south of Columbia. B-More was twenty-two miles north of Monet's residence. She washed her face with cool water, returned to the kitchen, checked her cell.

I don't know where he's at, Trinity had texted.

"Girl, he came home. Tried to start an argument with me, then when I didn't say anything, he left. Wasn't here long enough for me to dash my homemade seasoning on his portion of the meal." Monet removed the container from the refrigerator. Certain there was plenty of shrimp fettuccine Alfredo, with fresh basil and diced tomatoes, for her girlfriend, Monet generously sprinkled spices all over the eggplant before placing the cookie sheet in the preheated oven.

Monet opened the front door and sat on the porch, waiting for Bianca. She texted her mother, **Are you okay? I miss and love you.**

Miss and love you more. Miss the girls. It's not you. It's me. I need to focus on myself for a while, Trinity replied.

An aching pain surfaced in Monet's lungs as she inhaled deeply. Gasping to take in oxygen, she was relieved to see Bianca heading toward her.

Bianca parked in the circular driveway, hurried up the stairs, sat next to Monet, and hugged her. "Oh, my gosh, you're trembling. Breathe. You're going to be just fine. You're the strongest woman I know."

She wasn't always that way. In this moment Monet wanted to curled into a fetal position while her mother cocooned her body. Why did women have the responsibility of holding the family together?

Stroking Monet's hair, Bianca rocked, side to side, holding Monet's hand. "What's wrong, honey?"

Monet shook her head. "Maybe he needs a permanent break from me. I'm the only woman he's been with in twelve years. My mother says Kingston needs space. You think she's right? Maybe I should chill out." Monet cried aloud. "I'm scared, Bianca. What if I'm pushing my husband away for real?" she asked, laying her head on her best friend's lap.

"Humph. You know I love Trinity, but your husband is in Atlanta. Without you and the girls. I couldn't raise two children by myself the way you do. Sit up. Look at me." Bianca held both of Monet's hands. "I say take half, get all the way out, and don't look back. Kingston is cheating on you. With a man," Bianca replied.

Of all the exaggerations Bianca could've created to prove her point, she, too, accepts the rumor that all men in Atlanta are gay? Monet shook her head, choosing to believe her girlfriend was simply being supportive.

Monet had to defend Kingston this time. "Every man in Atlanta isn't gay. Kingston would die before letting a man touch his dick."

"If you say so." Bianca sandwiched her fingers between her knees. "I know what I saw at the hotel. Straight men do not be in public with—"

"He's not that way, all right," Monet objected. "I've been with him since he was seventeen. I would know. I love Kingston. My life centers around him. I've never applied for a job in twelve years. I don't know how to start a business. All I've done was be his wife."

More afraid to be on her own than to stay married, Monet stood. Paced back and forth on the porch.

"All the more reason to file for divorce, Monet. What do you like doing?" Bianca inquired, following Monet with her eyes.

No ideas surfaced. "I am Mrs. Kingston Royale," she said.

"That's it!" Bianca sprang to her feet, stood in front of Monet. "Take acting classes until you figure it out," Bianca suggested.

"In Columbia?" Monet couldn't imagine pretending that she was someone else was exciting.

"No, honey. In Hotlanta. You don't need Kingston's permission. His money is yours. Buy your own house." Covering her face with her hands, Bianca slowly spread them apart. "A pussy palace with all designer shit. Real pink ponies for the girls—you know you can take ponies on the plane now—and put glitter in their manes."

Monet's sorrow turned into laughter.

Bianca became more animated. "I'm serious. Buy a home, a thousand square feet more than this." She stretched her arms wide. "Move down there with your girls and don't give Kingston access. It's unlawful to put him out. Not to lock him out. And if I were you," she whispered as though someone was eavesdropping, "I'd keep this house and I wouldn't tell him I moved."

In slow motion Monet shook her head. She wished her decision was as simple as Bianca suggested. "You would do some shit like that?"

Laughing, Bianca said, "You damn straight. Why should you be unhappy while he's living his best life without you? Let me set you up on a date with a handsome, intelligent, sexy man from my on-line account."

Ignoring her girlfriend's last statement, feeling relieved, Monet smiled. Her dilemma wasn't over. "Come inside. I have to feed my kids. And you're staying for dinner."

"Perfect. The girls can eat while I show you the men in my in-box. Can you say 'dessert, dessert, dessert' three times? These guys will have you licking more than your lips."

CHAPTER 21

Victoria

"Willy, we need a vacation." Victoria wiggled seductively in her seat. It was their usual Saturday date night. She reached across the table to grip his tie and pull him close. "I'ma give it to you good tonight. You just wait."

Surviving both of his wives, Willy was a man that enjoyed being married. For her, companionship sufficed. He didn't care much for traveling. Would rather drive to a destination than get on a plane. But she wanted to show him a different country.

Reclaiming his tie, Willy asked, "What's gotten into you, sugarplum? You're acting like a teenager."

Victoria wanted to spice up their sex life and strengthen their emotional connection. Tahiti. Bora Bora. A tropical experience would be good for them to share. Or venturing farther away.

"I'm happy. What's wrong with that? How's Australia?" she asked.

TuitionCougars rejuvenated her. Praise the Lord, she was saving the world, one young educated man at a time. Scrolling the app, she shivered. *A real-life Zeus. Why-oh-why, Lord Jesus, did You make this man so sexy?*

Rattling her head, Victoria repeatedly thought, *Yield not to temptation.*

"Australia. Who's that?" Willy laughed. "I'm not going all the way over there to see a kangaroo." He slid the bottle of wine closer to his side of the table, placed it under his nose, then sniffed. "What they put in here? Don't start smokin' that cannabis just because Georgia finally made it okay."

Legalization of marijuana in Georgia was for medicinal purposes. Victoria had explored the puff-puff/pass-pass back in her day. But it might not be a bad idea to ask her doctor for a prescription and get Willy high as a kite.

Victoria dissected her salad. Ate small bites of butter lettuce. Willy had become more attractive to her since she'd started dating younger men.

"Since you're in a good mood, I have something to share with you, Victoria." Brother Copeland's face became expressionless. "This time is good as any other."

"Victoria"? No "sugarplum"? Bracing herself in the booth as though he'd tapped a little too hard on the brakes, she replied, "What is it, Willy? You don't want to fly? Drivers in Georgia kill more people on the street than people die from falling out of the sky."

Willy sucked in, then swallowed a mouthful of Cabernet.

Hmm, he never gulps that way. Victoria's eyes narrowed as she stared at him.

Resting his elbows atop the dining table at Bones, Willy stared at Victoria. Became quiet. A live jazz band on a small stage across from them started performing "Stormy Weather." The bottle of red wine sat nearer to his almost-empty goblet. Dim lights on the chandelier above their table cast a yellowish tone over Willy's face that she hadn't noticed until now.

Victoria shivered again. This time because her vagina involuntarily twitched. Perhaps it was due to the hot, passionate sex she'd had this morning instead of breakfast.

Victoria said, "This sounds serious. Willy, come." She patted the cushion on her side of the booth. "Sit next to me."

Standing, she allowed him to sit on the inside. If Willy said something she didn't like, he wouldn't be able to leave without explaining himself.

Another session scheduled for tomorrow evening with a thirty-something from the app had her spirit glowing. But the thought of training Zeus was doing something new to her. She hadn't had a single hot flash the entire week.

Motioning for the waiter to come to their table, Victoria requested, "A glass of ice, please."

Willy scooted closer to her. "Sugarplum, I'm going to have to amend my trust," he said, reaching for his goblet. His hands clung to his glass. If he squeezed any harder, he might break it.

Lord Jesus, this must be a test, she thought. Or maybe she hadn't heard him correctly. "Repeat that."

"Don't go getting upset. You'll get half," he said.

"Whom? What? Why? Let go of the glass, Willy. I've been your mistress through both of your marriages. I never married because of you." That last statement was a lie, but he didn't need to know it. "You owe me." That was the truth. "What is this about?"

"It's only fifty percent, sugarplum." His brows raised.

"In the name of Jesus, I've come too far for whatever nonsense you're talking about." Victoria's voice escalated. "I refuse to share one penny. All of your money is mine." Hissing an inch from his face, she added, "Do . . . you . . . hear . . . me, William Copeland?" then leaned back.

Willy's head hung low as he revealed, "Tracy says she's my daughter."

"*Tracy?* The congregational whore, *Tracy?*" Victoria laughed out loud.

Brother Copeland held his head up, then nodded.

Victoria's expression froze like ice. "She's a liar!" Victoria's tone escalated above the music.

In the name of Jesus! Victoria didn't want to have to put a hex on Tracy.

"Actually, she is. She brought over a—"

" '*Brought over'!*" Victoria exclaimed. "She's been to my house? That's my house you're living in. Everything you own is mine. Just like mine is yours." Knowing the good Lord would call Willy home to glory first, she said the last part to make Willy feel better.

"Hear me out," Willy requested, placing his hand on Victoria's thigh. "She brought over this home kit DNA test, she said it was.

She swiped a stick in my mouth, then in hers. We waited a few minutes. She read me the results. Tracy is my biological daughter."

"William Copeland. You're too old to be a new fool." Victoria didn't move his hand; she covered it, instead, with hers.

The waitress brought their orders to the table.

"Box it up," Victoria told her. "This conversation will continue at my house." Getting to know Zeus could wait. "That bitch is lying. And you're not taking my name off of anything."

Victoria might have to crack that masturbation egg over Willy's skull tonight, then suck him back to his senses.

Victoria would cast a spell that would make Tracy Benjamin throw herself into an early grave before she allowed Tracy to swindle a penny of Willy's money.

"In Jesus' name, let's go, Willy!" The Lord knew her heart.

CHAPTER 22

Kingston

"How many times do I have to explain to you, I'm not leaving my wife." Kingston regretted inviting Theodore to Columbia. "And stop walking like that!"

Theodore pranced in the hotel suite, circled around the chocolate leather chair Kingston sat in. "I served in the military." He saluted Kingston. Theodore stopped parading. Started kicking as though he were in formation. "I protected your wife, your children, and your life while you had the privilege of making millions of dollars running up and down a basketball court. It's not my fault that you were injured." Theodore stood in front of Kingston with his hands at his side.

Kingston could really use a cigar right now to calm him. The entire property was nonsmoking. He blew hard. Filled with air, his cheeks rounded out. "Bruh, back up off of me. I'm asking you politely."

Theodore didn't move. Kingston wasn't going to get into a physical altercation that could potentially lead to media exposure.

Staring up at Theodore, Kingston asked, "What do you want from me?"

"Your heart, sir." He saluted.

Picking up his cell off the circular glass tabletop, Kingston ordered Theodore an Uber from the hotel at Baltimore Harbor to

BWI Airport, then stated, "I'm legally obligated to make my marriage a priority. When you get to Atlanta, remove—"

"Don't you mean when *we* get to Atlanta. I know you're not planning on staying here with her. I'll show up at *her* house if I have to. I know exactly where she lives." Flopping in the chair near Kingston, Theodore folded his arms across his chest.

They were both willing to die. Theodore, once upon a time, for his country. Kingston, always and forever, to protect his family. Although she might not believe him, Kingston would sacrifice his life for Monet. This was a situation where Theodore thought he could win by bullying. But he couldn't. Kingston canceled the Uber.

Instead of asking Theodore to get on his knees and suck his dick, Kingston knelt before Theodore.

Unbuckling Theodore's belt, Kingston slowly undressed him from the waist down. He could dive right in, devour Theodore, and make him cum, but Kingston's approach had a scripted ending that would get him exactly what he needed.

Kingston licked his lips. Not in a circular motion. Sliding his tongue over his upper lip, he curled it back over the lower.

"I'm sorry. I can't help how I feel about you." Theodore's hands rested on the arms of the chair. He reclined until his ass was on the edge of the seat.

Planting kisses on Theodore's frenulum, Kingston began circling his tongue around the head of the penis. Slowly he eased the shaft into his mouth. He felt Theodore's excitement grow longer and harder. Glancing up, he saw that Theodore's eyes were shut.

Heavy breathing and moaning from both of them ensued. Kingston wanted to join in the orgasmic pleasure, but he thought better of it and stayed focused. The familiar taste of salted sauerkraut oozed from the pores of Theodore's dick, indicating he was ready to climax.

Slightly increasing the pressure and the pace, Kingston stroked and sucked until Theodore grunted, "I love you." Semen squirted into Kingston's mouth.

Pretending to swallow, Kingston entered the bathroom, rinsed with mouthwash, then returned to the living area. "If you love me, like you said, I need for you to do this one favor."

Theodore stood, nodded, fastened his buckle. "What?"

"I need you to take the next flight out. Remove all of your be-longings from my Airbnb tonight. I'm ending the stay."

Theodore propped his hand on his hip. "The stay or our relationship?"

Slowly Kingston shook his head, clenched his teeth, told himself, *Don't react. That's what he wants.*

"And what about you? Are you moving out, too? Are you staying here? Am I flying back the same way I got here, on a private jet?" Theodore questioned. His hand and hip remained motionless, but not his neck.

"There's just no pleasing you," Kingston complained.

Theodore protested. "What's your obligation to me? I'm the one who comforts and closets you. Now you're tossing me out like leftover meat?"

Kingston appreciated Theodore's time and companionship, but he'd never have clarity about his sexuality if he abandoned his family.

"I've never mistreated or disrespected you. I need time to sort things out. That way, if we reconnect, I can do so without feeling guilty."

What Kingston realized was that he wasn't going from being a married man to committing to a man. Holding hands and kissing in public was strictly for Monet.

"If?" Theodore retorted.

Counting ten $100 bills, Kingston handed them to Theodore. "For your time. Or mine. However you want to look at it."

"How about you not contact me again." Theodore slapped the money out of Kingston's hand, unlocked his cell, showed Kingston that he was blocking him, then strolled out of the room with his carry-on suitcase.

Kingston closed the door, then waited fifteen minutes before checking out and ordering a car to take him to a hotel in Columbia.

Showering in his new suite, he dressed, then splashed on cologne. The upside of his having sexed a man was there was no trace—lipstick, perfume, or hair.

En route to his house in Columbia, he texted the entry code to Lilly, then added, **Get all of my things out of the Airbnb now.**

And do what with them? Lilly replied.

Kingston texted Trinity, **I need a different Airbnb tomorrow.**

Keep them at your place until I get back, he answered Lilly.

Entering the gate code to his property, Kingston instructed the driver, "Let me out in front of the steps."

Kingston pressed his thumb on the pad, stepped inside, then stood in the foyer. He prayed for the Lord to take away his urges to have sex with men, and for his wife not to shoot him. No need to text Theodore an apology. He wouldn't get it.

"Daddy, you're back," Nairobi said, then called out, "Daddy's home!"

Lifting Nairobi up, he held her close. "I'm here to stay . . . for a little while."

"You're always here 'for a little while,' silly," Israel said, then gave him a quick hug. "I'm going upstairs by Grandma."

"Wait for me," Nairobi said, wiggling until Kingston put her down. She ran until she caught up with her big sister.

Monet walked by him without speaking, exited the front door, got in the car with Bianca. Kingston supposed he deserved that.

The one thing he knew for sure was Monet would be back and he'd be there waiting for her. Now was the perfect time to talk with Trinity. Calling out her name, he poured a glass of cold, fresh lemonade.

He texted Victoria, **I'm in Columbia. I'll be back in Atlanta next Sunday.**

"Well, look who's here," Trinity said, joining him at the kitchen island.

"I could say the same," Kingston sarcastically replied. "When did you return??

Moving closer to him, Trinity stated, "Enough, already. Obviously, you're not here to stay. You don't have your bags."

Kingston hunched both shoulders.

"Then why are you requesting another Airbnb?" she questioned.

Oh, yeah. That's right. That has to be rhetorical, he thought. "Thanks for renting the first and the second Airbnb for me. I got myself into an uncomfortable situation."

Trinity helped herself to a glass, filled it with freshly squeezed orange juice. "What's the verdict?" she asked, texting him his new reservation.

Kingston sat on a barstool and looked at his mother-in-law; she had proven she'd do anything for him.

Truth was: "The jury is still out."

CHAPTER 23

Monet

"Make love to me, Kingston. The way you used to," Monet said.

Craving his touch. The feel of his naked body against hers. Monet lay atop her husband and pressed her lips against his. If they were going to make their marriage work, one of them had to initiate an effort.

Kingston's long fingers gently glided along the crevice in her spine as he kissed her. "This is all my fault. I shouldn't have left you here with the girls. I'm going to do better. I promise." Rolling her onto her back, her husband spread her thighs.

"It's my fault, too," Monet said as she looked into her husband's eyes. She loved him so much that it hurt her to think about losing him. "I should've been more patient with you."

"Shhh." Kingston eased his way to her sweetest spot. Parted her labia. Slowly he sucked her clitoral shaft in his mouth. His enormous lips traveled all the way up, then back down to her clitoris.

Monet moaned. "I miss this. Go slow, baby."

Sliding back the hood of her clit, exposing her pearl, her husband patiently circled his tongue, then suctioned her shaft faster.

Her body tensed due to how he was sucking. Monet felt her entire vulva becoming engorged. Her husband pressed his tongue at the opening of her vagina, swept upward, engaged her clit again, suctioning all the way up, again and again.

Where had he learned that technique? It felt sooooo good, she had back-to-back small orgasms. Whatever woman Kingston was cheating with definitely had schooled him well.

Kingston's repetition picked up momentum.

Monet thrust her hips upward. Held the back of his head. Clamped her thighs over his ears, then grunted with pleasure. It was hard for her not to scream; if she had, she'd have awakened the girls.

"I want to feel all of you inside of me, baby." Monet pushed the crown of her husband's head, moving him away from her vagina.

Kingston tightly squeezed her ass. He began devouring her as though he were determined to make her cum.

Recalling the times when Kingston stroked deep inside her womb, and she could feel every inch of him, made her crave his dick, not his mouth. "Stop." Monet scooted toward the headboard. "Let me get on top." In case he'd be gone an additional four weeks. "I need you to beat this pussy all the way up," she pleaded.

Kingston froze. Stared at her. "This is all about your needs, not mine."

Shaking her head, Monet began to cry. She never had to beg her husband to fuck her. Kingston positioned himself on his back. Monet held his flaccid shaft in disbelief. She opened her mouth. Gripping him at the base, she passionately performed fellatio on her husband. The faster she sucked, the harder he became.

Monet climbed atop her husband, guided his head to the opening of her vagina. As she was bouncing and grinding, his limp dick unexpectedly slipped out.

"Shit." Reaching behind her back, she tightened her fingers around his shaft, tried positioning him at her slippery opening.

Kingston held her hips. "That's it, baby. Ride your dick," he said, forcing her down harder and harder until he said, "Cum with me."

Was he serious? Struggling to match his rhythm, she said, "Okay. Okay." Her breathing was weighted with frustration.

"You ready?" he asked.

For what? Faking she was on the verge of climaxing, she said, "Yes. Yes. Yes." More important than having an orgasm, Monet needed what only her husband could give her. Reassurance. "Baby, why did you leave us?" she asked, using her vaginal muscles to push out the head of his limp penis.

"Baby, I apologize. When my career ended, a part of me died inside. My being away wasn't your fault," he said, embracing her.

She placed her cheek on his chest. "I felt abandoned. Even with the girls and my mother here, at times," she admitted. "For the first time since we were really young, I felt like you didn't care . . . about me. About my feelings. You were cold-blooded, Kingston."

His hug became heavy. Seemed as though his concerns had evaporated.

"Do you still love me?" Monet asked, looking up into her husband's eyes.

His hesitation spoke volume.

"Of course, I do, baby. Didn't you hear me say a part of me died. The one thing I was great at is gone for the rest of my life. I don't know who I am anymore." Tears escaped the corners of his eyes.

She heard the sadness in his voice. It was different from when his team lost a game. "Are you blaming yourself for you guys losing the championship?"

"Worse. No one calls to check on me. No 'Kingston, how you doing, man? How's the family?' Nothing. I thought joining church would give clarity to who I am off the court."

Kingston rolled her onto her side, then got out of bed.

"You are a loving, kind, caring husband and father," Monet said.

He entered the bathroom. Staring at the ceiling, she heard the shower. Kingston entered his walk-in closet, appeared fully dressed, holding a designer carry-on bag.

"I know you're not leaving," Monet said.

"I have to usher at church tomorrow. I'll call you when I get to Atlanta." Kingston left their bedroom and closed the door.

Shaking her head, Monet was too confused and disgusted to cry.

CHAPTER 24

Chancelor

"Let the church say, 'Amen.'" Pastor Baloney scurried back and forth behind the pulpit as though he were a moving target about to break out into a sanctified dance.

Chancelor laughed, looking at Brother Melvin, who was sitting alone, until he heard a familiar voice shout, "Amen!"

Tracy clapped her hands. From the side of the choir stand, Chancelor saw that Brother Melvin was seated on the pew behind the deacons, rocking side to side. A new guy was sitting on the last pew next to Tracy, following her lead. Leaning her shoulder into his, Tracy smiled, then stood. He jumped up, too.

They need to sit their asses down!

Fake whore. Lying bitch!

That was the last $4,000 she'd get from him. For a total of seven grand, Chancelor owned Tracy, and he wasn't going to stop pursuing her until he got what was rightfully his. There should be a way to have her arrested for scamming men. Obviously, she didn't discriminate. This one was white. Dressed in a suit. Clean-shaved. Grinning from ear to ear.

Chancelor stood next to Victoria with his eyes fixated on Tracy. Interrupting his plot to take Tracy down, Victoria nudged him, then motioned with a nod for him to step into the back.

"How well do you know this Tracy Benjamin?" Victoria asked.

"Not well enough to know if Benjamin is her real last name or some fake shit she came up with to fit her thieving personality," Chancelor stated, then asked, "What's up?"

He was embarrassed to tell Victoria he'd CashApped Tracy more money than the first time.

"She's convinced Brother Copeland that she's his daughter and now I can't talk him off the ledge. He's getting ready to put her on his trust. I'm going to stop her." Victoria seemed more desperate than angry.

Chancelor rubbed his palms together furiously enough to spark a fire. Shaking his head, he tightened his lips. "Let's ask Jordan for legal help. Tracy needs to go to jail," Chancelor said, happy to have Victoria join him on team "Get Tracy's Ass Back."

"Okay. I got this. We have to go back inside." Victoria entered first.

Briskly walking to the altar to join Kingston and Jordan, the four of them faced the congregation. *Why the fuck doesn't Tracy sit on someone else's side?*

Rolling his eyes at Brother Melvin, Chancelor should've apologized. Brother Melvin flashed a fake smile. *Damn!* Both of his front teeth were missing. Oh, well. That was Brother Melvin's fault for fucking that ho Tracy. Had Melvin seen her pussy?

Chancelor took the wicker basket from the woman on his end. Handing the collection plate to Peaches, the "give the Lord $5 and save the rest for wigs and weaves" member, he mumbled, "Next time throw in a couple tracks."

Her stare didn't scare Chancelor. He was Tracy-proof!

Finally making it to the second-to-last row, Chancelor stepped to the left, handed the basket to Tracy.

"Hello, Brother Leonard. You sure are a blessing." She passed the basket to the white guy seated next to her. Sliding his jacket aside, he put his hand in his pocket, removed a stack of hundreds, peeled off one Benjamin, added it to the collection.

Chancelor didn't know which one to stare at longer. The white guy's FBI badge or his wedding band. Trick-ass Tracy got an officer of the law. A sponsor and a bodyguard. Bet she gave him some pussy. Chancelor should kick his teeth out, too.

That was okay. Neither the FBI, CIA, nor APD was going to keep Chancelor from making sure Tracy went to prison. Taking advantage of a senior like Brother Copeland was a crime in every state.

CHAPTER 25

Jordan

"Only one bottle of wine today?" Levi asked Jordan as he uncorked, then partially filled two goblets, placing the other in front of Victoria.

"I have a date later with Terrence Russell," Jordan said, glad he hadn't given up on her.

"I'll be right back with your usual, fellas." Levi pointed at Chancelor, then at Kingston.

"Make mine a double, bruh," Kingston said. "Shit getting hectic with Monet. It's not enough I went to visit her. She wants to move here with the girls."

Levi replied, "Beef last longer than fish, man. She'll ruin your good thing. You're single. In Atlanta. Just sayin'."

"Duplicate my cognac," Chancelor added, then told Jordan, "We need you to do a background check on Tracy Benjamin."

We? Jordan smiled at him. She was not entertaining Chancelor's foolery. His spiked Afro, locked at the blue-dyed tips, appeared as though he'd been running his fingers backward against the frontline. Chancelor began looking the way he was acting . . . unstable.

"I don't know who *we* is, but I could've had an opportunity to get laid, aka get me some dick, aka get fucked so incredible in every hole that I'd become comatose. But no!" Jordan pushed her finger against Chancelor's temple.

Frowning, he massaged the side of his face.

"All because of you and your ego assaulting Tracy and kicking out Melvin's tooth—"

"Teeth," Chancelor corrected.

"Whatever. I had to apologize to Terrence and come here to counsel your dumb ass."

Levi's gasp was heard from the register. "Let it go, Chancelor. My best advice, bro."

"As far as I know, Tracy hasn't done anything illegal. You need to move on," Jordan insisted. "I'll check anyone new that any of you have met on your app."

"*We* includes me," Victoria said. "Tracy is claiming to be Willy Copeland's daughter. And she's convinced him to leave her half of his estate, which is supposed to be all mine." By the time Victoria stopped sipping her wine, her glass was upside down.

Levi slid up to the table, placed drinks in front of Kingston and Chancelor. "Repeat that, Victoria."

For the same reason Jordan didn't want to represent Donovan, Jordan wasn't getting involved in a situation that could deem her intent unethical. "Brother Copeland can leave all his money to a bitch or a dog. That's his right."

"Or a bitch *and* a dog," Levi added.

Kingston chimed in, "Correction. A bitch is a dog."

Victoria gripped the bottle by the neck, narrowed her eyes at Jordan, Kingston, and Levi, then filled Jordan's glass to the rim. "Enjoy."

Jordan winked at Victoria, emptied half of her wine into Victoria's glass. "Don't get an attitude with me. If you think you can compete with Tracy, secure your position."

Possession was an advantage in most cases. But there was no guarantee that because she was currently the sole heir, Willy wouldn't change his mind. Victoria could have had sex with Brother Copeland seven days a week. Yet, on his dying bed he reserved the right to will his assets to the person of his choosing.

"The problem with women is y'all try to control the man," Kingston said, then laughed. "Women like Tracy rule the heads. Dick first."

Chancelor frowned. "What if you've never seen the pussy?"

"Jordan is right. You are dumb, dude," Levi told Chancelor. "Control the dick and the brain will follow. Most women don't know how to take charge," Levi commented from behind the bar.

"Are you guys serious? I've been screwing this man for over forty years. If you won't help me, Jordan, then tell me how I can prove Tracy is *not* his daughter." Victoria sat on the edge of her seat, awaiting a response.

God will make a way . . . somehow, Jordan thought.

A text registered from Terrence: **Can't wait to see you, Jordan.**

Ms. Jackson . . . if you're nasty, she replied.

Ms. Jackson it is, Terrence answered.

"Jordan," Chancelor said, commanding her attention. "What if Tracy has conned *elderly* men out of their money? How many fathers does that ho have? If we can prove she's a thief, can she go to prison?"

Jordan sighed. Long as they'd known her, her friends didn't understand the law. Brother Willy Copeland was of sound mind. Was he naïve? Probably not to the extent that Victoria might believe.

"I love each of you, but don't ask me to do your dirty work. Chancelor, leave Tracy Benjamin the hell alone. Victoria, you can try to change Willy's mind, but don't deal with Tracy. I thought you guys were smarter than this. Smart young pussy always wins in the end."

Jordan stood, then looked at Kingston. "Stay out of their business. You have enough to worry about. See—"

"Wait," he said, holding her hand. "You don't know me."

"If I didn't, you wouldn't be at this table," she countered.

Jordan background checked everyone in her circle. Her investigation extended well beyond what was online. She never wanted to be in the presence of a criminal or pervert and not know it. She wondered how long Kingston would withhold the fact he was married. Vital records were the easiest to confirm—birth, death, and marriage certificates—but most of her female clients never checked online to find out if the man was lying.

"See you guys Sunday," she said, then exited the bar.

* * *

Heading home for a shower and change of clothing, Jordan put on a fitted sleeveless white dress that stopped six inches above her knees. Stepping into black-and-white stilettos, she drove to one of her favorite restaurants, The Capital Grille Buckhead.

Terrence was seated at the bar, facing the door. Welcoming her with open arms, he whispered in her ear, "You look and smell amazing."

"Thanks." Jordan was holding to her "always let a man like/love you more" rule.

After they were seated at the table, Jordan silenced her phone, then tucked it in her purse. "No interruptions this time," she said, praying Wilson Ealy didn't need to contact her. And that Donovan didn't mysteriously appear.

"Tell me one thing about yourself that if I dug to the bottom of your soul, you hope I'll never find out," Jordan said. "Don't overthink it. And please don't respond with the obvious."

"I like you, Jordan. If I share this with you, you have to promise not—"

"If there is anything I do well, it's keep pertinent information confidential," Jordan replied.

Terrence suctioned in his lip.

"What? Is there something wrong?" she asked.

He shook his head, then said, "You asked me a question. Followed by an interruption that was an assumption. I was going to say you have to promise never to throw anything I share with you in my face. That's my biggest pet peeve with women."

Well, her pussy instantly lost interest. Hopefully, she wouldn't do the same. "Fair enough. Same here," Jordan said.

"Goes without saying," Terrence replied.

Jordan firmly stated, "That's not true."

"Forget it. I'm not telling you." Terrence pushed away from her as though he were an angry adolescent. "I've seen how this story ends with professional black females in Atlanta."

He was not convincing her that she was the problem because she interjected, "If you're not feeling this, say so. Don't attack me."

The sound of a puff of air escaped his nostrils and entered hers. Terrence stood, extended his hand. He escorted her to the entrance. "Get on the elevator. Go downstairs. And decide. If you come back up, we'll start over. If you don't, leave me like the rest and have a great life."

Offended or impressed? On her way down Jordan thought, *Terrence Russell could be amazing or he could be a total psycho asshole.*

One thing was certain. She'd never know.

As she stepped off of the elevator, the unexpected commanded her attention. The guy was tall, fit, and handsome.

He smiled.

She grinned.

"Wow. You are stunning," he complimented.

And you are fuckable, she thought.

"Allow me to introduce myself," he said, extending his hand. "My name is Langston Derby."

"I'm Jackson. I mean Jordan. Jordan Jackson." No man had made her breathless in years, including Donovan and certainly not Terrence.

"Care to join me for dinner?" he asked. "I just closed up my shop next door. I hate eating alone."

"I'd love to," Jordan said, stepping back onto the elevator.

CHAPTER 26

Victoria

"Not right there," Victoria advised the delivery guy. "Six inches to the left. Pick it up. No dragging."

Morning had progressed to noon. Victoria was excited to get her project under way. Since she was a perfectionist, anything out of order would become a distraction and cause her plan to fail.

"Ma'am. We've shuffled your extremely heavy furniture back and forth, and from one side of the room to the other, for the last four hours," the delivery guy complained, holding his fingers. Massaging his hands, he said, "Respectfully. Can you please make up your mind?"

"Or we can come back tomorrow," the other worker suggested. "We have six more customers to serve today. At this rate we won't get off until midnight."

And they'd do as she said for another four hours, if necessary. Victoria didn't blink as she stared at them. She'd paid for white-glove service and that was exactly what she was going to receive.

"Scratch it and you'll have to take it back and deliver a new one," she stated.

The third guy mumbled, "That might not be a bad idea. Let somebody else deal with her."

"I heard that. Do not try me, young man." Victoria stared at the man. "One mark and I'll specifically request each of you come back tomorrow with a new one or be terminated for insubordination."

They each frowned at Victoria, then shook their head in unison.

Her inheritance depended upon the perfect positioning of her new counter-height voodoo altar. The black-stained beech wood weighed seven hundred pounds. Among the three of them, lifting what appeared to be their collective body weight shouldn't be difficult.

"You all should thank me. You can skip going to the gym today. One inch toward me, gentlemen," she commanded, then cheered, "Perfect! Thank You, Lord Jesus!"

"Goddamn," guy one said. "You're hard to please, lady."

"That's it. The customer is always right," guy number two added, handing Victoria a pen. "Sign here, ma'am."

Guy three commented, "Good day, Ms. Fox."

Posting up in front of the altar, the three men lingered. She knew exactly what they wanted. And the truth was, they deserved a generous tip. Victoria opened the box that was in the corner. She proceeded to pull out her voodoo dolls, then meticulously placed them on the altar.

"Are you serious?" one of the guys asked. He didn't take a single step toward the front door.

Victoria slid her hand into a single front pocket on her mustard-colored maxidress. She pulled out three $50 bills and handed one to each of the workers. "Thanks, guys, you can leave through the side door. Don't discard any rubbish on my property. Take all of the packaging with you."

One delivery person said, "I'm out," then left immediately. The other two followed pursuit.

Good riddance, she thought, following them outside. Victoria stood in the driveway and watched the moving truck exit her security gate. She waited until the gate completely closed, then hurried inside.

Eager to set up what she knew would make Tracy Benjamin want to crawl under a manhole and stay in the sewer, Victoria was distracted by an incoming call. Removing the phone from her pocket, Victoria answered with a smile. "Hey, Heavenly. Baby, can we reschedule?" she asked. "I have to view a few residentials before they go on the market."

"Awesome. Can I go with you?" Heavenly asked, sounding like a kid. "I'd love to learn about real estate investing."

Hmm. Heavenly was a great student in the bedroom, fun and, thus far, loyal to her commands. A "yes" would educate and elevate that young black man while increasing his bottom line. A "no" meant she'd have to finance their roller-coaster ride until it stopped. Dependents often became stalkers. Better for a man to have his own so he could move on. Victoria did like this one, though.

She placed seven black candles on the altar next to a two-ounce bottle of root oil, loose cowrie shells, real chicken feet, feathers, a beak, and several small onyx energy stones. Victoria gently placed the black mortar and pestle in the center of the ingredients.

A text registered from Willy: **I have to cancel our standing. My daughter is taking me to dinner.**

"You can meet me. Under one condition," she told Heavenly.

"What's that?" he replied.

"You agree to attend my church this Sunday." Victoria had a few ways to get Willy and Tracy's attention without speaking a word.

An early preheat of her body's temperature threatened an escape of perspiration.

"I'd love to," Heavenly said. "Text me the time and location where to meet."

"Will do. And rain check on accompanying me to the properties. Something came up. I have to go," she told Heavenly, ending their call.

Victoria went to the kitchen, filled a glass with ice, pressed it against her wrist, then returned to the room.

She'd focus on a potion for Heavenly and Willy later. It was time to create a scent for Tracy that would stink worse than a skunk's spray every time Tracy opened her mouth.

CHAPTER 27

Kingston

Desperate times sparked Kingston's best creativity.

The third Airbnb Mama-T had reserved on his behalf would be the last. Since Theodore stated he had blocked him, Kingston was having sex at the new location with as many men as he wanted, and he was no longer risking anyone seeing him coming out of the basement on Cheshire Bridge Road.

Touring a residential property that was on a private road surrounded by tall trees, with no close neighbors, and far away from the main intersection, Kingston hugged Lilly.

"This is perfect," he complimented. "Buy it. All cash. In your name only."

Lilly was the prettiest Puerto Rican he'd ever met. Kingston was certain her long, curly hair, with golden highlights, her well-defined hourglass waistline, flat stomach, and rotund derrière drove men insane. But none of that excited him. Not even her seductive Spanish accent.

"You're going to have to give me emergency contact information. In case something happens to you back here in these woods. Especially since my name is the only one that will appear on the title," she said emphatically.

"Lock in Monet and her mom, Trinity," Kingston said, sharing their cell numbers. "Thanks for agreeing to be my straw buyer.

We'll sell the property soon as I move my family to Atlanta." Kingston roamed the empty house, imagining he could live there with Theodore.

The little boy locked in the janitor's closet cries for help. Counting to fifty might turn into fifty years of hiding his sexuality. If I could sit at a table with Langston Derby, sharing a bottle of aged cognac, what would I say?

Lilly gently touched his arm. "Are you okay? You seem a bit out of it."

A single tear escaped his right eye. Struggling to hold it all together, Kingston had to tell someone. Mama-T held general secrets, but that wasn't the same as confiding in someone with details.

He asked Lilly, "Can I trust you?"

"Uh, yeah." Holding his hands, Lilly sat on the floor, then folded her legs. Not letting go, she stared up at him, then replied, "It's just the two of us here. I will never share anything that you say is confidential. That's my job and I'm great at it."

Kingston sat facing Lilly. He folded his legs, too, then asked, "How can I tell for sure if I am gay? I've never been anally penetrated. But I enjoy the company of men."

"How much?" she questioned.

"A lot. Theodore Ramsey loves me. But sometimes I get angry at him and with myself because I'm not that way," he explained.

"A man seldom treats his wife the way he expects another man to treat his daughter." Lilly squeezed his fingers. "You have two girls. I have one. How would you feel if Israel or Nairobi were married to a man like you?"

Whoa. Kingston nodded, but didn't respond.

Lilly released her hands. "Personally, I'd want to kick his ass if he did that shit to mine. Not because he was gay or bisexual, but because he was a fucking liar and a cheater of the worst kind."

"Let's close this transaction and forget we ever had this conversation." Hopefully, Lilly wouldn't make him regret opening up to her. Mentioning Theodore by name was intentional, in case there was ever a physical altercation.

"No problem." Lilly stood. "I'll notify the selling agent in a few minutes of my all-cash offer of the asking price. I'll notify you when it's done. Whenever you're ready to change the title into your name, let me know."

Escorting Lilly to her BMW, Kingston wrapped his arms around her. "I'll say a prayer for you at church this morning."

Lilly let out a cute laugh. "Do that. If you need me for anything else, let me know," she said, closing her car door.

Kingston drove to a nearby café, sat at a table in the corner with his back to the wall, and surfed the VirginsSeekingVirgins app.

"What would you like?" the waiter asked.

After ordering a light breakfast, he saw several titillating prospects.

The waiter placed a piping-hot cup of black coffee and a raspberry-and-cream-cheese pastry in front of Kingston. Enjoying a bite of his croissant, Kingston read several more profiles. All with features, measurements, hobbies. None of them had body pics of abs, dick, or ass, like BottomsUp.

A text registered from Theodore, **Where are you?**

Kingston ignored it. Continued scanning and sipping coffee.

If you don't respond, I'll show up and call you out at your church this morning.

Theodore's second message warranted a response. **Maybe that's what I need.**

Bravery about his sexuality wasn't what Kingston wanted to confront. If Theodore did it, Kingston knew his sins weren't worse than Pastor Baloney's and the first lady's. The entire congregation accepted their humanness.

Church didn't start for another three hours. They were ushering the late service. Contemplating whether he should drive to Cheshire Bridge Road and connect with a stranger, or invite Theodore or Levi over to the Airbnb, Kingston kept scrolling. He'd promised himself no more basement sexcapades, but he couldn't lie. There was something about the griminess of fucking without knowing a man's name or number.

Texting **Checked into a new Airbnb. I'll text you my address later** should comfort Theodore and keep him away from Hope for All Church today.

His new soon-to-be residence was tranquil. From toothpaste to towels, furniture to sheets, dishes, forks, paintings, rugs, and more, Lilly would hire Cassandra Guy to decorate each room beautifully. All Kingston had to add was his wardrobe.

Company, not companionship, was what Kingston desired this morning. He texted Levi the address of his current rental, then added, **Come over now.**

Moments later, Levi replied, **omw.**

Swiping one last time, Kingston's croissant slipped from his fingers. "No fucking way."

Kingston stared at the in-box note: **Interested in getting together?**

The user's name: Derby69.

CHAPTER 28

Monet

"Bye, Mom." Israel got out of the car. She strolled up to a group of her friends that were waiting for her inside the gate.

"Love you, Mom!" Nairobi held her cell, tossed her new backpack over one shoulder, closed the rear passenger door, and ran to the schoolyard, yelling, "Look, y'all!"

Assuring that the girls were safe within the surveillance of the security guard, Monet drove away. Cruising along the B-W Parkway, she started to text Bianca, but changed her mind and decided to call. Continuously complaining to her girlfriend about Kingston had made Bianca dislike him more.

Monet commanded Siri, "Call my best friend."

"Calling your best friend, mobile," the Australian male voice replied.

"Hey, girl. I was just getting ready to call you. Are you ready for that tall cup of black coffee this morning?" she asked with excitement. Bianca's single life on the outside definitely appeared to be funtastic.

"A little coffee in the morning never hurts," Monet answered.

"That's the right attitude. I'm glad you let me set you up. I have all of his information. Remember, it's just an icebreaker to prepare you to get back on the dating scene, if necessary. Call me soon as you leave the—"

Cutting Bianca off, Monet said, "I gotta go. That's my mom calling, which reminds me to turn off my tracking."

Ending one call and accepting the other, Monet answered, "Good morning."

Trinity replied, "Is everything okay?"

Monet cleared her throat. Her pitch was slightly higher than usual. "Yeah, why?"

"You sound . . . uncomfortable. What is it?" her mother questioned.

Dang. Two words and her mom had drawn that conclusion. "I'm headed to my first acting class," Monet lied. "I signed up online this morning."

"So if I went to your house, logged on to your computer, and checked your cookies, I would find"—she paused, then added—"the link and your application?"

Knowing her mother, Monet was sure Trinity was going to investigate the situation. And she'd find the registration link. But by the time she left her home, went to Monet's, found out where the one-hour introductory class was supposed to be, the session would be over.

Traffic was light on the highway. Monet exited two miles north of where she lived, then parked in a grocery store parking lot. Before arriving at her final destination, she turned off all locations.

"Monet, what just happened? You stopped at the grocery store, now I can't see exactly where you are," her mom frantically said, then asked, "Are you in a bad location? Is there something wrong with your phone? Check your bars."

"No, Mom, I'm not in a bad area. Soon as I get to class, I'll check my phone and make sure my locations are working."

"Text me the address of the class, Monet. Right now," her mother insisted.

"Okay. Will do. Gotta go." Monet lowered her visor, checked her hair and makeup.

Post Monet's confession of having gone to Atlanta without her mother's knowledge, her mom was trying to track her every move.

"Monet?" her mother blurted. "What do you have on?"

Eight o'clock in the morning was rather early for her to be wearing red Everlasting matte lipstick and a snug snakeskin jumpsuit, but Monet didn't care. If she were heading to the class, she'd definitely be the focus of everyone's attention.

"Bye, Mother."

"Listen to me," Trinity commanded. "Just because Kingston is acting inappropriately does not mean that you should carelessly venture into new things on a whim."

Inappropriately!? That is an understatement. "I have the right to live my life the way I want to."

"I know you're wearing your wedding ring, diamond jewelry, an expensive watch, and designer everything else. Pull over, take off your valuables, and secure them in your trunk with your purse. You do not know those people. And nowadays you cannot trust anyone."

Monet sarcastically asked, "Where's my husband?"

"Fine, do whatever you want," her mother said, sounding annoyed.

"No disrespect, but I'm no longer waiting for you to decide when you're available to help with the girls. Nor am I sitting around waiting for Kingston to find his way back home. I'm a grown woman, and from this day forward, I'm acting. And I'm hiring a live-in nanny, a maid, a tutor, and a chef."

Trinity gasped.

Monet's decision was not debatable. Trinity was being standoffish since Kingston had left again. Monet ended the call with her mom, then drove to the café situated on the northeast side of Columbia, to meet the online date Bianca had arranged for her.

Entering the café, immediately he stood gesturing for her to come over. Her stroll toward him was so sinful; she was certain it wouldn't get her into the pearly gates of Heaven. Approaching her destination, Monet had already undressed him with her eyes.

Well-endowed, no doubt. The bagginess in his slacks couldn't hide the girth of the imprint against his thigh. Her body experienced an orgasm before she made it to the table. Climaxing without any physical contact, that wasn't a first. Her husband used to have that effect on her.

Slowing her pace, she contemplated doing an about-face, returning to her car, and heading to acting class.

God wouldn't have sent her a man that fine. Temptation lingered on her clitoris. That man must have been sent by Satan himself.

"Hello, gorgeous. I'm Cairo. And before you comment, my mother really named me Cairo," he explained, pulling out a tan wooden chair.

Whoa! What were the odds of her meeting a man with a uniquely beautiful name befitting his pronounced Egyptian features?

"Hi, Cairo. I'm 'Irresistible.' And, no, my mother didn't name me that, but that's what you can call me." Monet couldn't believe she was lusting over and flirting with a complete stranger.

She sat as he asked, "What would you like?"

You, she thought. *Naked. In bed. Eating my pussy.*

Eight customers waited in line. If he ordered now, that would give her time to regroup and bring down her libido a few notches.

"A medium triple caramel chai latte." She had to look up to avoid staring at his dick.

"May I get you something to eat?" he offered.

This time she stared at his bulge. Her pussy said *yes.* "No, thanks."

What you need is to get your thirsty ass up out of this chair and go to that class you paid for. Monet had not realized how sexually deprived she was until now.

Resisting reaching out to touch his thigh, she knew the time had come for her to prepare an action plan for having a substitute husband in order to sustain her marriage. The lyrics to Maurice Moore's "Destination Unknown," which were floating in her mind, were complementary to her present situation.

A ringtone registered on her phone. She knew exactly who it was. Maybe that was a sign. Removing her cell from her purse, Monet read, **Hey, baby. Don't be upset with me. I'll be home soon.**

Cairo's hand touched her shoulder. "Hungry? Or you gotta go?"

Redirecting her focus, Monet silenced her phone, then gave Cairo her undivided attention.

"Just a chai latte. Thanks." Monet smiled softly. Quietly took a deep breath.

Silently he eyed her wedding set. "I'll be right back, Mrs. Irresistible."

Returning with two hot beverages, Cairo sat across the table from her. "If you don't mind, start with why you as a married woman are pursuing a single man?"

Monet held her cup with both hands, but didn't lift it off the table. She looked into Cairo's eyes and explained, "I've been with the same man for the last twelve years. I'm interested in a deviation from the norm. I'm hopeful this encounter will help me understand why my husband is neglecting me."

Cairo raised his brows. "You? *Neglected?* I'd never do that to you."

"How about we start with your taking the edge off?" Monet boldly said, surprising herself.

"Cool. When?" Cairo asked.

"Since you're single, your place. Now." Monet wasn't seeking a long-term relationship. She wanted to fuck and be fucked real good.

A one-morning stand with a man she'd never see again was what she needed.

CHAPTER 29

Jordan

"How long have you been celibate?" Relaxing in her rose gold spa tub, Jordan spoke through the Bluetooth speaker that was built into the wall behind her.

"Nine months times seven equals five years and three months," he said, adding, "I really like you."

Right away she knew Langston was lying. It was a good thing she hadn't met him on the app. They'd have to change it from CelibateNoMore to CelibateWhores. Men always admired her, in the beginning. Their enthusiasm lasted until they realize she had a phenomenal head on her shoulders, a mansion with everything she ever wanted in it, wealth beyond their imagination and what she'd spend in her lifetime.

She would've asked him that question the night they'd accidentally met (which reminded her she needed to text Terrence a thank-you). But she didn't want to come across as being desperate.

Nine months times infinity wasn't the answer she was anticipating. Maybe closer to nine hours or nine days, considering most men in Atlanta held the Bible in one hand and their dick in the other.

At the top of the fuck chain were recently released inmates. Behind bars they found religion, but day one on the street, they chased women, including the men who preferred men. She couldn't believe the number of females in the ATL that allowed just-released convicts to move into their homes. Jordan had been an attorney long enough to have represented countless men that were users and losers.

Holding a handful of bubbles, Jordan curled her fingers. "Wait a minute. Multiplying is cheating. My count is higher than yours. Legitimately."

"All men are dogs," Langston said. "So I have to times mine by seven, but you can't do that. I'm glad yours isn't more than five years, because if it were, I'd have to end this damn conversation. You'd be a born-again virgin. If that were the case, no man could get into that pussy no matter how hard he tried." He laughed.

Humph. Mr. Derby, like most men, believed he was funny, when he was not. Jordan carefully stepped onto the bath mat. She wrapped a large white fluffy towel around her dripping wet, sudsy body. Removed the shower cap and head wrap from her hair.

"So you know I'm about to explode," Langston said. "Let's Face-Time and indulge in mind-fucking. I love a woman who stimulates me all over."

Was that how he remained celibate?

"Langston Derby. What's your government name?" Jordan asked in order to complete his background check as they spoke on the phone.

Some men in Atlanta had multiple identifications. And they could get away with using an alias because women seldom checked to find out if they were lying. Langston Derby could be Derby Langston, or Langston Williams, or the great-great-grandson of Langston Hughes! Jordan had heard it all.

"Langston Derby, no middle name. I have nothing to hide," he answered.

"And you're thirty?" she asked.

Langston confidently replied, "You have a problem with making virtual love with a younger man? I find you attractive. I want to see your pussy."

Jordan was not flattered, but she found his statement interesting. "Sorry, but that was a 'yes' or 'no' question," she said, sitting on the wet towel at her home office desk.

An incoming call registered from Langston requesting to Face-Time. Jordan declined.

"To be continued in person. I have to get ready for church," she said.

"Mind if I attend?" he asked. "I need to be saved. By you."

"I do mind. Meet me at Bar Purgatory *next* Sunday afternoon. I'll text you a time."

Langston countered, "You mean today."

She was sure he'd heard her correctly the first time. "I said what I meant. Next Sunday afternoon, Mr. Derby. I'll let you know what time."

"Sure thing," he said. "I'm a patient man. Until then, keep smiling, beautiful. And don't sell a bit." He laughed.

Ending the call, Jordan entered the limited information she had into their legal background-check database. Langston did in fact own a men's clothing business with Theodore Ramsey. His net worth was four million. *Hmm.* His birthplace was Columbia, Maryland.

Her online net worth was four times his. Add another ten million to the sixteen and the online reporting would be closer to accurate. He could be worth a lot more. Or less.

Jordan's gut instinct urged her to cancel the date.

Her curiosity overruled.

CHAPTER 30

Chancelor

Chancelor stood in front of Hope for All Church; he was desperately waiting for Victoria to arrive.

"Good morning, Brother Chancelor," a member said.

Chancelor responded with a friendly greeting. Church was starting in twenty minutes. Victoria was unusually late, at least by ten minutes. He dialed her cell. There was no answer. Chancelor called again. No answer. He'd impatiently waited all week for this day to come. Victoria couldn't disappoint him. They both had a reason to take Tracy down together.

"Aw, shit," he said. *Victoria best hurry up.*

Noticing Tracy approaching him with Brother William Copeland on her arm, Chancelor pointed his phone at them and started recording live.

"Good morning, Brother Leonard," Brother Copeland stated. "Allow me to introduce you to my long-lost daughter, Tracy Benjamin."

Fumbling his cell, Chancelor made a quick recovery, snatching it in midair, then held it against his vest. He could be Brother Copeland's son-in-law. That would really piss Victoria off. The live video was still active. He held the camera in Brother Copeland's face. "Repeat that."

Brother Copeland stuck out his chest. "Allow me to introduce

my long-lost daughter, Tracy Benjamin. She's cute as a dumplin'."
He stood tall. Smiled wide with pride.

Tracy was in a sleeveless white dress, with green-leaves print and
splashes of pink, that was shrink-wrapped to her titties, waist, and
her ass. A speck of pollen couldn't squeeze under that outfit. Tracy
hid behind large-framed dark sunglasses and a pink wide-brim hat.
She had short green lace gloves on her hands, like she was going
to the Kentucky Derby after service. Chancelor wished she were
headed to a funeral. *Hers.*

Toggling the camera in his direction, Chancelor spoke to his fol-
lowers as if he was making the church announcements. "Brother
Copeland, you can't trust Tracy Benjamin. She's a liar. She's a
thief. And she's not your daughter. What happened to the white
dude she was with last Sunday? And Brother Melvin the Sunday before that? Where he at? I'm warning you. She's a whore after your
money, man."

Chancelor toggled his camera, held it in their face like he was
reporting the news. Tracy didn't say one word on the live.

"Brother Leonard," Brother Copeland said. "I imagined your
vocabulary to be a bit more extensive than . . . Shall I say, a third
grader could speak better. Brother Melvin is probably recovering
from having two front teeth implanted."

Tracy laughed. Chancelor wanted to kick her teeth out. All of
them. *Whore!*

Tracy never let go of Brother Copeland. They climbed the stairs,
arm in arm.

"What you doing out here?" Jordan asked, startling him. She
stepped from behind Chancelor to his side. "Whatever you do,
don't say shit to Tracy. I already warned you."

Too late. Ending his live video, Chancelor replied, "I don't have
anything else to say to her. I'm waiting on my new girlfriend,
Shanita. I invited her to church today," he lied.

"*Shanita*, huh?" Jordan shook her head.

"That's right. Besides, Tracy is already inside the church with
her new sponsor. Brother Copeland."

"I saw them. See you at the altar." Jordan gracefully made her
way up to the front doors.

"Bruh, what you doing standing out here like you on a beat? Let's go," Kingston said, approaching Chancelor.

"Man, I'm waiting on Victoria. She's not here yet."

"See you inside." Kingston followed in Jordan's footsteps.

Chancelor was on a beat of sorts. Missed his opportunity to hancuff Tracy to him, the way she was holding on to William Copeland.

The moment Chancelor saw Victoria, he approached her. "What did you come up with?" he asked, playing his live video for her to see.

"Already seen it." Nonreactive to the footage, Victoria nonchalantly commented, "If I tell you, you'll ruin it."

"I promise you, I won't," he said, eager to hear the details.

"And I promise you, you will," she retorted.

Chancelor followed Victoria indoors, whispering, "You missed it. Tracy came with your man. Brother Willy seems like his willy is happy without you. Tracy might inherit all of his shit." Chancelor hoped to irritate Victoria into sharing their plan, but she remained calm. He continued, "Brother Copeland was at her house last night, so I know he wasn't with you. Don't y'all do it every Saturday?"

Soon as they were in the rear, out of the view of the congregation, *wham!* Victoria slapped his face.

"Ow! That hurt," he said, rubbing his cheek.

"Say something else. I'll beat you like you stole the offering." Victoria placed her hand in her uniform pocket. "And I'll use this on you, too."

"Use what?" Chancelor didn't see anything.

He had a date later this week with a woman he hoped would make Tracy jealous. Her name, Elite, was suitable to her sweet telephone personality.

Victoria cracked the door, stared.

"You looking at them?" Chancelor questioned. "What's that serpent Tracy doing? Let me see."

Victoria stepped aside. Tracy mouthed the word "bitch" at him, stood, then claimed her usual seat. Last row. Outer end. That was okay. Chancelor had her bitch, all right.

Victoria stood alone, sprinkling something in her palms.

"If that's holy water, give me some." Chancelor reached for the bottle.

Shifting the small black bottle to the side, she yelled, "Don't touch it!"

"Damn, Victoria," Jordan commented.

"Yeah. You act like it's acid," Kingston added.

When did those two come in? Chancelor thought.

"Or poison," Chancelor said. Drawing back his hands, he smiled. His eyes grew with excitement.

Victoria dug into her uniform pocket, pulled out a doll that had a face resembling Tracy's, then splashed it with the contents from the little black bottle. "It won't kill her, but it might make her wish she was dead."

A sinister look consumed Victoria's face. Her eyes squinted. Lips curled.

Jordan said, "I do not want to be an accomplice to whatever you're plotting against that woman. See y'all inside," then left.

Kingston followed Jordan.

Victoria warned Chancelor, "Whatever you do, don't touch Tracy. Stay away from her, forever."

He frowned, thinking, *Forever?*

CHAPTER 31

Victoria

"Forgiveness is for the soul of the sinner. For we all sin. I have sinned. My wife has sinned. Can you picture a world without forgiveness? I can't. I want each of you to open up your heart. How can you ask God to forgive your debts, but you refuse to forgive your debtors?" Pastor Baloney stomped from one end of the platform to the other in a purple robe, with a long gold stole.

Well, the Lord knows my heart, and I'm not asking Him for permission, but I will pray for forgiveness, Victoria thought, then said, "Amen, Pastor!" as he concluded his sermon. The organist played "Be Blessed" by Yolanda Adams.

Standing at Chancelor's normal post, Victoria was on the same side with Tracy. She nodded across the row at her usher partner. Brother Willy Copeland was two rows back on her side. He avoided making eye contact with her. He must've felt guilty and asked Tracy to sit elsewhere. There was no way Tracy would part from marking her territory.

But it was too late for Victoria not to follow through with her plan. The damage was already done. The entire congregation had seen her man with Tracy. What Victoria had to do was stop Brother Willy from signing her inheritance over to Tracy. And she had just the right potions to make certain that the two of them being seen

together at church didn't repeat. One for Tracy and the other—
she'd administer later—was for Brother William Copeland.

Gracefully Victoria stepped to her left again and again. Each time
she received the basket from the person on the end of the row, she
passed it to the first person on the next. The collection traveled toward Chancelor. Alternating watching Victoria and Tracy, he moved
to the last row. Seeing each parishioner drop their tithes in the basket, Tracy's head was turned in Chancelor's direction. For the first
Sunday in nearly a year, the man next to Tracy didn't appear to be
her sponsor.

Tramp probably thinks she's hit the jackpot with Willy.

This was a time when history did repeat; Tracy did not make a
donation. Victoria placed her hand inside her right uniform
pocket. She grasped the voodoo doll, then tossed it in Tracy's lap.

Startled, Tracy's head snapped in Victoria's direction. Tracy
picked it up, held it. She stared at the doll whose face mirrored
hers, then looked at Victoria. "Bitch, what is this?!" Tracy threw the
doll toward the basket.

Victoria snatched the doll in midair as she splashed oil from the
little black bottle into Tracy's mouth. Wiping her lips, Tracy appeared confused.

"Oh, my, what is this?" Victoria asked, as though Tracy had given
the look-alike to her. She quickly stuffed Tracy's mini-me into her
pocket before anyone else touched it, because they, too, would receive the curse.

Leaping from her seat, Tracy swung at Victoria's face, nearly
connecting with Victoria's eye. Oohs and aahs resounded in unison from the congregation. Victoria swiftly moved to the center
aisle, then stood behind Chancelor.

The man next to Tracy grabbed Tracy's bicep, pulled her down
into her seat, then said, "Forgiveness, Sister Benjamin."

Roaring laughter escaped Chancelor's mouth as he bent over,
breaking his silence, holding his stomach with one hand. Standing
tall, he said, "It's a baby doll, you guys." Staring and walking toward
the altar, Chancelor whispered to Victoria, "Whatever you did,
good job."

One could hear chatter among the church members.

The man seated next to Tracy said, "It's okay, Sister. It was a rag doll."

Facing the guy, Tracy said, "It wasn't a regular doll! It had my face on it. It was some sort of voo—"

"Oh! Damn!" He pinched his nose.

"What the hell?!" Tracy said, covering her mouth.

People around Tracy scattered as though tear gas exploded.

"The doors of the church are closed! Service is over," Pastor Baloney said. "It smells like every one shitted on themselves. I'll bless the offering in my office. Damn!"

The first lady pinched her nose, held up her pointing finger in the air, and ran to the back.

Victoria, Chancelor, Kingston, and Jordan quickly took the offering to the pastor, then evacuated immediately through the rear exit.

Willy busted out of the back door, gasping for oxygen. "Who in the hell was that?"

Pleased with the outcome of Tracy's spell, Victoria felt a celebration was in order.

Tracy would quarantine herself. Even if Willy wanted to get to know his fake daughter, it would have to be over the phone. But Victoria already had Plan B to interrupt all forms of their communication.

CHAPTER 32

Kingston

Cheshire Bridge Road summoned his dick like a moth to a flame. Midspring, Mother Nature's high had maxed at a never-seen-before ninety-two degrees, but the heat index registered over a hundred.

Kingston drove from church to a gas station. A quick change of clothing from his usher uniform into a black zipped-up, long-sleeved lightweight cotton jacket and matching sweatpants, baseball cap, tennis shoes, and he found himself back in the basement.

Searching the dimly lit room, he saw a man's physique that matched that of the suitor's profile on the app NoStringsIntended. Kingston sat next to the guy, then whispered his code, "Sushi."

"Purple," the guy replied, using his secret word.

They didn't waste time relocating to a private room. Kingston lowered his waistband to his knees. No need to remove his pants. They were going into the trash soon as he got back to his new home.

"Hit it raw, man. It'll feel better," the guy said, removing his shorts.

Ignoring him, Kingston rolled the condom to the base of his shaft. Penetrating the guy from behind, Kingston felt the guy's sphincter muscle contract tightly around his shaft. Each time Kingston tried to pull out all the way, he only managed to get one inch out; then he was stuck again.

"Hey, man, ease up," Kingston said.

"You should've taken the condom off," the guy said. "No worries. I took care of it for you."

Kingston gripped the base of his shaft, then pulled. When he was halfway out, the guy suctioned him all the way back in.

"Man, I'm not going to do this with you. Let go of my dick," Kingston demanded, wanting to punch the guy in the back of his fucking head.

People in Georgia were being arrested for stupid shit, like destroying someone's cell phone. Plus, if Kingston were to assault this dude, he'd publicly expose himself. Frustrated, he stroked fast and hard until they ejaculated.

Pushing forcefully with his muscles, the guy ejected Kingston's penis, then the condom, from his rectum.

"Didn't that feel great, man?" he asked. "Angry sex is my favorite. Once you got worked up, you were a rough maniac, man. Just the way I like it, dude."

Kingston removed the soiled condom from the crotch of his sweats, tossed it in the trash. He ripped two cleansing towels off the rack, wiped himself off, then threw them in the can. He wasn't a kid anymore. But he still didn't want anyone to catch him coming out of a place that he shouldn't have been in.

Pulling his hood over his head, he opened the door, trotted up the stairs, exited the facility, then jogged to his car. En route to his home, Kingston had to admit to himself that he enjoyed the experience and was definitely going to start going raw, but only with Theodore.

A quick shower, change of clothing—white-and-black button-up, white slim-fit slacks, and black leather Italian shoes—and he was on his way to Bar Purgatory to meet up with the group.

A call registered from Theodore. Kingston answered, "Hey, man, what's up?"

Truth was, he missed Theodore. But he wasn't willing to admit it.

"Come by my clothing store. I have some things I know you'll like," Theodore said.

"Cool. Can't come right this minute, but I can stop by, say, around six o'clock." Kingston knew the shop closed at that time. He had intentions on trying more than clothes. "Gotta go. Call you when I'm headed over."

"I miss you," Theodore said, then quickly ended the call.

Parking in the lot, Kingston strolled inside the bar. "I'm never fucking you over," he told Victoria. "What in the hell did you do to Tracy to make her breath smell like everybody in the church took a dump in that woman's mouth?" Laughing, he held his hand in front of his face, then huffed. "Don't do that to me. The stench was like a public toilet filled with feces that had been left unattended for a month of Sundays."

He noticed Jordan staring below his beltline. Kingston winked at her, then sat in his usual seat.

"Until I choose to break the spell," Victoria said, holding up her glass, "flies will be the only company eager to be intimate with Tracy. As long as Brother Copeland is alive, Tracy will be undesirable."

" 'Do unto others' . . . that bitch got what she deserved. But why do I have to stay away from her?" Chancelor questioned. "The next round is on me, Levi. Give Victoria and Jordan their favorite. I'm feeling generous."

Levi was a good lover who'd gotten better the last time they were together. Kingston's top guy remained in position and he couldn't wait to reunite with him. Listening to the others, he texted Theodore, **Get a bottle of cognac.** Then messaged Monet, **Miss you. Kiss the girls for me. I'm going to try and come home in a few days.**

"No telling when this offer will repeat." Jordan removed her bottles—one empty, the other unopened—from the table, placed them in her insulated bag. "Bring a bottle of your finest Cab, Levi."

"God knows my heart. Tracy won't die from halitosis," Victoria said. "Bring two clean goblets, Levi. And we're going to need to double up on the wine, so bring two bottles."

Typical, Kingston thought. "Why females always elevate their libation preference whenever a man offers to pay?" Reading Theodore's response, **Can't wait to hold you in my arms. Ready to have sex when you are . . . man,** Kingston took a deep breath. Exhaled slowly to release the pressure in his heart.

"I'm the sweater in this group," Victoria said, staring at Kingston. "You all right? Need a glass of ice?"

Holding up one of her wine bottles, Jordan yelled to Levi, "Google this and give me the closest comparison."

Kingston nodded at Victoria. "Baby mama tripping," he lied, before telling the truth. "She wants to visit me. And bring my girls."

Jordan tightened her lips, rolled her eyes at Kingston.

Chancelor stated, "Stick to your initial decision, dude. Don't do it, man."

"Second that," Levi added, delivering all of their drinks on a round black tray. "Next thing you know, they'll be living with you. Trust me. You'll regret that."

Setting the empty tray on the bar, Levi texted Kingston, **Got this solid film deal in the works. Let me hold ten racks. I'll repay with interest.**

Ignoring Levi's message, Kingston tossed back his cognac in one shot. "Another, Levi, bruh."

Levi approached, smiling, took the glass, abruptly walked away, then returned.

Theodore never asked him for anything monetary. What made Levi think he'd loan him ten thousand dollars via a message? Monet hadn't replied. Kingston texted Theodore, **Missing your ass,** then wiped his forehead.

"If I ever piss you off, Victoria, even a little, let me know immediately," Jordan said, holding her empty glass up to Levi.

Setting Kingston's drink on the table, Levi stood and his stare lingered. He filled Jordan's goblet halfway. Twirling the bottle to prevent the vino from dripping, he topped Victoria off from her bottle.

"I'm sealing the deal on a feature, you guys. If you want in on this hedge fund, now's the time."

Kingston didn't miss Jordan rolling her eyes at Levi.

A congratulatory solicitation from the group would've done

what? Made Kingston consider transferring the funds? This time he avoided eye contact with Levi. Kingston was generous like Chancelor, but he was no fool. He questioned Levi, "Your budget solid, bruh?"

Levi's seductive glance felt damaging. Kingston scanned the faces of his friends. Jordan rolled her eyes again. Best not to question an attorney. Her body language was a clear indicator Levi was on some hustle bullshit.

"I fully support you, but I'd put a root on your ass for sure if you lost my investment money . . . again." Victoria gulped her wine.

Everyone else was silent. The tension was sufficient for Kingston to text, **I'm good on the 10K, bruh. Sending up prayers.**

Levi removed his cell from his front pocket, smiled without looking up. Left. Returned with another round for Kingston and Chancelor. "I have networks fighting over this one. I'ma net at least a few million."

Oh, shit! Levi misinterpreted Kingston's text. Kingston would never loan money to a man who didn't repay his debt to a woman. No need to embarrass Levi. Kingston would tell him in person the next time they lay together.

Thanks, man. I'ma pay you back. I promise, Levi texted.

Kingston believed a person saying "I promise" was like starting a sentence with "to be perfectly honest." If Levi had an ulterior motive from the beginning, Kingston might have to cut him off altogether. Doing that would mean he might need to stop hanging out at Bar Purgatory indefinitely.

Kingston stood in front his chair. "I've got a date. See y'all at church next Sunday. And, Victoria, can you make Tracy stay home?" He laughed.

Levi stood behind the bar, staring at Kingston. "Watch out for these women, bro. All of them aren't female."

Jordan commented, "Kingston knows the difference between a natural woman and a transgender woman."

Chancelor continuously shook his head, then said, "Man, Levi is right. Sometimes the transgender females look better."

"Kingston, go," Jordan insisted.

"Yeah," Levi stated. "Go."

"Oh, Kingston. Tracy won't be going anywhere anytime soon," Victoria said. "You won't see her for a while."

Chancelor laughed. "You are my good-luck charm, Victoria."

"Speaking of date. If you guys want me to background check for you, my offer still stands. I'm having dinner with a guy I actually met in person, at a restaurant, while on a date with Terrence."

Shaking his head, Kingston was glad his wife wasn't that type. Monet had what Jordan and Victoria secretly wished for: a handsome, successful husband with deep pockets.

Jordan continued, "He's meeting me here next Sunday for an early dinner. Langston Derby . . . don't you just love that name." She smiled with her eyes.

Sweat covered Kingston's face, neck, and arms. He didn't sit; he fell down on his seat, almost tumbling backward onto the floor.

"Repeat that," Kingston insisted. He had to be 1,000 percent certain he'd heard her correctly.

CHAPTER 33

Monet

Cairo was what Monet needed. Patient. Passionate. Under-standing of her situation. Monet hadn't told Bianca that she'd given Cairo her direct cell number or that she'd continued seeing him. Now she had a reason to look forward to dropping off the girls at school. Even if Monet divorced Kingston, she couldn't imagine introducing her children to another man and have them call him "Daddy."

Nairobi would have to live the number of years her sister had been alive (plus an additional nine months) for Monet to have her first opportunity to live alone. And that would manifest in spurts when her girls came home for spring breaks, weekends, and holidays.

Ignoring a text from Kingston that read, **Kiss the girls for me. We need to talk. I'll be home in a few days.** Monet shouted from their home salon, "Israel! Hair time."

"Coming, Mother!" she replied.

That meant she'd be another few minutes. Monet called her best friend.

"Hey, lady," Bianca cheerfully answered.

"I don't know what to do. Kingston keeps texting, but I'm so angry with how he's . . ." On the verge of crying, Monet paused. Not wanting to freak out Israel whenever she walked in, Monet held back her tears, then asked, "Can you meet me at the café in an hour?"

"Girl, of course. Working out can wait. Let me change clothes and I'm on my way. Hang in there," Bianca said. "Kingston has lost his mind. And don't think that I forgot about getting the deets on your date with Cairo. Maybe telling me all about that will cheer you up. If he wasn't a match, I'll hook you up until we find you some emotional relief."

Monet texted Cairo, **Can we do lunch instead of breakfast? I can come over at noon.**

What she really needed to do was confess to her girlfriend that she had an affair with Cairo. And she'd planned on continuing to see him. Monet felt a bit better that after dropping off the girls at school, she'd at least be able to vent about her husband and clear her conscience about sexing another man.

Her elder pranced in, modeling her pink, purple, and white plaid designer tennis shoes. Red glitter decorated her orange laces. "Mother, I want two giant Afro puffs. One on each side, please."

Monet spritzed Israel's hair, brushed the front hairline back, then tied a ribbon to secure the hair from falling in her child's face. She slicked the baby hairs along the edges, using a soft toothbrush.

Israel protested, "Mother, no. I had this style Friday. It's Monday. A part down the center of my head will only take a few minutes. Please."

Children weren't sounding boards. Monet didn't want to impart negativity on her girls regarding their father. "Tell your sister to come down."

Making a sucking sound with her mouth, Israel stomped her way out of the room. Monet ignored that, too. Monet cared, but not enough to discipline her daughter while she herself was upset. Styling Nairobi's hair the same, Monet told the girls to make sure they had their homework and iPads. Today she was not making an unnecessary trip to deliver anything to them at school that they'd forgotten.

Checking herself in the mirror one last time, Monet wore a pink sleeveless fitted jumpsuit with green stilettos. No ponytail today.

Parted two inches in the center, her hair flowed over her shoulders and down her back. Fuchsia ever-stay liquid stain coated her lips.

Ready to take on her bittersweet day, she calmly said, "Girls, let's go."

Monet glanced in the rearview mirror and watched the kids secure their seat belts; then she exited the driveway. Seeing her daughters scroll on their phones and not communicate with one another, Monet withheld her tears, again thinking this routine couldn't possibly be her life for the next decade. Neither of the girls asked, "Mother, are you okay?" Now that Nairobi had a cell phone, she communicated less with her sister.

Were her feelings important to her family? Her husband, mother, kids? Or were they accustomed to her being the strong black woman of her household every day?

"Bye, Mom," Israel and Nairobi said, getting out of the car.

"Hugs and kisses." The words had replaced her actions. If Monet didn't solicit affection, she seldom received it. "Love you guys," Monet said.

Israel closed the door, ran in the direction of her friends. Nairobi followed her big sister, then skipped to her group of classmates on the playground. Monet texted Bianca, **Dropped off the girls. omw.**

Bianca was seated at a booth by the window. Monet sat next to her friend, plopped her designer bag on the edge of the burgundy leather.

"I am trying hard to hold it together. I'm not going to chase my husband. I'm not going to sit and patiently wait for him to decide our . . . my future. I—"

Bianca interrupted. Her tone was firm. "Breathe as I speak. Hear me on this. I cannot cheer for your marriage when you're the only one doing flips. Fuck Kingston. You like Cairo? Y'all had a good date?"

"I do. And, yes, we did." But Bianca didn't know how well Monet liked him.

"Have an affair with him. My work is done," her best friend stated.

Scooting over enough to face Bianca without having to turn her head, Monet frowned. Had she heard her friend correctly? "Repeat that?"

Holding up her hand, gesturing for the waitress, Bianca requested an egg whites–only vegetarian omelet, with country potatoes, a side of spinach, and coffee.

"I'll have the same," Monet told the waitress to simplify the order and get back to their talk.

As the waitress walked away, Bianca stated, "You said you had a good time. I haven't heard you sound happy in months. Girl, give him some. Keep yourself a man on the side until Kingston gets his shit together. What's wrong with that?" she asked.

"Excuse me, waitress," Monet said. "I'd like Baileys with my coffee. More Baileys than coffee."

"Make that two, please," Bianca said, then reiterated, "Get yourself a man on the side until Kingston gets his shit together. Don't be naïve, girlfriend. Kingston is in Atlanta upping his body count, just like he did when he was in the league. Only now, he has more time. More time equals more men. He's probably at Magic City, Onyx, Allure, the Pink Pony, in search of *d-i-c-k*, hon—"

"Stop it, Bianca. My husband is not gay. Besides, this is not what I need to hear right now." Monet debated if she should tell Bianca about having had sex with Cairo.

"Well, that's not what I need to hear right now, either," Bianca lamented.

Deep inside, Monet knew her friend was wrong about Kingston. Picturing him being penetrated by a man, Monet had blocked that from her mind years ago. Losing her first best friend, the father of her children . . . Perfect timing for their beverages to arrive.

Monet placed her lips on the edge of the cup. The first sip was always the best. Maybe counseling would help.

"I'm your friend. Your best friend. I'm not telling you to leave your husband the way I left mine. But we know how these ballers get down. If you're going to stay married to Kingston, you must find your own happiness and stop going in and out of depression. Right now, the woman I see is miserable, heartbroken, confused, angry, in denial, and the next stop is bitter. Before you realize it, you're going to wake up and hate yourself, when Kingston is to blame. The only person who can stop this train from crashing is you. If you already have all the answers and you just need your friend to listen, I can do that." Bianca became quiet.

"That's not it. I respect your opinion. It's just that Kingston is the only man—"

Bianca completed Monet's sentence. "That you've fucked. I know that. And I know that makes it difficult for you to imagine being with another man. Honestly, I think that's what you need. You're going to mope and wait for your husband to divorce you? Get you some side dick. If nothing else, maybe that'll release your stress. And mine, too."

Monet took pride in the fact that her postmarriage body count was two. But perhaps Bianca was right about her having an extra-marital affair. What was Monet trying to prove by being faithful to a disrespectful husband? "I hear you. I don't think cheating is the right decision for me, but I'll think about it."

"Well, if that's not the right decision, I have a solution. I'm taking your ass to the pleasure store and buying you lots of dildos and vibrators. You need to do something. Eat up so we'll have time to pick out your toys before the girls get out of school. And if you don't feel comfortable, I'll buy you some shit that don't look like a dick. Either way you're going to orgasm yourself out of this funk."

Monet had plenty of advances from Kingston's teammates, but she never told him. Men approached her often. Whatever her hus-band was doing had influenced her to make her decision to move on, too.

"That's an alternative I can get with," Monet said, then smiled.

"Good. Then Kingston's treat. I can use some new toys," Bianca said.

She laughed with her best friend.

Monet texted Cairo, **Something unexpected came up. How's 6pm?**

CHAPTER 34

Chancelor

"You want to see my pussy?" she asked, then purred.

Chancelor massaged his hard-on. Whenever he wasn't work-ing, he was thinking about sex or Tracy. Not necessarily in that order. His new girl was a welcome distraction.

"I bet she's pretty. Please let me see your pussy," he begged as he continued pleasuring himself underneath his desk.

Dressed in a white shirt, red tie, and black socks, his dick wasn't as small as most women claimed. Chancelor didn't see what the big deal was about having an enormous penis, when those men had to work harder to get and maintain an erection. Seemed if the whole thing couldn't fit in a woman, that was a hazard.

ChristianFornicators did not disappoint. Elite took her time dancing in lingerie in front of the camera. He was tempted to speed up his pace, but he didn't want to cum, or make her aware that he was naked from the waist down to his ankles. Chancelor's stroke count outside of a vagina was considerably higher.

"I can show you, but I'ma have to charge." Elite lowered the right side of her gray wife-beater enough to expose her areola.

Shit! It was two shades darker than her deep brown skin. He knew her nipples were huge. He saw them poking through her T-shirt. *Keep going, baby.* If she got closer to the camera, he'd lick

Mary B. Morrison

his screen. "Take it off. Let me see all of your tits. Please," he pleaded. "Lift it up."

Elite stepped back, slid the hem of her top down, then tucked it between her legs.

"Damn, you don't have any drawers on, do you?" Chancelor was about to cum. He had to stop stroking himself. "I need to see that in person. Come over."

He texted Elite his address. She messaged him her CashApp, requesting $500.

How about $50 now and the rest when I see you?

Elite turned off her camera, ended the conversation, then texted, **I don't leave my house for $50. Either you find another 0, or you're the missing 0.**

Chancelor surfed the app for Elite's replacement, but all he thought of were her nipples and almost seeing her pussy. Did she have hair like a grown woman? Was her stuff bald like a young girl? Copying her code, he sent her the full amount. He'd spent more than that at Bar Purgatory last Sunday.

Got it! Thanks, Elite replied.

Cool. What's your ETA? Chancelor inquired.

I have an opening in my rotation next Thursday at 10:00 a.m., Elite replied.

Chancelor contacted CashApp, stating he'd sent the money in error. Someone from the company advised him he'd need to contact the person, and, hopefully, the person would return the funds to him. Otherwise, there was nothing they could do to assist him with getting his money back.

Atlanta women were turning him into a fuck-and-done dude. All those bitches were whores. Shanita. A woman with that much going on, it was just a matter of time before she tried to use him, too. Elite made him think about Tracy. Angry, he surfed the dating app until he found a good Christian accepting of a complimentary hookup. Her arrival time was two hours out.

He showered, dressed, drove, then parked three blocks from Tracy's. Removing his drone, he flew it around her house. All of the shades and curtains were drawn. Victoria had warned him not to be in contact with Tracy. But how dangerous could it be to confront her?

Chancelor headed home to meet his date. If she didn't look like her profile picture, he'd have sex with her, then pretend he had a last-minute appointment and escort her out the door.

CHAPTER 35

Jordan

"This case is breaking my heart." Jordan sat alone in her office and watched the video of Donovan's son being shot and killed. She'd viewed the footage nineteen times this afternoon.

Exhibit A, B, C–Z, lawyers never showed emotions when presenting a case. Inadmissible evidence that was crucial to the favorable outcome for her clients outraged Jordan, but also challenged her to find another way to win.

She pressed rewind. This time watching it in slow motion. If she hadn't met DJ, didn't know Donovan Sr., Jordan wouldn't have an attachment to the victim or the victim's father. But she did.

"DJ wasn't a criminal. He was in his freshman year on a full scholarship," she said aloud. Code Blue made indicting a police officer virtually impossible. Particularly, a white female rookie in Atlanta.

Anne Whitehall wasn't threatened. DJ handed her his driver's license and proof of insurance. He sat in the car while she went to hers. When Anne returned to DJ's luxury foreign two-door sports car, her hand was on her gun as she'd commanded, "Get out of the car! I need to search your vehicle."

DJ placed his hands on the steering wheel, politely denied her request to search his vehicle, and exercised his rights by requesting her supervisor come to the scene.

　　Slapping the door handle that was fleshed with the car, Whitehall shouted, "Get out of the damn car!"

　　Her partner approached DJ's metallic red Tesla Model 3 on the opposite side. "Is there a problem, boy?"

　　"No, sir. She demanded I get out and then she smacked my car," he said.

　　"You getting smart with me, boy?" the partner questioned.

　　"No, sir. But I know my rights. I feel threatened. I want your supervisor to come before I get out," DJ said.

　　The partner laughed. "This nigger thinks he has rights."

　　Whitehall joined in the laughter.

　　DJ asked, "Why did you stop me? You're supposed to let me know."

　　"Get out of the car!" Whitehall shouted. "Now!"

　　DJ slowly removed his hand from the steering wheel.

　　"Boy, you got a gun?" the partner asked.

　　DJ placed his hand back on the wheel. "No, sir" were DJ's last words.

　　Whitehall drew her gun and unloaded the bullets into DJ's chest.

　　"Holy shit!" her partner yelled, then repeated, "Holy shit, rookie!"

Jordan felt both officers should be prosecuted. The police chief differed. Whitehall's partner was not placed on administrative leave, but Whitehall was off duty, collecting her regular salary.

　　Turning off her monitor, Jordan called Langston.

　　Right away he asked, "Hey, we're still on?"

　　"Yes. Let's start with a drink at Bar Purgatory. I'm heading there now. Then we can leave and go to dinner." Jordan needed to decompress. Her first date with Langston was fun. If her melancholy mood didn't change, she could fake a headache and go home early. If things went well, he was scoring in the bedroom tonight.

　　Driving to the bar, Jordan received a call from Donovan. She considered not answering, then said, "Hey. How are you?"

　　"I need to see you. Now. Where are you?" he anxiously said.

　　Already she'd regretted taking his call. "I have plans. But I can talk for a few minutes. What's up?" she asked.

"I have new supporting evidence I need to share with you," he said.

No amount of evidence was going to bring his son back. The case wasn't going to trial anytime soon. Jordan didn't believe Donovan understood that regardless of what firm represented him, his trial was going to be lengthy and costly.

She gave him an alternative to present what he had in person. "Let's discuss it in the morning. I'll have my assistant schedule you for ten o'clock. Cool?"

Donovan snapped. "My son is dead!"

"I didn't kill him!" Jordan retorted. How dare he disrespect her after all the exceptions she'd made for him.

"You might as well have. I knew I shouldn't have counted on you. You always were 'Team Jordan.' That's why we aren't together now. And you call yourself an attorney?" The real irate Donovan had showed up. "You're fired, and I want my retainer back—every penny—or I'm going to expose your naked pictures on social media."

Honk! Honk! Honk! Jordan continuously pressed her horn. "Damn, Donovan. You almost made me have an accident."

She vividly recalled why she'd stopped dating him. Inhaling deeply, Jordan replied, "I'll have my assistant wire fifty thousand dollars to the same account my firm received it from. Check your account in the morning. I wish you the best, Donovan Bradley Senior. I always have. Good—"

"Stop being irrational. I know you didn't kill my son, but if you give up on him, it's going to feel like DJ died twice. I need you, Jordan. *We* need you." Donovan cried. "I'll be there at ten."

Jordan was not getting on the roller coaster with Donovan. He'd done that same shit when they were in a relationship. Turning off her engine, she placed her cell on speaker, then said, "Good. Then you can pick up your cashier's check in person," then ended their conversation.

Checking her makeup, she exited her vehicle, then went inside. Langston waved at her from the bar. A bottle of wine and two goblets were near him. He stood, pulled out her barstool. Opening his arms, he embraced her for at least half a minute.

"You are more gorgeous than the last time I laid eyes on you," he said.

His greeting was soothing. Jordan exhaled into his hug, wrapped her arms around him.

"Hey, Jordan," Levi said, opening his arms. "You look like you could use more than one." His hands rested on her shoulders; then Levi returned behind the bar.

"You're all set because I'm teaching Langston what you like. It's the same wine Chancelor sponsored." Levi partially filled each glass.

Standing by her side, Langston held the back of her stool until she was comfortable. He handed Jordan a glass, then held his high. "Cheers. To new beginnings."

"To new beginnings," Jordan said, burying her thoughts of the conversation she'd had with Donovan. Giving her attention to Langston, Jordan asked, "How was your day?"

"I don't want to recap the past. I'm focusing on my future. With you," he said.

Levi turned toward them, leaned on the counter. "Guess who Langston knows," he said. Not waiting for her to respond, Levi added, "Kingston."

Langston nodded as he smiled at Levi.

"Kingston Royale?" Jordan questioned, recalling how Kingston had loss his footing and fell back into seat when she'd mentioned Langston Derby.

His nod continued.

Jordan shifted her eyes back and forth from Langston to Levi. Connecting with Langston, she asked, "How, and how well, do you know Theodore Ramsey?"

"Jordan!" A familiar voice resonated behind her. Donovan suddenly appeared beside her. Stood between Langston and her, then said, "We need to talk. Now."

Langston placed his hand on Donovan's chest. "What you need to do is show some respect."

Donovan had to quit popping up on her. If she gave in, he'd do it again. And again. "I'm busy, Donovan."

"You heard the lady," Langston said. "Back the fuck up."

"I ain't gotta do shit. She's my attorney, and before she was my lawyer, she was my—"

Langston's fist landed on Donovan's lips. Donovan stumbled backward.

Donovan touched his face, stared at his bloody hand. "You witnessed that, Jordan. That's what you want? A beast." Donovan took another step back when Langston pushed back his stool, then stood.

People in the bar looked in their direction, then resumed whatever they were doing.

"Expect a lawsuit, from Jordan," he told Langston.

Levi approached Donovan, grabbed him by the collar of his polo shirt, then forced him outside.

Langston inquired, "That's the guy who was on television? His son was killed by that cop?"

"Yes. And yes." Jordan was beginning to think Donovan's interest was more than professional but he wasn't man enough to be open and honest.

He'd ruined her chances with Terrence Russell. Langston Derby wasn't going to be her next relationship casualty. Donovan was making Jordan's decision to no longer represent or communicate with him clear.

Interrupting their silence, Langston asked, in a sarcastic tone, "He's your client?"

"Was," Jordan said out of frustration, then asked, "How, and how well, do you know Kingston Royale and Theodore Ramsey?"

The only information Jordan was attempting to attain was confirmation that Langston co-owned a men's clothing store with Theodore.

Langston placed his glass on the counter. Removed Jordan's glass from her hand, set it next to his. "Let's continue this conversation over dinner. At my place. That way we won't be rudely interrupted by your stalker client-*boy*friend."

CHAPTER 36

Kingston

Jordan Jackson. No specifics. A text from Derby69, Mr. Langston Derby, registered on Kingston's cell, followed by **No time to explain. Come by my place now.**

Another text, this time from Levi, registered with his bank account and routing numbers.

Jordan needed to hear the truth about Langston's sexuality, but not from Langston.

Kingston arrived at the Buckhead address Langston Derby had texted him. The expensive cognac brand he'd brought was intended as a generous gesture. Kingston was hopeful they'd toss back a few shots to loosen up, and Langston would reveal the reason he'd gone down on him (in the third grade) and Kingston would confess why he allowed it to happen.

He had to hear Langston state why he was on an app for gay men. And what was his intentions with Jordan.

Unlike Kingston's hidden gem, Langston's home was practically in plain sight off of a busy highway near Peachtree and Lenox. Kingston's shaking finger pressed the doorbell. Kingston paced two steps to the right. Four left. When the door opened, he traveled two steps back to the right.

"Hey, man. How crazy is this shit? Come in," Langston said, then closed the door. "We were finishing up dinner. You're just in time for dessert."

We? Handing a liquor gift bag to Langston, Kingston said, "I brought a little something for the house." He followed Langston through a gallery of framed basketball championship posters hanging on the wall in the foyer and living area. When he looked into a room off to the side, multiple big screens were mounted in a media room. Finally they'd arrived in the dining room, which had a large circular table with four gold Victorian-styled chairs. No straight man's décor would be so elaborate and meticulous.

"Thanks, man," Langston said, opening the Hardy XO Rare. "I take it no introduction is needed here. Have a seat, man."

Fingering her natural hair, Jordan was dressed in business attire. Shaking her head, she said, "Don't sit. Kingston, I know the two of you grew up together, but why are you here?" She protested as though he were the sun ready to dry out whatever wetness she'd managed to secrete.

Langston answered, "Don't get all sensitive, babe. You wanted to know how, and how well, I knew Kingston. I told you I have nothing to hide. So I invited him to stop by. He won't be here long." Langston French-kissed Jordan for damn near a minute.

Whoa. He had serious game. Perhaps that was because Langston had gotten the head start on seduction well before him. Jordan didn't contest that shit.

Langston looked at Kingston, then licked his lips. "This woman is sweeter than honey."

Maybe Kingston's conclusion based on the décor was premature. Jordan's red lipstick hadn't smeared. Watching them, Kingston felt a bit jealous.

Rubbing the nape of her neck, Jordan said, "It was inappropriate of you to invite Kingston without first consulting with me."

"If I'm going to be your man, babe, you need not treat me like a client." Langston opened the oven.

Her what? Jordan was far too intelligent to fall for the bullshit. Kingston laughed to himself, then thought about his wife. Convinced he was right the first time, if Jordan started dating Langston, her relationship with Langston would be the same as his with Monet.

The scent of apple cinnamon pie escaped the oven as Langston blew a kiss to Jordan. He removed the cookie sheet from the oven, centered the hot dish on a cooling plate on the table. Taking a pint of butter pecan ice cream from the freezer, he placed it next to the pie. Four crystal bowls were positioned adjacent to the same number of small plates and silverware.

"We'll give the pie a moment to cool off and the ice cream to thaw." Langston pulled out a chair, sat, then said, "Thanks for coming. Have a seat, man," then told Jordan, "You can quiz him and compare notes."

As she scanned the table, Jordan's thoughts probably aligned with Kingston's. *Who else is coming?*

"You know you want to ask," Langston told Jordan.

A *humph* sound escaped Jordan's lips.

Kingston sat to the left of Jordan. Langston was to her right and directly across from Kingston. The awkward situation made Kingston uncomfortable. He'd come for answers, not questions.

Small talk ensued. Langston dished up four slices of pie and an equal number of scoops of ice cream for each setting. Tight-lipped. Jordan tilted her head sideways, shifted her eyes from Langston to the empty seat.

"Oh," he said, smiling. "That's for the less fortunate. Keeps me grounded. Some people don't know when they'll eat again."

"Kingston isn't going to be here all night. Just ask him your questions, babe," Langston insisted.

"How, and how well, do you know Langston?" Jordan twirled her spoon into her ice cream.

"Am I interrupting?" Kingston asked, delaying a response.

Langston replied, "After you answer, you're free to go, man. Excuse me. I have to use the restroom."

Kingston was ready to leave now. "Look, Jordan. I hadn't seen or heard Langston's name since third grade, until you mentioned him by name at the bar. We attended elementary school together. That's it."

A text registered from Langston: **Let me take Jordan upstairs and put her to sleep. Hang out in my media room. When I'm done with her, I got you. We're grown now. Bisexual men don't have to choose sides.**

Wow. Kingston never thought of it that way. But he knew Monet would never knowingly accept his sexing her, Theodore, Langston, and other random guys.

"That's what Langston said." Jordan whispered, "I like him. Since you're here, what do you think? Should I give in and have sex with him?"

"Let me put it this way," Kingston told her. "Women hold out. Men don't. If it's not you, it'll be someone else. That's for sure. Whatever you decide, make sure you use protection."

If Langston were a scammer, he wasn't in search of pussy from Jordan. It was something more valuable. But Kingston was certain that Jordan had performed a thorough background investigation and didn't require his support.

Jordan smiled at Langston as he entered the room.

Kingston wanted to open up to Langston, but he might lose Jordan's friendship if he stayed.

Langston kissed Jordan again. "Missed you, baby. You're so sexy. Mind and body," he said, then reclaimed his seat. "Isn't she lovely, man?"

"I'ma get out of the way," Kingston said, then texted Langston, **My dick is hungry for your ass. Hurry up.**

The fourth setting was for a mutual friend, but after seeing you, I uninvited him. Langston's text engaged Kingston's curiosity. Was it a woman? Or a man?

"Yeah, do that. And I'ma take my dessert upstairs," Langston replied, then discreetly rubbed his foot against Kingston's leg underneath the table.

Reaching for Jordan's hand, Langston said, "Let yourself out, man. Thanks for stopping by on such short notice and clearing things up for my lady."

CHAPTER 37

Kingston

A commercial flight was preferred today, since he'd traveled solo. Landing at BWI, Kingston retrieved his carry-on from the overhead compartment. Settling into the back of a reserved Town Car, he reflected on last night, texting Langston, **Who was the uninvited guest?**

Sex with Langston was total body orgasmic! Oh, how both of them had grown in many ways. Torn between two lovers—Langston and Theodore—Kingston's departure from Atlanta was needed to regroup, but he could hardly wait to let Theodore spoil him.

Getting out of the car, Kingston was pleased his wife's car was in the driveway. He pressed his thumbprint again the keypad, then entered the front door.

"Baby, I'm home!" Kingston shouted, dropping his black leather bag at his feet.

Designer head-to-toe Monet strutted into the living room, sporting a fitted dress. The hem stopped well above her knees. Open-toe stilettos drew his eyes to her shiny legs. Her purse dangled from her forearm. Ponytail was perched high and hung low. Dark sunglasses hid her eyes.

"Oh, hey, Kingston. Good you're here. I'll tell Trinity you're picking up the girls from school at three o'clock. Dinner is prepped and in the fridge. Let it sit out for thirty minutes, then put it in the oven on three hundred fifty for forty. Bedtime is eight sharp."

His wife smelled sweet and rosy. Her red lips were glossy. Where was she going at ten in the morning dressed like that? He'd taken the early flight to spend the day with her before she'd get the girls.

"You look nice," he said politely, yet pissed, looking her down, then up.

Monet smiled cheerfully, placed her hand on her hip. "Thanks."

She stepped to the right. Kingston moved to his left. Monet shifted in the opposite direction; Kingston did the same.

Deepening his voice, he questioned her with authority. "I asked you, where are you going?"

"No, you didn't," she answered boldly.

"Well, I'm asking now." Kingston moved closer to his wife.

Calmly Monet replied, "Out."

"Out where?" Monet Royale was still a married woman and he had the right to demand answers.

"I'm not doing this with you, Kingston. You show up here, acting like you didn't ignore my texts, hang up on me, and abandon your family. Go back to wherever you came from. I'm running late. I have to go." Monet attempted once more to exit through the front door.

Kingston refused to allow her to leave. All of what she complained about was in the past. He'd asked the question, a basic one that deserved a response. It didn't matter what she thought, he was here and she wasn't leaving.

"What the fuck do you want?!" Monet yelled.

"You, baby," he said, leaning down for a kiss.

For the first time, Monet stepped back. "I'm finally getting accustomed to your not being here, and now you want to act as though you never left and you expect me to be excited to see you. When you played ball, I understood. But this right here, Kingston . . . move."

Monet shoved him, but he didn't budge. She wasn't leaving him. He grabbed his wife by the arm, snatched her purse, then threw it to the floor. "I know what you need," he said. "Let's go to the bedroom."

He never imagined his wife cheating on him. But he was not stupid. Nor was he allowing her to walk out of their house—the house he paid for—to go screw another man.

Monet removed his hand from her bicep, picked up her purse. Staring at him, she didn't respond.

Kingston grabbed the handle and pulled the bag away from her. "I mean it, Monet. You're not going anywhere. If you want to leave, take off all of your clothes, leave my car, and get out."

His strategy to get his wife naked failed miserably when she politely responded, "I'm wearing my half." Monet eased her bag out of his hand.

Kingston refused to let his wife walk out the door. "We need to talk."

"I don't want to talk," she said quickly.

"Then listen to me," Kingston stated. "It's only been a few months. I almost have everything in place."

Monet repeatedly punched him in the chest, then screamed, "If you want a divorce, be a man about it! Don't string me along! You want me to respect you? Miss you? Love you? I've been taking care of our girls while you do what in Atlanta? Huh? What, Kingston? You promised the girls more gifts. And you're too busy to send them? Showing up unannounced doesn't make you a father." Monet cried.

Damn. Lilly forgot to send the other packages to his girls. He'd deal with her later. Or perhaps he needed to thank her. The brand he'd requested was no longer popular with African Americans.

This was the moment Kingston had waited for. Seeing his wife break down, Kingston thought, *Now I know she cares.* It was his job to build her back up. The way he wanted. Moving closer to his wife, he put his arms around her, leaned her head on his chest, then said, "Baby, you're right. I'm sorry. Tell me what you need me to do."

Leading his wife to the bedroom, Kingston dried her tears. He knew what he needed to do to get his wife back to a submissive state.

"Let's take a shower and let me show how much I love and miss you." He kissed her lips, her forehead, her cheeks, her neck, then led her to the bathroom. Unzipping her dress, he let it fall to the floor.

Kingston started the water to fill up the Jacuzzi tub. He removed his clothes, neatly folded them, then placed them in the laundry room. Monet frowned at him as she removed her shoes, leaving them in the middle of the bathroom floor.

"Let me show you something that I bought for you," Monet said. "It's a surprise." Exiting the bathroom, she wiggled her ass.

"That's my baby." Kingston added lavender, eucalyptus, and baby oil to the warm water. Getting into the tub, he relaxed, hoping that his wife had a really sexy surprise for him when she returned.

Kingston began stroking himself to get ready for Monet. His dick didn't get hard. Recalling last night's events with Langston, he almost came.

He called out, "Monet! Baby, what's taking so long?" There was no answer. If he ejaculated, he probably wouldn't be able to recover quickly. He waited a few more minutes, then called his wife's name again. There was no answer. Getting out of the tub, Kingston wrapped a large brown towel around his waist.

He searched the bedroom walk-in closet, but his wife wasn't there. Kingston trailed water to the living room. Monet's purse was where they'd left it. Opening the front door, he saw his wife's car was gone. Picking up her pocketbook, he found it was empty.

Retrieving his cell to call his travel agent to book him on a late flight back to Atlanta, Kingston read the response from Langston: **My uninvited guest was my male partner. I think you'll like him. Will introduce you soon. Cheers.**

Whoa. Langston had loose, low-hanging balls that swung both ways. Kingston had to find a way to let Jordan know.

If Monet wanted to be with another man that badly, let that nigga take care of her.

Kingston sat on the sofa, signed into VirginsSeekingVirgins in hopes of finding someone in the area to help release his frustration.

CHAPTER 38

Victoria

"You so sexy," Heavenly told Victoria, reclining in the passenger seat of her car. "When I graduate, get a real job, make lots of money like you, I'ma make you my wife."

Typically, what he'd uttered warranted a verbal thrashing. Curiosity prompted her inquiry. "What do you consider a *real* job?" Victoria enjoyed his infectious energy, bulging muscles, amazing smile, transparency, and good dick.

It wasn't seven, eight, or nine inches long. More like a stiff six and a half. And Heavenly was an eager and fast learner. He had an extra inch of introverted dick that she could pull out of him. But Victoria didn't think he'd be around for the six months that it'd take her to complete the painless process.

"An AI developer," he said confidently.

Humph. Artificial intelligence, when his major is communication? It was a common and consistent concern with men; when they saw how she balled, they often superficially elevated themselves to her status in some sort of way.

Victoria turned off of Peachtree Road, onto West Paces Ferry Road Northwest. "Ever considered real estate investments?"

Heavenly laughed, then said, "I'm smart, but I'm not smart like you. I'd need two cougars to make that happen. Maybe three."

"Or perhaps the right one." Victoria reduced her speed to twenty miles per hour.

His voice became melancholy. "I didn't mean literally. What I meant was, I don't have that kind of money. I apologize if I offended you."

Heavenly, like most men, was confused. But he wasn't disrespectful, which made Victoria appreciate him more. "Why don't I turn this tour into a lesson for you. The first thing you're going to do when investing is check the foreclosure list and property tax sales with the county and the bank. Then I'm going to take you to an auction. The most important thing you need to do is research, drive the neighborhood. It's good to know where the cell towers are located, as well as who the developer is."

Success in any field required self, online, and textbook education, passion, and a greater humanitarian purpose. Victoria knew she wasn't perfect, but she'd always be a child of God. She thought about Tracy and the spell she'd cast upon her and felt no remorse. Even the Bible stated an "eye for an eye." As long as Heavenly didn't cross her, she was willing to help make him independently rich.

"That makes sense. People want to make sure they have great reception," he said, nodding.

Okay, maybe not independently rich, she thought.

"Wrong. Cell towers are believed to cause cancer, and too many of them in a concentrated area lowers property values," Victoria explained.

"Dang. I never knew that." He stared at her with loving eyes. "I'm serious about marrying you. You're intelligent. You know that?"

Driving through an upscale area of Buckhead, Victoria pointed out various houses. "How much do you think that property is worth?" she asked him.

"Well, it's pretty big. I guess it's about one-point-five million dollars."

"That's a good guess," she said to encourage him. "What if I were to tell you it sold for four-point-one million before going on the market?" She knew, because she'd brokered the deal.

"You mean Buckhead has some kind of secret ole boy network?" he asked.

"It's all about who you know. Brokers and investors rule Buckhead. It's ninety percent white. Ten percent black."

Heavenly shook his head, said, "I thought Atlanta was primarily black," then he massaged her inner thigh. "I might not know much about houses, but I've learned a lot about you. I'm never going to let you go."

His immaturity and lack of understanding of women blended together in an attractive kind of way. He seemed more impressed than calculating. A call registered from Jordan.

Answering on the car's Bluetooth, Victoria said, "Can I call you back later?"

Unexpectedly, Heavenly cheerfully said, "She's busy right now."

Parking her car curbside, Victoria told him, "Get out." She pressed a button and the wing doors lifted like an Eagle taking flight.

"What? I was joking," he protested.

"Well, I'm not. Out. Now," Victoria demanded. She waited, then lowered the doors.

"Damn, he'd better act right before you cast a spell on his ass," Jordan said, laughing.

"He'll be okay. I'm not going to abandon him in Buckhead. Especially now that he knows the population ratio. And white people around here will call the police on him in a nanosecond."

Heavenly paced back and forth alongside her car.

"Trust me, I know the stats all over Georgia. Anyway, I wanted to give you the deets on Langston Derby and Kingston Royale before our meetup after church tomorrow."

"Okay, girl. Let me get this fine-ass man back in my car. He's staring in my window. Somebody probably already called the cops. Text me first. Bye." Victoria reopened the doors.

"I see I can't even play with you," Heavenly complained.

Arguing with a man his age was pointless. If he announced his presence again without her permission while she was on a call, he'd have to get himself a new cougar. Driving along a side street,

Victoria said, "Just pay attention to the neighborhood first, then hone in on the pockets. Buckhead is affluent. Where you don't want to invest is Lindberg. The ROI, that's 'return on investment,' is minimal. Those are the things you educate yourself on.

"If we're still together your senior year, I'll gift you a fixer-upper. And teach you how to flip."

"Oh, shit! For real? You would do that for me? For real? Wow! First you pay my tuition. Now you're going to teach me how to make money. Man, this is unbelievable, and you're beautiful and you're intelligent and you're sexy. I'm going to pay you back with interest. I'm going to call you my lucky charm. Can we go back to your house? I want to eat your pussy until you fall asleep."

Or until he fell asleep. Victoria definitely could benefit from a great orgasm. And although Willy was coming over later, the good Lord knew her needs. Merging onto Interstate 75, Victoria headed home.

Heavenly stood outside her car door, followed her into the house, went straight to the bathroom, then removed his clothes. Staring at his tightly curled pubic hairs, Victoria thought, *Thank You, Jesus, I almost forgot.*

"Let me clipper shave that," she said, pointing below his navel.

"I've never had that done. Will it hurt?" he questioned, frowning.

Victoria shook her head, opened the bottom drawer, removed the clippers and a clear glass bowl. She brushed between the grooves to make sure there were no long straight strands left over from Willy. She placed a towel on the comforter. "I'm going to need you to lay right here on the bed for me."

Setting the bowl beside Heavenly, she powered on the cordless clippers, then gently shaved his pubic area, upper inner thighs, and his balls. Carefully collecting every clump of hair, she rolled them together in her palms, then dropped them in the dish.

"Get in the tub. I'll be back." Hurrying to her voodoo room, Victoria set the bowl on the altar, closed the door, then returned to the bathroom.

With a wide smile Heavenly asked, "Wait. Let me see my hairs first."

"Focus on how bigger and prettier your dick is." Victoria firmly stroked his shaft.

Heavenly propped his fists on his hips, stared at his erection. "Damn, thanks. I am bigger." He picked up a vibrator, said, "This is for you," and got in the shower.

Victoria joined him.

Lathering Victoria's body all over, Heavenly gripped the handle of the showerhead, then knelt before her. Pointing the stream toward Victoria's clit, she watched him open his mouth. Powering on the vibrator, he traded places, sucking, teasing, until she screamed his name.

When she nearly lost her balance, Heavenly stood quickly to his feet, caught her in his arms. "I'll never let you fall," he said. "I love you. Do you love me?"

Love. Was that the appropriate way to describe his true feelings and hers? Victoria had a strong *liking* for him, but she wasn't *in love* with any man. Never had been. For her, *love* and *in love* were two totally different emotions.

Heavenly dried her off, tucked her in. "I'll see you next weekend. But if you have some free time during the week, I'd like to take you to dinner."

"I'll let you know," Victoria said. "Thanks for everything. Order yourself an Uber, Heavenly."

"Thanks," he replied.

"Lord knows you definitely hit the spot today," she said, cuddling the pillow.

"No, thank you. Nobody has ever loved me like you do," he said, then left.

CHAPTER 39

Chancelor

The baddest bitch in all of Atlanta was worth his wait. Chancelor grinned, admiring—more like lusting for—Elite. He wasn't the only one. Surveying the room, he caught a few men and females checking out his woman's body.

Yesterday he'd gotten a haircut, manicure, and pedicure. This morning he'd shaved, scrubbed his balls and the crack of his ass, and cleansed his dick thoroughly. He'd added a spritz of sandalwood cologne to his genital area. Chancelor didn't want to give Elite any reasons to reject him.

"Sky blue is my favorite color. Did you know that?" he asked, placing his hands on her waist.

The fitted dress was a second skin, smooth to the touch. The halter plunged down almost to her navel. Her nipples protruded. Chancelor could hardly wait to bite them. If he hugged her again, the way he'd done when she first entered, he'd feel the firmness brush against his chest.

Elite planted the sweetest spearmint kiss on his lips. "Of course, I know. That's why I wore it." She kissed him again.

Sliding his hand down her spine, he cautioned himself not to disrespect her the way Tracy had done him. Elite's ass sat higher than Tracy's. Waist was smaller. Titties were huge. He didn't care if every inch of Elite was manufactured off of an assembly line straight out of the Dominican Republic. He loved it and her.

"I'ma spoil you," he said as they sampled the Cabernet at the black-owned winery in Avondale Estates. "Purple Corkscrew was a great recommendation. Your mama named you right. You have exquisite taste."

Chancelor gently touched her ass with one hand. Pulled her closer and inhaled. Elite's breath was minty and fresh. A cool breeze went up his nostrils. The experience was nothing like Tracy's. He snickered at the thought of how Tracy had cleared the entire church after opening her stinky mouth.

"What made you post on ChristianFornicators?" she inquired.

He loved that she hadn't backed away or moved his hand. "I'm looking to take a lucky lady off of the market. Settle down. Get married. Start a family."

Really? Are her lips pressed against mine again? Damn. They are.

Chancelor closed his eyes, opened his mouth. Suddenly all he felt was air. Looking at Elite, he realized her nose almost touched his. But her mouth didn't. If he puckered, he could reconnect.

"I want a man like you to stuff me with twins." Sliding her hand between them, she rubbed her stomach. "I only plan on being pregnant once." Stepping back, Elite created a gap wide enough for a child to separate them.

Like me? "Why not me?" he questioned. "We'd make the perfect power couple."

Swirling the next sample of merlot, she told him, "It's not your fault. My standards are too high for you."

How could she draw that conclusion? "Explain yourself."

"See that comment. You're doubting yourself," she said. "That's inconsiderate of you."

Chancelor frowned, then replied, "No, I'm not doubting myself at all. I know what I'm capable of." Wanting to back away from Elite, he couldn't. His back was to the bar.

"Now you're defensive. You know men think having a baby is easy. Y'all not responsible after you get the pussy. Most of the men I meet want to be head of household, but they don't want to be husband and father to their family," she said. "I need a real man. Like you."

Like? What the fuck did she think he was? He kissed Elite, then reassured her, "*I am* your guy."

"Prove it. CashApp me a push gift deposit right now. A grand if you want to be exclusive. Ten thousand for a deposit to snap this body back, if you want me to have your baby. And five hundred if you just want a fuck buddy now and then." Elite turned her back to him. Backed her ass up to his dick. "I'll give you a minute to think about what you should already know the answer to."

"I'm not looking for a whore," Chancelor lamented in her ear.

"And I'm not interested in a broke man who thinks after dinner his dick is dessert. I can have any man I want, but what Elite," she said, referring to herself in the third person, "will never do is suck broke or cheap dick."

Chancelor wasn't willing to lose the investment he'd already made. "Why don't we see if we're compatible first."

She responded, "Cool with me, Daddy. But I haven't received your funds."

Her ass was tight. His dick was hard. Chancelor imagined lifting her dress and penetrating her at the tasting while holding on to her breasts. The guys who were still periodically staring at Elite could cheer him on.

"Add this to the five I already gave you?" He sent Elite her minimum. "Now we officially go together."

Victoria had to cancel the spell she'd put on Tracy. How else was Tracy going to see his new woman?

Elite pulled out her cell, started typing. Facing him, she asked, "What type of woman do you honestly want?"

Fed up with her head games, he felt his dick go limp. "Let's just enjoy the moment, then cap the date off at my place, where I can answer any other questions that you have."

A tall, handsome dude entered the room. He approached Elite. "You ready, babe?" he asked Elite, taking her hand into his.

"It was nice meeting you, Chancelor," she said as though she wasn't *his* date.

"Hey, man," Chancelor said, tapping the guy on the back. "You owe me a grand or you need to keep walking without my woman. I bought her."

The man stopped. "Excuse me for a minute, baby," he told Elite, then turned to Chancelor. Speaking in a low, deep tone, he said, "You're disrespecting my girl. You want to repeat that?"

He could be brave, but doubted he'd be Elite's hero even if he won the battle for her. Was this a new kind of pimps-up ho stroll where females no longer had to fuck for food or funds?

Chancelor left. Got in his car and drove away. He might as well take Tracy back if he had to deal with this bullshit. Parking a half mile away from Tracy's home, Chancelor set up his drone.

Having it hover over Tracy's place, Chancelor lowered the drone outside her bedroom window. Tracy was naked, on all fours, on her mattress.

"What the hell?"

He zoomed in closer on the guy's face, then scanned down to dude's dick. Watching him slide all of his sausage inside of Tracy. Her mouth was closed, but her ass was wide open.

Chancelor yelled, "Stop right there!"

As though she'd heard him, Tracy looked toward the window. Her mouth opened wide. Dude scrambled to get up. Hopping on one foot, he stumbled into his pants, one leg, then the other. He pinched his nostrils before running out of Tracy's home.

Chancelor laughed so hard, his drone crashed into Tracy's window.

CHAPTER 40

Jordan

"**R**equest denied! Ms. Jackson." Judge Goodwin banged her gavel on the block.

Nothing Jordan had said warranted the judge yelling at her. Jordan had presented cases before her for years. This level of aggressiveness was new.

Calmly Jordan contested, "Your Honor, we have circumstantial evidence we'd like to present. You can't deny our client his right to—"

Bang! Bang! Bang! The judge hammered. The block popped up, hitting her on the forehead. Jordan concealed her laughter, but others didn't hold back their gasps or saying, "Oh."

"Order in the courtroom," Judge Goodwin demanded, placing the block back in its original location on her desk. "You're out of order, Ms. Jackson. Are you suggesting that I'm incompetent?" she questioned.

Incompetent? No. Inconsistent. Yes. Racist? Maybe. Black people discriminate against our own kind, too.

Was Judge Goodwin overly protective of city law enforcers, like Anne Whitehall? Absolutely!

A chilling room filled with people awaiting their cases to be called became quiet enough to hear a pin drop. Today's case was unrelated to any officer of the law. Jordan's partners, against her opposition, had unanimously decided to represent the wrongful-death lawsuit for Donovan Bradley Sr. against Anne Whitehall and the police department. Someone's decision had changed Jordan's firm's ability to get an ordinarily favorable ruling on any of their cases. From community service to probation, the odds had shifted from eight wins out of ten, to one dropped case out of ten, including misdemeanors of obstruction and trespassing.

Judge Goodwin's outward display of innocence—long, loose bouncy curls, pearl earrings and necklace, and mocha lip gloss—didn't match her acrimonious disposition.

Filing a request to have Judge Goodwin removed from the case would be a waste of everyone's time, especially her client's. Jordan whispered in her client's ear, "Don't worry, we're going to figure this out."

The prosecutor spoke, "Your Honor, I recommend four years of probation with ninety days' jail time. With seven days of credit for time served."

Oh, he'd gotten bolder with his plea offers since he knew the judge strived to make Jordan's firm withdraw representation for Donovan. Jordan's team had the highest number of cases won in Fulton County.

How easy, Jordan thought, *for a young white male solicitor to make an unjust recommendation for a nineteen-year-old black man who was an honor student, college-bound, that had never been in trouble with the law.*

Feeling defeated, but refusing to give up, Jordan avoided looking directly at the young man's family seated on the front row. The mother, a single parent, sat between her two sisters. The young man, her only child.

Eyes filled with tears, her young black client cried. "I swear I didn't do anything disrespectful. The police officer was harassing me. I'll lose my mind if I go back to that cell. Fulton County is the worst county prison in America. Don't you guys read?"

"Counsel, control your client," Judge Goodwin said, then asked, "Have you ever thought about committing suicide, young man?"

That was a new low for Judge Goodwin. Jordan felt the statement was intended to encourage acceptance of the deal.

Jordan's client frowned. Quickly she covered the gap between his lips with her hand, then whispered in his ear, "Don't answer that question now or ever. Suicide watch and isolation are ten times worse than being in general population."

"We declined the solicitor's plea, Your Honor. And request a trial, Your Honor," Jordan said.

"Bail is set for five thousand dollars," the judge said, then slammed that damn gavel again. *Too bad it doesn't smack her in the face again.*

"Next time be better prepared, Jackson," the judge said.

No. What Jordan should've been was bed partners with the governor, police chief, and their inner circle of friends, like Judge Goodwin. Jordan wasn't asking for leniency, but they all knew evidence mattered, and without it there was no way a jury could unanimously find her client innocent based on the lies the officer had written in the report.

The boy's gaze upon his mother pleaded for her to rescue him. His mother lowered her head toward her lap.

Jordan knew his mother didn't have $500 to bond out her son. But she did know her client could serve months or years awaiting trial.

Approaching the mother, Jordan said, "We'll get him out. It's just going to take a little longer than anticipated."

One sister handed the mom a $100 bill. The other gave the mom $50.

Lawyers were like journalists. They weren't supposed to show emotions or get involved in situations where they represented clients or reported events. Leaving the courtroom, Jordan had to make a decision. Was she going to try to save every client that Judge Goodwin ruled against, or was she simply going to do her job and nothing more?

Exiting the building, Jordan stood on the steps of the county courthouse, then texted Victoria, **I need a HUGE favor.**

Returning to her office, Jordan told her assistant, "Hold all calls."

The first thing Jordan did was kick off her heels and close her door. She knew Victoria would bond the man out, but Jordan already felt guilty for asking.

She phoned the one person she knew would make her heart smile, Langston Derby.

"Hey, babe. How's your day going?" he asked.

"Horribly," she answered. "The system sucks."

"Well, fortunately for you, I do, too," Langston joked.

Laughing, she said, "What do you have for a headache?"

"You forgot? I have magical hands, and I'm running out to get your favorite bottle of wine, and I'm going to swing by the grocery store for butter pecan. Come by."

Jordan already felt less stressed.

Her assistant buzzed on the intercom. "Hold on," Jordan said, placing Langston on hold.

"Yes, Tia," Jordan said.

"Donovan Bradley Senior is here. He won't say why," her assistant stated.

Unmuting her cell, Jordan told Langston, "I have to take this."

"No problem, babe. I'll be waiting and I'll cook your dinner and bathe you tonight," Langston said, ending with, "Text me your ETA."

This was the last time she was allowing Donovan to ignore protocol. If he wanted to meet with her, next time he'd need an appointment.

She told Tia, "Send him in."

Entering her office, Donovan wore a navy-colored slim suit with his jacket opened. A tan shirt was buttoned up to the collar. Nearly one hundred degrees was the high for the day. Buzzed haircut. Clean-shaved. His cologne greeted her before him.

"Don't say anything, I won't be long. I came to thank you for helping me to get justice for my son, but I'm concerned about the number of cases you're losing. By the way, you look hotter than all outdoors. Maybe that's why you're not winning. Tone it down when we go to court. No one is going to take you seriously in that tight dress. If I may, I'll send you a stylist."

Jordan stood, placed her hand on the doorknob. "Tia," she politely said.

"Yes, Ms. Jackson," she answered.

"Introduce Mr. Bradley to our male partners. I think his concerns are more suited for the opposite gender. Do have an amazing day, Donovan," Jordan stated.

Barely waiting for his ass to cross the threshold, Jordan closed her door.

CHAPTER 41

Kingston

"**L**et's get out for brunch. Go to Copeland's. Then we can go to my shop. I've been dying to get your other measurements," Theodore suggested. Rolling onto his side, he rested his elbow on the mattress; with his chin in his palm, he fluttered his eyelids. His fingertips touched his cheek.

"All you can eat" deliciousness came to Kingston's mind immediately. Lilly had taken him there on a Saturday. Fried catfish nuggets. Omelets made to order. Crawfish étouffée. Shrimp creole. Red beans and rice. Lamb chops. Freshly carved ham. Grits. Bacon. Eggs. Chocolate chip cookies. Banana pudding. Pasta. Salads. Alcoholic beverages starting at 12:30 p.m., but that was on Sundays. All that, and live music. Kingston's mouth watered at the thought of the Creole jambalaya. He got full thinking about the calories.

"I do want to make it to your clothing store. That'll be dope." Now that he was permanently in the ATL, Kingston could establish and promote his unique style. And Theodore could be his assistant.

Tempting as the bottomless feast was, being seen with a man who'd exhibited feminine ways wasn't happening again. Secretly Kingston felt embarrassed witnessing that Theodore couldn't completely contain his public display of affection while they were in

B-More at the Inner Harbor. Kingston had never been on a da-da-da-da-da-date with a man. Theodore being comfortable with his sexuality made Kingston the opposite.

He'd pretended not to see Bianca in the lobby at the hotel in Baltimore. Kingston prayed she hadn't coupled him with Theodore. Kingston became upset at the thought that Theodore believed he could (but couldn't) mask his mannerisms whenever he chose. But how could Kingston ever stay angry with a lover so sweet.

"Tell you what. I'll consider it, but not today," he lied. "Why don't we order in, chill outside on the deck, and make . . . I mean have sex in the sunshine," Kingston said; then he raised his head and kissed Theodore.

Neither of them was under the sheet. Both of them were naked. If he had been at home with Monet, she'd be buried in cotton up to her collarbone.

Kingston's cell vibrated. Stretching his arm to the nightstand, he picked it up. Held it in front of his face.

Theodore stared at him. "Can we have one day," he asked, holding up a finger, "to ourselves without any outside interruptions? You don't see me picking up the phone every time I receive a text or a call."

"You don't have kids. I do." Kingston silently read the text from Langston, **What's up?**

Kingston scratched the nape of his neck to suppress the urge rising in his groin, then replied, **Nothing much,** then read an incoming message from Monet, **Thought you'd want to know the girls are in a play tomorrow.**

Why did you wait until the last minute to tell me? he responded, then read Langston's comment, **Your place. Tonight. 7pm? Somebody's gotta be on top this time, man, I'm about to bust for you.** It was followed by a scrumptious dick pic.

Thank God for whoever created privacy screens, Kingston thought, noticing Theodore leaning toward him.

Clearing his throat, Theodore interrupted, "Can you stop it? I'm lying right here next to you. The outsiders can wait their turn. Or I can leave now."

Why was bruh being extra? Always threatening to bail when

Kingston didn't give him his undivided attention. "You're right," Kingston told him, simultaneously responding to Langston, **Cool,** knowing it would be Langston on the bottom or another round of quiet and sloppy fellatio. Man, it had been hard not to scream and awaken Jordan.

Placing his cell underneath his pillow, Kingston rolled onto his side, facing Theodore. "When did you know you were different?"

"Oh, this is going to be good. Let me order our food first. I'll surprise you with something savory and delicious," Theodore said.

Kingston texted Monet: **What time tomorrow? And what play?** He was close enough to make it if he tried.

Watching Theodore tap on his phone, Kingston admired the joy in his friend's eyes. Every part of Theodore's face lifted a fraction of an inch as he uttered aloud, while using his thumbs, "One juicy rib eye steak, a rack of lamb, both medium-well. A lil pink is okay." He measured a slit of space between his thumb and pointing finger. "Don't send me no bleeding cow. I promise I'll send it back with a box of maxi pads."

Theodore paused. He glanced at Kingston. "Give me kiss." Continuing, he typed and talked. "Add a scramble of red potatoes, sausage eggs, and jack cheese, country potatoes, grits, brown rice, a large side of spinach, and two tall pineapple juices. You want coffee?" he asked, then said, "Of course, we do. It's not like you have any in the kitchen. We need to go grocery shopping today."

That heavy of a meal was going to make both of them lazy after eating. "I have to hop a flight later. We only have three hours. Plus, my relator wants to show me a property she thinks the family will like," Kingston lied.

"Huh? What? The order is in. Should be here in forty minutes. You're going to have to push that appointment back. After we eat, you're next," Theodore said, then licked his lips. "It's going to take me at least five hours to digest everything."

What Theodore had said sounded good, but in three hours tops, they were going to be completely dressed from head to toe and on the other side of the front door. Kingston would make a few stops, then double back to the house.

Putting the focus on Theodore, Kingston said, "Answer my question."

"When did I know I was gay?" Theodore clarified.

Propping his elbow on the firm pillow and his cheek on his fist, Kingston gave Theodore his undivided attention, praying what he was about to hear would help him move forward in making a decision.

"God made me this way in the womb." Theodore moved his mouth as though he were chewing.

Kingston didn't mean to, but he burst into laughter. "Bruh. God didn't do that to you."

Defensively Theodore stated, "How you know? You ain't God. I was never sexually attracted to girls. Then when I found out they bleed from down there." Theodore's eyes protruded; he pointed toward his penis, then flopped onto his back. "*Eew!* That was it for me."

A menstrual cycle was like a self-cleaning oven. Kingston knew HIV wasn't a gay man's disease, but he believed it was easier for a woman on her period to transfer blood to a man during oral sex than to contract it sucking dick.

Kingston laughed at his lover, then asked, "What was your first anal experience like, bruh?" recalling being in the janitor's closet.

Theodore sat up. Pressed his back against the headboard. Bending his knees, he buried his face between his thighs and wept.

Kingston retrieved his cell, powered it off. He went to the kitchen, grabbed a bottle of cognac and two snifters. Filling both glasses, he returned to Theodore's bedside and tried to place one in his hand.

Shaking his head, Theodore cried, "I hate him!"

Swallowing a gulp of liquor as though it was a shot, Kingston set the empty glass on the nightstand, scooted next to Theodore, then embraced his trembling body.

"I'm sorry, bruh. For real." Kingston had been emotionally distraught before, but he didn't hate anyone. He empathized with his friend, wondering what truly happened. "Were you raped?"

Theodore nodded and sniffled. "He hurt me. They hurt me."

Fuck! *"They?"*

Nodding again, Theodore said, "An officer broke me in."

What the hell? Is Theodore serious? "A police officer?" Kingston wanted, and didn't want, to know more. What good would that do? "Fuck that. He'll get his."

"Military officer. You're the first person that I've told." Slowly lifting his head, Theodore warned Kingston, "You've got to be careful who you meet off- and online. Men are cruel. Human trafficking in Atlanta doesn't only happen to women. One-point-five million black men are missing in America."

Now Kingston wanted to hear the rest of Theodore's story. "It's going down like that in the military?"

Had the military guy done it to establish dominance? How many men had he done that shit to? Or did he take advantage of men because there were no females in his camp and he hadn't had sex in months?

Same-sex relations were going down in professional sports, but they, too, had a "don't ask, don't tell" policy, like the military used to have. What really made him attracted to men? Kingston questioned himself.

"As a straight man, which you're not, but if you were, what would you do if you were stationed overseas and didn't see—I mean, as in 'laid eyes on'—a woman for years, with an *s*?" Kingston knew if Theodore opted to masturbate, that much jacking your dick was unhealthy.

Theodore's body slid flat against the mattress.

Hmm. He realized the answer wasn't easy. But under no circumstance would Kingston force himself on a woman or a man. What had happened to Theodore was criminal.

"I love you, Kingston. There's nothing I won't do for you. Leave your wife and come out so we don't have to hide." His gaze focused on the motionless ceiling fan at a time when Theodore should've made eye contact.

Kingston enjoyed the company of a man, but he never wavered from the fact that he didn't want a relationship with one. "I hear you." And he was nobody's fool. "Sit up, bruh."

Handing a glass to Theodore, Kingston refilled, then held up his. "To friendship forever. What's most important was your opening up to me." *With that make-believe story,* he thought. It was a good try by Theodore to win his heart, but Kingston didn't believe that military officers raped men. Women, yes. Dicks were confused.

Clinking their glasses, Theodore sipped, then passionately kissed Kingston on the lips. "I'm going to freshen up. When the delivery comes, sign for it. It's paid for."

"Cool. Use one of the guest bathrooms," Kingston replied.

Theodore mumbled, "Humph. That's a first."

"Close the door behind you." Soon as Theodore was out of the room, Kingston powered on his cell, texted Langston, **Send me something naughty to get me started.**

A picture of Langston's asshole appeared. *Damn! That is tight.*

Kingston never had a yearning to penetrate his wife's rectum. Maybe he was meant to be with Langston and not Theodore. Perhaps Langston's equally yoked masculinity better matched his personality.

Don't leave me hanging, Langston texted.

Kingston had no naked photos of himself saved in his phone. Whenever he'd taken one, he'd delete it right away. **Give me a sec.**

Spreading his thighs, Kingston positioned the phone at his groin. He lifted his balls. Raised his knees to his ears, then clicked the side button. It wasn't the greatest angle. He lightened the pic. Zooming in on the hairs, he smiled proudly, thinking that was definitely a virgin butthole. He shared the picture with Langston.

Are you and Jordan still involved? Kingston inquired.

Why not? She's fine as hell, great in bed and at giving head. Plus, if I ever need a lawyer, she's an orgasm away.

Bastard. **You can't do both of us. She's going to find out.**

How? Langston texted back. **You want exclusivity with me?**

Kingston recalled his moment at Langston's place. Considering both of them were toppers and virgins, Kingston wanted to be Langston's first, but under no circumstance would he be Langston's or any man's first bottom.

Your asshole, bro, Langston texted, then added, **#Priceless.**

Ding. Ding. Ding. The doorbell chimed.

Opening the bedroom door, Kingston called out to Theodore from the foyer, "I got it, baby."

CHAPTER 42

Kingston

"I like how you added a personal touch to this Airbnb. I can trick out whatever home you buy. Develop and add your branding. Let me house search with you," Theodore pleaded.

As he opened the front door, sunlight blinded Kingston. He placed his hand above his brows. The sky was a bright blue. A perfect afternoon to end with Theodore, and prepare to share with Langston.

Kingston held his cell in front of his face. No new messages from his next guest. Pretending to be looking at the trees surrounding his place, he had to get Theodore off of the premises before he crossed paths with Langston.

"Nah, nah, nah. That would be inappropriate, bruh." Kingston kissed Theodore. "Tell you what, I'll give you a call when I'm done with Lilly," he lied, then lied again. "I'll invite you back over to spend the night."

"I thought you had to catch a flight." He placed his hand on his hip.

"That's exactly why I need you. Forgot that quick. My girls' recital is tomorrow," Kingston lied.

There was no way Kingston would let Theodore know that this was his property.

A short huff was followed with, "When you're done house shopping for her, meet me at my men's clothing store. I can introduce you to my business partner and we can give you a private showing. Together," Theodore said. His lips curved as he tilted his head, then looked at Kingston out of the corners of his eyes. Standing in the doorway, Theodore awaited a response.

A ménage à trois. Hmm. The thought was intriguing. *Might have to take Theodore up on that offer soon, depending on what his partner looks like.* Kingston only liked men who were physically fit.

Sex between the two of them was filled with passion. That was cool, but if Kingston wanted intimacy all the time, he'd go home to Monet. Now that he'd experienced his inner-beast, animalistic side, Kingston preferred it rough—thrusting, banging, shoving, grabbing, groping. Furniture-moving, accidentally-breaking-a-lamp kind of sex had never happened with Theodore.

Redirecting his attention from the underground sexcapades he'd solicited before and after church on Sundays, Kingston left the door opened, then escorted Theodore to his car, which was parked in the private driveway.

Lying was becoming second nature to Kingston. "If I finish by eight, I'll stop by."

Thumb in the front, fingers on his back, Theodore propped his hand on his hip. "We're not going to be sitting around waiting for you to show up." Theodore stood outside his car, staring directly into Kingston's eyes. "I need a commitment."

Theodore's tone was more personal than professional. Kingston bit his bottom lip and thought, *Get your sensitive ass the fuck outta my face.* He never wanted to regret physically harming Theodore. But Theodore wasn't helping the situation by trying to force a relationship.

"Are you seeing someone else?" Theodore questioned.

Annoyed with Theodore's procrastination about leaving, Kingston replied, "Nah. I'm not seeing anyone," hoping to piss him off enough to make him go.

"Anyone *else.*" Getting in his car, Theodore lowered the window, then said, "Don't let me catch you cheating on me. You'll be added to that number of black men missing." His tires screeched against the pavement as he sped out of the driveway.

A dirty cloud trailed Theodore's car. When the smoke cleared, black tracks remained on the concrete. Astonished that men could be more desperate than women, Kingston got in his SUV, exited through the gate, then drove to the nearest liquor store.

Kingston purchased two bottles of Rémy Martin XO cognac. Returning home, he went directly to the kitchen. Kingston placed the brunch leftovers into skillets, tossed the containers into a trash bag, and disposed of it in the can in the outdoor garage.

He generously sprayed air freshener and opened windows throughout the house, giving a few extra squirts in his bedroom. Quickly changing the linen on his bed, he fluffed his pillows.

A text registered from Langston: **At your front door.**

Damn, bruh! No heads-up. And he'd gotten through the security gate without a code. How? Kingston texted Lilly, **What's up with the security gate on this property? Just had a visitor show up at my front door?**

Lilly promptly replied, **Okay, we need to do a reset on all codes. You probably have an 1111, 9999, or simple combo that previous homeowners used for landscapers. I can stop by now and show you how to reprogram your system.**

Kingston messaged her back, **No. I'm walking out right now. I'll let you know if I can't figure it out.**

Kingston hadn't showered. Theodore's bodily fluids were all over him. Opening the front door, Kingston was caught off guard with an aggressive kiss.

Unsure if he should respond in kind or resist based on the intrusion, Kingston stepped back. "There's time for that, bruh. Let's eat out on the deck."

The backyard was Theodore's and his haven. Kingston shouldn't taint the energy by chilling there with Langston, but it was Kingston's house.

"Man, you know what I came for. I already ate. Plus, I don't like outdoor adventures, if you know what I mean. Let's have a drink in the living room. Don't want to scare the snakes when I whip out mine." Langston laughed.

Truth was, Kingston wasn't hungry, either, but he was accustomed to being the one in control. Turning off the burners in the kitchen, he missed Theodore already.

An incoming text prompted Kingston to remove his cell phone from his pocket. Theodore had messaged, **How's the house?**

I don't like this one, Kingston replied, then asked Langston, "How you liking the ATL?"

"Not nearly as much as I'm about to," he said, nodding as he sat on the sofa. "On second thought, I am hungry. Fix me a plate," Langston ordered. "I want to start this moment off right, like I did with Jordan."

Kingston retreated to the kitchen. Already his mood changed from being enthusiastic to wanting to kick Langston out of his house. Preparing two cocktails, he reentered the living room, handed a snifter to Langston, then set his glass and the bottle on the end table.

"Man, it smells good in that kitchen." Langston downed his drink in one swallow, then refilled his glass. "Go get my food. I told you I'm hungry."

Kingston retreated to the kitchen, carried two red square plates into the living room. "You ever been violated?" he inquired, then handed Langston his meal.

"That's my role. Indirectly. Got a date with Jordan tonight. Give me that." He took Kingston's plate, placed both on the coffee table, then handed Kingston the cocktail that he'd left on the end table. "Lighten up. No, I have not."

Disgusted with Langston's personality, Kingston gulped his cognac in a single swallow. Was Langston avoiding letting Kingston question what happened between them in elementary school?

Langston refilled his glass. "This time wait for me, bro. Let's take it to the head at the same time on the count of three."

"One. Two. Three. Motherfucker." Kingston tossed back his cognac. "I want to know what made you suck my dick in the janitor's closet?"

Following his lead, Langston did the same, then refilled their glasses. "You were weak. A follower, not a leader. An insecure little boy. You still are. All those years a standout player and you were never captain. You can't stand up to your wife. I'd fuck her in front of you."

"I've lost my appetite," Kingston stated. "You need to leave, bruh."

Picking up his plate, Langston stared at Kingston, then began eating the steak.

Kingston left his food untouched, checked his cell. Theodore texted, **Are y'all done yet?**

I don't like this house, either. Heading back to the Airbnb, Kingston replied, then told Langston, "Why the fuck you staring at me like you 'bout to do something?"

Calmly Langston said, "I am."

Another text from Theodore registered. Kingston's vision started to blur. He struggled to read it. He screenshot the message, went to his photos, enlarged the text, then read, **I know you don't like it, because you never saw it. Out of all the men you could've cheated on me with, you chose my business partner, Langston Derby. I warned your ass!**

Kingston blinked several times. He paused, rubbed his eyes, leaned back. As he struggled to focus, Langston's facial features became cloudy. Kingston could barely see his hand or the phone in it.

"Shit, bruh." Kingston's body slid off of the sofa onto the floor. Slowly his eyes opened, then closed. He fought to reopen them. His mind said to get up. His body couldn't move.

"I told you, bro. Somebody's gotta be on top." Langston rolled him over, facedown on the carpet.

The last thing Kingston recalled was when his pants were pulled to his ankles.

CHAPTER 43

Victoria

Victoria texted Heavenly his new gate and door code.
Dropping a pinch of matcha green tea powder into sixteen ounces of water, Victoria vigorously shook the bottle, then swallowed without stopping.

She spread a towel atop her nightstand, then filled the red Crock-Pot with water from the bathroom vanity. Carefully carrying the pot to her bedroom, she centered it on the plush cotton, plugged in the cord, then turned the switch to medium. Returning to her en suite, Victoria started their bathwater. More hot than cold water flowed into the Jacuzzi tub. The temperature should be a perfect lukewarm for her to bathe Heavenly when he arrived in an hour.

Kneeling on the padded bench in her casting room, Victoria's nakedness allowed each of her seven spiritual channels to become exclusively receptive to positivity. She laid a pair of medium purple boxer briefs, with a black waistband, on the altar in front of her. Purple because the most important aspect of sex was creativity.

To her left was a seven-inch-long (cloaked in red, yellow, and green linen) doll stuffed with straw. Red for passion. Yellow for optimism. Green for growth. She'd meticulously hand-painted Heavenly's features onto the face as she'd done with Tracy's image, which was on the bottom shelf below Willy's replica, which was perched on row two. She loved the way Willy's energy balanced her. At her right was a stack of money. Ten $100 bills.

Victoria intertwined a pair of black wooden beads between her fingers, then chanted, "Heavenly will forsake all others as long as he monetarily and otherwise benefits from all that I contribute to his well-being."

She placed the doll in a clear bowl, covered it with the beads, then filled the bowl with holy water. Victoria dripped blessed rose water on the stack of money. Racing to the Jacuzzi, she turned off the water, retraced her steps, to curse Heavenly's underwear.

Rubbing spiritual oil in her palms, she laid them on the crotch of the boxer briefs. "Heavenly's dick will get aroused for me and me only. The goddess in me takes total dominion over the god in Heavenly. No other woman shall stimulate Heavenly mentally or physically."

Carefully removing the beads and doll from the bowl, she placed them on the purple boxers, put the stack of cash on top, then rolled everything like a wrapped sandwich.

Victoria added lavender, sage, bitters, rose water, and oil to the clear dish where she'd stored his pubic hairs, then poured part of the potion onto the wrap. Warding off all females of interest, she prayed over the doll, "Heavenly will keep faithful unto me, Lord Jesus. Should he think of another female, his heart will truly skip a beat and his body shall twitch uncontrollably."

She placed the wrap inside an open pure amethyst stone by the window. Raising the blinds, she concentrated on how sunshine would beam on Heavenly as long as he kept unto her.

Cautiously she poured the remaining potion into a small glass bottle, sealed, then safely stored it on the top shelf, ensuring she had the same exact mixture to break the spell.

Returning to the bedroom, Victoria retrieved two pink crystal eggs. She inserted one in the pot, the other she'd buried in a glass of crushed ice, along with a waterproof Slim Jim and Luxe clit stimulators.

"Hello," Heavenly called out. "I'm here."

An hour had passed quickly. That, or he'd arrived early. Victoria made certain to completely close the door to the casting room.

"Hey, handsome," she said, lightly planting a kiss on his lips. "Wait for me *in* the Jacuzzi."

"That's what's up." He smiled, rubbing his palms together.

Oh, she'd almost forgotten her final step. While Heavenly entered her bedroom, she hurried to her casting room. Removing the bottle from the top shelf, Victoria returned to her en suite, drizzled three drops of the voodoo love potion that would make Heavenly unable to get an erection every time he thought of another woman.

"That smells good," he said, then turned on the jets. "What is it?"

Victoria answered, "Love oil."

Not leaving anything to chance, Victoria drizzled three more of her special love drops into the Crock-Pot, then soaked two face towels. An incoming call redirected her attention. Placing the open bottle of love potion on the nightstand, she quickly put a glass container of Kama Sutra oil inside the pot, then secured the lid.

"Hello," she politely answered, knowing that it could be a robo call or important business.

"Is this Victoria Fox?" a woman asked.

"Please state the nature of your call," Victoria insisted.

"Hold on," the woman stated.

Picking up the small bottle of love potion, she placed the phone between her shoulder and ear, then retrieved the top.

"It's getting lonely in here," Heavenly sang.

She pressed the mute button, then told him, "Give me one minute, handsome."

Unmuting the call, Victoria walked to the casting room to store the bottle on the top shelf. The woman said, "I was double-checking. You're listed as William Copeland's emergency contact. Is that correct?"

Victoria stood still. Her breathing became heavy. "That's correct."

"Mr. Copeland suffered a heart attack and was pronounced dead on arrival at the hospital."

Victoria, the bottle of love potion, and her cell phone fell to the floor.

CHAPTER 44

Chancelor

Build it and they'd come.

Chancelor entered the Gathering Spot, proceeded to the conference room he'd reserved for the day. Membership afforded the luxury of his not having to enter into a long-term lease of office space and furniture.

He powered on his computer.

Developers in Atlanta were learning that despite their best efforts, people weren't instantly gravitating toward their shopping communities and luxury apartment complexes simply because their properties were new.

One. Two. Three. Four. Five. Six. Seven people approached the glass-enclosed room. Chancelor waved, motioning for them to come inside.

"Welcome," he said, repeating, "Welcome. Help yourself to a hot or cold beverage. Sit wherever you'd like."

Helping start-ups was his preference, but established corporations compensated him a lot more. His phone screen illuminated. Tracy's photo appeared. His heart raced; he wanted to answer. The call went to voice mail. He prayed she'd leave a message.

"Any questions before we get started?" Chancelor asked.

"Ready when you are, Mr. Leonard," the CEO announced, holding his cream-colored mug with one hand, but not using its handle.

Noticing his wedding band, Chancelor scanned the ring fingers of the others. Based on symbolism, he was the only single person present.

Great. The earlier I finish, the sooner I can hit up Tracy.

"I've reviewed your package. If you want to elevate your brand, you're going to have to invest millions into marketing. Here's why my company is the perfect match for yours." Chancelor began his PowerPoint presentation with statistical data of his success rate in the Atlanta metropolitan area based on client surveys and their consumers' satisfaction.

His phone lit up again. It was her . . . again. He hated ignoring Tracy, but he had to. For now.

"Let's take Ponce City Market and compare it to the Shops at Buckhead. What do they have in common?" he asked the developers, who were preparing to break ground on a mixed-use three-hundred-thousand-square-foot building in midtown.

The all-white, predominantly male group looked at one another. The guy at the opposite end of the rectangular-shaped table, next to the CEO, spoke. "They're both purportedly being acquired by new owners."

"Correct. New management is one thing, but the sale of real estate originally intended to be held is an indicator that there's a problem. We know that," Chancelor said, then asked, "Why is this occurring?"

Silence filled the air. Either they were reluctant to give an uninformed answer, or did they think his presentation was rudimentary? Tracy's face reappeared on his cell. Her incoming calls and their being mute was unnerving. He prayed his services were contracted.

Chancelor was no fool. As much as he loved Tracy, making money came before bitches and whores.

Clicking to the next slide, Chancelor continued, "Research shows that many customers aren't aware of which retailers are located in those malls. The majority of the restaurants in both developments are not on the out-of-town visitors' top places to dine. One is extremely high-end and costs over one hundred dollars for two people to eat. The other has eateries with reasonable prices, but they also have menu items that don't cater to the majority. Kids want burgers, not veggies and fries, not sweet potatoes. Neither location comfortably accommodates families with children. Failure happens whenever there's a disconnect between the product and the people.

"You have to consider the income bracket of individuals relocating to Atlanta. And from what part of the country and the world they're coming from. Your proposal to build in midtown is only going to yield a return on your investment if you start by marketing it properly."

Observing seven poker faces, Chancelor was convinced that he needed this group more than they did him. He had to say something to create readable expressions.

As he moved along with his presentation, one of the developers interrupted with, "Midtown will take care of itself because the millennials are becoming the majority."

"Millennials on average don't waste their money on material things. They don't lock themselves into thirty-year mortgages or a high-cost rental. Hostels over hotels. Few of them commit to relationships. Fewer of them get married. And the women are opting on average to have kids around thirty-five."

Ready to end the meeting, and connect with Tracy, Chancelor began pacing.

Victoria had warned him, but what harm could he do touching Tracy? Dude had fucked her. Maybe Chancelor could stop off at the store and get himself a gas mask. That was it! Why hadn't he thought of that sooner?

One of the two women pushed away from the table, uncrossed, then crossed her legs in the opposite direction, before inquiring, "What do you suggest, Mr. Leonard? Marketwise."

Really? This was how she wanted to express herself? If Chancelor stared at the gap underneath her skirt, she'd be offended. He'd noticed her savvy sexiness when she first entered the room ahead of the rest. Her voluptuous curves were in all the right places, but he wasn't interested in what was between her creamy thighs.

Glad she'd asked, Chancelor replied, "I have trendsetting exclusives for you guys. I'll submit your proposal within the next three business days."

"What's it going to cost us?" one of the guys questioned.

"Somewhere between two-point-one and two-point-six million if you want to retain me for the first four to five years." Chancelor turned off his PowerPoint, placed his laptop in his brown leather cross-body bag.

"If you don't mind, we'll continue using the conference room," the CEO said.

Typically, Chancelor would stay and work on his plan, but not today. "Stay as long as you'd like. It's available until six o'clock."

Exiting the glass door, he had to find out what Tracy wanted.

Instead of calling, Chancelor decided to drive directly to Tracy's home. Parking in front of her gate, he dialed her number.

"Hey, Chancelor. Thanks for coming. I'm glad you're here." Tracy's voice was sweet. "Park in my circular driveway."

Chancelor got out of his car, trotted up the steps. It didn't matter why she'd called. He was there and happy they were back together again.

Tracy opened the door, wearing a leopard see-through top and short-ass jeans that hugged her ass the way Chancelor wanted to. He stared at her camel-toe imprint, then up at her face. She mumbled with her mouth closed.

Damn! I need that gas mask.

Frowning, he couldn't understand anything she'd said. Tears fell as Tracy reached into her back pocket, then handed him $4,000 and a note.

He was more impressed with the fact that anything other than her fit into those jeans.

Chancelor read: *I'm so sorry, Chancelor. I can't live in my house the rest of my life. Please forgive me. Give Victoria my condolences and ask her to undo whatever she did to me that day at church.*

If he made contact, was what Victoria told him true? Handing Tracy the money, Chancelor kept the note to show Victoria. "Don't worry. I'll make her break the spell," he said to impress Tracy, knowing he had no control over Victoria's actions.

Tracy hugged Chancelor, then leaned her head on his chest and cried without parting her lips.

"I love you." Consoling her, Chancelor added, "It's okay, baby."

Cupping her nose, Tracy stepped back, then slammed the door.

"Tra . . . Oh. Damn!" Chancelor cupped his hand over his mouth, ran down the stairs to his car.

Texting Victoria, **I'm on my way to your house. I have a $2.6 million deal to present in three days and my mouth smells like shit!!!!!!!**

He sped out of Tracy's driveway.

CHAPTER 45

Jordan

Since she'd dated Donovan Bradley Sr., Jordan hadn't placed a picture of a man on her desk. Bloodsucking vampires looking for a comeuppance were posting inappropriate images and comments on Donovan's social media pages. Representing him was beginning to feel more like having an asshole celebrity client than a mourning dad.

The photo of Langston wasn't one that he'd given her. Or one from his profile on the app CelibateNoMore. Brown snakeskin hard-sole shoes, a tan slim-fit suit, with a pink button-up shirt, matching fedora, dark sunglasses, and his left sleeve pulled up just enough to see the face of his designer watch. She'd found that seductive pic in her search engine.

Sitting at her desk, Jordan thought about her new guy and her next orgasm. Langston was definitely worth her waiting for the right man. She closed her eyes, recalling how attentive he was in bed. The tingling in her pussy radiated throughout her entire body. That old feeling of being in love, when she didn't think it was ever going to happen again, made every moment of her day easier.

No judge, solicitor, or juror could ruin her high. Skimming through her client's file, Jordan was determined to have a ruling in her favor today.

She sent a text to Langston: **Can't wait to see you tonight**.

He replied, **I have a surprise for you. I'll text you the address. Can you be there at 6pm?**

Yes, she messaged back.

Blowing a kiss at his picture, Jordan placed her client's folder in her briefcase. Exiting her office, she told Tia, "I won't be back after court today. Forward my calls to my cell. After six hold all calls, except for Wilson Ealy's."

"If you don't mind my saying, Ms. Jackson, you are glowing." Tia smiled. "Whoever the new guy in the photo is, he must be a keeper."

"We'll see," Jordan stated, not wanting to appear anxious.

En route to the courthouse, Jordan received a text message from Victoria. "Siri, read my recent text message."

Siri said, in an Australian man's voice, "You have one unread text message from Victoria Fox. 'Just left the morgue. Had to identify William Copeland's body. Found a handwritten will on his dining-room table, leaving half of his estate to Tracy Benjamin. Getting ready to burn it! Then flush it down the garbage disposal where it belongs.' Would you like to reply?"

Jordan wasn't shocked regarding the note. Victoria hadn't mentioned William Copeland had been ill or killed. No need to worry about the unknown. As with DJ, there was nothing Jordan could do to bring him back. Her client who was on trial today was her priority.

"No," Jordan commanded Siri. She wished Willy hadn't put that information in writing, especially not for Tracy Benjamin. Victoria was a friend worth protecting, but her tampering with evidence was illegal. If Jordan were in Victoria's position, she would've done the same—except she wouldn't have told a soul.

Brother Copeland had lived a good life. There was no need to mourn his passing. He was never on the sick and shut-in list. He hadn't had a major surgery. Nor was he in hospice or given comfort care. Whatever happened was probably brief, because Willy looked fine at church last Sunday.

Jordan smiled at the thought that perhaps Tracy's breath sent Brother Copeland to an early grave. Parking in the lot at the courthouse, Jordan deleted Victoria's last message. Another incoming text message registered on her phone. This time from Levi.

He asked, **Have you heard from Kingston?**

No. Why? I'm heading into court now. Have a date tonight with Langston. I'll reach out to Kingston. What do you want me to tell him?

I have a table for the concert tonight at Mable House. Ask if he's interested in going. And he was supposed to wire me $10,000.

That was nice of Levi, but the money was his initial concern. Seemed as though he and Kingston were becoming good friends. A table at that venue was normally for six people. If Kingston was there with Levi, Jordan didn't have to worry about him popping up on her date with Langston.

She texted Kingston while walking: **Levi has a concert ticket for you for a show tonight. Call him . . . now.**

Checking the calendar outside the door, she confirmed that Judge Goodwin was presiding. Jordan strutted inside, dressed in a crimson suit, white blouse, and four-inch stilettos. After checking in, Jordan greeted her client.

"Let me speak with the solicitor. If she offers a plea deal for forty hours of community service, I recommend we take that deal. Anything more, I suggest we go before the judge." Jordan was not going to be intimidated by Judge Goodwin.

The judicial system was corrupt. Attorneys knew that. While judges could be removed from their jurisdiction, a judge could never be fired. That meant they would move from one location to another. Jordan believed that judges weren't above the law; in many instances, they circumvented the law.

Jordan informed the solicitor that her client was a forty-five-year-old black male, never in trouble with the law, and his charge was a misdemeanor, not a felony. To her dismay the solicitor offered one-year probation, forty hours of community service, and ten anger management classes. All based on obstruction because he'd asked why his father was being arrested.

Her bigger question was, was this a case worth taking to trial? After the judge was seated, Jordan requested to approach the bench. Surprised the judge had approved, Jordan asked that the case be thrown out due to the fact that her client had the right to inquire about his father.

Motioning for the solicitor, the judge heard his side of the case. She looked at Jordan's client, who was dressed in a navy long-sleeved, button-up shirt that neatly hung outside of his slacks, then said, "Case dismissed."

Speechless, Jordan quickly escorted her client out of the court-house. Repeatedly he thanked her, as she'd done the same to God. Whatever had altered Judge Goodwin's attitude, Jordan hoped the old judge that she knew was back.

She texted Langston, **I finished early. Can meet you at 5pm**.

Cool. Can you bring a bottle of Rémy Martin XO cognac, baby?

Since this was his first time asking her to bring something, she stopped at the liquor store, purchased the alcohol and a bottle of wine for herself. With traffic the ETA to her residence was thirty minutes.

Showering, Jordan slipped into a spaghetti-strapped outfit that granted easy access to her vagina. She skipped the underwear, then texted Langston, **omw!**

Running a few minutes behind. Let yourself in, he replied, includ-ing the gate and door codes.

Jordan instructed Siri, "Call Victoria Fox."

"I'm picking out an urn, let me call you back," she answered.

"No, you will not hang up this phone. Didn't you just identify Willy's body?" Jordan turned off of the highway and onto a side street.

"I have to have Willy cremated before the vultures start circling, demanding an autopsy that I'd have to pay for. By the time his next-of-kin is notified, one, he's deceased, and two, they're not get-ting shit, the services will be over and I'll be away on vacation." Vic-toria never would've been a lawyer. Her skills and schedule were more suitable for real estate. Jordan seldom had time to get away.

"I'm on my way to meet Langston for a date. I'll pin-drop you my location when I arrive. Bye." Jordan ended the conversation, laughing at Victoria.

Jordan drove onto a private road that led to a gated home surrounded by trees. Granted access, she parked in the driveway, pranced up the stairs with the bottles in hand. Pressing the code on the keypad, she shoved open the door, using her hip.

Tracking through the foyer, she entered the living area, then froze. Wine and cognac slipped from her fingers. A broken lamp lay on the floor. On the coffee table was one plate of food covered with flies that buzzed around a framed photo of Kingston with a man. That man was Levi. Dark, spotted trails stained the carpet leading toward the garage exit.

As she walked backward, the room resembled what Jordan was all too familiar with . . . a crime scene. There was no need to text Langston or Levi.

Jordan left the door open, and she was certain that her fingerprints, footprints, tire tracks along the road, would link her to whatever had happened.

CHAPTER 46

Kingston

Creeeak.

Here we go, he thought.

As a man, he felt being raped was emasculating. Having been a standout athlete that children and adults looked up to, he wasn't going to seek sympathy for what was happening to him. Nor ask his wife to forgive him. There was only one person he had to make things right with. Going from the top to the bottom, for the first time in his life, Kingston prayed, "God, please let me die."

Wumpth! The sound of the door closing meant it was that time again. A time when Kingston knew he was going to be violated. Again.

Click. He hoped he never heard the sound of a door opening, closing, or locking for as long as he lived, but that would be unrealistic, unless he'd become deaf. As life-threatening as his situation was, he didn't wish evil on anyone, including his predators.

Fuck that lie! He wanted to castrate every last one of his rapists, starting with Langston. Kingston was conscious enough to feel Langston penetrating him, but whatever drug he'd put in his drink made him too weak to fight back.

"I saw the ad online. How much for today's special?" Kingston heard a man eagerly ask.

He wasn't the first to make such an inquiry. Kingston had lost count days ago, around 101. Nothing Theodore claimed he'd gone through compared to what Kingston was enduring. Maybe being set up by Langston was God's way of punishing him for lying to Monet about his sexuality.

Gagged, lying facedown on a mattress with no sheet, Kingston constantly heard car engines starting and stopping. The *swish* sound of fast-moving cars and frequent, extended horn blowing in the distance (at certain times) meant he was possibly close to a freeway.

His arms ached from being stretched wide, and his legs, too. The assaults had occurred so many times, yet each situation was psychologically detrimental and physically traumatic as the previous one.

If he could kill himself right this second, he wouldn't hesitate. The humiliation had already squashed his pride.

"Five hundred for fifteen minutes," someone stated with the same male's voice he'd listened to for what might be a week, but felt like an eternity. "He's famous. And newly broken in. Definitely worth the price."

"Newly broken in," my ass, Kingston thought, having heard dude tell that lie each time. Whatever they were power-washing his rectum with caused him to tighten up after each offense.

Blindfolded, Kingston couldn't confirm if it was day or night. The sound of cars was his greatest indicator. He'd never felt sun on his back. The room was always cold. Colder when the predator's sweat slushed against his body. What Kingston could calculate was feeding time. Soon he'd eat the same meal.

"How much to do him raw?" the man questioned.

You don't have enough money to run up in me with no protection, Kingston thought. *Men are fucking dogs.*

How would Kingston explain to his daughters that he was a liar and a cheat? How could he protect them when he couldn't trust his own judgment about loving Theodore Ramsey or hating Langston Derby?

Theodore was mad at him, but Kingston prayed he'd never set him up like this. Or had he? They'd met on a dating app. Suddenly, he wished he'd asked Jordan to do a background check on Theodore.

Kingston believed whether he'd gone to the shop to meet Theodore's partner or stayed at his house that was currently in Lilly's, he'd still be facedown about to be fucked again. Certain that Langston had slipped something into his drink, never again would Kingston's lips savor the taste of alcohol.

"An additional hundred," the familiar voice enthusiastically quoted.

Kingston could've answered that question.

Not sure of what the customer had paid for, Kingston knew not to protest this time. He'd find out momentarily. Shaking his head, moving his body, any of those things could result in his being tortured after hearing, *creak, wumpth, click,* signaling the customer was gone.

Movement along the sinking mattress crept slowly from his ankles, to his legs, to his knees, then to his inner thighs. No cool, slippery solution slithered between his butt cheeks, which meant dude was going in raw. Next there was the sensation of a stiff poke that glided inside him until he felt balls pushing against his.

Men are fucking dogs! He now understood that to be factual. Before his abduction into human trafficking, Kingston would readily say "some men, not all." The number of predators, including the one on top of him, made Kingston realize he was a different type of abuser—not a rapist—but he was definitely a serial cheater, if only to his wife. For that, he prayed he'd live long enough to apologize to Monet.

Kingston began counting the seconds. One thousand one. One thousand two. One thousand three.

The man began to grunt. "You're right. This is good shit."

If no one was watching, guys would do anything to cum.

One thousand five hundred sixty-two. The man oinked like a pig. Stroked harder. Thrust faster. Kingston's already soaked blindfold became wetter as he wept. Enduring the pain, he didn't feel worthy of asking God for mercy. If he could bite his lips, he would. But the ball secured inside his mouth made motion impossible.

His tongue. His teeth. His face. Every part of his body was in excruciating pain.

One thousand eight hundred forty-nine. Fifty-one seconds remained.

"Oh, shit!" the man yelped. "I'm cumming," then added, "Shit, I'm fucking cumming inside a famous dude."

Praying this man would pull out, Kingston's countdown was five, four, three, two, one. Done!

"Your time's up," the familiar voice stated. "Pull out now."

"That was fucking awesome, man! Blasted that one off in the nick of time. If you're running the same special tomorrow, I'll be back," he said, sounding like a regular.

Click. Creak. Wumpth.

"Time is money. Clean him up. Feed him. The next customer is booked in ten minutes."

The ball gag was removed from his mouth. Someone shoved lumpy mashed potatoes into his mouth. It was the same meal each time, followed with a few ounces of water. A tube slid into his rectum. Pressure. Suction. More pressure. More suction to vacuum out his feces and the last guy's cum. Next came the urinal, then the wet bed pad was replaced with a dry one.

"Okay, that's good enough. Let the next guy in," the familiar voice directed.

"Wait," a woman's voice interjected. "Look. He's on television. Reportedly missing. We have to release him."

"Bitch, you crazy? When he dies, if we don't kill him first, we'll change his name, ship his body to our mortuary, cremate his ass, then scatter his ashes in the forest like all the rest. Or sell him. But we never release them. Like I said, let the next guy in," the guy with the familiar voice commanded.

Levi might've been in on Kingston's abduction. He was probably upset when Kingston refused to loan him $10,000. The only person Kingston needed to believe was not involved was Theodore. He had to look into his eyes and ask if he knew what was going to happen. Langston was definitely a culprit. Then there was Lilly sitting on the deed to his home that was paid in full.

None of this would've happened to him if he'd stayed in Columbia.

"Hey," a man way too jovial for Kingston's fragile state of mind said, "how many more runs can we get on this asshole?"

Wait! No *click, creak,* or *wumpth.* That meant bruh was in the room the entire time.

That's him! His voice was familiar and he was hearing it for the first time. Kingston was positive it was Langston Derby. It sounded exactly like him.

"'Bout one-fifty, two hundred tops, if we speed up the pace," the guy who was giving orders from day one casually stated. "The media might pose a problem."

"The police aren't out there looking for missing black dudes. That's why I don't kidnap bitches, especially the white ones with blond hair and blue eyes. And I'm keeping his lawyer friend preoccupied."

Kingston felt lips against his ear. "Outside of her cases all Jordan Jackson can think about is my dick."

The other man stated, "Don't get sloppy or comfortable, man. That's how niggas get busted."

Langston bragged, "I've been selling ass for ten years. Never been caught. Just in case, double up. Run him 'til he's done. Don't let his daily drop below thirty grand," he said with that arrogant Langston tone when he demanded being served food that night at his house.

"Gotta go check on my other moneymakers," that bastard said.

Kingston felt a finger slide in his rectum. "Great job on the cleansing and tightening. I'll be on-site making rounds for a few hours, if you need me. I'll send in the next customer."

Click. Creak. Wumpth.

Kingston heard, "Yeah, man. I responded to an online ad."

Now Kingston prayed he'd live long enough to kill the little boy that violated him in the janitor's closet.

CHAPTER 47

Monet

"Ah . . . yes." Monet inhaled slowly.

Cairo's middle finger had been inside of her the entire time they'd watched the morning show. She relaxed as he massaged her G-spot. Using his other hand, he teased her clit.

"Right there. Yes. Yes. Don't stop. Right there. Right there." Monet inhaled, then exhaled a long *"Yasssss."*

Perhaps it was better not to have known what she was missing. Cairo was better in bed than Kingston. Sex with her husband was amazing—not lately—but being with Cairo was next-level mind-blowing orgasmic.

Cairo replaced his finger with his mouth. Softly sucking her clitoris nonstop, he continued stroking her G-spot. He stopped performing oral copulation. Started. Stopped. Started. Stopped. Each time he switched it up, Monet's excitement grew stronger. She stared at the television, trying not to cum.

The pressure inside of her vagina was ready to explode. But she didn't have to tell him that. There was something different about Cairo. He understood her body more than her husband did. Monet wasn't sure if that was a learned or natural ability he shared with all of his women, or it was just her. The answer didn't matter.

Sucking her clit firm, while fast fingering her with the same motion, he didn't stop this time.

"Yes. Yes. Yes." Inhaling, Monet completely relaxed. Exhaling, she firmly bore down, using her vaginal muscles to push.

Juices squirted and gushed in Cairo's face, drenching his mattress pad at the same time. Cairo massaged his face with her fluids. Circled his tongue around his lips. Picked up the wet pad, folded it, left the room, and returned without the pad.

Lying on top of the flat sheet, Monet cuddled in his arms, then said, "I need some dick to go with this squirt," as if she were ordering breakfast from a menu.

Getting on her hands and knees beside him, Monet faced the foot of the bed, then tilted her ass up, looking at him over her shoulder.

"You know it's about to go down, right?" Cairo ease behind her, rubbed his engorged head from her vaginal opening to her clitoris and back. "You ready for this hokey pokey?"

Monet laughed, smiled, then nodded.

Slowly he put the head in, then pulled it out. He put it back in two inches this time instead of one. And pulled back an inch. Massaging the small of her back, he went deeper three inches and pulled back one

Monet scooted toward his balls.

"Whoa!" Cairo shifted his hand from her back to her ass. "The kitchen. The living room. All that's yours. You know you don't control anything in this damn bedroom. Let me do my job, woman."

"Well, c'mon, man. I'm ready," Monet said. "Give it to me or I'ma hafta take it. And you know what—"

"A Columbia, Maryland, man is reported missing. He was last seen on surveillance camera at a liquor store in the Buckhead area of Atlanta, Georgia. You may be shocked to learn who this person is. If anyone has seen or knows the whereabouts of Kingston Royale"—Monet fell flat onto Cairo's bed. She stared up at her husband's photo on the screen as she listened to the newscaster continue—"contact the police department immediately. Again, Kingston Royale, the retired star basketball player, is reported missing."

Monet scurried atop the eggplant-colored Egyptian sheet. Cairo was still on his knees. Stunned, Monet sat on the edge of the mattress, motionless.

Was this a stunt for Kingston to live two separate lives? Report himself missing, then disappear from her life? Her husband had been voluntarily missing since he'd left his family, but it wasn't official if enforcement hadn't contacted her. Regretting not trying harder to effectively communicating with Kingston, she stood.

Cairo spread his arms, then hunched his shoulders. His hard dick pointed toward the ceiling.

Walking away from him, Monet entered the closet, then slid her dress over her head.

She stepped back into the bedroom. "I've got to go," she quietly told Cairo.

A hot shower to rid herself of his bodily fluids would've been appropriate, but time didn't permit. Sitting on the foot of the bed, she put on her stilettos.

"Why are you going, baby?" Cairo questioned.

"Because I have to!" Why couldn't he respect that? Monet lowered her voice. "Sorry. It's my fault. You don't deserve this."

"I don't understand what Kingston Royale going missing has to do with us? Why are you leaving me?" Cairo stated.

Shaking her head, Monet wished he'd stop talking. She looked at him. Monet didn't have any answers. Not good ones. She hadn't lied to Cairo, but she hadn't told him to whom she was married. She'd assumed he'd Googled her.

Just as Monet picked up her cell and took it off of silence, a call registered from Trinity. "Please give me a moment," she told Cairo, then answered, "Hey, Mama, I just saw the news. I have no idea where Kingston is."

Cairo's eyes narrowed. Lips tightened. He stared at her mouth as though he was reading her every word.

"Monet, where are you?" her mother firmly inquired.

"I'm leaving dance class right now," she lied. There was no way she'd confirm the affair her mother had alleged. "I'm heading to the school to pick up the girls early."

Leaning against the headboard, Cairo folded his arms high over his chest, then crossed his ankles.

"The acting school called you twice, and then they contacted me as your emergency person. The girls are upstairs at home. I got then. Why didn't you answer my or their calls? Where are you?" her mother questioned again.

Cairo got out of bed, entered his bathroom. *Good,* Monet said to herself.

"Get your story straight. It was acting classes you were taking. Stop lying to me. You dress up in the morning like you're going out at night. The second you started switching your ass, talking breathy, and being extra happy, it was obvious. The only thing that can make all of that happen overnight is good sex with a man. You're cheating on my son-in-law."

Everything her mother did was to protect the lifestyle Kingston had provided for each of them. Cairo entered the bedroom, hugged Monet from behind, rocked her from side to side, kissed her on the nape of her neck.

Rejecting his affection, she gently pushed him away, then shook her head.

"I recently added on the dance class to release my stress," Monet lied, emphasizing, *"Mother."*

Apparently, Trinity couldn't care less if Monet was miserable. She continued listening to her mother's abrasive tone.

"You're releasing your stress, all right. I need you to come home right now. There're some things I need to share with you, but not over the phone." Her mother whispered, "We can't take a chance on the authorities eavesdropping."

We? Monet huffed, knowing she had nothing to hide.

Cairo puckered to give her an enduring kiss on the lips. Monet covered his mouth. "I'm on my way," she said, ending the call with her mother.

Reaching for her purse, Monet said, "Sorry, but I have to leave."

"I can see that." He blocked her hand from gripping the handle on her bag. "Before you go, don't you think I deserve an explanation?" He wrapped his arms around her, then seductively pulled her to him.

Men! she screamed in her head. *If he had to go, he'd expect me to understand. What in the hell is wrong with him?*

This wasn't the proper time to tell him any more than he already knew.

"I want you to know I respect your home front. If you need to confide in me, I'm here for you. I have feelings for you, Monet. But I don't want to play games. You're a gorgeous woman that I'd love to call my own one day. I know what I've gotten myself into. Promise me you'll text or call and let me know how you're doing."

None of what was happening was Cairo's fault. He was a sweetheart.

Opening her mouth, she closed her eyes. When she felt their lips touch, Monet slid her tongue into his mouth, then suctioned his tongue into her mouth. Softly she caressed the nape of his neck.

As long as she resisted, she knew he'd find a reason to keep her there. Breaking their bond when she felt his hand on her breast, she agreed. "I promise."

Hurrying home, she parked in her garage and entered her house. She found her mother sitting alone in the living room.

"Are the girls still upstairs? Do they know what's going on?" was Monet's first question as she tossed her purse on the leather sofa.

"Of course, they know. They both have cell phones," her mother sarcastically mentioned.

Choosing her battles, she knew this wasn't one worth fighting. The only way the girls should've known their dad was missing was if their principal, their teachers, or her mom told them, because students weren't allowed to use phones during class.

"I've spoken with Israel and Nairobi. I've taken their phones and they're not allowed to watch TV until we agree on what to tell them."

Monet knelt at her mother's feet, placed her head on her mom's lap, and cried.

Scooting to the edge of the sofa, Trinity said, "Hush. Kingston will be okay. Grown men his age and size don't disappear without a trace. There's something I must share with you."

Sitting next to her mother, Monet grew angry as she listened to her mother explain how she'd secretly rented an Airbnb for Kingston. That wasn't enough. Her mom rented a second Airbnb and a third. Her mother had honored Kingston's request to keep his locations a secret between them. There were moments when Trinity claimed she had no idea where Kingston was living. Nor had she spoken with him recently.

Speechless, Monet created enough space where both of her children could've comfortably sat between them. Rocking back and forth, she shook her head. Gravely disappointed in her mom, Monet softly asked, "What else do you know? If you're going to lie again to me, Mother, I prefer you don't say anything at all. Because right now, I don't believe you don't know where Kingston is."

"The truth is, Kingston went to Atlanta to explore his—"

"What, Mother? Huh?" Monet prayed Bianca wasn't right.

Trinity hesitated, then said, "To explore his sexuality."

"So you're telling me that you know my husband is gay and you never told me?" Monet stood, then shouted at Trinity, "You told me not to pressure my husband! To give him time! Give him space! And all along you knew he was cheating on me with a man?"

This was the first time Monet was angry enough to punch her mother in the face.

"Lower your voice, Monet. The kids might hear," Trinity insisted.

"You didn't give a damn about my kids"—Monet slapped her chest repeatedly—"when my husband was out fucking a . . ." The next word was trapped in her throat.

Trinity stood, stretched her arm behind her back, then swung at Monet's face with an open hand. After she slapped her daughter, Monet shoved her mother on the sofa, straddled her, then held her biceps. "This is not a fight you want me to finish."

If it were true that her husband preferred being with a man, that was his right. She'd rather suffer through the woes of divorce than be married to a liar.

"Mommy! Mommy!" The girls ran toward them with their tablets in tow.

"Why are you fighting Grandma?" Israel asked, tugging at her arm with one hand. "Let her go. You're hurting her." She placed her iPad on the floor, then used both of her little hands to pull her.

"Thank you for rescuing Grandma." Trinity quickly stood.

"Grandma slipped and fell on the couch, honey. I was trying to keep her from falling to the floor," Monet lied. "You okay?" she asked her mom.

Trinity rolled her eyes, but did not respond.

"Where's Daddy?" Nairobi cried, pointing to the article about their father on her electronic notebook.

This was one of the few times Israel mimicked her sister. Tears ran down their faces.

Monet wasn't going to lie to her children. "I don't know, but I don't want you girls to worry. We're going to find him. Until we do, both of you will have to miss a few days from school."

Imagining the worst, Monet prayed Kingston was alive. But how did children cope with the death of a parent? She never considered that.

Drying her tears, Israel pleaded, "What good is staying home going to do? I'd rather go to school. I'll tell the kids my daddy is on vacation or something and he'll be back soon. The media makes mistakes all the time." She hunched her small shoulders.

"I don't want to go to school until Daddy comes home." Nairobi ran upstairs, crying.

"Go check on your sister," Monet insisted.

An incoming call registered from Bianca. Monet answered, "Hey, girl, I know you've heard."

"I'm on my way to your place," Bianca said, then asked, "You home?"

"I'm coming to your house," Monet stated. "Be there in a few minutes."

Looking at her mother, Monet said, "If Kingston is dead, it's all your fault."

Monet would've preferred to stay in bed with her new guy. She liked Cairo more than she'd admit. If Kingston was dead, she wasn't sure what to do with her side situation. No matter what had happened, Kingston was still her husband and her best *friend* for life.

Driving to Bianca's house, Monet parked her car, then hurried to the door, which was open by the time she got up the steps.

"Girl," Bianca handed her a large goblet filled with chilled Chardonnay.

Monet sipped, sipped, and sipped again, then sat at the dining table with Bianca. "I came here so I could call Lilly Ortiz without having my mother in the conversation. She's the Realtor that Kingston supposedly had looking for a house for us."

Bianca snapped her fingers. "Do it!"

Monet dialed Lilly's number, then placed the call on speaker.

Immediately Lilly answered, "Have you found him?"

"*Me?* I need you to tell me everything you know about my husband," Monet demanded.

Bianca tapped her fingernail against the silver cloth placemat.

Lily confessed that Kingston purchased a property, an all-cash deal, and deeded it in her name. She explained, "He did it because he didn't want you to know where he was living." Lilly added, "I have no additional information to offer."

"That's my house. You're going to transfer it over to me immediately," Monet declared.

"Not so fast," Bianca countered. "We don't know if Lilly is lying. Let's find out where Kingston is before you draw any attention to yourself."

"I agree," Lilly said. "I have no problem signing the property over to you, Monet. I've already given the same information to the police."

Why in the hell didn't Lilly start with that piece of information? "Do you know any of his church/drinking buddies?" Monet questioned.

"No," Lilly said. "And all women in Atlanta are not whores. I don't understand why you're not taking this seriously. Your husband is missing. I have to go." She rudely ended their conversation without giving Monet the chance to respond.

Monet was more in search of the truth regarding her husband's disappearance. She'd talk to the cops when she was ready.

A text registered: **You don't know me, but I know your husband. Call me.**

Showing Bianca the message, Monet asked, "What do you think I should do?"

Her best friend replied, "Right now. Not a damn thing. That might be his side chick."

CHAPTER 48

Victoria

"Fine! Chancelor. Meet me at the church. Bring Tracy with you, but don't either one of you open your mouth," Victoria lamented. Mumbling, she added, "I warned his ass. Lord, forgive me for cursing in your presence."

"Thank—"

She punched the red phone symbol on her steering wheel. "Lord Jesus, help me make it through this day," Victoria prayed.

Kingston was missing. Jordan was acting out of character. Chancelor had disobeyed her and connected with Tracy, which meant they both smelled worse than dog and horse shit mixed. Neither Kingston's nor Chancelor's emergency was hers. All Victoria wanted to do was complete Brother William Copeland's service before his family members came busting through the doors of the church.

She'd deliberately printed invitations for them with a start time two hours later than everyone else's. She'd prepared to take home his teddy bear urn and place him on the new rocking chair in her casting room.

A call registered from the one person with whom she looked forward to speaking with. Victoria answered, "Hey, Heavenly, how far are you from the church?"

"I'm parking in the lot right now," he said, then asked, "How are you doing?"

"I'm fine," she said. "I'll be glad when everything is over. I appreciate your being by my side today. Think about where you want to go on a weeklong vacation. Sit on the first pew," she instructed. "I'll meet you inside."

Turning off her engine, Victoria sat in her car in the rear lot. She bowed her head and closed her eyes, then prayed aloud. "Thank You, Lord Jesus, for blessing me with a companion that comforted me for over forty years. I know I haven't been a perfect Christian, but I am Your child and You know my heart. Tell Willy what he already knows . . . I love him. And I'll see him, but, dear Lord, please don't make it too soon. I pray for another forty years of blissfulness with Heavenly. Forgive me, God, for casting a love spell upon Heavenly. But what good is having all of Willy's money if it cannot bring me happiness? Willy would want me to have a companion. Amen."

Dressed from head to toe in a sky-blue outfit, Victoria entered through the rear doors of the church. Greeted by Pastor Baloney, he and the first lady expressed their condolences.

Chancelor and Tracy walked into the back of the church together.

"Greetings, Brother Leonard and Sister . . . Lord, have mercy on us." Pastor Baloney's eyes protruded at Tracy. "Whateva you do, don't open your mouth again. Victoria, I'm telling you, if Tracy speaks, you'll have to perform Brother Copeland's services by yourself. She damn near killed everyone in here. I'll be in the pulpit. C'mon, First Lady." Pastor grabbed his wife's hand and entered from the rear into the church.

Chancelor stared at Victoria, but didn't speak.

"Let's go in the pastor's study for a moment." Victoria led the way for Chancelor and Tracy.

Congregating behind closed doors, Victoria removed a small black glass bottle from her purse. Pouring the same potion she'd used to cast the spell upon Tracy, Victoria massaged oil into her palms. "Close your eyes." She touched Chancelor and Tracy on the foreheads at the same time.

Victoria chanted, "Let the spell be broken right this moment." Then she added, "Okay, you can open your eyes now."

Tracy stared at Victoria, but still didn't speak.

Frowning, Chancelor questioned, "Is that it?" He huffed into his hand, then inhaled.

Following his lead, Tracy did the same, sighed heavily, then laughed. "Thank you, Victoria." Tracy bowed before Victoria. "I promise I'll never use another man for money as long as I live. Just don't do whatever you did to me again."

"Honey, I wouldn't make that promise to anyone. That's what women are supposed to do. Use men for whatever they're good for. Just don't make the mistake of trying to use any of *my* men. That's where you fucked up . . . Excuse me, Lord Jesus . . . Other than that, we're good. You can stay for the service if you like. I'm sure Willy would approve."

Exiting the pastor's study, Victoria saw Jordan enter into the rear of the church. She was wearing all black. "Have any of you heard from Kingston?"

I'ma need the Father, Son, and Holy Ghost to make it through this day. Can You help me get through the service, Lord Jesus? Victoria silently prayed, then said, "Kingston is a man, darling. There's no telling where he's at or whom he's with. Kingston Royale is too big to be missing."

Jordan pulled her arm, escorted her away from Chancelor and Tracy. Standing in a corner, Jordan whispered, "There's something I didn't share with anyone."

"Girl, you haven't killed Kingston, have you?" Victoria joked. "I'm kidding. Whatever it is, it can wait. We need to start the service before the ratchets arrive," Victoria lamented. Didn't anyone give a damn about her situation?

Blocking her in, Jordan spoke low: "Langston Derby set up Kingston." She lowered her voice even more. "I don't know if the police are trying to discredit me for representing the Donovan case or if Langston is a con who sought me out to help him get Kingston, but I need your help."

Obviously, Jordan was serious, but what could Victoria do at this moment to help her? "This is confusing. Give me all the details after the service."

An officer had entered the church, approached them, and said, "Jordan Jackson?"

Quickly Jordan placed her phone in Victoria's hand, then confirmed, "Yes, Officer. I'm Jordan Jackson."

"We have to take you in for questioning. We have evidence that you were the last person seen at the property where Kingston Royale resided."

Lord Jesus, help me so I can get Willy Copeland home, where he belongs, on an express cloud.

"That's ridiculous," Victoria vehemently defended. "Why would Jordan be at Kingston's residence? There must be a misunderstanding here."

"If you don't change your tone," the officer advised Victoria, "I'm going to arrest you for obstruction."

Victoria next heard, "Where that bitch Victoria at?"

She might be better off if the officer arrested her.

Jordan stared at her phone, which was in Victoria's hand, then said, "I'm innocent. I'll fully cooperate. Don't worry about me, girl. Take care of Willy's service. I'll use my one call to contact you later."

Jordan wasn't her usual, confident self as she exited the rear of the church in handcuffs, as though she'd committed a crime. Victoria told Jordan, "Willy is already dead. There's nothing I can do to bring him back from glory."

A young woman pushed the door and entered into the rear of the church.

Victoria told Jordan, "I'll leave now and head to the police station."

"I'm going with you," Chancelor told Victoria.

"Bitch, you ain't going nowhere!" the woman said.

Chancelor pointed at himself.

"She know who the fuck I'm talking to. What the fuck kind of service is this with a teddy bear! Where's my uncle's body?" the woman yelled at Victoria.

Victoria prayed Pastor Baloney would appear and intervene.

Looking at Tracy, Victoria instructed, "You stay here. Make sure everything goes as well as it can and there's five thousand dollars in it for you. Make sure you get, protect, and keep the teddy bear for me. Sit in my place on the front pew, next to my new man, Heavenly. And don't—"

Tracy interrupted, "I got you. Don't worry. I've learned my lesson."

CHAPTER 49

Chancelor

Women were unnecessarily complicated. Liars. Cheaters. Unpredictable. The more beautiful they were, the more fucked up in the head they were. The worst part was they got pleasure out of breaking a brother's heart.

Browsing the adult store off of Cheshire Bridge Road, Chancelor was in search of toys for himself. Everything he saw was for women. He picked up a cordless waterproof vibrator, pushed one of the six buttons.

"Goddamn! What dude could get a chick to cum after she'd fucked with this shit?" he said.

The head spun in one direction, and the shaft with pearls on the inside spun the other way. The soft rabbit ears danced for her clit, and the tickler for the booty slapped back and forth.

"Women don't need us for dick," he said aloud to himself. Powering off the pink glitter monster penis, which was bigger than his, Chancelor returned it to the display shelf.

Laughter resonated from across the room. The guy behind the register approached him, then asked, "Man, what are you looking for? Maybe I can help you out. This section has toys for females. Over there are rings for men. My name is Blu. Pronounced like the color, but I dropped the *e*."

"Blu. My man. What do you have for the fellas other than dick rings?" Chancelor inquired.

"That joint that you just put down. Believe it or not, dudes come in here and buy that and other female sex toys for themselves. Toys are damn near becoming unisex, you feel me?"

Shaking his head real slowly, Chancelor replied, "No. Not for me."

"Cool that. What do you like? Our next most popular are the masturbation sleeves and pussy pockets. A lot of them feel the same on the inside. The more expensive, the better the sensation and quality. The one-and-dones get you off, too. Just depends on whether you want to stick your dick in a pussy or an egg."

Chancelor laughed.

"Seriously," Blu told him. "We also have gloves. Feels better than jacking off in your palm. Then there's nutcrackers, ball busters, super cock rings, vibrating dick pumps to make your shit fat and long. Personally, I love real pussy that's attached to a female. Ain't nothing like it . . . except our twenty-thousand-dollar sexbot. Wanna fuck her?"

This could be the answer to his prayers. "Hell yeah," Chancelor replied. His dick had already begun rising.

Following Blu into a back room, Chancelor stared in disbelief at the brown-skinned mannequin that stood at least five feet, five inches.

"Fuck her anywhere," Blu said, handing him a condom. "Come out when you're done."

Chancelor poked her in the mouth, shoved his fingers deep as he could. "Wow." The roof of her mouth had ridges. Her tongue had buds. Good, her teeth were smooth.

Unfastening his belt, he shoved his pants to his knees, then covered his dick with the condom. Pussy? Mouth? When he stuck his finger inside the vagina, it contracted.

Definitely pussy.

When he stood close to the sexbot, her nipples vibrated against his. While he penetrated her, she said, "Your dick feels good, Daddy."

"Oh, shit!" Chancelor didn't know she could communicate. "Squeeze my dick harder."

She did.

"Vibrate faster," he commanded.

She did that.

"Make me cum," he told her, then screamed, "Fuck!" before pulling and damn near passing out.

Chancelor cleaned himself up. Found Blu in the lube section.

"How'd you like the experience?" Blu asked, laughing.

Chancelor handed Blu his black Titanium Card. "I need my own one of those, man. Ring my new baby up. I'm taking her home."

Rolling the box on a dolly, Blu and Chancelor couldn't get the sexbot into his car. She felt heavier than the one in the store.

"Let's take her out of the cardboard." Chancelor was eager to get her in bed.

"Tell you what. It's damn near a hundred degrees. Why don't I have her delivered, in the box, within the hour?" Blu suggested. "You don't want to damage her. The warranty doesn't cover meltdowns."

"Here's my address. I'm heading straight home. If she's not home in an hour, I'll be back." Chancelor drove directly to his house.

Opening the refrigerator, he removed the marinated steak from the refrigerator, poured a glass of cognac. The liquor made him think about Kingston. He retrieved his cell, clicked on messages.

A call from the number he'd been waiting for was registering. Chancelor tapped his forehead, chest, left, then right shoulder. Clearing his throat, he answered, "Chancelor Leonard here."

"Congratulations, Mr. Leonard, our company is accepting your proposal for two-point-six million dollars," the owner said.

Dancing around his kitchen, Chancelor felt highly favored. Victoria's spiritual energy was rubbing off on him. He could respond by saying, "you definitely made the right choice," but he didn't want to come across as being arrogant.

"Thank you, sir. You won't be disappointed. Have a great weekend," Chancelor excitedly said.

"You as well, Mr. Leonard. We'll e-mail you the next steps. Good-bye," the CEO said, then ended their call.

Dashing to his office, he picked up the framed photo of his mother, hugged it to his chest. Everything he'd accomplished he owed to the woman that birthed him, Kelly Leonard.

Based on the proposal, he knew he had one week before starting his deliverables. It was time to celebrate, but with whom? Not Tracy. Definitely not Elite. Shanita came to mind. Maybe he could give her a chance. But none of them were his first choice. And Tuesday was four days away.

Checking the time, he calculated his new companion should arrive in less than thirty minutes. Chancelor set an alarm on his phone. He needed to come up with a name for her. She was primarily for sex, but he'd still respect her.

Seeing how worn-out Jordan looked after being questioned by the cops, she probably needed to get out. Chancelor texted her, **How are you doing? Any word on Kingston?**

I'm not a suspect. YET. No word. Hopefully, they'll find him soon and clear me.

Scratch Jordan off the celebration list. Seemed like the group was falling apart. That wasn't fair. Chancelor messaged Jordan: **Just landed a $2.6 million deal. Want to celebrate with me?**

It's easy to be a team player when there's no opponent. We have to stick together. Rain check. Working late on the Donovan case. #stayfocused was her response.

Damn. Okay. She didn't have to piss on his deal. That should've read: #stayingfocused.

Perhaps he'd have better luck with Victoria. **I Just landed a $2.6 million deal. Want to celebrate with me?**

Huge congrats! I'm out of town on vacation with Heavenly. Hit you up when we get back. Rain check. She ended with a champagne bottle emoji.

Dude's ashes weren't even in the urn for a week and she was already frolicking with the new guy. Women really were bitches. Some were bosses *and* whores like Victoria. Others were nasty for no reason.

Why bother getting married? he thought.

Returning to the kitchen for his drink, he debated on whether or not to text Kingston. Maybe he was out of town like Victoria, with a chick, lost his phone, and hadn't seen the news. Chancelor went for it. **Just landed a $2.6 million deal. Celebrate with me.**

Running out of options, he messaged Shanita: **Just landed a $2.6 million deal. Want to celebrate with me? I know it's not Tuesday.**

An incoming call registered with her name.

"What's up?" Chancelor asked.

"Oh, my gosh! I'm so excited for you! You *are* the man! When? Where are we toasting you?" she wanted to know. "Can't wait to meet your mom and your friends."

Shanita's enthusiasm boosted his ego. With all of his accomplishments, he felt women typically wanted to use him. That would be all right if they were spreading.

"It'll be just us," he clarified.

"Oh," she said. "Okay."

Entering the foyer, he opened, then shut the front door. Damn! He could hardly breathe in the hot and humid air.

"How about I pick you up so you don't have to drive. Or I can send a car for you. Whichever you prefer," he said, trying his best to respect Shanita.

"Are you kidding me! Pick me up." She went from cheery to concerned. "How should I dress?"

Neither Tracy nor Elite would have asked that question. They were always tempting for any man's appetite. "Appropriate for a Michelin star restaurant."

"Where is that?" she inquired, making him reconsider his offer.

Education—or the lack thereof—could create degrees of separation. He didn't want to stay home hugged up with his sexbot. "No worries. Put on your sexiest dress and highest stilettos. That'll be fine. Text me your address. I'll see you in an hour."

Back to sounding cheerful, Shanita said, "Okay. I've got to go. I've got to find someone to cover my shift and get ready. Bye."

Ding. Dong. He put the steak back in the refrigerator. Hurried to the door.

"Bring her in, gentlemen," Chancelor happily said.

The lady of the house had finally arrived.

CHAPTER 50

Jordan

Gold open-toe spiked heels greeted the sweltering black asphalt. Shimmering bare legs dazzled in the sunlight. A statuesque woman wearing a tight white halter dress that stopped above her knees emerged from the rear passenger side of a luxury SUV.

Her hair, slicked to her scalp, gathered in a neatly intertwined bun, was positioned more to the left side of the back of her head. Red lipstick. Glittered, pointed nails. Hoop earrings nearly touched her shoulders. After she removed her sunglasses, her dramatic eyelashes batted once.

Jordan had represented her type a thousand times over. Youthful and sexy, Monet Royale definitely resembled a baller's spouse and trophy wife.

As she greeted Monet with an "I'm Jordan Jackson," she thought, *Why would any man want to abandon such a beautiful goddess? She must be more ratchet underneath than refined on the exterior. Or she's the type that secretly wants more attention than her husband.*

"Thanks for meeting me here," Monet expressed. "Where is Lilly Ortiz?" was her first question. "I thought the two of you were coming together."

Humph. Monet was the unrealistic, assuming kind. *Interesting.* Would've been appropriate, but she never promised Lilly would show up.

Unless the police deemed her to be a "person of interest," Lilly was adamant about not voluntarily getting involved in Kingston's disappearance. After Jordan had questioned Lilly about the house being in her name, Lilly agreed to transfer the property out of her name and into Kingston's. Not Monet's.

Jordan had conducted a background check on Lilly. Nothing derogatory was revealed. Zero complaints were filed against her with the Georgia Real Estate Commission Board. Lilly was an up-standing Realtor with a multimillion-dollar portfolio of her own. Jordan deduced that Lilly legitimately accommodated Kingston's request.

"She gave me the code, but she's not coming," Jordan stated, showing Monet her cell. "Here it is."

"I have it, too," Monet stated. "What's the point of being here if she wasn't turning over the keys to me?"

Hmm. "It's supposed to be a SmartHouse." No keys. Only codes. There was reportedly an app to control everything. Jordan stepped aside wondering who else had the series of numbrrs.

Monet batted her lashes several times. "Oh, you mean like the house I own in Columbia. The one with thumbprint recognition." Pressing a series of numbers on the keypad, Monet opened the front door.

Jordan warned Monet, "Brace yourself for what you're about to see. If your schedule permits, I'd like, when we leave here, for us to go to my office and discuss the next steps in finding your husband."

Monet heaved, covering her mouth as she entered the living room. "Is that what I think?" she questioned, moving closer. "Is that my husband's blood all over the carpet? Was he hit in the head? Stabbed? Where are the damn cameras?"

"There are no cameras. According to Lilly, that was your husband's request." Staring at the floor, Jordan noticed a new stain pattern, or so she thought. Maybe she simply hadn't noticed it when she was set up by Langston.

"Well, how does she call herself a professional if she didn't make sure a celebrity like my husband had surveillance?"

Jordan hadn't come to engage in a debate with a disgruntled wife. "Obviously, there was a struggle." Jordan believed the stains were Kingston's, but she wasn't saying to Monet they could've been Langston's.

Jordan was equally concerned that she hadn't heard from Langston since the date that never happened/disappearance incident. Langston could be the one missing and Kingston could be in hiding.

Consumed with her own forensics, Jordan hadn't noticed that Monet had left, until she reentered the room, holding a framed photograph. Tears flowed down Monet's cheeks, then plopped onto her cleavage. "I didn't want to believe it, but my girlfriend told me . . . This other guy is so handsome."

"And he's a fantastic lover and liar." Jordan added, "I know, because Langston Derby told me to meet him here. When I arrived, this is the scene I walked in on." Well, almost. *Where is the photo of Levi and Kingston?* She wasn't hallucinating having seen it on the end table.

Monet's tears stopped flowing. Her eyes widened. Her brows raised. "You're involved?"

"Hell no!" Jordan was convinced that men were not worth investing in emotionally or otherwise.

"Then why were you at my house for a date with a man that's not my husband?" Monet questioned.

Bitch! "Back all the way up off of me," Jordan demanded.

Jordan once believed Donovan would marry her. She trusted Langston was an honest person. With her level of education and the background checks she'd performed, she realized the one thing she wasn't was clairvoyant.

"I have to go. If you have time to come to my office, I'll explain everything I know to you as best as I can, the same as I did with the police officers. You deserve to know what I know. I don't need to see anything else here. You can leave whenever you're ready."

"I'm not ready," Monet said.

Monet headed toward the master bedroom. Jordan, not wanting to leave her there alone, followed Monet.

The room was tidy. She opened several drawers. Packages of sexy men's underwear were in one. Lubrication and condoms were in another. The third drawer she reached in and then pulled out a framed photo.

Jordan gasped. "Oh, my Lord!"

"I'm the one who should be saying that. That's my husband hugged up with a different man."

"That man is Theodore Ramsey." Jordan hadn't met him in person, but she'd seen his pictures online when she ran a check on his name and business. "That man with Kingston is Langston's partner at the men's clothing store."

Monet's discovery may have uncovered another layer into the investigation. Jordan took a screenshot of the photo, then texted it to the police officer, along with the name and address of the men's clothing store.

Returning the frame to the drawer, Monet stated, "I'm done with this. My husband isn't missing. He's living a secret life."

"Don't give up. I know it's complicated," Jordan stated. "Let's go to my office and discuss everything. After hearing me out, if you feel you're done, I'll respect that."

Monet frowned, questioned, "Who reported my husband missing?" Then she added, "You?"

There was no simple answer. That was why she wanted Monet to come to her office. Levi had initiated her involvement with a text to Jordan, asking if she'd spoken with Kingston. After several failed attempts to contact Kingston, Jordan informed the police he was missing. Langston hadn't answered any of her texts or calls.

Jordan responded, "Yes. I did," then walked toward the front door.

"Humph." Monet exited the house behind Jordan, closed the door, then asked, "Do you have children, Ms. Jackson?"

Jordan stopped, faced Monet, and answered, "No, I don't." As she followed Monet to the SUV, a gentleman quickly got out of the driver's seat, then opened the rear passenger door.

Monet said, "*My* children need me. I'm taking the next flight home. There's nothing I can do to further assist you."

Further assist her? "How about you assist in finding him. Kingston is *your* husband. Please come to my office and hear me out," Jordan pleaded.

Sliding on her sunglasses, Monet firmly stated, "I don't think he's missing, but call me if you find him."

Jordan watched the SUV drive along the private road . . . until it was no longer in sight.

CHAPTER 51

Kingston

"I told you I'd be back. I wish I could take him home. What's his name?" the guy asked. "I promise not to tell anyone."

Bet he wouldn't be so chipper if he were in Kingston's position.

The all-too-familiar voice that was constantly resounding in his ear replied, "If I told you, seriously, I would kill you."

"Oh, well. No need to be an extremist," the man said. "Here's my six hundred."

One thousand one . . . Kingston wanted to say that he couldn't breathe. But maybe this was the blessing he'd requested of God. He wasn't sure how long or why he endured this level of assault and degradation, but he was ready to let go. He couldn't confess his sins with his mouth, but he did believe in his heart that he meant to harm no one, especially Monet.

One thousand sixty-two. Eight hundred thirty-eight seconds remained.

Boom!

"Everyone down! Get down! Now! Everybody! Facedown on the floor, hands where I can see them! You! Get your fucking dick out of him and get the fuck off of him!"

"Ah!" The man inside of Kingston pulled out, yelling, "Let me go! Please don't shoot! I have a wife and three kids. I'm a Christian. Forgive me, Lord, for I have sinned."

"Get your bitch ass on the floor facedown or you can tell your Jesus face-to-face," Kingston heard as someone removed the blindfold from his face.

Opening his eyes, he was blinded by light. They removed the ball from his mouth. Felt as though all of his teeth fell onto the mattress.

"Aw, shit! Are you fucking kidding me! Do you know who this is? I should ice every last one of you sorry motherfuckers. Call an ambulance now!" a man commanded. "Christian, my ass," he mumbled. "I'd put a bullet in your head right now if I wouldn't have to trade places with you for doing it."

Kingston's right arm was freed from bondage. Then his left. Then both of his ankles were released, but Kingston couldn't move. His body felt like a two-hundred-pound weight was on his back. He'd probably lost more than twenty pounds.

Kingston wanted to cry, but couldn't.

God, why? he questioned. *Why, in what appeared to be my last few breaths, did You save me?*

"Don't turn him over. Wait until the paramedics arrive," the guy who appeared to be in command ordered.

Kingston heard what sounded like handcuffs clicking.

"Please don't arrest me. My wife will kill me if she finds out I was here. I'm not gay!" The man who was just inside of Kingston cried like a bitch.

No falser words had been spoken. Kingston totally understood. The time had come for him to face his own reality. He had to publicly announce he was gay. Or pray for God to help him for the rest of his life suppress his urge to have sex with men, and seek fulfillment with Monet. If she'd have him.

What did the man who'd come back to penetrate Kingston again look like? Was he white? Black? What did any of them look like? Kingston didn't want to see the man's face, not now or ever. Living with an image of a man who'd violated him meant he'd have to relive seeing that face every day for the rest of his life.

Kingston felt a hand on his.

"Oh, my God. Not my idol," someone said, then asked, "Kingston, can you squeeze my hand?"

Kingston tried, but his fingers barely moved.

"Can you turn your head to the opposite side?" someone else asked.

A fraction of an inch toward the left felt like someone had stabbed him in the nape of his neck with a million ice picks.

"Okay, don't move," the guy told Kingston, then ordered someone, "Get a morphine drip. We're going to have to heavily sedate him before we can move him out."

"I'm going to put the needle in your arm. You may feel a sharp pain," the paramedic said, then added, "You're my hero."

Kingston was ready. But he was nobody's hero. And no complete stranger should idolize him.

"Next I'm going to start administering morphine, and then we're going to place your body on a gurney, put you in the ambulance, and take you to Grady Hospital. You're in a safe place now, Mr. Royale."

Give all of those trafficking bastards a lethal injection, Kingston thought. He didn't want God to have mercy upon them. Their souls belonged to Satan. Some people deserved to die. Others, like Kingston, wanted to die because of torturers and bullies, like the ones he'd encountered.

Human abduction into sex slavery for the love of money, which would be taken away and given to the state. Kingston's kidnappers hadn't realized they, too, were in captivity. Physically. Mentally. Emotionally.

"Get all of those sons of bitches out of here right now! I'm glad Georgia's law to prosecute human traffickers to the fullest extent is right on time," the person presumed to be in charge stated about the state-level decision.

The so-called heartbeat bill had passed before the law to prosecute human traffickers that made women, men, and minors their sex slaves. Kingston wished he could say something in this moment, but he couldn't.

With a deep country accent, another voice said, "This is a good day, boss. The entire motel is swarming. We rescued twenty more sex slaves. Can you believe they're all black men? Plus, we've caught ten more traffickers."

Feeling the sunshine on his face, Kingston heard, "Stop! Stop, I said, or I'll shoot!"

Whoever it is, Kingston thought, *shoot now and don't miss.* No rounds were fired. *Why is it that the cruelest people get to surrender and innocent victims are killed?*

"Boss," a different voice shouted. "We got that motherfucker this time. And he's going down!"

"Wait. I have to see this. Y'all caught Langston Derby?" the boss asked.

"Yee-haw! Sure did. Langston Derby, the ringleader! Finally got that motherfucker!" someone shouted.

"Well, I'll be damned," the guy they'd called "boss" said. "I don't know how Jordan Jackson escaped him. She was his target."

"She was next on his list," someone said. "Langston Derby was circling back to her and he'd arranged to ship her pretty ass overseas."

The last words Kingston heard before a sheet was draped over his body were "Damn! Show respect. No media and cameras allowed, people."

CHAPTER 52

Monet

"Ah, yasssss. Grind deep inside this pussy." Monet moaned.
Cairo did. As though he were trying to strike oil.

It was easier for Monet to let go of the guilt for Kingston after she'd seen the photos in his house in Atlanta. There was too much speculation around who'd done what, and there was the possibility of her getting caught up in his mess. Kingston not relocating her and the girls to the ATL was a blessing she hadn't prayed for.

All of Cairo's Mandingo-ness was inside of her. Cairo rolled his hips from her left butt cheek to her right. Repeating the slow motion, he pressed his thumbs into the arch of her back while holding on to her lower waist. Monet tilted her head back as far as she could. "Pull my hair." She released a sound that emanated from her gut.

She wasn't acting.

Cairo jerked her hips toward his pelvis, then held her there.

"That's right, baby. Let it all out. I got you. And I'm never going to let you go," Cairo stated.

Kingston never loved Monet more than she'd loved him. Perhaps it was because he wanted something different, but he hadn't been man enough to say so. Regardless, after seeing the photos in Kingston's house, Monet never wanted his dick inside of her pussy again.

Monet was willing to give Cairo more than her body. She was willing to give him her heart.

Collapsing onto her stomach, she rolled onto her back, bent her knees, reached for the remote, and turned up the volume on the television.

Taking the controller from her, Cairo lay on his side, facing Monet. "When are you going to let me meet your girls?" he asked.

A news report stated: "A human trafficking operation in Atlanta was broken up today by a SWAT team. More than twenty people were arrested. Over twenty victims rescued. Now the hardest part starts with reuniting sexual assault victims with their families. The person over the operation is reportedly cooperating with the police department. With the new law against human traffickers in the state of Georgia, all of the traffickers, if convicted, may spend the rest of their lives behind bars."

Monet sat up in the bed, looked down at Cairo.

"I know you don't think your brother, Kingston, is involved. Or do you?" Cairo questioned.

When the time was right, she'd tell him her truth. "Sorry, but I have to go," Monet stated, teary-eyed.

"It's like *Groundhog Day*. I wish you'd tell me exactly what's going on so I can help. You don't have to deal with this by yourself." Cairo leaned toward the edge of the bed, wrapped his arm around her waist. "Come back to bed. Baby, please. There's nothing you can do until they contact you."

Shaking her head, Monet put on her shoes. Cairo plopped onto the mattress. He didn't bother getting out of bed to stop Monet from doing what she was going to do, anyway.

"When you're ready to talk, I'm willing to listen. Besides, I need to get some work done this morning. You have a nice day."

Stepping into her romper, she straightened her ponytail best she could. "I'll call you later."

Cairo didn't respond. Exiting his home, Monet called her mother from the car.

Trinity answered, then scolded, "I told you not to let my grandbabies go back to school. Just because you've moved on doesn't mean they can deal with what's happening with their father. I'm in transit to get the girls. I'll meet you back at the house."

An argument on her end wasn't happening. Monet wasn't officially notified that her husband was one of the victims. Kingston could be laid up with a . . . Monet couldn't say the word in her mind.

Starting her engine, Monet said, "Thanks."

An incoming call registered from Jordan Jackson. Monet told Trinity, "Bye, Mother. I'll be at the house by the time you get there."

Pressing the button on her steering wheel, she ended the conversation and started another. "Was Kingston one of the men?"

"Yes. I'm at the hospital, but I'm not his relative, so they won't let me see him. You should've come to my office when—"

Monet interrupted, "I'm a grown woman. Kingston is grown, too—"

Jordan cut Monet off. "Don't be that way. You should get here immediately. The doctors aren't sure if he's going to make it."

Monet burst into tears. Cried out loud. Instead of going home, she drove to the airport. As she parked in the short-term lot, a call registered from Bianca.

"I apologize, Jordan. I'm on my way. I have to catch this call. Text me the information on where Kingston is."

"That's what I—"

Ending the call with Jordan, crying and shaking, Monet answered, "Hey," then kept crying.

If Jordan had contacted her to give her information, she should've led with that instead of a tongue-lashing.

"Where are you?" Bianca asked.

Monet struggled to speak through sobs and sniffles. Eventually she replied, "At the airport. I have to go to Atlanta."

"Not without me," Bianca insisted. "Drop me a pin. Stay right where you are. I'm on my way."

A call from Lilly registered. Monet sent the call directly to voice mail. Cairo called. Her mother called. An unidentifiable number from the 404 area code appeared numerous times. "Stop calling me!" Monet yelled.

Her phone wouldn't stop ringing. Most of the numbers she didn't recognize. Afraid someone might tell her Kingston was dead, she dropped a pin to Bianca, then ignored all of the incoming calls.

Unstrapping her seat belt, Monet curled in her seat into a fetal position.

A tap on her window startled her. It was her best friend, Bianca.

"Girl, open this door." Bianca waited for her to get out of the car. They headed to the ticket counter and purchased two first-class seats on the next flight to Atlanta.

Sitting at the gate, Monet handed Bianca one of her earbuds. "Listen to the messages with me."

Hearing the fourth message—"Hello, this is the nurse from Grady Hospital calling for Monet Royale. If this is Monet Royale's number, please give us a call back at . . ."—Monet cried out loud.

She couldn't imagine life without Kingston. She regretted not hearing what Jordan had to say while she was in Atlanta. All of those emotions were real, but Monet was clear. She didn't feel remorse for having a relationship with Cairo. Irrespective of how she processed what'd happened, Kingston had brought many things upon himself by lying to her and disrespecting his family.

Settling into their seats, Monet asked her best friend, "What if he's dead?"

Looking at Monet, Bianca replied, "That would be the easy part. The harder question for you is, what are you going to do if your husband is alive?"

CHAPTER 53

Victoria

"I love you, Victoria," Heavenly said.

Victoria cracked an egg. Separating the white from the yolk in two bowls, she wondered what she could do to break the love spell she'd cast on this innocent man-child.

"I love you because you take excellent care of me. I see why Mr. Willy stayed around so long. Now it's my turn." Heavenly inhaled, thrusting his chest out. His smile was wide and beautiful. That of a boy trapped in an adult's body.

"Let's not talk about Willy Copeland until I say it's okay." Victoria wasn't asking. She didn't want to emotionally share her beloved with his replacement.

No man could fit her Willy's shoes. Heavenly was the new guy. And would have to build his own foundation.

"I really, really love you, Victoria." This time his smile switched to a grin.

Pouring the egg whites into the skillet, she wanted him to kiss her all over. Any part of his body caressing her made her temporarily forget about Willy. Slowly she added smoked salmon, scallions, red pepper flakes, and mushrooms, then lightly stirred them together.

"Let's take another vacation," she suggested. "Where would *you* like to go?" Cracking another egg on the side of the bowl, she let the white fall, then tossed the yolk.

Without hesitation, enthusiastically he shouted, "Vegas, baby! I've never been, heard it's spectacular. We should fly in tonight. I hope Cardi B is there," he said, rubbing his hands together. "And if I get lucky," he said, slapping Victoria on the ass, "I might hit another jackpot."

"Hmm." She had herself to blame.

Heavenly visiting her house every day, as opposed to their sharing twenty-four hours in each other's company at an all-inclusive resort, was new. She didn't mind when they were out of town, but he couldn't move in on her.

Victoria said, "Oh, yeah. Do tell." Putting a dish in front of him, she said, "Blend these pineapples and blueberries with crushed ice and mango juice."

"I could get lucky at the casino. And if I'm really on a roll, we can go to one of those places where people get married."

And do what? Be witnesses. Oh no! Victoria thought. Making an omelet, she carefully lifted the edges, ensuring it didn't overcook.

"Why not make me your husband?" Heavenly spun the fruit bowl.

"I've never married." Committing to Heavenly or any man would make that teddy bear in her casting room come to life.

Her lifestyle wasn't conducive to marriage. As a single woman, she'd had great dick and incredible companionship. Now she had one and wondered if she'd ever regain the other.

"Neither have I." Heavenly moved from the counter-height chair, stood behind Victoria, close enough for her to feel his growing erection.

Thinking of Willy, Victoria was no longer in a sexual mood. "I've lost my appetite." She turned off the fire, handed him the spatula.

Sliding the omelet from the skillet onto a plate, he helped himself to a fork and started eating. Willy would've served her first.

"I'm never going to leave you. Like *ever.* This tastes good, but not better than you." Talking with his mouth full, Heavenly told her, "We might as well make it official tonight. Is Vegas a go?"

That wasn't the potion speaking. That was an opportunist. He wasn't the first. "You stay here and eat breakfast. I'll make and then take my smoothie into the bedroom and get ready for church."

Heavenly added her scramble on top of his omelet. Capturing her hand, he asked, "You miss him, don't you?"

Victoria tried to swallow the lump in her throat. Victoria eased her hand out of his grip. "Hurry up. Finish eating and get dressed. Otherwise, we're going to have to take two cars."

She showered, dressed, then told Heavenly, "If you're not ready in fifteen minutes, I'm leaving."

Heavenly devoured the rest of his food, washed it down with the remainder of her smoothie, disappeared, and then reappeared all within ten minutes. "Ready, my love." Genuinely, he had the most adorable demeanor. Innocent. Young. His spirit was younger than his age.

Victoria didn't want to be alone, yet she didn't want him in her space every day. Flying to his suggested destination wasn't a bad idea. Why not?

Getting in the car, she said, "I'll book our tickets for Las Vegas tonight."

"We're going tonight!" He leaned over and kissed her.

"No." Struggling not to become annoyed, she explained, "I'm booking the tickets tonight. I'll have to check my calendar first to see what day we're leaving."

"This is the best summer of my life!" Easy for Heavenly. He was off from school without a job.

Victoria had to run a business.

Driving along Peachtree, she saw it was going to be another scorching day. Victoria parked in the church's front lot. They walked inside, holding hands. People stared. Mumbled. She didn't care. Honestly, Victoria didn't give a damn. It was her life. And she was Willy's mistress for over forty years. The church members didn't frown upon that and they'd eventually get used to seeing her with Heavenly.

"Sit wherever you like," she told Heavenly. Touching his face, she softly kissed his lips to give the haters a real reason to gossip, then made her way to the back of the church.

The gang was there standing in a circle. Tracy had volunteered to replace Kingston until—or if—he returned to Hope for All Church.

"Hey, Victoria. Come here," Jordan beckoned.

Jordan was in uniform, but cuter than usual. Her natural hair was flat-ironed, but the ultrabright red lip and witch-pointed nails were different.

Joining the new group, she said, "I'm going to stay back here until it's time to collect the offering." To Tracy, Chancelor, and Jordan, she said, "I'll be fine," before they started questioning if she was okay.

Retreating to the pastor's study, Victoria closed the door, turned on the television, and watched the service that was happening up front.

"This song is dedicated to Brother Kingston Royale." The choir started singing "Never Would've Made It." They followed with "Jesus Is Love." Victoria cried through both.

"Let the Church give thanks unto the Lord. Brother Kingston Royale is expected to have a full recovery. It's not going to be overnight, nor will it be in his time, everything is in God's control."

Pastor Baloney marched behind the pulpit. "I want the congregation to become the eyes and ears of our community, for here at Hope for All Church, we are family."

Victoria bowed her head, closed her eyes. This was the first Sunday after Willy's disastrous service. Looking up at the screen, she glanced around the church, hoping Willy's ratchet family would honor the restraining order Jordan helped her get in exchange for bailing out her young client.

"Sister Monet Royale, we welcome you to become a visiting member," Pastor Baloney stated. "Of course, if you should decide to move to Atlanta, you'll always have a home here. Whatever your needs are, let them become ours and God's. You don't have to walk this journey alone. Brother Kingston is part of our sick and shut-in now and we'll make sure to visit him throughout his healing process." Pastor Baloney paused, rattled his head, then continued: "As the ushers come forward, preparing to collect the offering, know that you cannot outgive who?"

The congregation responded in unison, "God!"

Victoria dried her eyes with a tissue, then hurried to the altar. She stood on the inner aisle next to the front pew and faced Chancelor. She glanced at the space where Brother William Copeland once sat. Chancelor handed the basket to the person seated on his end. He glanced at Victoria, then mouthed, "Are you okay?"

She nodded at Chancelor, then looked at Heavenly, gave him a half smile.

They had a blast traveling the Abaco Islands. Lots of sunshine, swimming in the ocean, sipping on cool, refreshing cocktails, massages on the beach. The only site she adamantly refused to visit was Piggyville. But now it was back to her reality until they left for Vegas.

Glancing over her shoulder, she saw Jordan was on the center aisle with her back to Victoria.

Victoria reached into her pocket. Those closest to her gasped. Leaned in Chancelor's direction.

"That's impressive, you guys. Truly," Victoria said.

She left the small glass bottle hidden. In or outside of the church, if she'd learn that a particular person or persons were involved in any kind of way with what was rumored to have happened to Kingston, she'd cast her "I've fallen and can't get up" spell. Then she'd throw away the remains so it would never be broken. Like the spell with Heavenly.

Victoria was side by side with Jordan, facing the altar. Chancelor was behind her. Tracy stood beside Chancelor. Never had Victoria believed she'd see a day where Tracy was solo and serving the Lord.

Walking along the aisle as she approached Heavenly, he reached out and touched her hand. For a brief moment, Victoria held on.

Continuing walking toward Pastor Baloney, Victoria again looked at Brother William Copeland's empty seat. The members had dedicated the space to honor him.

When they all reached the altar, Victoria continued walking. She strolled until she arrived at Brother Copeland's seat.

"Lord Jesus. Why didn't You give me a sign?" she cried.

Falling on her knees, she leaned into his seat and wept uncontrollably. She placed her head on the bench. Hugged the empty space. She cried and cried and cried.

Two members of the congregation knelt beside her, rubbed her back.

"Let her be," Pastor Baloney said. "Sister Victoria and a lot of people hold on to their grief. Believing they can move forward in their daily lives as long as they do something different. Just keep busy. Or love someone new. But true love can never be denied."

Blessing the offering, Pastor Baloney opened the doors to the church. "If there is anyone who would like to give their life to God, please come now. Brother Copeland was saved. Can you say the same thing?"

Victoria found the strength to sit in Willy Copeland's seat. Pastor Baloney's arms were spread wide, palms up. He preached, "Don't wait. For the time to be saved is right here. Right now."

Monet stood, walked to the front of the church, then knelt at the altar. Tracy followed in her footsteps.

"This is the last call. Much like the one when you are at the bar. If you're fortunate to make it back, there'll be another. For you do not know when you walk out the door"—he pointed—"what is on the other side. If you are not saved, you'll never know what Heaven is like."

Heavenly stood, approached the altar, knelt next to Tracy.

Victoria watched the two of them, thinking Heavenly did deserve a younger woman. One closer to his age. Not Tracy, but someone he could grow with.

She'd spilled the love potion when she had gotten the news about Willy. Silently she prayed, *Dear Lord Jesus, if this man is mine, let it be of his own will. If You should have him be with someone else, including Tracy, I won't complain. Amen.*

Soon as service ended, Victoria was glad it was time to head to Bar Purgatory for a bottle of wine.

In transit she asked Heavenly, "Do you really want to be with me? And before you respond, please know there is no wrong answer."

Caressing her inner thigh, he said, "I love you, and, yes, I want to be with you."

She wasn't sure if it was the potion speaking on his behalf or if that was how he truly felt. But in that very moment, Victoria realized she needed Heavenly more than he needed her . . . and that was okay.

CHAPTER 54

Chancelor

"Thanks, Chancelor. The movie was okay, but the cinema was amazing! Where I go, there are seats and snacks. I've never been to a theater where you can order a steak, vegan burger, truffle fries, chicken and waffles, and popcorn, plus cocktails." Shanita inhaled. "The guava margarita was so delicious, I can still taste it."

Chancelor touched the driver's-side handle to unlock the doors, then sat behind the wheel. He would've opened the door for Tracy and Elite, but Shanita wasn't that type of showgirl.

Shanita was different in an intriguing kind of way so he took her out again. She was the girl he'd fuck, but not fuck with. Too many parts of her personality weren't ladylike.

"Would you like to go to my house?" he asked, pressing the button to start the engine. "Or I can take you home."

Chancelor had a lot of work to do on his new contract, but he also wanted to reap the benefits of his generosity. He envisioned Shanita's mouth on his dick. She was probably a great rider.

"Are you kidding me? Of course, I'd love to go to your house. I don't have a clean pair of underwear, so I'ma wash the ones I'm wearing by hand, then put them in your dryer tonight. I need to be home by six in the morning." She turned up the music without asking.

Chancelor lowered it. What good was a conversation if he had to talk over the songs? Why was Shanita planning on staying, without an overnight invite? Chancelor sensed that Shanita hadn't been treated well in her past relationships. Maybe that was true. Maybe not. Some girls just weren't accustomed to getting much, so everything excited them.

He drove from CinéBistro in Brookhaven to Phipps Plaza in Atlanta. A short two-mile drive and they were at the mall.

"I thought we were going to your house?" Shanita asked.

"We are. Let's go inside for a minute." Getting out of his car, Chancelor led the way to the entrance.

"Wow! This place is over-the-top." Her eyes roamed up, down, side to side. She stopped. "Look at those shoes in the window. Oh, my goodness. I've never seen so many sparkles on designer tennis shoes. Wow!" Her expression was like that of a kid looking into a candy store.

"Let's go inside," Chancelor casually suggested.

Shanita's mouth was wide open, and then she said, "The backpacks! Oh, my gosh. I'd love to have one of these for school, but I'd have to spend a whole year trying to pay for it. I don't have rich people's money."

Chancelor told her, "Pick out whatever one you want and a pair of shoes. I got it."

"Oh, no, I can't let you spend that much money on me. You paid for the date. And we're not even in a relationship." Was Shanita talking to him or the backpack?

Chancelor told the salesperson, "Give her whatever she'd like."

After paying for a backpack, a pair of tennis shoes, and a watch, Chancelor and Shanita walked through the mall. He had one more stop to make for her. They entered the lingerie store.

Again, Chancelor told her, "Pick out whatever you'd like."

He'd never say that to Tracy or Elite. Shanita placed her bag on the floor. He left it there.

"All of these things are pretty, but it's not the freaky kind of lingerie. Where're the animal prints? This looks like stuff for rich white people."

Chancelor eyed the salesperson, shook his head.

Picking up a set, Shanita stumbled over her bag. "A thousand dollars for a bra and panties. This is ridiculous. People actually pay this price?"

"Excuse me, miss. The thousand dollars is for the bra only," the salesperson explained. "The panty is an additional eight hundred—"

Chancelor interrupted, "Pick out whatever you like." He was ready to leave.

"I'll have the purple set. That's my favorite color. But I have to tell you," Shanita told him, "I'm never going to wear it. This is my good stuff."

The hell she wasn't! Chancelor laughed. She was putting that on in approximately one hour. "Let's go."

Parking in his garage, they entered his home, into the kitchen.

"Oh. Wow! Give me a tour of your mansion," Shanita requested immediately as she circled the island. "Your burners are over here. Where's the stove?" She glided her hand along the countertop.

Good, Chancelor thought. Shanita had left her bags inside his trunk. That way, in case they had to leave abruptly, all he needed was for her to hop in the passenger seat.

"Oh, shit!" Chancelor said.

"What?" Shanita asked, lifting her hand. "Did I do something wrong?"

"Nothing. Have a seat in the living room. Better yet, make us a cocktail. There's champagne in the refrigerator and a wet bar in the theater room."

Chancelor entered the master bedroom. Vanessa was sitting up in the bed with one knee bent, holding a book. He hadn't thought of where to store her when he had company. Placing his hand behind her back, and the other under her knees, he picked her up.

"I forgot to ask what do you like in . . ." Shanita froze.

The book fell on the floor. "Get out of my room," he demanded.

Shanita moved closer to him and his doll. "What is that? And why is she in your bed?"

There was no way Chancelor could lie his way out of this situation. He decided to tell the truth. Sitting Vanessa at the foot of the bed, he explained, "This is my sexbot. Women nowadays come with a lot of drama. I wanted to see what it would be like to come home to something unique." He was lying, and he added another lie, "I bought her before I met you."

Rubbing Vanessa's leg, Shanita asked, "How much did she cost?"

"Vanessa was twenty grand," Chancelor said, moving Shanita's hand.

"Twenty what! I can get a new car for that price." Shanita felt Vanessa's breasts. "These things feel real. If I'm going to be around, she has to go."

"She's not going anywhere, because you, like the rest, will probably find a way to use me, too." Chancelor removed Shanita's hands from Vanessa's areolas.

"Does she have a real pussy?" Shanita poked her fingers in Vanessa's vagina before Chancelor could block her hand. "Oh, my gosh! She has a G-spot. Can she squirt?" she asked, jabbing repeatedly.

"Stop it!" Fed up with Shanita, Chancelor commanded, "Vanessa, tell Shanita not to touch you again."

Vanessa stared at Shanita. "Shanita, do not touch me again."

"This bitch on some Alexa shit!" *Slap!* Shanita smacked Vanessa in the face. "I'm not going to have a bot-bitch telling me what the fuck to do or not to do."

Chancelor quickly stood between Vanessa and Shanita. Defending Vanessa, he said, "Keep your hands off of her."

Staring at Chancelor, Shanita reached around him and punched Vanessa on the ear. Vanessa fell sideways onto the mattress.

"I'll fight a bot-bitch."

Chancelor stepped aside, then said, "Vanessa, slap Shanita."

The doll sat up, swung, hitting Shanita in the face.

Shanita snatched off her earrings, hopped on top of Vanessa, and started punching—left, right, left, right, left, right, left, right—until Chancelor pulled her away from his doll.

Shanita kicked the air. "I don't hear that bitch talking now."

He carried Shanita into the kitchen and out the door. They were both quiet on the drive to her home. Parking in front of her house, he released the trunk.

"Get your things," he said, then asked, "You want to go to a concert tomorrow?"

"All right," Shanita said. "Tell Vanessa if I see her tomorrow, I'ma beat her ass again."

Chancelor returned to his house, went to his bedroom. "Vanessa, sorry about what happened. How are you, honey?"

She replied, "I am great. How are you, my love?"

"Horny," he said.

What Shanita had done had actually turned him on. Two women fighting over him was a first.

"I am here to take care of your every need. What would you like me to do?" Vanessa asked.

Removing his clothes, Chancelor left them in a pile on the floor next to the bed. Propping his doll on her knees in the middle of the bed, he slid underneath her, bowed her head to his privates, then penetrated her mouth.

"I'd like a blow job," Chancelor requested.

Vanessa tightened her mouth around his shaft. Moving as though she were blowing up a balloon, then swallowing all of the air, she repeated the motion.

"Stop," Chancelor commanded. "Your mouth is dry. I need lubrication."

"You can get your own or I can make my mouth wet, which would you prefer?" she asked.

"Make your mouth wet, bitch." Leaning back on the pillow, with his hands behind his head, Chancelor smiled.

He wasn't sure where the lubrication came from, but her mouth now felt like a moist vagina. And Vanessa tirelessly bobbed and sucked Chancelor into paradise. He began to moan, pretending she was real.

"I'm about to cum," he said. "Cum with me, Vanessa."

The doll continued sucking. The more she bobbed, the harder his dick became.

"Stop. I want to cum on your face." Pulling out of her mouth, Chancelor stroked himself. "Cum with me, Vanessa," he said again.

"Okay, I am cumming," she replied.

Releasing himself on the doll's face, Chancelor questioned whether this should be his permanent sexual companion.

Getting out of bed, he bent her legs, then laid her flat on her back. Fingering her pussy, he saw that she was wet.

Chancelor went to the other bedroom, returned with the special cleaning solution, then dampened the cloth. He thoroughly wiped the inside of Vanessa's mouth and her face. Spreading her legs, he used the brush to clean her vagina.

Chancelor picked up Vanessa. Struggling to put her back in the box after several attempts, he tossed in the towel, brush, solution, and the reviving powder, taped the box, then stored her in the garage.

"At least a real bitch can wipe her own ass," he said, slamming the kitchen door.

Chancelor texted Shanita, **Get dressed. I'm on my way to pick you up.**

He was actually starting to like Shanita. He realized that with her, he didn't have to try to be someone he wasn't in order to impress her.

Shanita messaged, **When I get to your house, that bitch best be gone, and she'd better not be wearing my earrings.**

CHAPTER 55

Jordan

J ordan stared at her cell: either Langston was stupid or he thought she was dumb.

Leaning back in her swivel chair, Jordan's desk was covered with legal documents. The highest stack was for Donovan. Another for Mr. Ealy. Pile three through nine for cases coming up later in the week.

Deciding to answer, she said, "You know I know, right?"

"Hey, sorry for blocking your number. I called to apologize for standing you up a couple of weeks ago, but I had an emergency situation," Langston said.

"Emergency?" Opening her bottom drawer, she removed the framed photo of Langston, tossed it in the trash can. "Like human trafficking?" Hearing his voice made Jordan cringe. "Apology not accepted."

"Baby, some shit went down that wasn't kosher. I *had* to get ghost. But I'm back in town. Whatever you heard on the news, I can explain the mix-up. There's this dude that looks exactly like me using my identity. He's my fucking twin damn near. And the worst part is, my fucking partner, Theodore Ramsey, he was in on that trafficking shit with setting up Kingston. The police is working to catch the right guy. That's why I'm out. Let me make it up to you," Langston begged. "I'll come to your place. That way we won't chance any misunderstandings or illegal interruptions. What's a good time?"

Really? Did he believe his fast-talking would overrule her judgment of him? Or she'd be a fool and trust him again? How disrespectful of her law degree. For goodness' sake, she was an attorney. He had to have known that she knew he was arrested for and charged with human trafficking. "I don't understand why Judge Goodwin set bail, when bail for you should've been denied."

Retrieving the framed photo from the trash, Jordan removed Langston's picture, shredded it, then tossed the frame in the bottom drawer. He wasn't worth losing the $400 she'd paid for the crystal.

"Exactly. She gave me bail because I'm innocent," he insisted. "Soon as the cops find my identical, the case against me will be dropped."

Well, if this was the game Langston wanted to play, game on! Jordan replied, "I'm getting ready to leave the courthouse. Let me call you back when I get home."

Abruptly Langston said, "Jordan."

"Yes" was all she'd replied.

"Don't call the police on me. It'll put the spotlight on you. Let the authorities do their job. Give me a chance to explain my side," he pleaded, sounding desperate.

Jordan had already spoken with the police. She wasn't a person of interest anymore. "That's fair," Jordan told him. "I'll text you a time to come over. See you then." She ended their conversation. No way was she meeting with Langston without notifying the police.

Langston Derby could step foot into her residence under one condition. More infuriated than with his self-invitation, Jordan was livid that he intended to involve her further.

An incoming phone call from Donovan registered. "Greetings, Mr. Bradley."

"I'm glad we're back on track. What're you wearing?" he asked, then laughed.

All too familiar with his jokingly sexist statements, she didn't flirt with his humor. Jordan firmly stated, "I was never off track, Mr. Bradley."

He hacked. Cleared his throat. "Hey, how's the case coming along?"

"We're in a good position. I need you to come to my office to-morrow so the team can give you an overview and answer any questions you may have. We're working on having Anne Whitehall fired from the department. That would put us in excellent position for the lawsuit. Hold on. Actually, let me take this call."

Jordan ended the conversation with Bradley, then answered, "Jordan Jackson, of Jackson, Johnson, and Jones."

"Greetings, Ms. Jackson. This is Trent Wade with the Federal Bureau of Investigation. We hear Langston Derby is meeting you at your house tonight." He was upbeat. "He may still be assisting with kidnapping victims and selling them into human trafficking versus holding them."

The agent had confirmed what Jordan suspected. Langston's phone was definitely tapped. If hers wasn't, it would be after this conversation. Not good for an attorney.

"How can I help? What's your question?" she asked.

"We'd like to wire you before you go home and post up near your house later. If he tries anything with you, we can arrest him immediately. Is that okay? If so, we'll have an FBI agent meet you at your office right before you leave."

"I have a trial at—"

Interrupting, Wade stated, "We know. Judge Goodwin won't hold the prospective jurors past five o'clock. How about we confirm six o'clock? You're on Langston's list."

Jordan's heart pounded. "For what?"

"Langston's list is not the only one you're on," Agent Wade stated. "Be careful who you confide in. We'll be at your office at six. Bye."

First he was sending someone. Now he was coming, too? Trembling, Jordan terminated one call, then initiated another, contacting the person that would tell her exactly what to do.

"Jordan Jackson, how are you today?" Officer Dale, of the Atlanta Police Department, answered. "To what do I owe this call?"

She spared no time informing him, "Langston Derby just called me. He's coming to my house tonight to explain he's innocent."

"Well, he's playing right into our hands. Can you come by the station now? I'd like to wire you. Myself and another officer can do the stakeout."

A stakeout seemed interesting when it was the FBI. Wearing a wire for two departments was frightening. Determined to get justice for Kingston, Jordan stated, "Trent Wade has that covered."

Officer Dale commented, "Good ole Trent taking over. Wonder when he was going to let us know? We'll let him do his job. Be careful who you confide in, Jordan. We're here if you need us. Good-bye."

There was no time to analyze Trent's or Dale's dialogues, but something was wrong with both of them advising her to be careful. Entering the courthouse, Jordan spoke with the solicitor regarding her client's charges.

"Yes, my client had four ounces of marijuana, but there were four people in the vehicle. And they were in Atlanta proper. The arresting officer should've issued four fines for seventy-five dollars and my client should've been free to go."

It was called job security. Police departments were going bankrupt with million-dollar settlements for wrongful deaths. If cops knew black people, like Offset, had money, they'd arrest them. If police believed a black couldn't afford to post bail, they'd arrest them.

"Mayor Keisha Lance Bottoms made possession of one ounce of marijuana punishable by fine, not time," she told the solicitor.

"But the report shows it was bundled in one package," he countered.

Jordan sighed heavily. Frustrated, but not emotional, she said, "It was separated into four small bags. But let's go to trial. Waste taxpayers' money, and see how many jurors we have to question before having my client found not guilty. Statistics show that more white people consume cannabis than blacks."

To Jordan's surprise, Judge Goodwin dismissed the case. Jordan's client was free to go, and so was she.

Taping a small microphone to Jordan's waist, Agent Wade said, "When you get home, change your top from white to black."

Viewing her security camera, Jordan saw Langston at the gate's call box. She hadn't given him a code, yet she witnessed him pushing buttons repeatedly.

Through her speaker, she asked, "Are you done yet?"

"Nah. I mean yes. I thought my old code was still working. You know."

Tapping on her screen, the gate parted, allowing him access. Instead of posting up in a nearby vehicle, the FBI agents were in one of her spare bedrooms.

Opening her front door, she greeted Langston by taking three steps back.

"You don't have to be cold like that," he said. "I'm the same Langston that made you scream when you came. And I'm a 'make you do it again' kind of man. I haven't made love to you yet, Jordan. Tonight is our night." Langston handed her a liquor bag.

Jordan opened it. Inside was a bottle of expensive red wine and a bottle of cognac.

"Thanks." She set the cognac on the end table. "Have a seat here in the living room. I'll get a snifter for you and uncork this for me," she insisted, holding on to the cabernet. Retreating to the kitchen, she placed the wine on the counter as she removed the cork, then texted Wade, **Can you hear everything okay?**

He responded, **Yes.**

"Who were you texting?" Langston asked.

Knocking over the bottle, Jordan said, "Shit! I didn't hear you enter the kitchen." Quickly salvaging enough wine to fill her glass, Jordan attempted to power off her cell.

"Let me see your phone," Langston insisted, moving closer toward her. Snatching the phone from her hand, he demanded, "What's your code?"

Fearful Wade couldn't protect her, Jordan wanted Langston out of her house. "I'm not giving you my code."

He held the phone up to her face. "It's not unlocking. What did you do?"

Jordan had no idea, but she was relieved. She took her phone from Langston, handed him a snifter, picked up her drink, then said, "Let's go in the living room. You need to do more talking about what I saw on television. And I need to listen."

Retrieving another snifter, Langston led the way back to the living room as though her home were his. He explained, "When I arrived at Kingston's place, it looked pretty bad, babe." He sat on the sofa.

As she sat in a chair next to the sofa and faced Langston, this was a moment for Jordan to let him continue lying. "When you left, why didn't you contact me to tell me not to go there?"

"Theodore Ramsey," he said. "He—"

Frustrated, she interrupted, "We'll get back to Theodore, but why did you give me Kingston's address?" The situation was becoming personal for Jordan.

Langston poured a shot of cognac, then downed his drink, as though it were water, then refilled his glass. "Have a drink with me, Jordan. What I have to do will hurt less if you have a drink with me."

Jordan stood. "I have to use the restroom right quick," she lied.

"Don't take long." Langston's eyes were filled with sadness. "I want to make love to you tonight before we . . ." He paused.

Before what? she thought. *Going to prison? Selling me into sex slavery?* Quietly closing the restroom door, she stared at herself in the mirror. Her stomach churned.

"Hurry up!" Langston shouted. "Don't make me come get you!"

She didn't want to risk communicating with Agent Wade again. Jordan reaffirmed that her microphone was still in place. Returning to her seat, she walked slowly, sat on the edge of the chair. Jordan's entire body perspired as she observed Langston shaking the bottle of cognac.

"You ready to get this over with?" he asked as soon as he saw her cupping her wine glass in her palms.

Jordan relocated to the chair across from the sofa, facing Langston, and resumed sitting on the edge.

Calmly he said, "You are going to drink your drink. Go ahead. Enjoy finishing your wine. Then we can have a shot of my favorite." He stared at her.

Maintaining eye contact, she held her goblet with both hands.

"Did Kingston tell you we went to elementary school together? I've been attracted to Kingston since we were in the third grade. I'd done some things to him then . . . and now, that I shouldn't have. I've watched his career grow and end," he said somberly.

Jordan squeezed her glass with both hands. If she held it tighter, it my break. Long as Langston was talking, she prayed Wade and his team were listening.

"Our accidental meeting was no mistake. I used you to get to Kingston." His head pivoted to the right as though he'd heard something.

"So, Theodore is to blame for what happened to Kingston?" Jordan wanted to run toward the bedroom but she realized people of all kinds, had hidden agendas for other people's lives. She had to help get this lying bastard off the streets of Atlanta before someone became his victim.

"Nah." Langston resumed looking at her. "I'd done my research. Knew what church he'd joined. Knew who his friends were. If I got to you, I could get to him. I've always known that Kingston was gay. I also knew that my going down on him in the janitor's closet in the third grade made him curious. But I never thought my partner Theodore would fall in love with . . ."

Jordan nodded praying Langston would complete his thought out loud. If she interrupted the story, she might risk the FBI's obtaining valuable information. "I'm listening," she said. "You're safe here," she lied.

Slowly he filled two snifters with cognac from the bottle. Langston stood, removed the goblet from her wet hands, replaced it with one of the snifters.

He sat on the sofa, stared at her, then said, "Have a drink with me, Jordan. I'm not asking." Calmly Langston returned to talking. "Have you ever been raped, Jordan?"

If the agents weren't in the other room, this would be the moment where she'd run out the front door and scream for help. Many cases crossed her desk, but she had no firsthand knowledge on what it felt like to be raped.

"No," she answered.

Langston held the cognac underneath his nose, inhaled. "When I was five, six, seven, eight, you can keep counting in your head as I continue, I was a child sex slave."

Was he telling the truth? Or had Langston made this up for empathy so she would trust him?

"Jordan, this is the last time I'm asking. Drink the damn drink," he demanded.

Placing the glass away from her lips, she paused, then asked, "So, is that why you became a trafficker?"

"Bitch!" Langston sprang from his seat, stood on the coffee table, then in front of her. He grabbed her jaws, then attempted to poured the drink in her mouth.

Sucking in her lips, Jordan swiftly turned her head.

Langston's trembling hand, reached for the bottle. "Tell Kingston I love him. And I never meant to harm him." Letting go of her cheeks, he gulped the cognac until the bottle was half empty.

Langston's last words to Jordan were "I don't want to be alone. Take a drink. Die with me, Jordan."

Officer Wade rushed from the bedroom with his weapon drawn. "Don't move! Langston Derby, you're under arrest!"

Langston's body fell to the floor like a tree in the forest.

Wade instructed the other two agents, "Handcuff him."

One of the agents placed his fingers against Langston's neck, then said, "Boss, he's dead."

CHAPTER 56

Kingston

"I've failed God." Lying on his side in his hospital bed, Kingston asked Pastor Baloney, "Where do I go from here?"

"If you're looking for pity, you're not going to get it from me. Worse things have happened to other people. What you should do is, get healthy, and while doing so, start a nonprofit."

As a survivor of sexual assault, Kingston decided he wanted to help others, but he never thought about launching a nonprofit for human-trafficking victims. "That's not a bad idea," he said.

Pastor Baloney opened his Bible app on his phone, then handed it to Kingston. "Read this aloud, son. The second chapter of Ecclesiastes, verses one through three."

Kingston read, " 'The futility of pleasure. I said to myself, "Come now, let's give pleasure a try. Let's look for the good things in life." But I found that this, too, was meaningless. "It is silly to be laughing all the time," I said. "What good does it do to seek only pleasure!" After much thought, I decided to cheer myself with wine. While still seeking wisdom, I clutched at foolishness. In this way, I hoped to experience the only happiness most people find during their brief life in this world.'

"I think I get it," Kingston told Pastor Baloney. "But what is your interpretation?"

The pastor placed his hand on Kingston's head. "My son, I want you to memorize what you read. When I return to visit you tomorrow, we will discuss the first verse."

Kingston expected the pastor to pray with him, for him, in his presence. But Pastor Baloney left him, instead, with what felt like a Sunday school assignment. "Thanks for coming, Pastor. I look forward to seeing you tomorrow."

The hospital was a lonely place for Kingston. He prayed, *God, let me get well enough to leave this place and go home to my family.*

What had he offered God in exchange?

A text message registered. Kingston stared at his phone in disbelief as he read, **How are you doing? I'd like to see you. Is it okay if I come by the hospital today?**

Kingston had a trillion questions swarming in his head. Questions that only the person who'd texted him could answer. Afraid of how he would react if that person walked through the door into the room and stood close enough for him to grab the person by the throat and choke the last breath out of him, Kingston did not respond.

His door opened. Three unexpected visitors entered. Kingston had to remain lying on his side or else sit on that huge donut that was on the sofa across the room.

"Jordan Jackson, get over here." Kingston hugged her with one arm. "I want you to know I prayed for you day and night. Man, y'all just don't know how good it feels to see the group. I know one of you has one of those Popeye's fried chicken sandwiches or some fried chicken from Ms. Icey's in the bag for me."

Kingston's smile was only on the outside. The group had lightened his spirit. But the trauma could never be erased.

Victoria opened her oversized purse. She pulled out a clear plastic bag that had a brown paper bag inside. Opening both, she handed Kingston a fried chicken breast. "Brother Copeland never had a surgery, but every once in a while, they'd admit him for testing. And I'd always sneak him in a fried chicken breast."

Holding the fried chicken breast with one hand, Kingston took the biggest bite he possibly could. "Somebody update me on what's going on."

The look on Jordan's face—partially widened eyes, slightly lifted brows—made Kingston say, "Keep that to yourself."

"I met this girl online that I actually like. A lot," Chancelor confessed.

Taking another bite, Kingston chewed and talked at the same time. "What's her name, bruh?"

Victoria's eyes shifted to the side. Jordan laughed.

"Shanita Williams," Chancelor said, appearing upset with the ladies.

Kingston nodded. "That's what's up. Why y'all laughing? She sounds like she knows how to kick ass and suck dick."

Victoria and Jordan laughed hysterically.

Kingston handed Victoria the bone. "I know I missed a lot, but I appreciate hearing y'all laugh."

"If you really want to hear what happened, I'll—"

"Save it for the next visit. We came to cheer you up," Victoria said.

The door opened. Everyone became silent. Kingston didn't believe the person he loved most would visit him, when she had justification not to.

Monet entered, carrying a lilac designer handbag. A magenta-cotton halter maxidress showed off her curvaceous figure. Her hair was in a high ponytail that hung low. Large gold hoop earrings nearly touched her shoulders. It had been a while since he'd noticed how gorgeous his wife was.

Kingston said, "Guys—"

Chancelor interrupted, "Say no more, man, we're leaving."

"Do me one solid before you're out," Kingston said. "Help me over to the sofa."

Kingston sat on the sofa in his private hospital room. The inflated donut cushion prevented him from applying pressure on his ruptured rectum. He'd have to take it home after his discharge and use it everywhere he went for six weeks.

Monet placed her purse on his bed, sat beside him, then held his hands. "Do you want to come home? Or—"

Leaning toward her, Kingston held the nape of her neck, then vigorously kissed his wife. Monet placed her hand on his chest and leaned back. Rejection wasn't acceptable. He needed his wife.

Kingston's sob started slowly, growing into an uncontrollable, hyperventilating cry for compassion. With trembling lips, he told his wife, "I don't deserve you. If you want a divorce, I'll sign the papers and give you half of everything."

Monet gently placed her hand on his cheek, softly wiped his tears, then said, "What reason would I have to divorce you? If you want a divorce, file for it yourself."

Now that he had the opportunity to solely make the decision, Kingston didn't want to accept his truth. "What if I don't want to divorce my family? I want to continue being a husband and a father?"

Would he be happier with a husband? That question had to be answered.

Knock. Knock. "It's Nurse Elizabeth. Can I come in?"

Kingston wanted to say no, but Monet got up and opened the door.

"Oh, I didn't see you come in," Elizabeth said. "I can come back."

"I'm Kingston's wife. Please come in," Monet said.

Entering the room, Elizabeth handed Kingston a sheet of paper. Monet eased it from his hand, then said, "Test results."

Kingston reached for the sheet.

Monet pulled it away. "Elizabeth, thanks. You can leave."

"What kind of test results? Let me see," Kingston insisted.

Staring at the sheet, Monet shook her head, sat beside him, then handed the paper to Kingston.

He scanned the results: *HIV 1+2 AB+HIV1P24 AG, EIA Non-Reactive; GONORRHEA Non-Reactive; HEPATITIS B AND C Non-Reactive.* Every result was the same.

He was shocked. "It's clean! What's wrong?" he asked his wife.

It was a miracle he hadn't contracted any sexually transmitted diseases. That was by the grace of God and perhaps from Theodore insisting he take meds to minimize his risk of infection. All that he'd done and overcome, and God still had mercy on his soul.

"What really happened in Atlanta?" Monet asked.

"It's too painful to relive right now," he said. That was real. "I will answer all of your questions, baby. Later."

Looking into his eyes, Monet said, "Kingston, I love you. I will always love you. And most important, with all my heart, I forgive you. I mean it."

He couldn't believe what he was hearing. After all he'd put her through, why would his wife forgive him? None of this would've happened if he had been born without ungodly urges. If he had been honest and told Monet that it all started in a janitor's closet when he was in third grade . . .

Jordan had offered to share what Langston Derby had told her. It didn't matter.

Commanding his attention, Monet let him know, "Baby, you've never beaten me or called me out of my name. Whatever you did was something that you did with others. I can't say I understand what you went through, but I do want to know. Everything. But I'm grateful that you're alive. I don't know what I would've done if I had lost my best friend."

With every word she spoke, his wife became more beautiful. She was unequivocally his best friend. He'd given her valid reasons to cheat on him. But she'd never given her pussy to another man. Kingston wanted to keep it that way.

Monet continued, "I know people are going to think that our family isn't strong enough to make it through this situation. They can believe whatever they'd like. The Royales are forever united."

Slowly shaking his head in disbelief, Kingston admitted, "You have no idea how much that means to me, or what they did to me." Kingston cried. "Being sodomized, all day every day. Baby, some men are fucking pigs . . . I wanted to die."

Struggling to force the pain out of his mind, Kingston bit his bottom lip. Langston Derby was dead. In many ways Langston was the luckier one.

"It's okay to cry," Monet said, moving as close as she could. "Look at me. We are not going to give those criminals our power. You are not going to give those criminals your power. All of them are exactly where they should be. And you are going to stand up in court and speak up for yourself and for all of the people that have been kidnapped and forced into prostitution. A lot of people think it only happens to females, but you are living proof that it also happens to males, and you have to be their voice."

That may be too much to ask, Kingston thought. "I'm embarrassed and ashamed. My face will be all over the media. Some people will say I deserved it."

"You can do this. You have to do it. What if that were to happen to our daughters? You don't want to have any regrets for not being the voice for black men who are missing. I will be by your side the entire time."

Kingston would never encourage Monet to go public if she had been raped. The "right thing" wasn't proper for everybody. His former teammates would assume he was gay while he was in the league. Strangers would post memes on social media. How would he recover?

"You are the most selfless person I know. You have taken care of me, our girls, my mother, your family, friends, and the list goes on. From this day forward I want you to live your truth. You have the right to be gay, bisexual, heterosexual. Whatever it is you want to be, that is your decision alone," Monet reassured him.

Kingston sought confirmation from his wife. "So you're not going to divorce me if I say I am bisexual?"

Monet didn't hesitate to respond. "I cannot promise you that I'd be okay with you having sex with men, then coming home to be intimate with me. But what I can promise you is I will always love you. As long as you don't lie to me about what is happening. Just like you make your decision, respect and accept mine."

His ass shifted on the donut. Kingston wanted Monet to say she'd always be there with him as his wife. Being a family man was socially acceptable. But the fact that she didn't dehumanize or abandon him made him feel like a man.

Monet kissed Kingston on his lips, then left the room.

Kingston did not know why God had blessed him with an angel, but he was grateful he had chosen the right wife. He made a commitment to himself that he'd never lie to or leave Monet again.

CHAPTER 57

Monet

"Hey, pretty lady. I'm glad you called. How are *you* doing?" Cairo asked. "Don't stay in Atlanta too long. I need my baby here with me."

Standing outside of her husband's room, Monet said, "It's hard seeing him having to sit on a donut, and knowing why. I think he's in denial about what happened."

Monet struggled to truly forgive her husband. She'd told him she had, hoping to lift him up. She imagined he'd endured more than he deserved.

"His spirit seems good. I'm glad he didn't die. He's my best friend, you know. Nothing will change that," Monet said.

Bianca was right. Kingston being alive was harder. Monet had to be the glue for her girls, her mom, and her husband. If she were the one to leave Kingston, how would society judge her?

"I know you love your 'brother,' but if there is room in your heart for one more best friend, Mrs. Royale, I'd like to fill that opening," Cairo stated in a naughty tone.

Feeling Cairo's energy resonate through the phone, Monet had to be truthful. "What are we going to do? I know where I want to be. But I could never divorce Kingston under these circumstances."

Cairo became silent. Monet watched one of the nurses take pictures of her. She hadn't had the decency to silence the clicks on her cell.

"Are you still there, baby?" Monet asked.

"You know how I feel about you. This is hard for me, too. But I'm not going to be selfish. What we share is magical. I doubt if I'll ever find another human being that complements me the way you do." Cairo became silent again. This time she heard a sniffle.

"I've been knowing that Kingston is your husband. And I understand why you're protective of him. After the news break, and your overreaction, I looked you up."

Monet wasn't sure how she felt about Cairo not mentioning he'd researched her. But she had no right to lie to him.

"Listen," he said. "You told me your marital status day one. That hasn't changed. Neither have my feelings for you." Cairo added, "I'm here to complement. Not complicate your life."

A lump gathered in Monet's throat, making it hard for her to speak. Looking at the man walking in her direction, Monet stood tall. It was him. The man in the picture with her husband.

"Let me call you back. We have an uninvited guest," she said, ending the call with Cairo.

Monet wanted to tell Cairo, "I love you," but their situation was truly complicated and she didn't want to mislead him.

Blocking the entrance into Kingston's room, Monet asked, "Are you Theodore Ramsey?"

"You must be the cock *blocker*," he replied, singing the last word. Placing his hand on his hip with his thumb in front, Theodore continued, "Kingston should be with me, not you. It's time for him to shave his beard. And you know this."

She didn't give a damn what he called her. "Nurse! How did this criminal get past check-in?" Monet yelled.

"Who you defaming, honey? I'd sue you if you weren't married to my future husband. I have not been charged or implicated, thank you," he said, trying to go around her.

"Over here, Elizabeth." Monet waved.

Theodore waved, too. "Yes, Elizabeth girl. Come quick."

Approaching the door, Elizabeth escorted them away from Kingston's room, then asked, "What's the problem?"

"She's trying to keep me away from my man," Theodore said. "I had nothing to do with what happened to my baby. Would I be here if I had? And for the record, I'm glad Langston is no longer amongst the living."

Monet wasn't here to challenge Theodore. "Langston committed suicide be—"

Elizabeth interrupted, "I'm going to have to ask both of you to—"

Even if her husband preferred men, Theodore wouldn't be his type.

"That won't be necessary," Monet stated. "There's one way to find out if Kingston is okay with Mr. Ramsey's visit."

Monet wasn't going to let Theodore harm her husband. She reentered Kingston's hospital room with Theodore right behind her.

"Hey, baby," Kingston said.

The moment he noticed Theodore, his eyes softened, then shifted to her.

Is my husband tearing up at the sight of a man? Instantly Monet realized her situation was bigger than a battle of the sexes. Her husband loved that man.

"Yea, though I walk through the valley . . ." Lord, give me strength. Monet swallowed the new lump that choked her, then cleared her throat.

Theodore sat on the sofa next to Kingston. Their thighs touched. Redirecting his attention to her, Kingston was silent.

"What? Don't look at me. Act like I'm not here."

Theodore may have not been directly involved, but he must've had something to do with what had happened to Kingston. Monet had heard of prostitutes going back to their pimps, but what was this?

"What did they do to my baby?" Theodore asked her husband. "I was going to die, or die trying to find you."

"Die then! Like Langston. Because you know damn well you knew where my husband was. You set him up!" Monet moved closer to Kingston. "Look at me." She pointed at Theodore. "He set you up."

"How are you? How long do you have to sit on *this* thing?" Theodore asked Kingston, ignoring her.

Composing herself, Monet said, "Kingston, I'll give you a minute to end these despicable theatrics." Exiting the room, she overheard Theodore asking her husband more questions than she had.

Monet's body was numb. She went to the café on the second floor, ordered a cup of coffee, then sat at a window that overlooked valet parking below.

She processed what she'd witnessed; that was a cowardly way for Kingston to show his truth. She dialed the necessary number.

"Hey, how are you guys, my dear?" Kendall Minter, Esquire, asked.

"I need you to draft our divorce decree," she emphatically stated.

"Sleep on it. If you feel the same after giving everything consideration, we'll discuss it. I have to take this. Call me later if you need to—"

"Wait," she said, then explained.

Minter had no idea. Monet didn't want to reveal her husband's personal life.

"I'm listening," he said.

"The guy. The partner of Langston Derby." She'd found a way not to say Kingston was gay. "He had the audacity to come to the hospital."

Minter's voice went from cheery to serious. "Where is he?"

"He claims he's not involved with the trafficking. Kingston let him stay in his room. What should I do?" Monet asked.

"What's his name?" Minter asked.

"Theodore Ramsey."

"From what I've heard, Langston made over a million dollars off of trafficking your husband. Theodore, if he's involved, may not be willing to let Kingston go that easy. Whatever you do, don't let Theodore take Kingston out of the hospital." Minter ended their call.

Determined to prove Theodore was no competition, and she was going to make sure he stayed away from Kingston, Monet's hands trembled terribly as she dialed 9-1-1.

A female responder answered, "Nine-one-one. Caller, what's your emergency?"

What was her emergency? Monet thought, then cried out, "Someone is trying to kidnap my husband from the hospital!"

Monet returned to Kingston's floor, stood outside his room, and waited.

Two police officers hurried toward her.

"Theodore Ramsey is in my husband's room," Monet reported.

Forcing open the door, both officers rushed in. Monet followed them.

She was not prepared for what everyone saw. Theodore's dick was in Kingston's mouth. Theodore looked up. Holding the back of Kingston's head, he kept stroking.

"Uh, what's the emergency again?" the officer asked.

Kingston tried pushing Theodore away.

The other officer said, "Theodore, he wants you to stop," then nodded his head. "Now would be a good time."

Embarrassed, Monet told her husband, "That's it. I'm done. We're getting a divorce. He can have you."

CHAPTER 58

Victoria

"Victoria Fox. Will you marry me?" Heavenly asked.

Hmm. A dating app had turned into what Victoria had never fathomed. A real relationship. Why did he have to ask her in a public place?

"Wedding proposal on aisle nine" permeated throughout the grocery store. She looked down at Heavenly, who was on one knee next to a large cardboard box of watermelons.

Victoria hadn't acquired her wealth to jeopardize millions on a feeling that could change as she aged. Fun and pleasure was what she sought. Not commitment.

The audience of men was becoming restless. The women cheered her on, adding applause. Kids chanted, "Say yes!"

She wasn't there for the applause. In fact, Victoria would've preferred that Heavenly had asked her in private.

Looking defeated, Heavenly's response was "You're not ready for me. Forget I asked."

That was something she could do.

"The wedding is off," he announced, still holding the ring up to her.

Poor thang. Victoria didn't need to be saved by Heavenly or any man. Only God had the power to do that. The person she loved

CAREFUL WHAT YOU CLICK FOR 281

was no longer among the living, but Willy Copeland would always have a special place in her heart.

She couldn't say the same about Heavenly. He could leave and stay gone forever. She'd miss him. *Maybe*. But his replacement was online or on an app.

Everyone in the produce section was staring at her. Leaning over, Victoria whispered in Heavenly's ear, "You should get up. Why did you do this here?"

"Why not? You too good for a grocery store proposal?" The oh-so-familiar man-child's smile spread across his face. Only this time it was contrived.

The crowd of spectators grew, presumably expecting a resounding "yes" to escape her lips any moment. But Victoria wasn't thirty-something like her lover. She was over sixty.

Since he was the one who'd popped the question in the middle of the store, he'd have to wait for her answer. "Get up. Let's finish shopping and I promise to give you an answer before we check out."

"Go ahead and say yes," one woman said. "You ain't getting any younger."

"She's just fronting. She know she's going to marry that boy," another woman commented. "She done turnt him out."

"Dude, she ain't the one. When somebody loves you back, they don't have to think about accepting your proposal." So said the short guy with the potbelly that looked her age, but was probably closer to Heavenly's.

The crowd began to disperse. Heavenly finally stood up, put the ring back in its box, then shoved it into his pocket.

Victoria hissed, "What were you thinking?"

After Heavenly's dog-and-pony, her answer definitely wasn't a "yes." But it wasn't a "no." The difference with a mature man, in Victoria's opinion, irrespective of age, was that he would think through a situation before verbalizing what was on his mind.

Sensing he needed it, Victoria hugged Heavenly. "Why don't we leave this basket right here, go to dinner, order steak and lobster and champagne. Then we can have the conversation we should've had before you popped the question."

In the car on the way to the restaurant, he asked the question again, in a different way. "Will you be my wife? I'm serious. I know what I want."

What on earth is Heavenly trying to prove, Lord Jesus? If he could dismiss his ego, then maybe she'd give him an answer over dinner.

Ordering a bottle of their best champagne, Victoria asked, "Are you willing to buy me a higher-quality diamond?"

"What's money got to do with my offering you my heart? I bought what I could afford," he retorted.

"Hmm." That was exactly what she thought.

Heavenly hung his head. Stared at the table.

"Look at me." Victoria said, "Are you willing to sign a prenuptial agreement?"

Shaking his head, he answered, "No."

"No?" Instead of saying, "What do you bring to the relationship?" Victoria asked, "How much is the remainder for your tuition and the total amount due for your credit cards? I think we should start there. If we're still together when you get your degree, you can decide if you'd like to ask me again. Fair?" she asked.

Then Victoria added, "One more thing. Why are you asking me to marry you? And please don't say it's because you love me. I already know that, but love alone is never enough." She recalled what Kingston had recently put Monet through.

Heavenly pushed his chair away from the table. Stood. Looked down at her. "I'm sorry things didn't work out between us. I promise you, you're going to miss me when I'm gone."

Thank You, Lord Jesus. You know my heart. If the spell isn't broken, don't let Heavenly become a stalker. Amen.

Raising her glass to him, Victoria sipped her champagne. She ordered the African lobster tail and the filet mignon, medium.

Nothing was lost in love and faith. Heavenly's replacement was already in her in-box on TuitionCougars, and Victoria had every intention on finding her next Heavenly.

Tonight.

CHAPTER 59

Chancelor

"Ha-ha, ha-ha. Stop tickling me. You are so silly," Chancelor said, then hugged Shanita from behind.

Their legs moved in unison as they strolled through Centennial Park. The day had cooled off to a warm summer evening of seventy-two degrees.

"I'm hot. Let's get ice cream," Shanita suggested. "What's your favorite flavor?"

"I'll give you one guess." Chancelor stopped. Faced Shanita. Slid his finger from the bridge to the tip of her nose.

"Strawberry." She gave a quick kiss on his lips. "That's like black people's red Kool-Aid."

"Nope. Guess again," he said, hoping for a second kiss.

"Butter pecan. All black people love butter pecan," Shanita said.

"No. That's your ghetto-booty favorite," he said. Walking beside her, Chancelor held Shanita's hand. "I am the luckiest guy ever. I found a woman who isn't my type and I like her."

"Well, I cannot say the same about you because I don't have a type. I like what I like, and I don't go out with guys that are liars and cheaters." Shanita's head moved side to side.

Maybe he'd spoken too soon. "No more guessing. What kind of ice cream do you want?" Chancelor asked, looking at all of the flavors.

"Surprise me," Shanita said. "I'm in an adventurous mood."

She tickled him again, but this time he didn't laugh. *Everybody has a type. Why the fuck aren't I her type?*

While he was deciding, Shanita snapped a few selfies, then took a few us-ies. "I'm going to put this on my page. We make a good-looking couple. And I'ma change my status from 'single' to 'in a relationship.' You do the same."

What in the world was this girl thinking? Chancelor couldn't have his corporate people seeing him online getting ice cream with her. Her braids were nice. Nails were neat. He liked Shanita's infectious personality. But he had to move on his relationship schedule. Not hers.

Was Shanita so anxious to have him as her man that she claimed him before he claimed her? If it was Tracy or Elite, he'd be okay with that. But they'd never claim a man even if he gave them thousands of dollars.

Shanita flashed her fingers in front of his face. "Fine, if you don't want me to post your picture, I won't. But I am going to change my status."

It was a battle not worth arguing over. She was grown and could do whatever she wanted with her status. *Wait. Could I snag Elite as my girl? Nah. Forget her.*

Shanita focused on her phone. Chancelor stared at her to see how long it was going to take for her to put the phone back in her back pocket.

A text registered from Elite: **Want to hang out today? There's an all-white invitation-only party happening in a few hours at this new spot. You can be my plus one.**

After how she disrespected him? ATL females had amnesia.

No thanks, he replied, then added, **I'm with my new girlfriend.**

Chancelor couldn't lie; he didn't know which one felt better: rejecting Elite or claiming Shanita. But that shit felt good.

Let me know if you change your mind, Elite messaged.

"Man, let me have two Cherry Garcias. One in a waffle bowl. And my baby's in a chocolate-dipped cone." Chancelor's patience with Shanita's obsession with social was wearing.

Signing into his social page and going to hers, Chancelor noticed Shanita had changed her status, but she also identified him as the person she was in a relationship with. Whatever. Might as well let her have her way. He realized he was fighting a good cause. Where had his single status gotten him? Females always seemed to be more interested when a guy was booed-up. If things didn't work out, Shanita had probably done him a favor.

Chancelor logged in to the ChristianFornicators app to deactivate his account. "What kind of shit is this?" he asked, then showed Shanita her active profile.

"Here you go, sir," the guy said, handing him the waffle and the chocolate-dipped cone.

"That looks delicious." Shanita reached for the chocolate-dipped.

"Nah, you ain't getting none of this. Fuck it, let's go." Chancelor tossed both ice creams in the trash, handed the guy a twenty, then started walking away.

Shanita followed him.

"Why is your profile still active on ChristianFornicators? Answer the damn question, Shanita."

"If you know my profile is still there, that means your profile is still there. Why were you on the app?" She answered his question with one, too.

"I'm not on it. You're the one posting we're in a relationship. I was getting ready to delete mine for you." *Women,* he thought. *Always trying to do the Jedi.*

"Well, when you stop checking, I'll delete my profile," Shanita lamented.

Shaking his head, Chancelor conceded. "It's cool. Keep your profile. See if the other men do for you what I've done."

"Stop acting like you own me. I don't have as much as you, but I'm not your property, Chancelor."

This time he waved his hand. "You should've said that before I paid your car note, your rent, got your hair and your nails done, took you shopping, and put money in your pocket. You didn't have an attitude then—what's up with your attitude now?"

"Like I said, you don't own me."

Walking faster ahead of Shanita, he texted Elite, **Still got that plus one?**

Shanita grabbed his arm. "I didn't mean to speak to you like that. Let's go back and get our ice cream. My treat. And we can sit under a tree and talk. I want this relationship between us to work."

Her crazy was irresistible.

"Why are you always so uptight?" Shanita asked. "Soon as we start having a great time, you do something to spoil it. It's almost as though you don't believe that you deserve my love. But you are a lovable guy."

No woman had said that to him before. He wanted to believe what she was saying was true and stop finding a reason to catch and release.

"Two Cherry Garcias," Chancelor ordered.

The guy said, "One waffle cup. One chocolate-dipped cone coming up. Or I can just keep the ice cream and you give me twenty dollars again. Are you really going to eat them this time?" Dude handed Chancelor two Cherry Garcias, then said, "On the house."

Sitting on the lawn under a tree, Shanita told him, "You know you're my man, right?"

Chancelor texted Elite, **Cancel that plus one. Got my baby back.**

CHAPTER 60

Jordan

"Has the jury reached a decision?" Judge Goodwin asked.

"Yes, Your Honor," the foreman stated, then read, " 'We the jury find the defendant, Anne Whitehall, guilty of murder in the first degree.' "

Donovan fell into Jordan's arms and wept like a baby.

Cries of "Yay!" and "Yes!" in the courtroom were deafening.

Judge Goodwin shouted, "Order in the court!"

People ran into the hallway. Exiting the courthouse with her client, Jordan knew justice was served. Microphones were shoved in their faces.

Jordan advised Donovan, "Keep moving."

Reporters trailed them. "How do you feel about the judge's decision?"

"Are you satisfied with the outcome? Will there be a civil suit?"

Anticipating journalists swarming her client, Jordan had pre-arranged for transportation. "Get in the car," she told Donovan.

"I hope you do as well or better with your civil suit." She was relieved the hardest part was over, happy for Donovan and for the big win for her firm.

"What are you going to do next?" Donovan asked her.

"Take a much-needed vacation." Jordan removed her shoes.

Massaging her foot, Donovan said, "Let me take you. Anywhere in the world you'd like to go. I promise you won't touch your purse from the minute you leave your home until the minute I get you back to your doorstep."

The offer was tempting. *Oh, God. The massage feels divine.*

He pressed deep into the ball. "I owe you an apology for acting an ass. I lost my mind, for real. Forgive me."

"How about we start with a celebratory adult beverage?" Jordan said, then moaned, "Damn, that feels good." As imperfect as Donovan was, he was her familiar.

"Your favorite place?" he asked.

Not today. Not tomorrow. Not ever again would she step foot into Bar Purgatory. The good memories outweighed the bad, but the bad ones were horrible. Jordan still couldn't believe that Langston was an evil, complicated, and depressed man. But she was relieved that he was dead.

"Come closer. Let me return the kindness and hold you." Donovan leaned her onto his chest, wrapped his arms around her.

Jordan desperately craved this kind of affection every day, but for now, this would have to do. "I'm never online dating or using a dating app again."

"Don't say that." Donovan kissed the back of her head. "Don't forget, that's how we met. Give me a second chance, Jordan, Ms. Jackson. And let me prove myself worthy of making you Mrs. Donovan Bradley. I think DJ would like that."

Jordan smiled. "I think DJ would like us together, too."

The worst day in America will be if all black women give up on all black men.

Men don't miss the love they have until she's gone.

Discussion Questions

1. Do you believe people are born with an attraction to the same sex?

2. Does molestation or sexual assault make a person promiscuous?

3. How many of the characters do you feel suffer from mental illness? Who and why?

4. What are the characters in search of when it comes to relationships?

5. Who's using whom? For what? Why?

6. What are the dangers of lying to a spouse about lying and cheating?

7. Which character is your favorite?

8. What character/characters would you classify as a womanizer/womanizers?

9. Do you believe Monet was justified in her affair?

10. Can a person be in love with more than one person?

11. What would you do if your mother knew your husband was gay/bisexual and didn't tell you until your husband was missing?

12. Georgia is the first state to develop a task force (of six) at the state level to prosecute traffickers. Why do you think it's taken the state this long?

13. Most people aren't aware, but why do you think 1.5 million black men are missing in America? And why isn't the conversation being had?

14. Have you ever lived your life being what others expected of you? Why or why not?

15. Are you okay with the term "she shack"? What would (or do) you call your home hideaway? Fantasize and create your space. What's in it? Where is it located in your house?

16. Have you met or do you know a man like Chancelor? Is Chancelor the type of guy women like?